A CAPPELL

ISSUE 10 · SPRING 2013

Bestiary:

the best of the inaugural demi-decade

Guest Editor
GINA OCHSNER

FOUNDING EDITOR
Colin Meldrum

FICTION EDITOR   POETRY EDITOR
Amanda Lyn DiSanto   Lisa McCool-Grime

COVER & SECTION ILLUSTRATOR
Anna Bron

A cappella Zoo (ISSN: 1945-7480):
a magazine of magic realism and slipstream.

A cappella Zoo was founded in 2008 as an independent, labor-of-love publication. Contributions to this special issue were selected by award-winning author Gina Ochsner (www.ginaochsner.com). All illustrations were done by artist Anna Bron except where otherwise credited to contributors Cheryl Gross and Gavin Faherty. Support *A cappella Zoo* and its contributors by sharing your favorite stories and poems with friends and colleagues. Enjoy.

www.acappellazoo.com

Contents

· 𝔖𝔞𝔠𝔯𝔞𝔯𝔦𝔲𝔪 ·

· 𝔄𝔳𝔦𝔞𝔯𝔭 ·

a conversation with
GINA OCHSNER

Gina lives in Oregon and divides her time between writing and teaching at Corban University and with the Seattle Pacific Low-Residency MFA program. She has been awarded a John L. Simon Guggenheim grant and a grant from the National Endowment of Arts. She speaks at universities, retreats, conferences, schools, and book clubs on creativity, magic realism, flash fiction, prose poetry, the intersection of art and faith, and other topics related to writing. Her stories have appeared in The New Yorker, Tin House, Glimmer Train, *and* The Kenyon Review. *She is the author of the short story collection* The Necessary Grace to Fall, *which received the Flannery O'Connor Award for Short Fiction, and the story collection* People I Wanted to Be. *Both books received the Oregon Book Award. Her first novel,* The Russian Dreambook of Colour and Flight, *was published by Portobello Press and Houghton-Mifflin-Harcourt.*

COLIN: **Based on your selections for this collection, how would you describe *A cappella Zoo*'s landscape?**

GINA: I'm struck by the frolicsome, mischievous nature of so many of these pieces. Though the subject matter of much of the work is deep—dark even—the treatment rarely is and I think that this suggests a profound love of language among these writers.

COLIN: **One of my favorite of your stories, "How One Carries Another," is a contemplative, unique sort of ghost story, and it's certainly not the only one you've written. We've seen zombie and vampire fads dominate popular media lately, but would you agree that ghosts have kept a more consistent seat at the story sharing table? Why don't we tire of ghost stories?**

GINA: I would agree that ghosts do in fact inhabit a more consistent seat. Ghosts will outlast any bloodthirsty vampire or brain-deprived zombie because the idea of ghosts being present among us speaks to a collective desire between both living and dead to remain connected. I don't know of any culture that doesn't have some kind of a "position" as to the presence and meaning of ghosts (either as the subject of rumor and tales or as accepted "witness" of another time/day). I don't think I'll ever tire of ghost stories because I find them fascinating forays into the world of the speculative. What happens when a person dies? Where does the soul go?

What happens if someone were to become stuck for a time between two worlds? What reason would a person have for hanging around and making noise? Is it just noise or is there some larger message meant to be pieced together? I suspect magic realists Gabriel García Márquez and Isabel Allende found ghosts to be useful manifestations of history, of adding complexity and texture to the narrative and to other characters. And what better way to show the contradictions inherent in living than by rousting a ghost who can hold up the mirror, so to speak.

AMANDA: **In a 2005 interview with *Writer's Digest*, you mentioned a special love for the short story form. Since then you've published your first novel. Now that you've experienced writing in both short and long forms, has your view of short stories changed? What do you think the short story form offers readers?**

GINA: I don't think I'll ever abandon the short story form. In fact, when I'm feeling quite stuck on a longer project (and this happens more often than I like to admit) I go to the creative sandbox, a soup of words and images, that place of wonder and astonishment and surprise. I go to play, to have some low down messy fun. And inevitably I'll emerge elbow deep in story. Short stories are like a burst of fireworks—energy only momentarily contained. I can't think of a more fluid, malleable form.

LISA: **Unlike many literary journals, *A cappella Zoo* is fiction heavy. While we hope to appeal to a broad range of readers, our intended primary audience is fiction readers, an idea we keep in mind even when considering poetry for publication. What's in store in this anthology's poetry for readers who don't normally seek out poetry?**

GINA: I think that the mark of a successful piece, whether fiction, drama, essay or poem rests in the strength of the imagery and language. The poems in *A cappella Zoo* are particularly image rich, image driven. Because of this, I find the poetry evocative and yet, accessible. These pieces are built of blood, bone, skin, and dreams you can sink a fork and knife into.

COLIN: **You were a keynote speaker at Western Seminary's 2011 Faith and Culture Writers Conference and you teach for a private Christian university. Does being a person of faith play a role in your sense of—or approach to—magic realism?**

GINA: Being a person of faith absolutely plays a role in my sense of and apprehension of what magic realism is and represents. I believe in the supernatural as fact, not fiction, and in the miraculous as a part of reality, not myth. Moreover, magic realism carries special implications for people of the book who believe in the Word and in the creative power implied in written and particularly, if you look at the biblical accounts, spoken word. With a few words, *let there be*, the universe was created. Light separated from darkness and with another word this world was sent spinning widdershins to give us night, day. And with a few more words the trees were taught to weep from their bark, and swift to swallow winter ticked toward spring. And who knows how many more words it took to tell the camelia to bleed first and the chrysanthemum last or what dreams the fish maintained silently in their deep. But the creation account was just one of many I grew up with and learned to love because what I learned was that there's power and life in word. My forays into the Old Testament confirmed that this world spins on the twin axes of mystery and the miraculous. And this belief, I think, fuels my vision and perception. Because I believe in an invisible God I can't see but who I know exists and moves and has being and power and manifestation, I will write of the natural and supernatural world that reflects this belief. So what I take up with in terms of subject matter is another way that matters of faith intersect with fiction. I'll confess, it's the somewhat nebulous region of story-land where I work out what I believe and hold to be true. This is the safest place I know to test out spiritual observations that can be collaborated by the physical world in which I wake and breathe.

COLIN: **As an editorial board, we at *A cappella Zoo* are on the lookout for especially memorable works. What are a few selections that you expect to remember for some time? What surprises did you encounter while reading for this collection?**

GINA: As I read through the submissions, I thought: lucky editors! Lucky me! How fun these pieces are, how vivid and marvelously constructed. I was delighted to see a wide range of magic realism represented and written with such steady hands. So much can go so wrong with magic realist pieces and I admired the clear cogent vision and articulation in these pieces. I admired each of the poems and found particular delight in "Ginny," "Magic Realists in Love," "Sigilism," "Tale of the Avian Saint," "Teaching a Post Lunar World," and "In the Emily Dickinson Museum." Though I've singled these pieces out, I'd like to note that every poem burns with a bright interior light, every piece offers unexpected movement, dynamism. The fragmented architecture in the story "Transaction" parallels a frightening world in which every action, word, or gesture holds potential positive or negative commercial value, a world not wholly unfamiliar to us. For sheer imagination and inventiveness I admired "The Sand Ship," "The End of the Objects," "Larva," "Proximity," and "Popper's Choice." Language, a keen attention to detail, and sound prevail in "Oldjohn's House." "Dearest Dirty," "Requiem For a Glass Heart," and "Three Times Red" employ the fairy tale format and tone in which we are promised a bit of wisdom, and in each case, these writers deliver.

LISA: **In your opinion, why do *A cappella Zoo* and other platforms for magic realist writing matter?** AMANDA: **And what can this collection offer writers who seek guidance or inspiration?**

GINA: I think journals like *A cappella Zoo* in which magic realism is presented as a viable and legitimate form for narrative and image-rich poetry are vital. *A cappella Zoo* reminds us of the primal need for narrative in which the otherworldly, the strange, the supernatural is allowed off the leash for a little while, allowed to visibly collide with the known "real" world. The collision sparks the questions: what is real and what isn't and how am I altered by what I believe or perceive to be real or true? What would happen if . . . ? Let's suppose for a little while that . . . Entertaining such questions, such speculative acts, allows for a re-seeing—a revision as well as discovery. Magic realism teaches us how to read extended metaphor, how to tweeze meaning out of disparate things, how to use our own imaginations to animate worlds in which anything can happen and likely will.

· Aquarium ·

. . . above-water, i'm belly up watching his
jugular inflate and deflate. i guess his heart does that.
"do you float?" it asks me. "i do," i say quietly . . .

—*versions*

The Creature from the Lake

HAYES MOORE

Tim's instinct is to kill. He is too civilized to kill. Instead, he saves things. Right now he is on a ladder saving the rain-gutters.

The creature is underwater. She drifts in circles along the pool's floor, following the side of the pool. I think she is searching for algae. I think she is hungry. Despite her enormity she is surprisingly nimble, as a whale must be. When the side of the pool suddenly gives way to steps at the shallow end, she strokes out a startlingly deft spin, accelerating with grace until she finds her wall again.

I think Tim likes it up there, on top of his house, saving the rain gutters.

After a week of rain and clouds, the sun is finally out. I am at the poolside Formica table, underneath a canvas umbrella. I am supervising. The creature bobs up for air and then sinks back down, bulbous and alien in her tinted goggles, hairpins, and the black one-piece I insisted on. Tim says the suit isn't natural. But, I say, neither are we.

It has been a humid summer. The begonias are thriving. The slugs are too. They slink around the granulated rim of the pool. A family of robins defends an elm from a blue jay. As the creature slipped into the water I watched a squirrel chase another squirrel across the edge of the faded-pink plank fence, up an elm, and then disappear in a leap on the tiled rooftop of the neighboring house.

The air is redolent of chlorine and leaves mulching in the last rainfall.

I glance at my watch and then get up to wave and shout for the creature to come out; it's feeding time. She complies. She waddles up the steps on the shallow end like a molluscan monster, like the blob. She has no toes. Water droplets sparkle like crystals over her body. She has a smooth, pallid hide. Patches of cellulite mottle her legs. Her back and arms are scratched from Lake Stonewell's rocky shore. Offset by her paleness, the scars glimmer scabrous red.

She has healed quickly. She needs to be returned.

When the creature's bathing suit is off and I'm towel-patting her dry in the shade of the umbrella, Tim climbs down from the roof.

Like her belly, the creature's breasts are full and heavy. She is a globular thing.

Tim is bare-chested, too. He does not come under the umbrella. Flecks of leaf are caught in his chest hair. Despite the heat, he has stopped trimming his beard. Like his shoulders and back, his beard is a dark, earthen-ware red. The unkempt hair on his head, which is dark brown, is flattened with sweat. His eyes, a darker brown, roam over the creature. "Should we take out the hairpins?" He says.

"No," I say. "She needs to eat."

He stretches, like a plant absorbing sunlight.

The creature observes us behind the tinted goggles.

The creature's eyes are pink and sensitive and swell up under bright light. I believe that she is accustomed to the darkness of lake bottoms. I believe she is nocturnal. For the past week, since we found her, we have kept the house lights dim. We are finally using our candles. I usher the creature into our cadaverous living room through the back sliding-door. It is cool and still and smells like scented candles—like vanilla, key-lime pie, and sweetened lavender.

Inside, I put Tim's bathrobe around the creature and seat her on the sofa. I go to the kitchen to heap a plate with lettuce. We have kept her fed by scavenging the dumpster behind the local grocery store. Her diet is a turtle's diet.

Tim comes in soon after the creature has begun to eat. He is still shirtless. She is on the sofa, the plate perched on her lap. Tim goes to the kitchen and comes back with a beer. He stoops down to kiss my cheek. I am sorry for him because I want him to shave his beard and I know that if I ask, he will. I will not ask. I am not his mom.

Tim goes to the creature and, standing before her, he says, "I'm going to take the goggles off now. Okay?" He mimes the removal of goggles, a bottleneck in his hand.

The creature watches him.

When he reaches toward the side of her head for the goggles, the creature squirms and, as he touches her, she yanks herself to one side. Rotting lettuce is flung across the sofa; the plate topples onto the floor. Tim continues to wrestle with her. He has her on her back on the sofa, his hands on either side of her head. His back is broad and knotted with muscles like stones along the lake shore. Her legs kick uselessly in the air. Beer runs down Tim's knuckles and drips on the carpet, but he manages to keep the bottle from spilling. When he draws back he tosses the goggles onto the lounge chair. Her mouth is open but she is silent. She can only make sounds when her hair is down. When her hair is down she wails.

She was wailing when we found her. That's how I found her.

Last Saturday Tim and I went to Stonewell Park. I was against the idea. The sky was bone gray and the air hummed with mist. But Tim was determined. He wanted to fish. He said that the best time to fish is during a storm—I don't think even he believes that.

I found my parka and decided to go with him. In a relationship it's important to do things together. While Tim fished, I planned to hike the forested hills that encircle the lake.

We parked just off the dirt road that leads to Lake Stonewell's visitor's dock. It was pouring warm rain. I burrowed into my parka. The only protection Tim had against the rain was a wide-brim hat. All summer he has said that he likes the rain. I believe him. He followed me into the woods with his pole and tackle box before forking down to the lake. On the trail, at least, the trees provided a canopy that took the brunt of the rainfall.

I had been hiking for barely ten minutes when I heard wailing. It carried over the water as a high, pig-squeal of a cry, part animal and part banshee. I couldn't see what it was and was afraid it might be a rabid animal. Before going any further I forked to the river, hoping for an obstructed view.

From a distance, squinting across the lake through the rain, I thought she was a human—someone who had thought to go for a nude swim and had slipped on the stones, cracked open her skull or broken her back. She was nearly fifty-yards down the lake, at a point in the shore where the lake's edge curves into a small inlet.

I ran back for Tim.

Tim was good—he lives for emergencies, for opportunities to save things. As soon as I broke through the trees and he saw my face he reacted, not even reeling in his line, but merely dropping his pole and running to me. All I told him was that someone needed help.

When we were close the shrieking overwhelmed all other sounds. He stopped running and stood in the middle of the trail. "God," he said. "It's gorgeous."

He was right, it was gorgeous: the two of us caught together in the middle of the forest, breathless with the same adrenal sensitivity, the same objective, while rain coursed over us, splattering off the leaves of the trees around us. I wanted to kiss him, for him to kiss me. Then I heard it, briefly. I glimpsed it then in his eyes but I have not been able to catch it since. The beauty of her voice escapes me like something just outside of my vision, a tonal register beyond the grasp of my auditory reach. I sense that it is there, but it eludes me. At that moment, though, for a brief instant, I heard it too; I was able to hear what Tim hears when she sings. The creature's crying is normally high and plaintive, like a cat's screeching against my ears—an unrefined expression of torment. But for a moment, there on the trail, a melody of some kind emerged from the wailing, a pattern that softened the grating shrieks and transformed them to something liquid, clear and cool and fluid. The tone rendered the anguish into a mellifluous beauty. I heard it for a moment and then it was gone, replaced by the same high-pitched squeal.

Tim was transfixed. I shoved him and told him to go and the spell seemed to lift.

He nodded vacantly, water dripping from his nose. His eyes were as wide and mesmerized with wonder as a child's. "It's unbelievable," he said.

When we reached the forest's edge she was thrashing on the rocks.

Tim shouted as he sprinted to her. She gave no reply, and he went out on the rocks and caught her from behind, pinning her arms down with his own. He lifted her up. His arms sank in her fat. Her feet kicked the air. She wailed.

Tim struggled to carry her away from the rocks and they fell together onto the land. Blood streamed from her and mixed with the clayey earth. I took off my parka and wrapped her in it. She was shrieking as I lifted her hair from her eyes, checking for open gashes on her head. That's when she stopped. When I lifted her hair over her head there was silence. Tim, on his back, labored to catch his breath and the rain fell against the forest, against the stones, against the lake, against everything.

I wake up fully alert to the sound of sirens. It's her. I am alone in bed and it is dark outside and in. Our bedroom door is ajar. There is a dark haze engulfing the hallway, lingering at the bedroom door.

The torrent of sirens that woke me softens. I listen to the song she is singing, searching for the beauty, straining to hear what Tim hears. Her voice is a pane of shattered glass; multifaceted shards of brokenness create a fragile web pattern, sharp and precarious. Perhaps I have been mistaken. Perhaps I do hear what Tim hears.

Tonight we agreed to return her. We were eating dinner by candlelight at the kitchen table. In the hall across from us the creature soaked in the bathtub in the dark.

"I think she has healed," I said.

Tim nodded in the dark. His jaw chewed.

"She's frightened here," I said.

He swallowed loudly and said, "She's whole." He hunched over to fork his salad. He shies from conflict with me. He has been trained to protect me. He glanced at the bathroom before his next bite.

Now, in the dark comfort of our bed, her song sends me drifting back into a half-sleep. I float there until, coming up, I realize that the wail has become a gurgle, the faintest flow of water, as if through stone.

Tim has still not returned.

I walk barefoot into the fog of darkness, my bathrobe untied around me. All the lights in the house are off; the bathroom casts a muted halo of flame.

I stand in the doorway to watch Tim breath in the candlelight. He is with her in the bathtub, stretched out beside the creature. His thigh is curled over her thigh, his knee in her belly. His forearm weighs heavily on her breast. I feel her watch me through the shadows of her pink, sensitive eyes.

I am sorry for him because he has fallen in love. I tell myself that I am not his mom. Love is not a choice, I say to myself. He must save himself.

We leave before sundown, agreeing to release her into the night. She is in Tim's robe, quiet in the backseat. It rained all morning but the clouds ispersed in the afternoon and the world was reborn by evening. I drive through the incandescent dusk, the world sparkling and vibrant and soft. Tim, beside me in the passenger seat, is silent.

I take the dirt road down to the dock to Lake Stonewell and park just before the dock. The sun is sinking in front of us. The dusk is alive with locusts and, echoing from further down the shore, croaking frogs.

I kill the headlights and the three of us walk out on the dock.

Tim moves in front of her and grips her arms. I remove her robe and take the pins from her hair from behind. She is facing the lake, gazing at Tim. She is vibrating, as if she has already begun to sing inside. When her hair is down, her voice pierces the twilight. I fold the robe and back off the dock, returning to the car.

Tim removes his hands from her arms and she walks past him and, still singing, dives into the lake; there is no hesitation in her actions. She is the proverbial fish returned to water. She disappears for a moment then resurfaces a short distance from the dock, floating effortlessly. Her hair spreads out behind her, caught on the lake surface, rippling the sun's last rays like flames in the water. Her song echoes off the lake. She is singing for Tim. Tim walks down the dock, closer to the water, closer to the creature, towards the setting sun. He stands there, on the edge of the dock. He is prepared to dive. His dark form is stolid and large, as inert and powerful in its dilemma as the stones jutting the shore. I lean against the car and watch, waiting for him to decide, knowing his nature.

Ginny

ELIZABETH O'BRIEN

They say her daddy stickleback, he make a warm nest for her
of snot and clotted seaweed. He make a splinter bone cradle
and inside put baby Ginny. He give her his cold blue eyes,
his sea spray voice, and every word he sing he forge like a barnacle,
                                        warble each on the last.
He give her the moon for a shipwreck legacy, he point it out up
through the water, and Ginny teethe on sea glass, she peer at the briny
string tangle. Ginny grow ripe with battered bottle secrets, grow
strong like a flood of dark mystery. She sharp-teethed and vicious,
                                        pretty as you please
with a mouthful of spiny green fangs. She have boyfriends, so many
boyfriends, like drops in the ocean their bodies go blue and won't float
up topside no more. She pull them to the depths, the smarmy deep, say
a prayer quick for her daddy, that old stickleback eelgrass-loving man.
                                        They say on clear nights
when heaven dip close like a shimmer projectory and the moon
open wide like a cold green eye, lean out: in the shell-mash mirror
of the upside down world you see her like a whisper on platinum
her hair slick with fireworms, Ginny under water catching starfish,
                                        catching men their deaths.

The Life Story of
a Chilean Sea Blob

THEODORE CARTER

The Chilean marine biologist stood on the beach, her black hair swirling in the wind as she spoke into the correspondent's microphone. Milt watched her on his TV screen from his worn recliner. Over the biologist's muffled Spanish, the English translator said, "It very well could be a new species, a giant squid, or perhaps just a rotting piece of whale carcass. It's too early to tell yet." A French scientist with a fully-funded laboratory had volunteered to run DNA tests. Milt took the bowl of peanuts from his lap and placed it on the side table. He shouldn't have been eating cholesterol-rich peanuts.

Milt hoped CNN's translation was accurate, that the female voice-over was being as precise as possible given the incongruities of the two languages. This was important. Already he was separated from the images by thousands of miles of cables, and his television screen bowed outward so that he could never be certain of the accuracy of the pixilated images. What if it was all a grand theatrical performance like *War of the Worlds*? But the running stock quotes at the bottom of the screen and the scrolling headlines assured him that this was in fact real. This was news. "This is CNN."

He heard Sylvia rummaging through the pots and pans in the kitchen. "Sylvie, you should come see this," Milt yelled toward the kitchen. "They found a blob in Chile."

"I'm not coming out there. I know it won't look like much. That's what it means to be a blob."

"It washed up on the beach. They don't know what it is."

The camera cut away from the marine biologist to the mysterious creature, a gray swirl of lava-like flesh that looked as if it had been poured from a pitcher onto the rocky beach. Men and women walked around the mound of meat with tape measures and cameras. The blob's breadth was impressive, forty feet wide, said the biologist, but it was only a couple of feet high at most—an animal pancake. The story hadn't earned the "Breaking News" graphic at the bottom of the screen, but the station had given the segment a catchy title: "The Blob: Sea Treasure or Sea Trash?"

Milt had seen the movie *The Blob* on Thanksgiving in 1958. Sylvia had been at home cooking a turkey. Though approaching thirty at the time, Milt had found it easy to forget his age inside the darkened theater and root for the misunderstood high-school-aged protagonists. Milt had watched Captain

Nemo discover the secrets of the deep in Disney's version of *Twenty Thousand Leagues Under the Sea,* just a few short years before Sputnik launched a race toward space exploration. *The Creature from the Black Lagoon* depicted a sea monster with human emotions who reminded Milt of a guy he'd known in the Army who'd never known the right thing to say. Creature movie kitsch wasn't so farfetched. It could even be prophetic.

Perhaps the Chilean blob had a working brain hidden in its enormity, firing synapses to create thought and an awareness of the scientists and beach goers standing beside it. He imagined a grainy black and white image of a handsome leading man standing on the beach in Chile, his face contorted into sheer panic, begging the Chilean biologist, "What does it want from us?!" A studio executive was probably on the scene already asking the biologist to sell the rights to her life story.

Milt yelled toward the kitchen again. "They say they're going to send the blob to a lab to find out what it is."

He could hear the sizzling sound of browning chicken. Since his last trip to the doctor, Sylvia always made chicken—boneless, skinless, saltless, flavorless. She did her best to dress up the heart-safe protein, but her culinary skills couldn't combat the sheer repetition of it.

"Of course they don't know what it is. If they did, they wouldn't be calling it a blob."

A few years ago Milt had opened the newspaper and learned that by examining a single skin cell, a scientist could map DNA. Analysts and ethicists had argued on talk shows about the realization of a *Jurassic Park* or *Frankenstein* scenario. Fantastic horrors seemed possible. T-Rex might walk down Wall Street or an eight-foot-tall, square-headed monster might ravage suburban homes. But the Frankenstein argument turned into Frankenfoods. The T-Rex scenario turned into Dolly the sheep, hardly a doomsday creature. Soon the whole debate digressed into an argument over stem cells and *Roe v. Wade*. Here was a chance for DNA research to redeem itself. DNA sampling could turn the blob into an honest to goodness sea monster.

CNN's blob segment had lasted only thirty seconds. Coverage turned toward war in the Middle East and a story about a canine beauty pageant. At the very moment that Brutus, a bulldog from Athens, Georgia, was crowned canine king, the Chilean marine biologist and the French DNA specialist were probably on the phone discussing the find. He pictured the biologist holding a test tube containing a slice of blob up to her laboratory's florescent lighting and looking at it quizzically. Milt knew the world's ocean experts were contacting one another to ask, "sea treasure, or sea trash?"

Milt's computer fit awkwardly into the shell of his antique roll top desk. There was no place to put it. The desk's shelving contained compartments for an inkwell, envelopes, paper, and pencils, but nothing for an IBM. Wiring spilled over the edge of the desk face like Medusa's untamed hair and disappeared into a power strip on the floor. He sat down in the black rolling chair ergonomically designed to prevent carpal tunnel syndrome in seniors because, as the salesman had said, "as an older man, it's extremely important to protect yourself against injuries related to computer work." Milt had disliked its comfort ever since. When Milt hit the power switch, the IBM sprang to life with a melodious chime.

Sylvia must have heard the tone over the sound of the sizzling chicken. "Oh boy, here we go," she said. "This blob is going to consume you, isn't it?"

"I just want to know what people are saying," he said.

Though a bit clumsy in his navigation, Milt believed the Internet was miraculous. It could be used to back almost any delusion, hope, or preconceived idea. The lingo that came along with the computer was also a plus. He was now a web "surfer," an "explorer." While maneuvering his mouse, he pictured himself flying through the world's circuitry in a rocket car, or dodging in and out of a curling wave of zeros and ones on a neon surfboard. Every now and then he'd do something that would crash his Internet browser and remind him of his lack of computer competence. When this happened, Milt pictured himself falling off his surfboard and splashing into a sea of electricity or his rocket car running into a circuit board wall. His IBM (or was it an H.A.L.?) would say, "I'm sorry, Milt, but that's something I can't allow to happen."

This time the IBM hummed along just fine, something Milt perceived to be a coincidence rather than the result of his own actions. After clicking through several short wire stories on the blob, Milt found seamonster-hunter.com. He'd never been to the site before, but it looked as though today's page design broke the usual motif. "Sea Monster Found in Chile!!!!!" scrolled across the page in blinking red lettering. Below the headline, plagiarized bits of Reuters and AP stories described the blob's appearance and quoted experts speculating as to what exactly the blob was.

According to seamonsterhunter.com, this was a genuine find, akin to the blob that washed ashore in Florida in 1896 but was never officially identified. Seamonsterhunter.com pointed out that mythology from numerous cultures described sea monster sightings. Vikings, pirates, naval officers, and conquistadors had all recorded encounters with aquatic beasts. Over thousands of years seafarers had meticulously reported their sightings in cave paintings, diaries, and journey logs. They couldn't all be imagining the same things. The blob was proof. Sea monsters did exist. Seamonsterhunter.com had been waiting a long time for this, ever since it launched in 1998. Almost five whole years!

The discovery of the blob also proved the Loch Ness Monster's existence, according to the site. While Nessie had fallen out of vogue after the rise of sonar, the website claimed that the plesiosaur likely burrows in caves and therefore eludes modern fish finding equipment. A page of text explained why R.K. Wilson's famous black and white photo of the serpentine head was a genuine article, despite the photographer's recent admission that it had all been a hoax. According to seamonsterhunter.com, Wilson was simply overburdened by the criticism of disbelievers, exhausted from a lifetime of defending his photo. Milt sympathized with the characterization of R.K. Wilson. Though Milt didn't really believe in sea monsters, UFOs, or Bigfoot, he was still constantly frustrated by the logic of disbelievers.

If R.K. Wilson had only had Sylvia's sound advice to guide him, he probably would have kept his Nessie snapshot safely in a frame over the mantle instead of selling it to the tabloid magazines. Sylvia had recently suggested to Milt that he stop reading his *Ghosts of the Nation's Capitol* book on the subway. "Milt, the thing is that people look at you like you're a crazy old man, like they expect you to start talking to yourself or scream at the hand rail," she'd said. "With that mess of white hair and your befuddled look, people don't know what to think of you." Sylvia had spent decades as a researcher for a downtown public relations firm and knew quite a bit about perceptions. She gently suggested that Milt get his fill of ghosts from Henry James or Shakespeare while on the subway. Sylvia would have given R.K. Wilson some lessons on artful discretion. He would have been better off.

Milt could smell the chicken breasts cooking in lemon juice. With an easy swivel of his ergonomic chair, he looked toward the kitchen doorway and saw Sylvia's shadow on the linoleum, her body remaining around the corner by the pantry. He heard her remove dishes and slam the cabinet door shut, then rustle through the silverware drawer. She emerged from the doorway and began laying down their two place settings, her slender hands moving with quick deliberateness, even athleticism. While Milt had grown pudgy through the middle, she'd maintained her sinewy frame and agility, always zipping from one important task to the next. No more weekend tennis or morning runs, but she still moved in the same way. Milt wondered when exactly her curly hair had turned from blonde to stark white, when wrinkles in her cheeks began to accompany her familiar smile. Before Milt could finish taking her in, she'd vanished again into the kitchen.

"So what are they saying about this blob? Is it going to come get us like in the movies? Should we board up the windows and hide in the cellar?"

Sylvia had a habit of starting conversations after leaving the room.

"Not quite sure yet. The scientists are saying it may be some sort of new species, maybe a giant octopus. Did I tell you that?"

"They really think it's a new species? I thought we already had everything neatly categorized and filed away in the Smithsonian."

She was teasing him. For thirty-five years Milt had worked as a curator carefully categorizing rare items for The Smithsonian Institution. He'd organized national treasures ranging from Abe Lincoln's embarrassing love letters, to Jimi Hendrix's dry cleaning receipts, artifacts so bizarre that they were not only hard to catalog, but hard to believe.

"Well, they said it could be just a decaying whale carcass or whatnot, but the scientist, she thinks it's an octopus."

"Remember a couple months ago when that Alaskan truck driver spotted the giant bird?"

"Yeah, fourteen-foot wingspan. Pterodactyl size."

"Well, you thought it was some sort of aviary monster that would change the animal kingdom, remember? You thought it was leftover from the Jurassic period, but a few days later they decided it was probably just a sea eagle."

"Ah yes, but they never saw it again, thank goodness. The truck driver may have been right. He may have spotted something completely new. It could still be out there nesting in a distant mountaintop, eating small children, or preparing to battle Godzilla."

He heard a snicker from the kitchen and then Sylvia emerged with a frying pan and spatula. She walked over to the table and slid a chicken breast onto each plate. For a second, Milt could have sworn her hair was blonde again, that it was thirty years ago and Sylvia was young and beautiful, that their kitchen was an H.G. Wells time machine. But then, she reached into her pocket and took out his heart pills and placed them on his dinner plate, and he felt impossibly old.

"Well, I'd bet it was just a sea eagle. I suspect you think as much, but you're just too darn stubborn to admit it," she said.

Sylvia retreated to the kitchen with her frying pan and emerged again to distribute unsalted, unbuttered broccoli and healthful brown rice, hippie rice Milt called it, between their two plates.

Milt walked over to the dinner table, took his seat, and looked down at his heart pills. "The Alaskans should make a myth of that sea eagle. Look at the creature economies in the Loch Ness area and in Roswell, New Mexico: Nessie's Breakfast Nook, Monster Mash Night Club, Alien Café, Martian Martial Arts Center. You should get your old PR company on this."

"Yes, radio spots saying 'Buy a pterodactyl time share in Alaska. And bring your binoculars!'" Sylvia said.

They'd been to both Roswell and Loch Ness, not as admitted destinations, but because while on a trip to the Grand Canyon in 1982, Milt thought they "might as well" make the four hour drive over to Roswell. Beside the military base's ominous barbed wire fence, the only other noteworthy stop in Roswell was a small museum filled with crude sketches of aliens drawn by museum staff. Years later, while traveling through Europe, Milt had spent hours figuring out how they could "make a quick jump over to Loch Ness." It had been more than a decade ago, but Sylvia still teased him, usually while they were on their way to a haunted locale, "as long as we're in the eastern United States . . ." Still, Sylvia had made a sport of it too, buying the worst merchandise she could find at each stop. Her prize find had been a compact purchased in Roswell that read "Government Cover-up" across the lid.

Sylvia came to the table. "Well, I hope this one turns out for you, this blob. Maybe it really is a new species."

"I hope so too," Milt said.

Milt wrapped his arms around the terra cotta pot and carried the bush in from the garden. His vision was impaired by the plant's stalk, but the three worn wooden steps marked his passing with a familiar squeek and told him he was on the right path. Right knee creaking a bit, he bent down and placed the plant deep on the porch up against the backside of the house where it would be safe from the August sun.

The pain came on almost like a memory, a recollection of his earlier heart failure. First, he noticed he couldn't quite catch his breath. The realization of it seemed to set in motion other symptoms. His chest tightened and each breath set off a deep, hollow pain. Dizziness set in, and Milt sat down heavy in a deck chair. The familiarity of the pain was somehow comforting. It made him think that he could live through it again. He knew he should yell for Sylvia, but he didn't want her there now. Even if he did decide to yell out, he wasn't sure he could make a noise. Maybe it would simply pass and he'd never have to tell anyone, just a quiet moment on the back porch that he'd keep to himself. A dirty secret.

The pain grew deeper. His chest felt as if stabbed; the muscles in his neck and shoulders twisted into an unforgiving constriction. Milt tried to replace panic with thoughts about afterlife, the unknown, the infinite possibilities, ghosts, mummies, but all that came to him was the thought of Sylvia walking out onto the back porch and finding him lifeless in a plastic patio chair. His heart was failing. His body was giving out. It was so ordinary.

He was lightheaded, sweating, and saw splotches of black. Looking out over the yard, the image of his favorite fir tree appeared blurred. He'd fainted once before, and it had been so easy to just fade off, to lose consciousness.

"Milt! Oh my God!" Sylvia said.

Milt looked up and saw her through a haze. She looked beautifully familiar as she stood in front of him, her face frozen in panic. He wanted to tell her he was fine, that he was just tired. He wanted to tell her he was dying. Instead, he said nothing and let her figure it all out.

Sylvia watched as Milt flipped between the only working channels on his hospital room TV: Univision and The Nashville Network. She wasn't sure if the whole hospital's system was on the fritz, or if he was the only patient restricted to Spanish soap operas and professional wrestling. "You only got in here a couple hours ago, Milt. Just behave yourself," she said to him.

Just moments later, Milt yelled at a nurse he saw walking by the doorway. It was the one Sylvia had named Ms. Ratched an hour earlier after observing her large frame and sour disposition. "Can you get this sick old man a ballgame on the TV?" he asked. Sylvia realized that in asking Milt to behave, she'd started some sort of game that involved the careful prodding of nurse Ratched.

Sylvia looked at the nurse with a sheepish smile. Ratched's expression didn't change. Her austere, pulled-back black hair looked to have stretched her features into a permanent scowl. "The important thing is you get your rest," Ratched said to Milt. Sylvia had noticed that Ms. Ratched was always very practical.

Milt asked Ratched for the ball game again an hour later. Sylvia knew it was more of an attempt to rattle Ratched than a genuine interest in watching the Orioles lose again. Ratched raised one thinly penciled-in eyebrow and replied, "Can I get you anything to eat?"

"How about a bacon cheeseburger, side of fries, and a T-bone steak for dessert?" said Milt. He'd obviously expected Sylvia to be impressed by his pestering, but she didn't feel like playing along. Sometimes Milt's antics grew tiresome. He was like a five-year-old standing on the edge of the diving board waving his arms to attract her attention before his next cannonball.

The nurse gave him a scolding look and Syliva half expected her to wag her finger at Milt in disapproval. Ratched returned a few minutes later and placed a spoon and bowl of Jell-O topped with Cool Whip on the tray over Milt's bed. Milt looked at Sylvia and smiled triumphantly as Ratched turned, her sensible shoes squeaking on the linoleum, and walked out of the room. Sylvia looked down at her lap trying hard not to show amusement.

"Do you want it? I'm not hungry," he said.

"Thanks," she said taking the Jell-O off the bed tray. Sylvia hadn't eaten anything since he'd been admitted.

Upon his arrival, the doctors had told her that Milt had experienced a mild heart attack. He'd need to stay for a few days "under observation." Sylvia wasn't exactly sure what that meant and wondered if they were keeping the more frightening details from her. What did it mean to have two heart attacks? Is the damage cumulative?

She relayed what she'd been told to Milt who acted as if he were on some twisted, Kafkaesque vacation where he could break from life's daily duties but was subject to medical procedures. "So I guess this is what it feels like to be 'under observation,'" Milt said. "What do you think Sylvie, will nurse Ratched look over my body with a magnifying glass? Or maybe the observation is done with a hidden camera somewhere in the room. Perhaps Ratched is an agent of Big Brother. Next time she'll come in here wearing a pea green military uniform wielding a state-issued thermometer. Perhaps the limited television is part of her propaganda war, an attempt to make me into a new breed of eighty-year-old Spanish speaking pro-wrestler."

Sylvia sat hunched over in her chair and studied the movement of her hands as she ran her fingers over a leaf she'd picked off the plant in the lobby. "I suppose they're going to check your arteries and your heart valves to make sure everything is okay now."

It was silent for a moment. Silence had always unnerved Milt. "You've been observing me for over fifty years," he said to her. She didn't know what it was supposed to mean, but understood that he was thanking her for something.

Sylvia kept her face pointed down toward her lap, "Yes, long enough to know you're a crazy old man. You can't lift a seventy-five-pound potted plant like you did when you were twenty-five. You shouldn't do things like that, Milt." She'd started several conversations like this since his first heart attack, and they always ended badly. While Sylvia accepted the predictable onset of arthritis and liver spots, Milt always looked as if he felt betrayed by what he saw in the mirror.

Sylvia, in part thankful he chose to ignore her statement, turned toward the television and pretended to be engrossed in the muted fishing show. After a few minutes, Milt turned off the TV. She realized the predictability of watching overweight men pull up only one kind of fish was probably torturous for him. He'd probably have preferred they catch an old shoe or a rabid muskrat.

He lay still looking up at the square tiles on the ceiling. "Hey, Sylvie," he said, "remember that sea blob that was on the TV yesterday? Did the lab results come back from France?"

"I picked up a paper in the gift shop this morning," Sylvia said. She reached under her chair, pulled out the newspaper, and turned to the back page for the miniscule wire story she'd noticed about Milt's sea blob.

Sylvia was about to read the article word for word, but Milt was sitting up now so expectantly. He clenched the edge of his blanket in two balled fists and his eyes grew wide in anticipation. She couldn't bear to send him back to watching muted bass fishing or to watch him study the ceiling. What Milt liked more than anything was to drive her into mischievousness. Sylvia tried hard to suppress a smile, but a small smirk snuck out anyway, which may have given her away, but it hardly mattered.

"It says here, that in order to perform accurate tests, the Paris laboratory asked that the entire blob, not just a piece, be transported from Chile to France. The creature was loaded onto a barge using a specially designed crane constructed by a Chilean engineer in just two hours." She paused and looked at Milt to see if he'd stop her. He didn't.

"While making its way around Cape Horn, the barge was hijacked by South Asian pirates. Apparently, when the pirates saw the armed guards on the deck of the barge, they assumed the ship was carrying precious metals. After a shoot-out with the armed guards, the pirates found nothing in the cargo hold but the giant blob. They were so upset that they took over the entire barge. So the blob never made it to France. A South Asian pirate gang is toting it around the Atlantic on a barge. The National Academy of Sciences is furious about the loss of this important specimen and has hired a mercenary navy fleet to meet the pirate-controlled barge for a battle off the coast of Brazil. So, we should know more later." Then, deciding an extra bit of detail was needed for authenticity, she added, "Oh, it says here that the name of the barge is 'Nautilus.'"

"Ha!" said Milt, clapping his hands together. "That's great. A sea monster captured by pirates. We'll have to see how this turns out, see if the NAS navy can win back that sea blob."

Milt's IV bag jiggled a bit on its metal stand. His sudden movement had pulled at the slack in the plastic tubes hooked into his arms. Sylvia stood up to make sure nothing had been jarred out of place.

"I'm allowed to move, Sylvie. The tubes are stuck in there. Tomorrow I may go for a jog."

Sylvia awoke from a night's sleep in the bedside hospital chair to start Milt's second day of observation. Nurse Ratched came in soon after to check Milt's vitals and fluids and wrote things down on a clipboard. They talked about her for a while after she had left, then about how Milt would be better soon, but that was about it. He looked ashamed tucked in his standardized bedding, machines beeping, nurses scurrying in and out talking in sterile language and necessary pleasantries. Milt had been so quiet that Sylvia started to worry that his second heart attack had clogged up a bit of his quirk. Their second day in the hospital was only bearable because every few hours he would ask her for the latest update on the sea blob.

Sylvia felt relieved at having a specific duty to perform. She would take the newspaper, now a day old, out from under her chair and give Milt the news. The NAS mercenaries had been victorious after a six-hour battle during the night. Still, the blob had not been transported to the laboratory because it had begun to melt while traveling by truck toward Paris. It was being temporarily stored in a meat locker somewhere in the French countryside.

Sylvia knew the conclusion of the blob saga would have to coincide with Milt's release from the hospital at noon the next day. Two hours before Milt's release from the hospital, Sylvia wracked her brain for the ending of her story. The Chilean biologist, the heroine of the story, had finally overseen the successful transport of the blob to the Paris laboratory and received the results, which of course showed the blob was indeed a new species. The saga would conclude with Sylvia's next installment. There were papers to sign and things to gather before noon too, but that would be the easy part of getting Milt home. With just a half hour to go before his release, Milt acted coy and asked, "So Sylvie, what's the latest on the blob?"

Sylvia opened up the newspaper and held it up in front of her. "The scientific community is in awe of the complex DNA coding contained by the mysterious blob, now officially named *blobous amorphous*," said Sylvia. "Officials are just beginning to understand the medicinal potential of this new species; however, they've already found that proteins from *blobous amorphous* can be used to extract cholesterol from cheeseburgers, potato chips, and peanuts. Chilean biologist Elsa Acosta will no doubt receive the Nobel Prize for finding what will likely become the miracle cure for heart disease. Conservationists have already agreed to fund research that will examine how scientists can grow blobous amorphous specimens in a laboratory setting and curb over-fishing of the now wildly valuable and highly elusive animal. The president of the United States is scheduled to speak today . . ."

Sylvia laid the paper down on her lap and looked at Milt's deeply wrinkled face that'd grown a bit sallow over the last few days. He looked sick, and the hospital room they sat in was barren and sterile. She wanted to tell him what had really happened.

She could tell by his worried look that he had an idea of what was going through her mind. Waving his hand at her, he said "No, no, you're doing fine. Keep going."

"But it's all been resolved. The DNA results came back from the lab yesterday."

He grimaced and waved his hand at her again. "You're doing fine. Go on, Sylvie."

She kept looking at him and curled the newspaper in her hands. "Milt, this is nonsense. The doctor says it was just a mild heart attack. You're really doing just fine, Milt. You don't have to worry. You'll be fine for quite some time."

"Sylvie, what does it say about the captured pirates? When is the trial?"

She realized they could only go on like they had the fifty-five years before. She lifted the paper to hide her eyes. Her voice grew shakey. "The International Anti-Piracy Commission has asked that the trial be held in the United States. They want the blob-nappers to be prosecuted to the fullest extent of the law. They say there is nothing more serious than endangering the life of a newly discovered sea monster. No one should ever do it." She folded the paper, placed it in her lap, and looked at Milt.

"Perfect, Sylvie."

His eyes were closed and his head titled back on the pillow as if he were inhaling the fumes of a fine cigar. Still seated in her chair, Sylvia leaned forward, reached out, and closed her hand around Milt's little finger.

versions

ALI LANZETTA

then we lay like that, tribal, warm-blooded, having
hooked our limbs like celtic knots, in our frenzy where
our breathing is bellows, where we smell like animals.
composure unravels like a bandage, a kite string. we
unfurl like flowers.

i uncrumple a newsprint flower, peeling the inky text
away like the skin of an orange. "if i was an animal,
what kind of animal would i be?" it says. the ink
smudges my fingertips like ash, oily, inside the
crumple it's warm to the touch. you look out at me,
glint where i tilt you to the nightlight. dust to dust. a
whole hidden mythology, spilt across the eyes.

"your smell," he says. "i do?" i say. "i missed it." he
says. "oh," i say, "that's not what i thought you said."

"i make love two times," says the guy behind me on
the bus. to time? to hide? what did he say? someone
must have squeezed his voice from his throat and
stretched it like a caramel, scraped it over the asphalt,
pockmarking it with little rocks, slivered by a crack in
a downtown sidewalk. you know him. midmorning
Banter-Listening, Bus-Riding Alone. we all are.

or, please don't open me near the sink. i don't know
how to swim.

"you're good at that," he says, unspooling the space
between us down his chest, his belly, between our
skins, our eyes. mine are like teacups, a tea-party,
pocket roses. saucers ladled with milk. his are
towering pine shadow, rain on the forest floor, dark
pools darting secret minnows. i tell him everything i
know.

these: bone against skin, knuckled, calloused from digging dirt under winter rainweight, lifting stones pocked with muscovite or moss, hard under supple, naturally occurring weaponry that swells up from the ground. i feel a little sick, my mouth and my mind mismatched, i lick my lip, backwatering him, tasting oranges.

i'm a tired-of talker with sleepy-eyes. dayafter. my mysterious dream affairs with water: i seem to be the cat and the goldfish, lonesome fighterfish, scrappy tabby, tailed, striped, circling the bowl. on the bus a man gets on and says, "i think she's been talking to me in her sleep." a girl is left on the corner, is wearing hair in her eyes, like glasses.

winter fountain spray of white, a spray of baby's breath. pressure and air makes the same amount of water more. thirsty for its plural form. i'm so sleepy, my head nods about, eyes flying half-mast. my conductor of dreamwater, fruit parts, a greenhouse, i think and think and look and grow a spare heart. a man cradles a clementine, his hand the color of cardamom. another has breadcrumbs, is the center of a sundial of pigeons. thirsty to be at the center of something, i balance an orange pencil on my lip and make up things for our eyes to be.

a man on the bus falls into another. men being softer than they think, they both bruise. a soft spot in the skin to sneak a worm, or a tooth, or a secret.

words rub up against me: it's not enough. i bite my lip to keep from wincing my voice out from my trappy throat. "a bird throat," he says, smoothing the feathers down. i'm writing a play where he's the only character, playing himself. a different animal plays him in every act.

in one version of you, your fingers always smell like oranges. you unwrap it delicately, tap a fracture in the peel, crack it open like an egg. there's something alive inside.

warm-blooded. freckle-back down. he sleeps. i inspect
his profile with my dream vision. i'm wearing my
dream glasses. the morning is color-scented. he has
tiny, sun-colored hairs coming out of his ear. what
kind of animal are you? i'm looking at him like a
farmer. the room goes apricot and i go kernelled,
hourglass, above-water, i'm belly-up watching his
jugular inflate and deflate. i guess his heart does that.
"do you float?" it asks me. "i do," i say quietly,
holding a flower in my teeth, not knowing how it got
there. suddenly i'm a little lost, somewhere between
one edge and another.

it's too much, it kind of hurts. a pulsing knot, arms and
legs sticking out. if only i could slide out of the mirror
of skin i'm wearing, leave my exoskeleton in our tin-
can rosebush, rusting along with history. i could rocket
myself to the moon. "fuck—" i say, instead, like it's the
only word i know.

The Sand Ship

CLAIRE MASSEY

We liked it when they built the ship. Before, there was just a big sandpit at that end of the playground. Sometimes it had dog dirt in it. But when we got there one Saturday morning, after we'd been to the shop with Dad so we could get our sweets and he could get his paper and his can, there was a ship in it. Gypsy said it must have sailed there in the night. I told her they'd built it during the week whilst we were at school.

The ship was painted red. It had portholes in its sides. It had a gangplank, which you could walk along, up onto the ship without touching the sand. We claimed the ship. I said I would be the captain and Gypsy could be the crew. First I made her scrub the deck to get rid of all the sand so that we could lay our penny sweets out. I always got cola bottles, fried eggs and gummy bears. I pointed at a big fat seagull that was watching us from the fence and nicked one of Gypsy's flying saucers when she looked up at it. Dad sat on the blue bench over by the football pitch, reading his paper, so she couldn't tell on me anyway.

A little boy tried to come up onto the ship, his Mum was at the other end of the playground pushing a baby on the swings, so I blocked his way. I told Gypsy to pretend she had a hook hand. He jumped down into the sand and ran right to the edge of the sandpit. He crouched there and stuck his hands in, started to dig. He kept looking up at our ship when he didn't think we were looking at him. I saw him pull something green from the sand. "Ben, time to go," his Mum shouted. He buried it again. Gypsy had to dig for a long time to find it when he'd gone.

It was our first piece of treasure. It wasn't like the glass we normally found at the playground. It was all scratched so you couldn't see through it, and it wasn't sharp but smooth like a stone. When Dad shouted us to go, we buried it and pressed two sticks into the sand on top of it.

The next Saturday there were lots of seagulls perched on the side of the ship. They flew up into the air when the playground gate clanged shut and we ran round flapping our arms and squawking to keep them away. I told Gypsy to dig for our treasure and I ran up the gangplank. The ship had been attacked. There were drawings and writing all over the insides, done in black felt tip pen. When she saw them, Gypsy said they must be pirate names. There were cans, too, they looked the same as Dad's. I tipped one up and the last of the smelly brown liquid dribbled onto my fingers. They were sticky for ages, even after I'd wiped them on my jeans. I told Gypsy to come and throw the cans overboard. Then, because she still hadn't found our treasure, I went to show her where to dig.

We couldn't find the glass. We shouldn't have left the X marks the spot on it, someone else must have dug it up. Sand hurts when it gets too far up behind your nails so I watched Gypsy dig deeper and deeper. She pulled a long dark rope of seaweed from the sand. It smelt funny, a bit like the fish section in Morrisons. Gypsy wanted to take it home but I wouldn't let her because it would have made our room stink.

Other Saturdays, we found other treasures. Lots more glass, my favorite pieces were pale pink, and the best thing was the shells. When we took them to Dad he said they were cockle shells. Said the council must have saved themselves some money by lifting the sand from a beach somewhere.

I laid the shells out on the deck to make pictures. Then, when it was time to go, Gypsy buried them underneath the gangplank. But every time she went to dig them back up they weren't there, they'd been scattered all through the sandpit again.

It was a hot day when Gypsy first started worrying about the sand. Dad had bought us Mr. Freezes, mine was a blue raspberry flavor one and Gypsy's was pink. I was making a picture of an octopus on the deck with the shells. Gypsy wouldn't dig for more, she said the sand felt funny, it kept moving between her fingers. She was sat next to me on deck when the boys came into the playground with their bikes. They circled round a few times then dumped them by the gate. They ran up and down the slide and pushed the swings so hard they flew up over the bar. When they ran up the gangplank Gypsy put her hands over my picture.

"What's that supposed to be?"

I didn't say anything. Through the nearest porthole I could see Dad wasn't looking, he was reading his paper. I wondered if I should shout.

"Looks like a cat with a lot of dicks to me," the shortest boy said.

The other two laughed. Then the boy who hadn't said anything walked right up to the picture and stamped on it. Gypsy got her fingers out of the way just in time. He stamped and stamped and stamped until the shells were in tiny pieces that slipped into the cracks between the planks of the deck.

When they'd rode off on their bikes Gypsy tried to dig the slivers of shell out and one piece stuck in her finger like a splinter. She had to pull it out with her teeth.

After that, whenever we got to the playground, Gypsy wanted to play on the slide, or the climbing frame, or, when they weren't tangled up, the swings. She didn't want to play on the ship anymore and she couldn't stand on the sand without falling over. I still liked the ship. I wasn't going to let some stupid boys take it. I guarded it from them and the little kids and the seagulls by myself.

It was a drizzly, windy day when Gypsy saw the tentacle. She stood at the top of the slide and she screamed and screamed. I couldn't see anything. Dad came running.

On the way home Dad wouldn't hold her hand even though she was crying. He said she was stupid, that she'd scared him half to death. It had just been a bit of black bin bag or something blowing in the wind.

When the wind blew the ship creaked. I liked watching it make wave patterns in the sand. I wasn't going to give it up but it wasn't as much fun without Gypsy. I told her she could have two of my penny sweets if she came and sat on it with me, then I tried saying she could have half my bag. She still wouldn't come.

It was a Saturday morning when there were no leaves on the trees. It had rained in the night. The sand looked wet. I jumped down into it from the ship and pretended I was sinking. I shouted 'help' just loud enough so that Gypsy would hear but Dad wouldn't.

She came running, but as soon as she stepped onto the sand I jumped back up onto the gangplank. I was laughing. She plunged downwards, so that only the top half of her was sticking out. She screamed and fought the sand, flinging her arms about. There was sand in her eyes and it coated her teeth and tongue. I screamed too.

Dad's paper blew away in the wind. I saw it fly overhead with the seagulls. He left his can on the bench. He jumped in and managed to push Gypsy out onto the gangplank.

We stayed there screaming until the old lady and the man with the dog came and told us to get down. Everyone says Dad can't have drowned in the sand, but he did.

selections from **In the Circus of You**

a collaboration by poet NICELLE DAVIS
and illustrator CHERYL GROSS

On Its Haunches

the neighbor's poodle sits, a well-trained performer—
opens wide as lion's song—shows me a place to rest
my head. Soft pink tongue. Trust, just another trick
to learn. On all fours, my face between teeth, I watch

children play in the street. They are eating bugs on
a dare. Worms raised above their mouths, they
patrol for each others' hesitation. None want to be
each. All demands others to act. Whole world con-

structed from match. If they make a show of sameness,
they'll beat judgment. It's the boy who wants this
least who goes first. No one follows. They laugh at him.
His mistake for believing. They leave him. *What are you*

looking at? he asks me. Kicks the dog. Yelp folds into bite.
My face is a circle of puncture. The boy calls me, *Freak.*
I turn red. *I'm telling your mother,* I say. He pulls incisors
out of the dog, like scissors from a drawer. Cuts himself to

pieces. Re-grows as replica from every severed limb.
Which one of me will you tattle on? they ask in unison.
On the root of you, I answer. His multiples laugh at me,
you'll never locate our cause. Give it up. Dog breath.

Sideshow Serpentina:
The Last of the Split-Tailed Mermaids

The poster shows her bare-
breasted. Areola painted
pink on yellow paper,
a picture of heat, stage
lights focus on the wet
split of legs, one limb pulls
into the loops of the other.

Nickel crowds, line to see
the boneless woman. Un-
ossified, she lays a rag
draped on planks. A man,
taken by her inescapable
need, buys himself fresh
fish off the ice at Market.

On the trolley, rolling
fingers over scales, he
feels her blonde curls.
Home, unwrapping trout,
newsprint damp, ink bled,
he hates himself for
thinking he could have

such shimmer,
        such silver.

LA SIRENA

A Secret Note from the Dream-Self

Search for the pig's head
blindly—with a spoon,
uproot the skull. Its empty
sockets house dream-
sight. Wear it. You'll see
the pulse of imagery.
Pictures occupy both living
& dead spaces—dreams
are made from such over-
laps. Make a ladder to
reach down the burrow of
your throat. Then trace
the sky's profile with a dry
tongue on parchment.
Rungs are made from tran-
scribed bird-song, but
keep its melodies to yourself.
Dreamers risk a butchery
of words. A bone helmet is no
protection against what
they'll call you if they find you
inside a hog, singing for
sky to dig you a tunnel to stars.

The Collector of Van de Voys

EDMOND CALDWELL

There was money, but there was nothing to buy, or rather nothing else. My wife and I had all the clothes and furniture we needed, so we looked to the walls, which were bare. This was the time when everybody was buying pictures, even shopkeepers like us, so we started to spend the money on pictures. We had no children.

We are a people who put great stock in having a family, so our barrenness grieved us. But we grieved in silence, because we are also a people who put great stock in not complaining.

The van de Voy was a picture such as a child would have liked, but it was my wife who picked it out. No doubt it reminded her of her girlhood on the coast. I say "no doubt" because she never spoke of her past; she was a woman of hard work and few words, which is why I married her in the first place. That, and she had some property (she was no beauty).

She was not a woman who insisted on having her way; in fact, except with customers, she had a yielding nature. So when we went to buy the picture—the van de Voy was our first purchase—her insistence was something I was so little used to seeing, at least in relation to myself, that it took a moment to come into focus as the determination of one who would not be moved. Yet this was just how she made her preference known, even after I suggested that we look at the other pictures. She lowered her head, but did not budge from her place. She had been a hardworking and uncomplaining helpmeet for many years and she had not been feeling well lately, so I agreed to buy the picture.

It was not the best van de Voy but it was a van de Voy, and since he had recently died there would be no more van de Voys. The market in general was high and the market in van de Voys along with it, and you could always resell a picture later. Besides covering bare walls and making a modest house respectable and cultured, pictures at the time were a good investment. I handed the guilders over to the broker for the picture to be wrapped and delivered to our rooms (we lived over our shop) later that day.

I could tell my wife adored our van de Voy by the shy, sidelong glances she gave it. She seldom looked at it straight on, and never in a spirit of reverie, but she was often to be found dusting its frame. The housegirl, Gertie, was forbidden to touch it.

I didn't know anything about pictures, but I knew this was not van de Voy at his best. I liked his earlier pictures better, the few I had seen on my busy rounds, but ours was one of his later pictures. The later ones were the most coveted—you might even think that he had painted them to appeal to the popular taste. As someone who had devoted his life buying and selling things, I should have felt more approving of this than I did. But it was strange enough that I should find myself thinking about pictures at all—I mean besides as another thing that could be bought and sold.

My estimation of our van de Voy was confirmed by a visit to my neighbor's house across the way. He was a tradesman like me and no expert in pictures, but he had had a slight acquaintance with van de Voy himself in the early days, when the young artist was first struggling to establish himself in our city. At the time van de Voy had been a painter of obscure seascapes which were not in the popular taste and had not found their market. At one point the painter had been unable to reimburse my neighbor for a small loan and my neighbor had generously accepted one of these seascapes instead. He had kept it all these years in a dark and little-used corridor in the rear of the house, where a narrow stairway ascended to the servants' rooms, and he was just moving it to the sunny front parlor now that the improvement in the market for van de Voys had been solidified by the painter's death—an irrefutable case of addition by subtraction, my neighbor joked (he was fond of jokes and quips, and especially of actuarial paradoxes).

At first my neighbor's van de Voy looked completely pointless to me: a picture, if you could even call it that, of the sea at night, with dark smudges of sky above and of wave below, a scatter of bright blobs suggesting the reflections of heavenly bodies, and no hint of a ship. A tradesman looking at such a picture would like to see a ship, so that he might muse about what kind of freight it was carrying, and which port it was taking that freight to, and would it fetch a good price. A storm at sea would have added an extra element of drama: would the ship survive without having to throw the freight overboard? Was it fully insured? But there was no ship in this picture, and no storm. It was as if van de Voy had been more interested in the shapes of the waves and the dark colors of sea and sky, and that place in the middle where the sky and the sea appeared to blur and blend (he seemed fond of blurrings and blendings of what should have been clear outlines and well-defined borders). It was almost as if he had painted the picture with no regard for the viewer or purchaser at all, which was absurd.

And yet I was fonder of this picture than of my own van de Voy, the later van de Voy that hung in our own front parlor across the way. There was no accounting for it, that I should prefer a picture that afforded no point of purchase for a viewer's interests, and yet there it was. I almost joked to my neighbor that we should trade van de Voys, but I kept my mouth shut, because my van de Voy was certainly worth four or five times what his van de Voy was worth, and while I did not trust my judgment of pictures, I was no fool when it came to money.

My wife, I say, rarely looked at our van de Voy straight on, at least when it was in the parlor. This was not so in her final illness. She took to her bed and stared at the bare wall across from the footboard and refused any soup. I recognized the same silent determination that had made me buy the picture in the first place, so I brought it in and hung it where her gaze directed. From then on, for those last weeks, she rarely looked away. But even then she said nothing about it, and insisted on no other alteration in the household routine while she composed herself for her death, which she did as quietly and efficiently as she had lived.

I was sitting with her late one afternoon and could see that she studied the van de Voy through the slits of her eyes. I left to visit the commode—a few years ago we had been able to afford having one of these installed off the second-floor landing so that we did not have to visit the shed at the back of our small garden, which the shop assistants and servants still had to use— and when I returned I found her in the same position, with her eyes barely open and her fingers on the counterpane. But I knew immediately that this was only her husk and that her spirit had flown to its reward, which is eternal rest in the bosom of our Lord Jesus Christ. One moment she was alive and the next she was dead, without the slightest change in the folds of the bedclothes. Her eyes still looked at the painting, but now this was just a figure of speech, because she could not see anything.

It was only when I looked at the van de Voy that I felt any sadness, and even then it was mild. I was sad because I knew that the picture had meant something to her, something I felt certain had to do with her childhood by the sea, about which I knew nothing except that it had taken place by the sea. That was her single point of reference, those few times she had had occasion to bring it up. "When I was a girl," she would say, "by the sea." Or: "When I was a growing up, by the sea."

Unlike his earlier paintings, there was plenty to look at in this van de Voy. It was a beach scene, with two young girls—sisters by the looks of them— in the foreground and the rocky cliffs of the bay curving out to open sea with a ship and some clouds in the background. The girls were dressed in bright smocks and aprons and bonnets such as our women wear, the ends of their flaxen hair and their ribbons tugged by the sea breeze. The older sister, seen in profile and wearing a rose-colored smock, was leaning against a rustic old rowboat overturned on the sand. She had her arm around the shoulder of her younger sister, who stood close by in a light green smock. This girl had a hand on her sister's leg and a little smutch of seaweed on her cheek. Their smiling faces were like sun and moon: the older girl gazed out to sea and the younger gazed up at her sister's face, the older pleased by what she saw and the younger pleased by her sister's pleasure. In the upper left-hand corner of the picture a great three-masted schooner was cresting into view over the horizon, its sails taut in the wind. You could just make out a tiny figure waving from the bow. This spectacle had drawn the girls' attention from their previous pastime, a picnic and collecting expedition among the sea-wrack. Some of the contents of the basket at their feet had spilled out on the sand—a tea cup and the whimsical touch of an hourglass—and a little pile of shells and odd flotsam lay nearby. Their puppy was just emerging from around the overturned rowboat, padding towards the girls with its head cocked at a darling angle.

A sentimental scene, innocent youth admiring the grand vista of the age-old world, nothing more. These sorts of images were popular at the time; our people liked to see them on their serving dishes and teapots and vases. This one had charmed my wife and soothed her passage out of the world, but the more I looked the more my sadness turn to disquiet.

At that moment Gertie, our housegirl, came in. I could hear her behind me rustling the bedclothes. "Such a waste," she sighed, "these fine linens bound for the furnace." There was more rustling, then a sudden intake of breath. "Mistress, mistress, what's this you've left us?" I looked at the picture and heard Gertie's soft footsteps approach. "Master, look at this." Gertie was a good servant but young and as headstrong as my wife had been yielding. "Look." Something flashed in the loose cage of her slender fingers. "Look, master, look."

She came so close that I could feel her against me, but I could not tear my eyes away from our van de Voy. I seemed to be seeing it for the first time— it was the same in every detail as a moment before, but the details now made a different picture. I had the sensation of the sturdy floorboards beneath our feet giving way and Gertie and I plunging into the void, but the picture plunged with us at the same speed and so continued, with a kind of mockery, to hang motionless in my gaze.

A sudden and treacherous storm was blowing up behind the three-masted schooner on the horizon; I could just make out the slight line of a snapped cable and one of the masts akilter. The tiny figure on the bow was waving in terror, the helpless plea of a lost soul. The ship was being driven into the cliffs where it would shatter to pieces, and those who were not drowned or crushed would be the prey of sharks, whose fins I had mistaken for small rocks protruding from the waters. This prospect the elder girl regarded not with pity or fear but with glee. Her fingers had wrenched up a handful of cloth on her younger sister's shoulder and a few locks of flaxen hair with it, as if her profound sympathy with the savage spectacle she was about to witness might lead her to tear her sibling apart. Yet the younger girl was her match for depravity: it was not seaweed on her face but the open rot of a congenital syphilis, and the hand on her sister's thigh was creeping to the older girl's private place, tugging up the apron on its way. The little girl's smile was a leer; she searched for a kind of obliteration in her sister's eyes. Darkness gaped between the grim ribs of the overturned hull behind them— it was the remains of a lifeboat from a previous wreck; the girls had come here hoping for one of the disasters that were endemic to this part of the coast. But in their heated delirium they failed to notice the flecks of diseased foam around the slavering chops of the approaching dog—a mangy stray and not a beloved pet after all. The last grains in the cracked hourglass at their feet mingled with the numberless sands.

I closed my eyes.

"Look, master, look." Gertie was pressing so closely against me that I could feel the weight and warmth of her body through apron, smock, and shift. Against my leg I felt the small pillow of buttery fat where her thighs met. "Master, look." As if through a curtain I seemed to see her eyes roll back into her head and her mouth open and chin lift, exposing a white throat. I felt her half-closed fist against my chest. "Look."

There is little more to tell. My business flourished, and I expanded into a wholesale firm. More success followed and I expanded again—shipping, this time. But a part of my fortune I held in reserve for seeking out and purchasing all of the canvases of the painter van de Voys. I bought them all, even those which had made their way overseas. And all of them I destroyed.

Or rather all save one, which I keep behind the doors of a locked cabinet by my bed, and which I plan to look upon when I compose myself for death. When I die the last van de Voy will die with me—I have ordered its destruction in my will. I know this commission will be carried out, because on it depends the inheritance of my fortune by my beneficiaries, the children I had with my second wife, Gertie: unless the picture is destroyed by fire in the presence of my attorney—a man of the greatest rectitude and absolutely no imagination—all of my properties will be liquidated into a charity fund for indigent painters. I brought my children up to cherish the solid values of our race: they will do anything to keep this from happening.

The painting I have temporarily retained is not the one my late wife was so fond of and the last thing her earthly eyes beheld—that was the first to be consigned to the furnace, along with the locket that van de Voy had inscribed to the memory of their too-brief summer together on the coast, when they were both so young and so poor. No, this van de Voy is the one that my neighbor kept first in his dark back hallway and later in his sunny front parlor, from the period before the artist's transformation into a painter in the popular mode. It is a small canvas—the pieces of the frame, rearranged into a square, would efface it—and so dark that you almost cannot tell what it depicts. Only the blobs of light give its subject away as the heavens reflected in a dark sea, as though someone had scattered silver guilders on the waters and the painter had caught them in the moment before they sank.

Brunhilde's Escape

DANYA GOODMAN

Brunhilde, the zoo's most duchess hippo, was rumored to last be seen near a clump of oak trees by I-95. We fret for the moistness of her skin, and we wonder about the hoof of a hippo. Can she withstand concrete? What if a shard of glass pierces her webbed toes? Nonetheless, she soldiers on. Heinz, her compatriot and consort, remains cowed in the lagoon, shunning the gate an errant zoo-keeper left to swing over night. We avoid his gaze, not wanting to remind him of his cowardice and his loss. Brunhilde, Brunhilde! We imagine him calling, his great teeth clacking in the sunlight. But no, he remains diminished, refusing even the frozen carp we tempt him with. So it is our voices instead, lacking Heinz's authoritative baritone, which call for Brunhilde. We split into even groups and tramp through the forest, being sure to stare suspiciously into every puddle. Brunhilde! We whisper, like lovers. Come back to us. Secretly, though, we each harbor delight that her proud and foreboding footsteps are now free to stomp on pasture and road alike. We leave offerings of salmon on our doorsteps, buckets of cool water. We hose our yards into refreshing glomps of mud, and in Brunhilde's absence, we roll in it ourselves. Cover ourselves in the muck until we are indistinguishable wet joyful creatures. Still, she does not return. As a city, bereft, we hunch ever-forward.

· Phylum ·

all he can remember is pleading in the cave
for the rest of his pack he so
placidly loved.

—*Reintroduction*

Proximity

JOSH DENSLOW

When it happens, it feels as though his head is being forced through a keyhole. His organs pile up on one another as he's rolled into a cylindrical tube. Then the pain cascades from his skull down to his toes, like his skin is being seared. The sensation only lasts for a few seconds, but he's never gotten used to it. It's why he says he's never going to do it again. Every time. But the thing is, Neil Brigman can teleport. It just hurts like a bitch.

And this time he has to. He locked his damn car keys in the house again. Well, not a house per se. More like the room above the garage at his mom's house. But whatever. He can't tell her. His mom just had the responsibility talk with him again last night. That's why he's going to this interview in the first place. Apparently, he can't work for Uncle Dalton for the rest of his life.

He pulls off his tie, careful not to undo the knot, and then unbuttons his shirt. His dad tied this plaid tie for him about five years ago, and Neil just has to drop it over his head when he needs to wear one. Which is barely ever.

The rickety stairs creak as he climbs up to his small studio apartment. He throws the shirt and tie over the railing and visualizes the spot between his bed and his computer desk. Really concentrates on it.

The pain rips through him. It's as though every bone in his body has been broken at the same time. Then the slight shift. He isn't outside anymore. He unclenches his eyes and his teeth, his undershirt completely soaked through with his sweat, and he finds himself now standing in that spot he pictured between his bed and his computer desk. And sure enough, his keys are sitting right there next to the printer.

He staggers across the room, his knees weak. Clutching the table, he whips open the small refrigerator and pulls out a bottle of water. Sweat pours down his legs. Should've taken his pants off, too.

He yanks the cap off the bottle and chugs the whole thing in a few big gulps. His eyes stop trying to jump from their sockets and decide to throb instead. He grabs a t-shirt he's thrown on top of the table and wipes off his face.

The clock on the microwave says 2:10. He has to be at the police station in twenty minutes. If only he hadn't slept until 1:45, he wouldn't have been in such a hurry. And he wouldn't have forgotten his keys.

And he wouldn't have had to teleport.

．　　．　　．

Small town police stations are great. This one tries as hard as it can to look important. The front archway is wide and imposing. Police cars are parked in a neat row out front, perfectly spaced and shining in new coats of wax.

Neil walks in and is immediately recognized by Frank Palouzo. His nose is even redder than the last time he saw him. "What are you doing here, Big Guy?"

"Didn't Dad tell you? I'm here to interview for the dispatcher job."

"You're as good as in then. So don't stress." Frank grins at him from behind his desk.

But that's exactly why Neil is stressed. He's going to get this job. His dad has been a cop here for twenty years. Pretty much everyone knows Neil already. He can hear his life locking into place and he doesn't like tight places.

His dad's out on patrol so Neil doesn't see him before sitting down with Shirley. She used to come to all of his birthday parties when he was a kid. For a long time, she was the only black person that Neil knew. Today she's wearing bright red lipstick, most of it hanging out on her teeth.

"You don't stop by anymore!" she exclaims.

"I've been busy."

"Oh yeah?" She's not buying it. "Are you even working now?"

"I collect quarters from washers and dryers. My uncle owns a self-service laundry."

"Norman owns a laundromat?"

"No, not Dad's brother. My mom's brother Dalton. And he doesn't call it a laundromat. I guess the word Laundromat was a trademark of Westinghouse, or something. It's like calling tissue paper Kleenex."

"Sounds like he takes it pretty seriously."

"He gets paid in quarters. He has to be serious about it."

"You'll like this job much better."

But this job is eight hours a day, not like the one hour he spends emptying the laundry machines. And he'll be working with his dad. His dad'll be out cruising the streets in his squad car and Neil will be telling him where he needs to go. In a weird way, it'll be like Neil is telling his dad what to do. Like a faux boss of sorts. This does not appeal to him.

And besides, should Neil really be working for the police?

The first time he used his power for questionable purposes was the year after his parents got divorced. Breaking and entering. Well, no breaking. Just entering. He teleported into Tim Sommers's house and played his Nintendo when he wasn't home.

By then, Neil had worked out the backpack system. Inside was his Thundercats thermos filled with water for the journey in and his Star Wars thermos for the journey out. He also put in one of his mom's light blue bathroom towels so he could soak up as much of the sweat as possible. It wasn't like those first few times, in Kindergarten, when he'd suddenly teleported home from school. He could control it now.

The day before, Tim had invited everyone over to his house to show off his new game system. It was four kids crowded around him watching him play. He didn't give anyone else a chance to even touch the controller.

Neil asked his mom for one and she said no way, not until he got his grades up. And suddenly, Neil figured out a great way to use his power other than to scare the crap out of his dog Mitzi and to sometimes skip the long walk home from school. He watched Tim and his parents drive away for a family dinner at Sizzler and then he concentrated on the space in front of Tim's TV.

A moment later he was shaking off the pain and sucking all of the water out of the Thundercats thermos. He wiped his hands and face with the towel. He'd never been in Tim's room without Tim being there. His dog, a boxer named Frederico, tapped around on the hardwood floor downstairs. Neil shut the door.

It was exciting to be somewhere he wasn't supposed to be. He clicked on Tim's television and waited for a picture to appear. Then he turned on the Nintendo. The logo splashed across the screen. Neil picked up the controller and began to play.

He didn't know they had come home until he heard Tim pounding up the stairs to play his video game before bed.

Neil didn't have time to teleport. He grabbed his bag and ran into the closet just as Tim burst into the room. He froze at the sight of the glowing television displaying his game.

"Mom!" Tim yelled in fear.

And Neil concentrated on his own bedroom.

Add a beer gut, some acne scars and a chipped front tooth to young Tim Sommers and you get the Tim Sommers of now; who happens to be sitting across the booth from Neil.

"Have you seen these pornos where you can change the angle of the camera?" he asks Neil before downing the dregs of his beer.

"Sounds like we've finally entered the future."

Barky's is packed with kids from the local community college with fake IDs. Neil doesn't recognize anyone though he's technically a student there. He just isn't taking any classes at the moment. This particular moment has been going on for two years.

Neil and Tim say they're going to try out a new bar, but they never do. The beer tastes like pipe cleaner. The floor is so gummy that Tim once walked out with a condom stuck to the bottom of his work boots. The whole place smells like warped wood. Like broken teeth and bloody noses.

But as their group dwindled, they craved some consistency. Some of the guys went to out of state colleges, one or two joined the army, and scarily enough, some of them were dads. Whenever these guys visited, or received a get out of jail free card from their families, they all knew they could find Neil and Tim right there in the booth at Barky's.

Jeremy Barnes is working the bar tonight and he's acting like everyone there is over twenty-one. He's not really fat, but he has a solid gut that hangs over the front of his pants. His hair is perpetually dirty and his skin is dry and flakey. But maybe Neil is hyper-sensitive.

The thing is this: Jeremy is dating his mother.

The same guy that all of Neil's friends thought was so cool. The guy who'd hook them all up with free shots. The guy who took pictures of Barky's customers' cleavage and hung them up in the men's room. The guy who lit his farts while standing on the bar. This classy fellow is his mom's boyfriend.

"You're staring at Jeremy again," Tim says.

"No I'm not."

"I think you're obsessed." Tim spins his empty glass around on the table. "You're upset that this guy is putting his little pecker in the same hole that you jumped out of."

"Don't be gross," Neil says.

"Okay, then go and say hello to him. Stop being so creepy. And while you're up there, get me another beer."

Jeremy is desperate to be Neil's friend. He catches Neil's eye across the bar and ditches the college kids to say hello. The look is in full effect. Not the one he wears when he's the party all night, free-drink giving, lascivious barkeep. This is the unabashed, please-like-me look. He opens his eyes wide and pulls his mouth into a tight smile, an enormous dimple forming on his left cheek. And he's so nervous that he keeps tugging at the back of his hair.

"Whatever you want, it's on the house," Jeremy says.

"I'll just have a beer."

"How'd the job interview go?"

Neil can't stand that his mom tells Jeremy stuff about him. "It went well."

"I bet you'll get it."

"That's what everyone keeps telling me."

Jeremy finishes pouring the beer and slides it across the bar. "You want one for your friend?" Tim's looking at them from the booth, the plaid tie around his enormous head.

"No thanks." Neil slaps a ten on the bar. "Keep the change."

Jeremy rubs his hands together and clears his throat. "So, we're going to be neighbors, huh?"

"What do you mean?"

"Oh, I thought she told you last night. I'm, uh, moving in with your mom." He tugs at his hair.

Neil's shoulders tighten and the beer sloshes around in the glass. Foam seeps between his fingers. So his mom is kicking him out so that Jeremy can move in. No wonder she had the responsibility talk with him.

"Don't worry, you don't have to help me move if you don't want." Jeremy grunts, which is probably supposed to be a laugh.

Neil walks away and slams the beer down on the table in front of Tim. "What happened?"

"Jeremy is moving in with my mom."

"No, I meant with the beer. Like half of it is gone."

"What did you do with my tie?" Neil's throat is so dry he can barely push out the words.

Tim reaches onto the seat next to him and holds up the plaid tie. Fucking Tim untied the damn knot.

Things were better a few weeks ago. Neil's mom said she'd met a guy in line at the bank. They'd eaten dinner a few times and he made her laugh like crazy. Her words. Something Neil's father could never do, according to her. "He was such a bore, wouldn't know a joke if it had a name tag," she always said about him. "And this guy's such an adorable burly bear."

How was Neil supposed to know it was Jeremy? Neil's mom arranged for them to meet over dinner at Jeremy's apartment prompting Jeremy to confess one night at Barky's. He had begged Neil to act like they didn't know each other. He didn't want to be the guy that Neil had hundreds of stories about. He wanted to stand on his own two feet. So Neil pretended they'd never met, as if he hadn't been at Barky's the night before, drinking until he puked in Tim's mom's car. He and his mother took the stairs to the second floor. The carpet was so worn that the slats of wood were visible underneath it.

Jeremy's apartment was threadbare and hastily cleaned for guests. Neil wouldn't want to see what was under the couch or crammed into closets. He had some movie posters on the wall with no frames: *Raging Bull, A Clockwork Orange,* and *The Big Lebowski.* He also had a plant that was desperately clinging to life. It sat in a large pot next to the television and was about five feet tall. Neil decided that was the spot.

If Neil can't picture where he'll appear, he can't teleport. He can't leap somewhere he's never been. It was worth sitting through the watery spaghetti and Jeremy's inane attempts at conversation just to find that one spot.

When he leapt into Jeremy's apartment the next night, he thought he'd never recover. He actually left through the front door when he was done. It seemed to get more painful as he got older. When he was in high school, he could leap in and out of Target three or four nights a week without too many problems. He'd fill a large trash bag with video games and movies and then sell them at school. As he approached his mid-twenties though, he'd feel his bones aching sometimes days after a leap.

Jeremy had an XBOX and at least twenty games that he kept stashed in a black TV stand. There was a pot, a pan, three cans of soup and eight boxes of macaroni and cheese all in one cabinet in the kitchen. The other four cabinets were empty. He had milk, butter and orange juice in the refrigerator along with a dozen half empty take-out containers. Clothes were stuffed into the six drawers in his room with no intelligent design. Also, nothing was folded. Three shirts were hung in the closet. But the bed was made. And Neil was sure that his mother had brought her own pillow.

The bathroom was smudged and grimy. Two toothbrushes sat in a Barky's mug on the sink. The rug on the floor looked brand new, light blue and plush. Jeremy had a copy of *On the Road* on the toilet. Neil walked into the front room and sat on the tattered couch.

It only took Neil eight minutes to look around the place, but it wasn't until he was staring up at Jeremy's ceiling that he'd realized he was disappointed. He'd wanted to find something that would make Jeremy look bad.

There was only one thing he could do. Neil went back into the bathroom and emptied all of Jeremy's shampoo and conditioner. Then he squirted all of the toothpaste down the drain. Neil was going to pull out all of his floss but apparently the dude didn't use any. But that surely wasn't bad enough to get his mom to dump him. He wanted to do something to Jeremy's toothbrush but he didn't know which was which. Neil stepped into the bedroom and looked around. Then he turned quickly and went into the bathroom again. He moved Jeremy's bookmark back two chapters.

In the kitchen, he dumped out the milk and the orange juice and returned the empty containers. But when he shut the refrigerator door, he noticed something he hadn't seen before. Mixed in with all the coupons and ads for food places was a small picture of his mother and Jeremy sitting at a table. She had her hand on his arm and his head was tilted slightly toward her. Neil pulled the picture out from under the Barky's magnet and slid it into the front pocket of his bag.

Neil turns the key in the dryer and opens the front. He holds the ratty cloth bag open and lets the quarters fall into it; the dry slapping of the coins sounds like a river. Why would it matter if Neil was living on top of the garage if Jeremy was moving into the main house?

He cinches the bag of coins and hefts it into the back room. He stuffs the bag into a large, rectangular safe bolted to the floor. He rubs his eyes and takes a deep breath before stepping back into the laundry area.

The loud chirp of a siren blares outside and a quick burst of police lights streak across the walls of the laundry facility.

Whereas Neil looks like he can't even lift half his own body weight, his dad looks like he could eat half of Neil's body weight in one sitting. He has big ruddy cheeks and small blue eyes. His mom always described his dad as beefy, which seems pretty accurate. Though she always said it in a dreamy way. Before the divorce.

Neil strolls up to the patrol car and his dad tosses him a long plastic bag. "I brought you a sandwich."

"Thanks."

"I heard you met with Shirley."

"Yeah, look Dad, I . . ."

All business. "Is Jeremy moving in with your mother?"

How does his dad hear this shit?

"I ran into Tim at the 7-11."

Neil shoots a short burst of air through his nose. "Tim's an asshole."

"You know he eats the hotdogs there? I don't even eat those things."

"I was going to tell you about Jeremy." Neil tugs at his left elbow, the sandwich bag squished in his armpit.

"I just didn't realize your mom was that serious." Neil's dad's eyebrows lower over his eyes.

Neil's parents have been divorced for fifteen years now. But Neil's dad is carrying an eternal flame. Sort of pathetic. He sends flowers to her office on her birthday. He keeps in touch with her parents and her brother. As far as Neil knows, he hasn't dated anyone else. He has her picture in his wallet.

"I'm sorry, Dad," Neil says. "If it makes you feel any better, Mom's kicking me out of the garage."

His dad's eyes light up briefly. "You can stay with me, buddy. I've got room."

Neil's dad's apartment is like a dumpster behind an Italian restaurant. Neil may not be the cleanest guy ever, but he does have standards.

"I'll work it out."

"What do you think of Jeremy? Do you like him? Is he good for your mom?"

Neil's chest tightens. "I don't know. I think maybe he just likes her because of the boob job." The words hang in front of him like a neon sign.

"I don't know why she ever did that."

A group of kids on skateboards cut across the parking lot, their shirts flapping behind them. Just before they turn the corner one of them yells "Pig!" and they all laugh.

"I think you need to put Mom behind you. There's nothing we can do about it."

"When I saw that she was calling the other day, I thought to myself, God, don't let me have a heart attack before I get a chance to speak to her."

"Why did she call?"

"She wanted me to help get you this job."

Now it makes sense; she's using his dad. Of course he'd try to help her out.

"She's trying to hijack my life. I thought things were fine the way they were."

"Now you know how I feel."

Neil leans against the vending machine listening to the thumping of a washer. His sandwich sits next to him, unwrapped. The place is empty except for a man wearing purple sweatpants and sunglasses. He rubs frantically at the collar of a white shirt. After a few minutes he gives up and tosses it into a large trash can by the door. He catches Neil looking at him. "My wife got me that shirt."

The brilliant idea hurtles from the trash can and smacks Neil directly in the middle of his forehead.

When he gets home, there's a post-it note on his door. *We need to talk.* There's no way his mom missed his arrival, so he quickly puts a few things in his dresser and wipes down the small kitchen table. He's been living in the studio over the garage for so long that he can't imagine living anywhere else. His mom must have picked up on this sentiment, too. She probably pictures a fifty-year-old Neil climbing the stairs after another night at the bar. Neil shivers.

As soon as he hears the first stair creak, Neil pulls open the door. The light from the main house casts a shadow across his mom's face, but he can tell she's wearing her serious face. This isn't going to be easy.

"You told Dad to get me that job?"

Her hair is pulled back and she's wearing beige slacks and a light blue cardigan. She gets about halfway up and stops, her manicured nails red against the brown railing. "It's a good job."

"But you went behind my back."

"As if you were going to take my advice."

She has a point there. "You're pushing me out so Jeremy can come in and take over."

"Oh honey." She straightens her back as she huffs up the last few stairs. Neil walks into the room before she can reach him. "This has nothing to do with Jeremy."

She leans against the door jamb, suddenly looking old and tired. "Don't you want me to be happy?"

She sure played that card early. "Of course I do. I just don't know why I have to leave for that to happen."

"I can't be fully happy until I know you're settled. We just want the best for you."

"Now you guys are a *we*?"

"I meant me and your dad." Neil's dad would probably shit if he heard her talk about him like that. "I know I should've told you about Jeremy moving in. But we had such a nice conversation the other night. And you sounded serious about getting started . . . I didn't want to ruin it."

"Sure. I'm a loser."

"I'm not saying that."

"What about Jeremy? He's about the biggest loser I know."

She purses her lips. "You don't mean that."

"I've known Jeremy for a long time. He's scummy. He's crass. He ogles girls. He wipes his boogers under the bar. For Christ's sake mom, the only talent he has is lighting his farts."

"Jeremy confessed that you two knew each other already. And I'm sure he does those things to get tips. Your friends like him. And I think you used to like him, too."

"He's just a clown. Someone to entertain you. He's not someone who dates your mom."

"Well maybe I could use a little fun in my life. I certainly don't expect you to understand that." She stares at him, her sadness palpable. Then she turns and walks quietly down the stairs.

"Fine, I'll start packing," Neil calls after her. But that's not what she wants to hear.

Buying tampons is weird. Neil spends so much time building up the nerve, that he's disappointed when the cashier doesn't even blink. He also buys red lipstick and some cheap perfume. And a pack of cotton panties. He puts it all in his backpack with four bottles of water and a towel. He's ready to go right now.

Neil's mom and Jeremy usually go out on Wednesdays. His mom calls it Movie Night. Neil pulls the blinds up and sits down at the table. From there, he can see the tail end of the driveway. Waiting is not his strong suit.

About an hour later, he opens the bag again to make sure he remembered everything. He did. He's wearing a pair of faded sweat pants and an old Pearl Jam T-shirt from high school. Maybe he'll finally toss these clothes out when he's done.

At about a quarter to six, as the sun falls behind the main house, Jeremy pulls up in his powder blue Volkswagon bug. He grinds to a halt and kills the motor. The sky is rippled with deep red stripes.

He springs out, his belly tucked into a green button-up shirt. Neil watches him jog up to the front door and ring the bell. Jeremy rubs his hands together as he waits. Then he tosses a quick glance to the studio on top of the garage. Neil instinctually ducks even though he's pretty sure Jeremy can't see in.

His mom opens the door, her hair bobbed, wearing dark blue jeans. She takes Jeremy by the arm and he leads her to the car. Opens the door for her. Jumps in on his side. Fires up the motor. Backs out the driveway.

It was that easy.

Now the hard part. Neil's a little afraid to do the leap. He's been talking himself into it all day. No time like the present, though. He hefts the bag onto his back and pictures that strip of carpet between the plant and the TV. He remembers it so well, it's like he lived half of his life there.

The pain starts at his neck, but something is different. He throws up on his table just as his body rolls in on itself. He tries to stop it, but it's too late.

A moment later, he finds his face pressed against Jeremy's dirty carpet, sweat dripping down his nose. He opens his eyes, sending waves of pain cascading over his scalp. Then he realizes he can't move his arms and that's when the panic sets in.

He's going to die of dehydration. His stomach roils. His ears ring so loudly it makes him dizzy. He pictures Jeremy coming home to find him curled up and dead next to his television.

Neil feels his legs come back first. He kicks them back and forth, hoping to roll himself onto his back. Then he finally feels his arms return. He heaves himself up onto one knee and yanks the back pack off. But his fingers are slower. The bag won't unzip.

He gets to his feet, his knees wobbling, and stumbles into the small kitchen. The sink is only a few steps away. He shoves his head under the faucet and turns on the water. The water splashes down his cheek and into the desert of his mouth. He can't seem to get enough to go down his throat, but what does burns as it travels through his esophagus.

Neil staggers backward and finally gets his bag open. He pulls out a bottle of water and gulps the whole thing. A dull ache permeates his every joint. His vision is blurry. He drinks another bottle of water and then stomps into the front room and sits on the couch. His breath rips through his throat. His eyes throb.

As he waits for the worst of it to pass, his arms twitch spasmodically. But his heart rate finally gets back to normal. He has a terrible headache, but he can think clearly now.

He's able to breathe without much pain, so he gets back to his feet and begins plotting. The panties should be on the couch. Another pair on the handle leading to the bedroom. Neil sprays the bed with the cheap perfume, as musky as the reptile cage at the zoo, and then leaves the bottle on the bathroom sink. He puts the lipstick on the nightstand. Then the kicker. A tampon in the bathroom trash.

When he's done, all that's left of the pain is the throbbing in his eyes and a soreness in his joints. And the memory, of course. There's no way he's teleporting home.

Neil lets himself out of the apartment, locking the door behind him, and walks to the diner down the street.

Of course, after all his preparing, he forgot to pack his wallet. Now he's standing on the sidewalk in front of the diner and he could really use a drink. He digs in the front pocket of his bag for a few crumpled bills or some loose change, but instead finds the picture he stole from Jeremy's the first time he was there. He remembers being disgusted by how close Jeremy and his mom were sitting. But this time, he notices her face. The crinkles around her eyes from the full smile on her lips. She's forgotten all about keeping her crooked front teeth covered. She has one hand on Jeremy's arm and the other lightly grazing the back of his head.

Neil purses his lips and exhales loudly through his nose. Then his cell phone rings. He answers it without looking at the display, and even though he gets the same call every evening, he's not ready for Tim's peppy question. "Feel like going to Barky's?"

"I'm pretty sure that's my shirt," Tim says as they slide into a booth. "I left it at your house one time when I slept over."

"You didn't even like Pearl Jam."

"But Christine Evenson did, and I wanted to nail her. Also, you look like shit."

Neil rubs his fingers on the side of his mug.

"You okay, man?" Tim asks.

"I think I might have done something bad."

"You mean how you stole my shirt? I forgive you."

"What if I told you I came up with a way to make my mom dump Jeremy?"

"You could just tell her he lights his farts."

"She knows already."

Tim shakes his head. "He must be good in the sack or something."

"Never mind. Forget I said anything."

Tim chugs his entire beer, then he wipes his sleeve across his mouth. "So, be honest with me. Why don't you think your mom should date Jeremy? Does he not make enough money? Is he not attractive enough? Because he doesn't seem all that bad to me. In fact, he sort of reminds me of you."

Neil's bones ache and his eyes droop. He wipes condensation from the mug onto his eye lids.

"So what was your big idea?"

Neil shrugs. "Putting women's accessories in his apartment so my mom thought he was cheating on her."

Tim laughs. "How're you going to get in?"

"I guess it's a bad idea."

"I'm not saying it wouldn't work. I just don't think you could figure out how to get in there."

"Yeah. It's a dumb idea."

"It would work like a charm though."

Neil's chest tightens, but he's pretty sure it's not from the leap earlier.

Tim snags Neil's beer and takes a long swig. "I wish my mom would ditch my dad and start dating Jeremy. And you can be sure I'd be taking as much free beer as he'd give me."

Tim drops Neil off at the laundry facility. After dumping the coin bag in the safe and checking in with Uncle Dalton, Neil steps outside and sits on the curb. He watches people walk in and out of the liquor store across the street.

Maybe he should get drunk and pass out in the back next to the safe. Very tempting.

But then a cop car pulls up in front of him, his dad's meaty arm hanging out the window. "Sorry, no sandwich tonight. I was out on a call."

"It's okay," Neil says.

"You'll never believe this. That nutcase Jeremy called in a burglary. But instead of someone taking his stuff, they left new stuff in his apartment."

Neil swallows. "What do you mean?"

"This is hilarious. He says someone broke in and put women's undergarments in his apartment. As if your mother is ever going to believe that." He laughs and his chin wiggles from side to side. "It was pathetic."

"Maybe that really happened."

"Come on. He cheated on your mom and she caught him. And he thinks that if he makes a fool of himself by calling the cops, she'll believe his bullshit story."

"Are they going to dust for prints?" At this point, it would be a relief to get caught.

"Waste of taxpayer money. And get this. Says it happened before. Except the last time they emptied his shampoo and the food in his refrigerator. He didn't call that one in."

His dad's face purples, a poster child for impending heart attacks.

"So that's it? They won't even investigate?"

"Still no law against cheating, unfortunately."

Neil gets to his feet and leans against the car. "You should call her."

His dad looks at him blankly.

"You should call Mom."

"No, things are back to normal."

"What do you mean?"

"Now we're both unhappy again." His dad grins and smacks him on the arm.

Neil takes a deep breath. "I've decided I want that job, Dad." But he hadn't really decided it until right then. He hadn't even been thinking about it.

His dad's face bunches up under his chin. "You should've called me, Neil. I sort of gave them the impression you didn't want it. They offered it to someone else."

Neil gives a short laugh. "Just kidding, Dad. Can you see me doing that job?"

"I guess not." His dad can't figure out if he should smile or not. "I know Shirley was upset. She was looking forward to seeing you more often."

"Tell her I'll stop by soon." Neil's legs wobble. "I should get going, Dad. Thanks for letting me know."

"See you tomorrow, right?"

"Same time. Same place." And that feels terrible too.

Neil tiptoes up the stairs. The main house is completely dark except for a dim light in his mom's room. He slips into his apartment and shuts the door. He doesn't turn on any lights and sits heavily on the bed.

He wishes he could go to the main house and tell his mom that he got that job. That it didn't matter what was going on with her and Jeremy; he was going to start working. Go back to school. Find his own place. Just like they talked about the other night.

Then he suddenly finds himself on his feet. He crosses the room and opens the door. The kitchen light is on now and his mother sits at the table sipping from a mug. Neil slips down the stairs and across the driveway. He hovers in front of the side door, debating if he should knock. He lifts his hand just as his mom looks up and catches his eyes. She looks tired but she still smiles. She gets up and walks across the kitchen to the side door. She unlatches the deadbolt and opens the door.

"What are you doing here?" she says.

"I was about to ask you the same thing."

"I should've listened to you. I think you were right about Jeremy." The sweet smell of hot chocolate dangles in the air in front of her.

"I don't think I was."

She takes a step forward and puts her arms around him. Suddenly Neil wants to cry. He hasn't cried since his dog Mitzi died in eighth grade. But there they are. The tears desperate to push through.

His mom lets go just in time and retreats into the shadow of the doorway. "I've never told you this before. And it's something I still can't explain to this day." Her lips quiver. "On your first day of Kindergarten, I dropped you off at the school. You were so upset. You begged me not to leave you there. I told you how much fun it was going to be. All the new friends you were going to make. But on the inside, I just wanted to scoop you up and bring you home with me. When I got in the car, I just stared at myself in the rearview mirror. I felt like a terrible mother. As if I'd abandoned you."

Neil crosses his right arm across his body and pulls at his left elbow.

"But I swear to God, Neil. When I got home. You were there. You were there waiting for me. As if your love for me had brought you back home. We spent the day coloring and baking cookies. Then that night, when I tucked you into bed, I told you that you couldn't do that again. That you had to go to school." Her eyes mist. "Sometimes, I'm able to convince myself that it never happened. But I know it did. Somehow, you made it across town faster than I could in the car. And you were waiting for me."

"Mom, I . . ."

His mom laughs loudly. "I'm crazy, right? Losing my mind."

"It's a nice story."

She nods. "Yeah. It sure is."

Neil rubs the back of his neck and sighs. "I better head upstairs."

"Thanks, Neil. Thanks for coming over."

"I was just worried about you."

She smiles again and puts her hand on the door, ready to close it.

"Give Jeremy another chance," Neil says.

She stares at him, her eyes two pinpricks in the dark. Then a flicker of recognition; as if she finally put a name with a face that had been eluding her. "We'll see," she says.

Neil walks slowly across the driveway and up the stairs. He looks down at the main house to see that his mom is once again sitting at the table with her mug. He reaches out and grabs the handle for the door. But it doesn't budge.

If he hadn't left his keys inside, he would have walked right in and turned on the lights. Then he would've turned on the radio and taken a hot shower. He would've put on a nice shirt and slacks and then driven over to Barky's. He knew Jeremy would be there. And Neil would walk right up to him and buy him a drink.

But Neil was stuck on the porch.

Dialysis

PATRICK SUGRUE

I knew a little bird once.
The little round type
That hops around.

He lay in a hospital bed
For months
Waiting for a healthy kidney.
When he got a new one,
The meds he was taking
Fucked him up so bad

He got an infection
In his brain and
He died.

The next morning,

My father paced
The sidewalk before first light.

I walked by.

He glanced at me,
Stuttered once,

Twice,
Then flew away.

Postcards from Home

JOHN JASPER OWENS

Wife number one has the strength of a grizzly and skin as solid as sandpaper. She is impenetrable—not an ideal quality in a wife—and so quiet that people project qualities upon her (intelligence, empathy, Catholicism) which she may or may not possess. She usually wears yellow and red. When relaxed, watching television for instance, she is so still that any movement she makes seems sudden, causing most of us to flick our gazes towards her. This interrupts the show we're watching. She sometimes apologizes.

Wife number two has great powers of hearing and eyesight, capable of finding me even in my most unusual hiding places. Once, I was standing at a deli counter in New Brunswick when my cell rang. "Just get the Black Forest ham and Swiss," she said, "the pesto on the roast beef would give you heartburn. And honey? You're holding up the line."

Wife number three is a sex machine. I'm not going to lie, that's why I married her. Perky breasts, an ass that bounces twice when I slap it, and always ready, with the total lack of inhibition normally seen only in wildlife documentaries, or in Embassy Suite penthouses atop piles of hundred dollar bills.

She also cooks a little, a skill I have yet to develop.

Wife number four is Mama, surrounded by children: hers, ours, and others—some neighbor kids are mixed in there—and trailed by the dogs and cats and hamsters who not-so-secretly love her best. The wives are not numbered in the order of marriage (I distinctly remember marrying Sex Machine first), but rather as represented in a flow chart Mama stuck to the refrigerator. I'm not sure of the order of wife accumulation beyond Sex Machine; if I need to know I'll ask wife number six, who has never forgotten anything and is excellent at games of chance.

When Mama calls, we all respond. The boys need compelling, the girls dissuading, checks are due to instructors, there are recitals to attend, teams to cheer on, and reminders to sit up straight that require, in this instance, a masculine voice. Gutters need cleaning, and hoods on cars are scheduled to be opened and peered into with a cluck in the back of the throat.

In a family our size chores can get pretty specific, and Mama assigns tasks like she's blocking a production of *Les Miserables*. We've got one son who polishes tines. I'm responsible for the stretch of upstairs hallway between the Bertbaugh lamp and the room the two oldest daughters share.

Wife number one handles the rougher discipline—she is the threat Mama hangs over our heads—as well as adolescent talks centered around "this is your new body and these are the dire consequences that await when used as intended."

Wife number five works a lot. She's never home, and we rarely talk outside of good nights and good mornings. She's the wife I sleep with because she's most reliably home and in bed at a decent hour. I hate to sleep alone. She also makes the most wonderful alarm clock, as she always wakes up at the same time. I am therefore pulled awake by her weight shifting beside me, sitting up, maybe a cough. Then, as she rounds the bed toward the bathroom, she reaches out and gives my ankle a shake. It is the gentlest possible way to be forced to face the morning.

On Fridays I avoid Sex Machine (sometimes this is not so difficult because she is suspiciously absent) because Friday night is when wife number five and I have what she calls her "end-of-business-week sex." Efficient in this as in everything (she's the most skilled woman at dressing, makeup, and out-of-the-house I've ever met), she'll have her third orgasm just as I can no longer keep control, after which she'll go pee, return to bed and mumble "One more in the books" before going to sleep. She golfs with clients most Saturdays, attends the same church as her company president on Sundays, and otherwise spends time with wife number two, who uses her observational powers to spy on wife five's competition, adversaries, and dear confidantes.

I walk into the family room and find wife six and Mama, heads together, with Sex Machine stretched on the couch and eating strawberries that she runs through an open container of Cool Whip on the floor. They fall silent at once, in the way of having been discussing something I shouldn't hear.

"You forgot your Lipitor again," says wife number two. "I can smell its absence on your breath." My knees weaken and I fairly fall into a chair. In addition to her sight and hearing I now have to worry about wife number two's olfactory sense? The way she nods at me makes me think she might also be telepathic.

A chance mention of a homework assignment while I'm remedying my statin deficiency evolves (or devolves, as you look at it) into me giving a lecture to the children about the nature of fossil fuels, the irreplaceable nature of oil and coal, the boogeyman future of their depletion. I rarely hold forth, so the children slowly gather to my voice and gesticulations, until they surround me on armrests, stairs, and the floor, entwined with the cats and dogs who sense the hand of Mama in all this and the potential for treats.

"Maybe that's what happened to magic," says Molly, one of our nerdier daughters. "Maybe Baba Yaga and Camelot and Atlantis used up all the magic, so today we don't have any, not a single unicorn." Mama rubs Molly's head and murmurs to her. "Merlin tried to warn us," Molly continues, already laughing at her own joke. "He lived backwards!"

At dinner, Jacob (who's going out for guard this year) piles fried chicken on his plate, depleting the family basket. "Limited resource," he tells me. "Get it while you can."

I slip out onto the balcony for some nighttime air, and the slightest movement catches the corner of my eye. Wife number one is pressed against the wall at the edge of the rail, a bas-relief smoking a cigarette. This shocks me because not only did I presume her impenetrable, I didn't know she smoked. The night is still and humid, so her exhalations do not scatter, rather, they rise up cohesive as a mist—dry ice—the remnants of a hair metal band hanging in the cornices and eaves. She's obviously upset.

"I was married once before," she says, and I nod. I remember. "I don't have any forgiveness left in me. He took every last drop." She reads my face and says, "No, you haven't done anything." I exhale. I'm not afraid of her, but I am aware that wife number one could snap my collarbone with the most casual downward sweep of her hand. It occurs to me as a revelation that this is the reason she is so still, so precise in her movement. She extinguishes the cigarette between her thumb and index finger. I wonder if forgiveness is a renewable resource.

I open my mouth to ask her who needs forgiving, but a second concern, newly ignited, pushes its way forward. I say, "I thought you were impenetrable. If you can smoke, maybe we could . . ." But she shakes her head. "I'm not interested in sex anymore, but if I ever want it again, I'll come get you. Besides," she places a palm hard as scar tissue on my cheek, "aren't all the other wives in this house enough?"

Wife number five jerks in a nightmare, waking me up. This is yet another development, and I'm starting to feel overwhelmed. "Ow." She says. "Ow. Ow. Ow." in a rhythm. I shake her shoulder, and she says, thickly, "The keyboard is jabbing my ass." She works so hard. Do we have a dream interpretation book in the library? I ease out of bed and creep downstairs but am distracted by some goings on in the kitchen—murmuring and candlelight. I sneak in.

"Forgiveness is a limited resource," says wife number seven, when I bump into her.

Wife number seven is easy to forget, and I apologize for waiting so long to introduce her. Her presence in the house is normally felt only indirectly—a cereal box moved, the television set to a different station than the one I left it on, a bathroom sink cleaner than Mama remembers—but she always appears in times of crisis. She's the one who hands me a flashlight, the one we can send to climb a short wall and wiggle through an open window, the one filling out our paperwork in the emergency room. Although always a pleasure to see her, it's also disconcerting. I associate her with cries for help.

Right now she's in the shadows against the wall by the door, watching the presentation at the kitchen island: kids out of bed too late; Mama foiled, snoring upstairs. Molly sets plastic dinosaurs out like a shell game for the siblings around her. She presents a downloaded picture from *Dragonheart* and shows crayon drawings propped on a picture stand (I hope the picture that belongs there is safe somewhere).

I have entered in mid-explanation: ". . . because the dragons lived the same time as the dinosaurs! Get it? They're even built like dinosaurs, so some of the skeletons in museums we think are dinosaurs are probably dragons. So then there was a meteor." Her visual aids here are a screen capture from some space site, which she passes around, and a much more vivid crayon catastrophe, all yellows and reds, streaking toward earth. "And it killed all the dinosaurs and dragons." Molly solemnly turns over the plastic dinosaurs, which rock on their backs like disabled turtles.

In the dark, wife number seven elbows me and says, "I hope our college fund's coming along."

"The dinosaurs got furnace-pressed into oil," says Molly, "and the dragons got pressed into magic, and magic was underground like oil but you had to drill for it, like oil." She switches pictures on the stand to a drawing she's done of Atlantis. She's depicted it as a city rising from the sea, but in a bit of eleven year-old logic has also drawn a dome over it. "Atlantis," she tells us, "was the Middle East of magic times, built over the biggest magic reserves. They made magic swords and flying carpets and genie lamps and all sorts of stuff from the magic they pumped up from the magic wells."

The children lean forward, candlelight painting their hair. They are heartbreaking in their earnestness.

"And they all said," (at this point Molly adopts a grown-up voice), "'We mustn't use up all the magic. We have to save some for the future', but they didn't, they used up all the magic underneath, and Atlantis sank into the ocean." She replaces the picture of Atlantis she'd drawn with a picture just like it, except where the city had been there was now just sea. It is surprisingly effective. "Then came the dark ages, and the rest of history is pretty much correct." Her audience (and I'm including myself here) is aghast—no more magic at all? "There's probably still some in places," surrenders Molly, "but it's increasingly hard to find."

Wife number five has mumbly nightmares on Wednesday night, and Thursday night too. The keyboard is still jabbing her ass. She's keeping a secret from her boss. Is her assistant happy with his job? Will this get me fired? It occurs to me how little I know about her office.

Wife number seven tells me, "I think you need another wife." When I ask her why she says, "I'm sorry, but the husband really is the last to know." Mama has plastered the refrigerator with Molly's art, and every time I go for a beer I'm confronted by yellow and red crayon, absolute destruction raining down.

"I'm having an affair," says wife number five. I make a note of the verb tense. It's Friday night and I must've felt something inside her needed addressing, because I've lit candles and broken out massage oil for our weekly lovemaking. Wife number five has just exited the shower—she's wrapped in a towel and crying as she speaks. She looks as if her tears have soaked her body and are pooling at her toes. I ask if it's her boss, and she shakes her head. "Worse," she sobs. "My assistant." I imagine nooners in a local No-Tell. I see my wife in a black cocktail dress and heels, dashing across a car-clogged downtown avenue, but the truth is sadder and more sordid. It's an affair of locked office doors and hiked skirts, of panties dangling from an ankle as a keyboard jabs her ass with each thrust, of two mouths and two sex organs in the four possible combinations—the efficient orgasm production I'd expect in an affair designed by wife number five. I ask her what she plans to do, except I say "we," as in, "What are we going to do?"

This house is drunk with children, garnished with pets, and supported by wives. Wives in the shingles, the wiring, the load-bearing columns; estrogen in the mortar, lipstick in the paint, comfortable silences in the walls. The word in the head of wife number five, even as it forms, makes the basement shudder. The pipes knock, rebellious at the intention. The foundation shakes, and as we are on the top floor, the effect is magnified, and I am jostled off the bed. "Maybe we should consider . . ." she says, and the entire house seems to drop, as if finally crashing through empty reservoirs we've tapped beneath it.

I sleep on the couch, alone (which I've mentioned I hate to do) and awake to a clutch of wives, their dawn robes, sweatpants, and tee shirts in the usual Saturday morning disarray. It's a frightening sight first thing in the morning. The wives almost never congregate, preferring loose alliances that shift and change from room to yard to deck. They're like the cats in that regard. And they never face each other without makeup—even Mama has time for concealer. Their blotchy skin and crows' feet make their faces seem bigger, slightly forward, crowding and overlapping each other like word balloons.

"That whore," says Sex Machine. "She could ruin everything." I remember many nights of lifting Sex Machine's drunken body from the rhododendrons and corralling her to bed, of phone calls ducked out before taken, the couple of kids around here with questionable genetic ingredients.

I stare at her but she does not drop her eyes (message received, read, discarded). "But you're the one I love," she tells me. "You're why I'm here. Lasciviousness is *my* department, she's the one who churches and golfs." She joins me on the couch and rolls onto her back, bites her thumb and lets the other hand wander down between her legs. All of a sudden this conversation can wait, because I really want to nail Sex Machine, right now, right on the couch with the other wives watching. "You'll feel better if you take it out on me," she says, and whereas that's true, it avoids the problem beneath. "Tie me down and ram me in the ass. Whip me while you make me lick Wife number two's pussy." My cell rings—it's wife number two out early, already at the farmer's market. "For God's sake," she says, "tell Sex Machine I can *hear* her."

Molly asks everyone she comes across that day to finish this sentence: "If you dig down deeply enough, you'll find . . ." Some of the answers she receives, which she records on an unlined pad: Oil, Lava, Magic, Bones, Sleestack, Morlocks, I don't know, Bats in caves, The Land That Time Forgot, Lava, Go away, China, Forgiveness, Courage, Fossils, What you're really made of, Lava, Buried treasure.

After answering "The Antipodes" Mama asks Molly for a sheet of her paper.

MWMw/K ISO SF race/age unimportant for LTR. Should work well in groups.

Ability to forgive a must. Plus size OK. NS, but S OK, D/DR OCC.

On our third date, I decide to tell Linda. I've kept the wives a secret but she'll be getting suspicious soon if she never gets to see my house. Best foot forward and all. She shakes her head and says softly, "That's okay, I understand." For a moment I'm afraid she's a milksop, a woman destined to be rolled over, the kind of woman who'd forgive a heroin addict as he carted off her vanity, and that wouldn't do at all. But then she pauses, her fork at an angle to her left cheekbone, and delivers it: "Some men are just like that." That is the look—it seems to hang in front of her face, frozen, like a picture in a frame, even as this conversation moves on—*that* is the look missing from our home.

I shop for a ring the next day. Wife number five will have to pay for it out of her yearly bonus—money she would normally keep for her own clothes, glitter and scent. I take enough to make her feel the sacrifice, but not so much as to pauperize her. "You have to make your own decision," I tell her, "but keeping your affair will be expensive." My engagement to Linda stretches on—she has weekends to juggle and friends and family to import—and on these preamble nights I lie beside wife number five and watch the back of her head as she stares out the window—black hair, black window—filtering her desires, digging down through the strata of wants until the shovel bites hard into needs.

Linda arrives to meet the family. I don't envy her. My wives form a hall within a hall she must pass through, hugging, "I've *heard* about you," shaking hands, showing daring, appraising brows. The children, and I never knew there were so many, turn out on the staircase and sit behind knees, scrunched against the molding. The pets scurry, leap, and fly to higher-up perches. It is through this gauntlet of life that Linda, clutching her purse but otherwise calm, walks through to meet me and Molly, who has taken up position at my hip.

"You must be Molly," Linda says, the way you do to an older child. "I got your letter." I stare down at the top of Molly's head, and from this angle I see her skinny arm come out to take Linda's hand. "And where is this basement you wrote of?" Molly turns to lead Linda to the cellar doors (Linda brushes my cheek with her lips as she passes) and we all follow—a solemn parade down the entry hall and along the great room partition wall, to the utility hall and the door at the end that opens to a staircase into the earth.

I've never cared to examine our foundation too closely. Yet here we pour, down to the basement, a place of Suessian ducts and pipes, crossing and threading, from the too big to the normal to the stringy. This is the complexity beneath us. I guess. What do I know; I never come down here. It is cold; I notice that. The furnace and water heater live here, coupled in a corner. Linda and Molly march ahead, and wife number five shoulders to the front. Hey! There are things from my youth down here! I kneel to open a box, and wife number one stops me with her implacable palm. Kids, cats, and hamsters flow around us. The floor here was built brick—the normal rusty red kind with three holes. Here and there I see where the bricks have been pried up, stacked like hills. Molly's work. I kneel to examine the holes bored into the Earth beneath the brick layer. I glance up at Jacob, who is watching from the stairs, arms crossed, some younger children around him. I turn my head and see the trio in the deepest part of the basement—wife, daughter, and wife-to-be. They are conversing heatedly in a witchy, Macbeth circle.

This hole I've found, in the foundation, fascinates me. The dirt's still loose, and since no one is paying attention, I dig in the tingling coolness. I dig with my fingers.

At some point, a shin brushes my shoulder. It's Mama. I look up and find the two of us alone at the floor of the foundation. I'm not surprised. When the wives who know fancy tricks have turned their attentions elsewhere, it is the children's mother who is the last to leave my side. She kneels on the ground beside me. I look in her broad, sweet face and see she's near tears. I take her in my arms. Above us we hear the faint sounds of a celebration underway—they've left us to our digging. Together we scoop the earth hoping for a shred, a trace, of the magic our daughter promised.

We lie filthy and exhausted on the foundation floor. The glow between us is damn near post-coital. My shoulders ache. "The ceremony will be on Sunday," she tells me.

I skip the wedding and take the honeymoon alone, to Sapelo Island, a place I find by globe, running my index finger down the east coast of the United States until Molly, palms over eyes, says, "Stop."

They send me a DVD of the ceremony; Linda is lovely in pale chiffon, wife number five acceptingly suave in her tuxedo. The reception looks rocking; Sex Machine got hammered. I wish I could've been there. Over the next two weeks I get postcards from home—Molly's blocky script on the through-the-looking-glass side of a glossy from our local museum (towering skeletons—maybe dinosaurs, maybe dragons), Mama's list of the chores awaiting my return.

I read them in the hammock, the dozen postcards that arrive daily, and I watch the vacationers around me. Northerners, mostly, come to lobster their shoulders in the Georgia sun, mothers in their singlets, some with skirts, husbands absent. I am the only man on the shore, I think, although there are boys among the jumping-bean children. Those boys carry yellow plastic pails and red plastic shovels, which they use to assault the sand, to dig.

three **Conrad** *poems*

KRISTINE ONG MUSLIM

How Conrad Came Back

Two knocks on the door. My father let him in.
Conrad wanted to talk about his trip,
but his tongue kept on sliding out of his mouth.
I told him to push it back. *Hard.* He did.
And the tongue was hinged back in.
He said there was too much to eat out there.
Thanks to Mrs. Kelly's surgical skills, he looked too human
and how the girls swooned and sometimes followed him home.
My mother insisted that he get some rest.
His skin flaps were starting to slough off.
I quickly wiped away the blood, and I discovered that his flesh
was like sugared sun. I remembered what Grampa said: *We were*
all yellow inside. That wrong shade of yellow—the color of the gods.
I smiled at the memory. "We'll fix that later," I said to Conrad.
He nodded. His chest gaped open at the motion of his head.
I saw something ticking inside. It was not his heart.

How Conrad Got His Revenge

Before he went out the door on his way to school,
I asked one more time: "Do you have the camera with you?"
My little brother nodded, grinned. I patted his tuft of hair
slowly so as not to disturb the glued flaps of skin underneath.
Yesterday, he arrived home with his right hand dangling from
its socket. I found him crying on top of the stairs.
He did not imagine that it could be *that* painful
when his makeshift human part was injured.
His classmates had bullied him. I knew. He insisted that
it was an accident. Pain had its prerogative; it gathered strength
in waves—one after the other—until he could not take it anymore
and finally confessed. I sewed the arm back into place.
Then I gave him the family's camera, ordered him
to take a snapshot of whoever did this to him. "Just one shot
will do," I reassured him. And that was enough to comfort him.
Tonight, I would develop the picture,
scissor the damned bully nice and slow.

How Conrad Fell in Love

Over family dinner, we tried to talk him out of it.
"Stupidest thing I've ever heard," my father said.
Conrad was about to say something.
I squeezed his hand to make him stop. It crackled.
"Don't worry," I whispered over a mouthful
of grass, earth, and dark river water. A family recipe.
"I'll weld the broken bones later. Just don't make
father angry." The feral cat-dog was whimpering
under the table. Mother shooed it away.
"Conrad, honey," mother cooed. "Love is only for humans.
You are somewhere up there in the food chain.
And *that* girl's hair has clogged our drain pipe."
Conrad bowed his head, and I knew that he would think about her
tonight, how she had clawed at him when he lifted off his face
and how she had called him a "monster, monster... ugly beast."
I would drag that girl into the kitchen tonight, keep her alive
for a while, make her understand what monster love was all about.

The Sacrosancts

RACHEL ADAMS

THE SACROSANCTS
SEASON 5
EPISODE 7
"Fatal Attractions"

DEDICATED SKETCHES AND RECOUNTINGS[1] OF
BETTE, ESTHER, AND GEORGE[2]

Bette Sacrosanct[3]

Bette is in the car, and a man in a brown suede hat runs up to the window. "I have mace," she tells him. "PKM, PKM," he says. "I've been living in Australia." "I'm not afraid to use it," she says. He has a mouth that is small like a bow. "It's me, O'rion. Remember that time in the bathhouse—" "No," she says, "No I don't." The studio audience laughs. She almost backs the car into a muumuu-clad octogenarian, who glares at her fiercely.[4] "I know it's you!" O'rion shouts. Warm audience laughter burbles up.

Bette mutters to herself on her way home. She is often stopped on the street by old friends and clients, and she is becoming a somewhat bitter woman in these later years of the series.[5] She doesn't remember, just doesn't remember. It is really hard for her to conceive of a Bette who called

---

[1] See also: Episode 55: *Summary and Analysis*

[2] *Dedicated Sketches and Recountings* do not exist for other *Sacrosancts* cast members at this time (to submit a *Dedicated Sketch and Recounting* for a different cast member, please email thesacrosancts@gmail.com)

[3] Bette (Alice Sand) is the sitcom mother; she has paler skin than the rest of the family, and she can't remember the seventies, but the seventies remember her

[4] This same octogenarian is almost hit by a Sacrosanct-driven car once per season (see Ep. 7, 15, 27, 34, and 41)

[5] In Ep. 46, *The Shrew,* this increasing bitterness was identified by the family as problematic but not alleviated or solved in any way

herself Princess Kittymittens and sold LSD. People tell terrific stories, and she drinks warm milk every night to help her sleep.[6]

Mr. Sacrosanct[7] has a lady coworker who drinks a two-liter bottle of Dr. Pepper twice daily. When he is very tired he can see it oozing out of her pores. He has his own pore problem: he's allergic to fluorescent lights. They give him bumpy skin, which never goes away anymore, even on vacation. Bette calls it gator skin, though really it looks more like plucked chicken.

Bette has a text message from her husband. She still doesn't know how to check text messages.[8] She thinks maybe some wine might help her figure it out. She rubs rosemary between her fingers. Sprigs and needles litter the chops. The pan goes into the broiler. Bette swigs the Rioja straight from the bottle, pours some into the marinade for the hamburgers, and squints at her phone.

Lily[9] is almost sideswiped by a pink Corolla, and this scares her up onto the sidewalk where she collides with a barbed wire–topped fence. The blue reflective vest gets torn a little but the barbs don't break through her wife beater. A pair of basset hounds weep at her through the chain link. She stares after the Corolla with a strange look, remounts her bike, and continues on her way.

Bette is lying on the couch with a cool, wet washcloth over her eyes. The empty bottle of wine is hidden in the kitchen trash (cue laugher). Her phone keeps buzzing. She doesn't know why. "Esther!" she yells. "Esther, come exorcise my phone!" And, "The pork chops—" And, "Oh shit." Esther has already left.

Lily tosses her bike on the lawn and walks in through the front door. "Mrs. Sacrosanct," she says. "Bette," she says. She sits down at Bette's feet. "What can I do?"

Bette stirs. "Lily?" This is one of the new plotlines this season, this sexual tension between Bette and her daughter's friend.[10] She removes the washcloth. "Darling, what do you think of that mustache of Esther's?" Lily

---

[6] This has been going on since the pilot itself, when she had an acid flashback and then began to be accosted by assorted eclectic personalities (see *Pilot: Summary and Analysis*)

[7] Mr. Sacrosanct is played by Denny Rich; some say he is the most underrated character on the show

[8] Despite the fact that she's had the phone for ten episodes now (see Ep. 45, *Enfant Oblige*)

[9] Lily (Greta Gould) was played by Marissa Lynch for the first two seasons and replaced by Gould in subsequent seasons; the reason for this replacement remains unclear (see *The Sacrosancts: Gossip and Speculation*)

[10] (see Ep. 50, 54)

looks at her red Mary Janes. "I think it's wonderful." Bette sits up and looks deep into Lily's eyes. "So do I," she says.

Esther Sacrosanct[11]

At twenty, she is growing a pencil moustache. Esther's recent arc: embracing her thin, androgynous body, cultivating not resisting. The hair creeps over her top lip with defiant residence like a drifter on a park bench.[12] When it first showed up, Bette said it looked sexy with her black, hip-length hair and blunt bangs. Bette is not one for compliments. Like the others, the writers are embalming her, painting her face, preparing her to be remembered fondly.[13]

Esther wears her trademark John Lennon sunglasses all the time now.[14]

She calls to tell Lily about the barbeque tonight, unaware of Lily's altered feelings towards her. In the background, George plays Jimmi Hendrix. Lily hears it and feels more things. "Yes, I'll come," she says. Lily wears a reflective blue vest when she rides her bicycle. Her manager calls her Safety Girl. "It's not even dark outside," he says. "I gotta go," says Lily to Esther.

Esther is at the Rocketship. She is demonstrating her mastery of "Freefalling." As usual, she has beer for George in exchange for the lessons. Esther talks to George and Genevieve about the prognosis from her recent hospital trip.[15] She has cancer in her right breast and not her left, and she tells them that this doubles her odds—more than doubles them—because she is right handed. (The audience guffaws.) This is not the case; she is left handed. We know this because she is playing guitar.[16]

---

[11] Esther (Margot Meeks) is the middle child, younger than Genevieve (played by Letta Howie); Genevieve is the least popular Sacrosanct and the only one not to appear in every episode

[12] There is a lively debate over whether the mustache is makeup or Margot Meeks' actual facial hair; Meeks makes few public appearances, and even then wears a veil just to fuel the rumors (see *The Sacrosancts: Gossip and Speculation*)

[13] There is a rumor that Season Five will be cancelled before completion of the traditional twelve episodes, but the official word from the network only confirms that this is the last season (reference: Associated Press)

[14] Since Ep. 50, in which she became hysterical over losing them temporarily—George borrowed them; fans triumphed, claiming they knew Esther's cool exterior would someday crumble

[15] This hospital trip occurred since the last episode; Esther's illness has been foreshadowed but never before directly mentioned

[16] (see also: Ep. 32, in which George calls Esther a "southpaw")

Genevieve says, "We should start a family band," and her siblings look at her. "Bette can sing lead. You two are on bass and guitar and backup vocals." "We've always wanted to," they tell her. "So you don't mind?" "Mind hell," says Genevieve. "I will learn drums, and we will call ourselves the Beetles. Three e's." Esther stares at her and plunks away.[17] George searches for his gerbil.

Esther has a ferocious need to pee when she gets home. George is driving because she doesn't trust herself to work the pedals. "Why didn't you just pee in The Hole?" George says. (The audience cracks up.) The Hole is a dark cavity in the bathroom floor where the toilet used to be. "Snakes," says Esther.[18] George puts a hand over his shirt pocket where the gerbil lives. "Shh," he says.

Esther runs through the kitchen to the bathroom, noting the oven-spawned smoke clouds on her way. As the water in the toilet froths and fizzes with her stream, the camera zooms in on a tiny wet spot on her underwear, a slightly darker blue, a drop of pee that escaped. (A chuckle ripples through the audience.)

Esther strokes her mustache with both fingers and looks at the blackened pork chops in the pan. "Don't worry, Bette," she says. "George and I will make things right." They look at each other, nod, and stride back to the pink Corolla. Bette straightens the washcloth on her eyes and moans softly. Trademark crescendo and fade to commercial.

GEORGE SACROSANCT[19]

At seventeen, he lives in the kind of squalor you only see in the lives of teenagers who are renting a trailer across town on the dime of their rich parents. He calls it the Rocketship. He calls himself the Rocketman; he pretends he has never heard of Elton John.[20] George is growing an afro in which to lose things. The thing he loses most often is his gerbil.[21]

The father is at work. He is thinking about the barbeque tonight. His job is a horrible job. This does not bother him because he has never had a

---

[17] She is actually playing rather good offhand bluegrass

[18] This is the first mention of Esther's fear of snakes in the series to date

[19] George (Stew Radner) is the youngest Sacrosanct

[20] This trick didn't work for the producers, who are currently in a balls-to-the-wall legal battle (see *The Sacrosancts: Behind the Scenes*)

[21] The gerbil has its own official fan page, in spite of remaining unnamed through four seasons (see *The Sacrosancts Character Bios: George's Gerbil*)

good job. George taught him to text message, but he is still very bad at it.[22] On break he texts Bette: "pork chops." This takes him ten minutes. Mr. Sacrosanct has never been named. He is the series scapegoat. He never complains about the way he is treated or the bad things that always happen to him. It is a running joke that the family does not laugh at the jokes he makes, no matter how good.[23]

George's head fills the screen as the camera zooms in on the gerbil, which is perched in his afro. (The audience laughs, pleased to come back from commercial to such an excellent shot.) He crosses his eyes looking at it. "Burrow," he tells it. "Go ahead." He does not plan to go to college but has nevertheless applied to twenty different schools, all of which have 100% admission rates.[24] The gerbil does not burrow but it does poop a little poop. "Aw, gerbil," says George and puts the pet lovingly into his pocket.

The father has been leaving work one minute earlier for the last month, at 4:59. It is 4:57, and he thinks it is time to shave off one more minute. He is ten months away from retirement, and he just doesn't have those extra sixty seconds in him. Those extra hundred twenty seconds. At 4:58 he stands up thinking, *oh hey boss, just, you know, just a little stretch before I leave*, but his boss is not there.[25]

George puts a handkerchief over his mouth and nose though there is actually very little smoke in the kitchen and ducks his way through imaginary clouds of fumes to the broiler. He extracts the charred pork chops. The gerbil peeks out, and George plucks some rosemary for it.

The father is almost out of the office when the female coworker stops him: "I've broken the copier again." He follows her to the mailroom and examines the machine. "That isn't mine," she says coyly of a Xerox in the tray, on which two apparently estranged breasts occupy distant corners of the page.[26]

---

[22] This is the same episode in which George gave up trying to teach Bette (see Ep. 48)

[23] In fact, there are only four episodes in which a family member laughs at one of his jokes; each time it's a different character, and the reasons are always satisfyingly personal and situational; this silence is enforced for the studio audience as well, and the lack of laughter or hints of stifled laughter offsets the hilarity of his jokes in an uncomfortable way

[24] George is far and away the favorite Sacrosanct, regardless of who you ask (see *The Sacrosancts: Surveys and Polls*)

[25] Whenever Mr. Sacrosanct is ashamed of himself, he thinks of George (see Ep. 22, *Say A Mother*)

[26] Another running joke is that women always hit on Mr. Sacrosanct despite his less-than-impressive looks; some fans think there are feminist underpinnings here but this has not been confirmed (see *The Sacrosancts: Gossip and Speculation*)

Genevieve comes in, drumming the air with her forefingers. She goes into the kitchen and fiddles with the stove knobs. The pilot light is not lit, and a steady stream of gas releases into the air.[27] "Do I look like a Princess Kittymittens to you?" Bette says. Lily has no idea what she's talking about. "Yes," she says. "Maybe." And because Bette looks sad, she kisses her.

The father looks at the clock. 5:04. The coworker is leaning against the door frame, playing with a lock of hair. "I have no time for this," he says. "I retire in ten months." He leaves her in the copy room, taking care to step over the pool of Dr. Pepper at her feet.

George waits for Esther in the cereal aisle at the grocery store. He pulls the gerbil out of his pocket so it can burrow in his afro. It is limp. "Oh man," he says. "I'm sorry about the rosemary, little buddy." He hums Simon and Garfunkel and cries a little. The audience sniffles or says 'aw.' The series will end soon. The writers, in their sorrow, will be sentimental[28]. We will watch to the end, and when it is over we will change the channel.

---

[27] *The Sacrosancts* is famous for loaded guns that appear but never go off, though sometimes they "fire" between episodes and we hear about the aftermath, and sometimes they are never mentioned again; because of the severity of the situation, fans speculate that this gun will never be fired

[28] Some fans predict that in the final episode, Mr. Sacrosanct will make a joke and everyone will laugh and say *we love you*, _____ and the blank will be filled with something other than an insult, diminutive, or title; some say this is wishful thinking

Larva

RANDOLPH SCHMIDT

The triangular head and leafy legs of the mantis lay torn and useless on
my son's Pooh Bear sheets. Billy sat in the crib chewing the body like a
stalk of wheat, his saliva oozing out of the corners of his mouth, green and
brown. He swallowed with an audible gulp, and then bounced on his
diapered bottom. Picking up the legs, he waved them in the air as if
conducting an orchestra and smiled at me, insect detritus wedged between
his baby teeth. Although Stephanie was hesitant, I demanded we take him to
the pediatrician.

"Does Billy do this often?" asked Dr. Wu.

"Yes," I said, my face contorting from nausea. Just the week prior,
Billy had played in the backyard, choosing to sit in the sandy areas near the
fence. His hands, sticky with saliva and grape juice, probed deep into the
loose dirt and came out covered with tiny ants and millipedes shining
metallic in the sun. He licked his hands like they were ice pops and shook
them at the sky. He then crawled deeper into the grass, searching out other
things he could play with and eventually consume.

Bursting into the house in a frenzy, carrying Billy in my arms, I raved
about him needing to go to the hospital to get his stomach pumped. There
were amoebas, clusters of bacteria, coursing through my son's intestines
from the filth he ingested. Stephanie dismissed my concerns with a wave of
her hand and the words: "Boys will be boys."

"Sometimes, but I don't think it's a big deal," Stephanie said to Dr.
Wu. "Like, he'll eat those roly poly bugs that crawl around near the vents."

"That's the least of it," I said. Stephanie sighed through her nose.

"It's fine," she replied, "my sister did it when she was that age right at
the front window. One after another, and she was okay." I looked at Dr. Wu
for a safe face, a face that would commiserate with me against this madness.
Instead, he nodded and smiled warmly as if waiting for a mug of hot
chocolate. Billy sat placidly on the examining table, looking at each of the
adults like he understood everything, like there were no limits to the depth
of his comprehension.

"He should be all right," said Dr. Wu, "Kids eat lots of crazy things.
Pennies, wood chips. Now I can add mantises to the list." He snorted and
scribbled something on a pad.

"If the body can't digest something," he continued, "it will either throw
it up, or you'll be in a lot of pain. So keep an eye on him and let me know if

he complains of a stomach ache. Then we'll take it from there." Dr. Wu stuffed the pad back into his pocket.

"But he doesn't talk yet," I replied.

Dr. Wu shrugged. "You'll know when he's upset," he said with a chortle, "you won't be able to escape him." I nodded, but Billy was always quiet and fearless in the face of pain, only complaining if hungry. When Stephanie had to stop nursing due to sore nipples, he devoured formula, applesauce, and yogurt. Anything we gave him disappeared in his gaping mouth. It wasn't too long after that when Billy crawled to me with a crushed cricket in his hand. It was large and had long, spiderlike legs: a cave cricket, as my grandfather would say. And like a dog lapping at its water bowl, Billy inhaled the insect with a single bite and erupted with a squeal of satiation.

Stephanie nodded her head thoughtfully at Dr. Wu and then turned to Billy, mussing his hair.

"Did you not get enough supper, little buddy?" she asked with a playful glint in her eyes. I wondered if there were more episodes than these, some so severe that Stephanie would conceal them from me. What else could Billy eat? My tongue felt limp in my mouth and I found it hard to swallow. As we left, Dr. Wu touched my elbow, cupping it in his hand.

"A boy needs to explore his surroundings," he said in a soft voice. "How can you become a man if you don't understand your environment?"

When we arrived home, I scrutinized Billy, but he seemed fine. He played with his blocks on the carpet, giggling when makeshift towers would collapse and turning back every so often, just to make sure his parents were there, watching.

His diaper was full. On the changing table, I opened it, expecting to find a soft bowel movement, but instead there was a dead mouse. Small and brown with mottled fur, its neck was cracked upwards with bones poking through the skin in odd places. Tiny black eyes sat immobile in their sockets, as lifeless as marbles. Deep scratches that I hadn't seen before were laced over Billy's fingers, undoubtedly due to the struggle between boy and rodent. Billy cooed with laughter.

After placing Billy back in his crib, I quietly tossed the diaper and carcass into the pail. The room seemed small, and all the hairs on my body brushed against my skin. There were things alive everywhere, on every surface. I remembered reading about tiny mites that live in the roots of your eyelashes, and I felt like tearing at my skin. Where did all of these things come from? In our clean house, this child was somehow able to find the monsters that normally existed only in darkness. I looked at Billy. He stood in his crib, watching me silently, a half-smirk painted on his face.

This was beyond my experience, and I clutched at Billy's cheeks and stared at his eyes to see if there were any signs, any answers. I watched passively as Billy's mouth enveloped my thumb and squeezed gently. Mild pain shot up through my arm, but I did not break my gaze. Dimples appeared in Billy's face, his lips curled into a smile, and he released me, leaving small indentations in my skin. The boy jumped up and down in the crib, screaming with delight. He chomped down onto the wooden railing and shook his head and growled like a beast.

I was desperate to understand. He was my son. I bent down and bit the grain of the railing. I slowly applied pressure, my teeth wobbling at first, but then digging deep into the wood. Soon after, flecks of splinter broke off, lacerating my gums and softening on my tongue. Blood and saliva seeped onto the wood and dampened the fibers. It was salty and bitter and sour and sweet. It was everything, and delicious. The room darkened at the edges. Stag beetles scurried out of cracks and dotted the walls. Crickets fell from the light fixture and rained down gently upon us. Mantises were perched on all four corners of the crib. Their eyes, bulbous and cloudy with black pinpricks in the center, observed it all.

Billy ripped off a chuck of wood and gnawed it, his eyes wild. Wrapping his small hand around my pinky finger, we ate together: wood, cloth, and flesh.

The Story of Jimmy Draws-So-Small

rendered in four poems

ROBIN PATRIC CLAIR

Rendering Disappearance

Sitting in a little desk—arranged in a straight row parallel the other rows and facing the blackboard—Jimmy Draws-So-Small placed his sharpened #2 pencil onto the white paper.

Once again, he remembered an image from a book, now tacked to the wall, that the teacher had shared with the class about art history, a history more ancient than his grandfather or any of the other elders in his tribe.

A wounded bison on the cave wall of Lascaux.

Jimmy Draws-So-Small had drawn the bison everyday. First, he removed the spear; then he healed the wound; finally, he rendered the bison strong and free. But then Jimmy Draws-So-Small did something his teacher called *so strange.*
He drew the bison smaller
every single day.

On the seventy-seventh day, he leaned into his paper, in pretty much the usual way—his shiny, black hair fell about his face, hiding him from view—yet this time, he placed a single dot onto the page. And then
Jimmy Draws-So-Small
stepped into the picture and
disappeared that day.

Rendering Reality

Pulling the inside of his elbow to his face, Jimmy Draws-So-Small adjusted to the pungent buffalo odor that surrounded him and invaded his nostrils. A bison snorted the human smell away. The boy nudged against a calf who generously gave her scent to him.

Jimmy Draws-So-Small joined the Buffalo Clan in this rather unusual way.

He ran with the buffalo and rode on their backs, sometimes straddling two at a time, daring fate to play, wind speaking to his face each day and the nights better yet, with warm companions, inhaling large breaths of air, exhaling slowly, inhaling into the gentle light of day after day, until, suddenly, lightning slapped the earth and seared the sky, jerking all awake, sending broken dreams to flight, forcing hoofs to strike like thunder. Relentless lightning whipped with fury; thunder claimed its name.

The herd raced to the edge of the wood, where giant raindrops splattered in torrential streams against their fur. Shivering now, Jimmy Draws-So-Small nestled in among the hunkered herd, but peeked over a wet shoulder, spying a cave.

Cave walls are inviting, although rough to the hand. Jimmy Draws-So-Small didn't mind as he smeared mud and dung and ocher-colored clay—capturing in broad strokes, the bison and their way. At the upper edge, he painted the entrance to a cave. Then
Jimmy Draws-So-Small
stepped into it and
simply slipped away.

Rendering Appearance

Jimmy Draws-So-Small looked up as the teacher walked up and down the aisles looking at students' papers. As she passed Jimmy, she put a finger to her nose, smelling musk and dung and mud and something else, she said, *so strange.*

Jimmy Draws-So-Small
smiled, gazed with satisfaction
at the print tacked to the bulletin
board on the wall—The Cave
Paintings of Lascaux—
and then placed
a new dot
upon the
page

Rendering Art; Rendering Life

.

When the Weather Changes You

AMBER SPARKS

The year the earth froze hard as diamonds and the sky rained ash, my great-grandparents met and married. That's the way the story always starts, with a well-established fact: two people met one another and were subsequently married. The details surrounding that fact are stranger, less certain. More like smoke than story. More like mirrors than memory.

My sister Anne and I heard the tale a thousand times from our mother. We never heard a word of it from my great-grandmother, an impossibly proud and silent woman. The only time I ever heard her speak was when I was very young and she was very old, and I was summoned briefly to her deathbed.

You have them, she said, her voice surprisingly deep and strong. You have them in your heart, too. Just like me. Her face was purple and mottled, and her mouth collapsed into itself like a rotten fruit.

What, Gramama, I asked, trying not to get too close. The sour smell of death saturated the bedclothes. What do I have in my heart?

Ashes, she said. Your heart is full of ashes.

That terrible long winter, the year that all of Yellowstone erupted like one massive volcano, ash and soot had filled the sky and mixed with the snow. The entire continent was forced to eat the ash, bathe in it, drink it. Bits of it floated about and stuck in the eye, scratched the skin and clung to the hair.

I wondered if that was what my great-grandmother had meant. If she had drunk of the ashes too heavily and somehow they clotted and clung in her bloodstream, thickened it, gave it a sluggishness and heaviness—a trait caused by pollution that, like the pepper moths' coloring, would be passed on via mutation to later generations.

But my sister Anne had another explanation. Loneliness, she said, that's what she means. We've all got it in our blood, just like her.

It's true. My family is a loose confederacy of loners, hooked to others only by the double barbs of blood and chance. It's a mean loneliness, and it sticks in the heart like ash. Nobody stays long. Not in love, not in friendships, not in houses, not even in the same town. We don't become handsome elderly couples, doubly blessed with long life and lifelong love. The first blessing might be often visited upon us, but without the lifelong love it twists back on itself, like the bad fairy's curse at the christening.

I suppose that would make my great-grandmother the bad fairy. She was an enigma, a widow in her nineties when I knew her: a woman who played Debussy's Children's Suite for us and made us giggle, who played Beethoven like a rolling storm while we clutched at each other in panic, a woman who was otherwise dour and silent and who did everything in secret. Even when she smoked it was like she was hiding something, hand cupped around her cigarette the way Nazis smoke in films.

She was severe, disciplined, and she never smiled. Her music was the only passionate, the only *living* thing about her. It wrapped round her in thick layers, curled and twisted about, and seemed her only channel for expression as she calmly played, back straight as a rod, hair still black and hanging to her waist until the day she died.

Her tale sounds romantic at first, like a love story—but if you listen to the cadences, the code words buried in Edwardian sentiment, you can hear a fire dying out. Cold water rolling over flickering embers.

I can never tell it quite right, not like my mother used to tell it. She was a born storyteller. But I tell it anyhow, because it's too important not to pass it on.

Listen, my mother would say, and we listened; we leaned forward to absorb the whole story into our skin and blood and bones. Because this is a story about the weather, and what happens when it changes you.

In her youth my great-grandmother was a beauty and became a minor star on the New York stage. She was light-skinned and black-haired, tall and slender, perfect—except that her lips were thin and wan. This was one of few signs that she might not be a generous woman: those lips and the extraordinary silence they enclosed. She spoke so little that you would have expected her voice to be rusty, to stick like a drawer with disuse; yet it came out deep, dark, coated with lacquer. She looked like Snow White, but her voice belonged to the Wicked Queen.

She had a fairy tale story, too. The little lost orphan left at the train station, the foundling taken in by a family of vaudevillians. That's where she learned to play the piano, and she grew up there on the stage. But unlike her family, she never took to comedy—or to film, where many of her adopted brothers and sisters ended up.

We saw her in a silent film once, my sister Anne and I. A short little piece called *Flowers for A Fallen Angel* or something like that. A silly film, full of the clichés borrowed from the stage that early silent cinema was prone to. But it was easy to see why her film career never took off. She was meant for the far-away of the stage; from the audience, you couldn't see my great-grandmother's eyes. You couldn't tell that her blood was cold, chalky, and that her eyes were dead and flat. From the audience, you were fooled by the deep, rich voice and the lively black hair. But on film, up close, there was a negative energy around her. Even in photos you see it—like someone sleepwalking and hungry.

My great-grandmother had many admirers, but she was not interested in men or women. She wasn't interested in sex or even in people at all; like

Greta Garbo, she only wanted to be alone. She was already writing in her veins the DNA of solitude that she would pass on to us. It was as though she had read ahead, could see that after that year she would never be alone again. She was shoring up the fragments of loneliness against her eventual ruin.

It was a bad year that started off like the end of the world. The bang, splash, sizzle of Yellowstone exploding was the trigger. It was like a punishment for Westward Expansion. There was much discussion—but theories, religion, superstition were useless. A whole chunk of Yellowstone had simply gone off and buried itself like Pompeii. And after it went, when the dead were mostly accounted for and the dust settled across the sky like a layer of lead, the new troubles began. Crops and animals perished, people, too, from starvation, cold, illness, depression, despair—it seemed the whole continent withdrew from the weather and from the living.

The shut-out sun led to the coldest spring on record in North America since the Little Ice Age. Gas prices, coal prices, the prices of wood and wool—they skyrocketed that April, as it became apparent that it wasn't getting warmer and the sky was still more black than blue. The poor were perishing in record numbers, whole families found frozen, huddled together in dark, iced-over tenements.

After a while, it became common to see strange snow angels here and there. Dead children splayed in dreadful poses, wingless and blue and covered in ice. The crows would circle in frustration, bewildered by the slow rate of decomposition and decay, unable to peck at the eyeballs hard as glass.

At this point, my great-grandfather makes his first appearance in the story. It is my great-grandmother's story, really, but he remains the pivot, changed nearly as much as she by that long winter.

He was the only child of the Washington Square Suffrage Society's leader and often attended Society meetings. If you were a young suffragette living in New York City, you would certainly have heard of him. He would strike you as he struck most observers: as a fat man with a slightly stooped back, pretty, almost girlish blue eyes, and an oddly confident air. But there was a reason for the confidence, a reason that owed everything to the cold spell.

It had been a good year for my great-grandfather. He had discovered the one thing women wanted more than admiration, more than pretty clothes, more than fine jewelry, more than food and even love: *warmth*. And he had discovered he could provide warmth in a very satisfying way for the young women his mother was surrounded by.

He had never had any luck with women before. He was young, it was true, possessed of mild, inoffensive features and thick black hair. He was wealthy, too. But he was also very large. Profoundly fat, in fact. And that had kept him from the thoughts or arms of any nice young ladies; he had been forced to buy his embraces before that long winter began.

I never met my great-grandfather; he died of a heart attack long before I was born. But by all accounts he was not a wicked young man. He never attended his mother's suffragette meetings with the sole purpose of seducing young ladies. He fell into his Don Juan role by accident and good fortune. He had long been dragged to those meetings by his overbearing mother, where he'd doted on many of the pretty young girls in attendance. And they'd never paid him any attention at all.

So you can understand why he might have been perhaps too eager to take advantage of this new miracle. When the prettiest of the girls, Hilda Stone, shared a sofa seat with him at a meeting and discovered the warmth radiating from his big bulky body, it all started so suddenly that he was quite overwhelmed. Certainly he had no intention of ruining the young women. Or, god forbid, his terrifying mother finding out. He always had his driver get them home before anyone could discover they'd been out. But he didn't really understand about women, and men, and babies—so the real miracle was that none of the women he'd wooed and warmed was carrying his.

Scientists promised the cold would end. But they fought bitterly about when, some saying six months, others guessing at two or three years, even a decade. And the public grew weary, diffident, tired, as secret obsessions began to take over civilized lives.

People began to inhabit their homes like mice, holed up in tiny corners, hiding from the cold and trying to remember where their passions lived. Intellectuals wrote books about desert climates, and polar exploration finally lost the last of its charm. Oasis Parties became popular among the very wealthy, who would build up bonfires in fire pits where guests would dance in wild costumes and drink absinthe. More often than not, these parties ended in orgies or house fires. Sometimes both. People were starting to lose their minds a little.

No one knows why my great-grandmother started attending suffragette meetings. I like to imagine a sort of frequency switched on in my great-grandmother's head at that moment, her brain open to all the streams of the world, the great minds of the ages. Feeds flying in from Ancient Greece, the Renaissance, the Enlightenment—all the knowledge of the human world tangled up in it, ready to be snatched up and studied. Backs of giants patiently waiting to serve as step stools.

Anyhow, the historical fact remains, and who can say why: my great-grandmother became, briefly, a suffragette. She was a bit of a local celebrity in the city, and added prestige to the Washington Square Suffrage Society. And the Society was, on the whole, delighted by her. She was an actress who smoked cigarettes, drank whiskey, and often wore men's tweed trousers. She was a woman who did what she liked, and they liked that about her.

At one of those meetings, my great-grandfather and my great-grandmother finally entered the same orbit. Like a magnet, the long weather could finally begin to do its work, exerting its pull on the two strangest branches of my family tree.

My great-grandmother found herself seated next to my great-grandfather. She could feel the heat radiating from him, strong and bright, could smell him—mild hints of animal fat and cheese, lye soap. She shuddered to think of breathing it in deeply; she hated the smell of people. Still, the heat he gave off was the heat she longed for all of the time, everywhere she went, even in her sleep and in her dreaming.

He smiled at her, and took her hand to kiss it. She had heard some of the other girls talking about him. She had not believed it. But now she knew the snow was piling up outside, dirty and foul, and her ankles would sink into it and her leather shoes would soak up the water, and her feet would ache with cold until she could sit in front of the kitchen stove with her stockings off. She smiled back at him, a finer actress than she had ever been on stage, desperate for a little fire.

There were no Oasis Parties or any other scandalous goings-on at my great-grandfather's house. It was a Respectable House, and his mother made sure it stayed that way. She had the servants put out the gas lamps at precisely nine o'clock every night to save fuel. She was a very practical woman, and besides, she believed it was unhealthy to stay up late. All decent, God-fearing people are asleep by dark and up by dawn, she would say, never an original woman. The fact that it was dim all the time then and dark by dinner did not alter her arrangements in the slightest. At precisely nine, she would say goodnight to her son, climb the staircase, and retire to her room. My great-grandfather would usually do the same.

On one especially cold night, my great-grandmother was waiting for him. She had leaves in her black hair from climbing the trellis, and a scrape on her cheek where a vine had brushed her skin. He recognized her from the meetings, and didn't wonder at what she wanted. It was plainly written in her shivering frame, in the wild look in her eyes.

His hands were warm as he held hers, and his cheeks were red, and she, who had never known love, never loved anyone but had stood apart, cool and calm—she allowed him to envelope her, to pool around her and inside of her and fill her with light and flame and familiarity. And she fell in love with warmth itself, became instantly addicted as if it were an opiate, fell in love with the *appassionata* of his body heat played out against her paper-thin white skin.

Food prices soared and farmers starved, surrounded by their frozen fields. Those in tenements were still dying by the thousands, including those who didn't freeze or expire from hunger but killed themselves hoping for the fires of hell. Some blamed the suffragists, called them New Eves, convinced God was punishing man for the vanity of woman. Some blamed the Catholics; some, the Jews. Faith reversed itself, cults sprung up around Prometheus and Ra, and few believed in the priests.

No one believed in the scientists. No one thought it would end.

One night, my great-grandmother slept in her own bed, a hot water bottle at her feet. The warmth was feeble, barely reaching her ankles before dying out. She shivered and thought of my great-grandfather, of his oppressive but necessary heat. The currency of cellulite. And she knew she would have to go back again, to that house, to him—because she had fallen in love with warmth itself.

And so it finally came to be: my great-grandmother changed her life forever, trading solitude for a chance to swim in the sun.

Poor Great-Grandfather. He certainly thought he loved her, but he was also terribly afraid she would leave him. She almost never spoke to him. She just seemed to want him near, especially in the dark, especially in the cold, when the fire had gone out and each of his heartbeats signaled the only warmth in the room.

At times she clung to him, made him feel proud, made him feel certain he would never need to be alone again. But at other times, he would catch her watching him, and her stare would roll through him like ice water. Then, he felt certain that she would eat his soul in the end.

When he was gone, she would lock herself in the conservatory and play the piano for hours, or stay cocooned in her bed under piled-up furs. She ignored the servants and her disapproving new mother-in-law and became a ghost, a succubus living on warmth and music alone.

But only a few months after they married, the sky began to clear. Temperatures finally began to rise. And when they were high enough, my great-grandmother left my great-grandfather's bed for good.

She had her baby and cried for the first time in her life when she saw the new creature, unnerved and horrified by what she had made. She knew it was her own fault. She'd eaten the apple. But she would punish him— punish her children and her children's children, and their children, too—by cursing her own rotten blood and spilling a little into their veins. Not enough to kill them. Just enough to consign them to the solitude she longed for, and would never have again. She bent over her baby's cradle, pulled a pin from the band of her hat, and stuck her finger until a single drop appeared. It hung like a ruby from her finger for just a second, then splashed onto the child's tiny tongue. The baby shifted in her sleep and licked her lips, restless, leaving a faint scarlet smear at the corner of her mouth.

My sister Anne has my great-grandfather's face; she is round and rosy like he was. She pretends to herself that the story doesn't matter. She has been married twice, but they were short affairs, bookended by solitude. Still, Anne thinks she can escape what's in the blood. Every time she begins a new relationship, she calls me and says, You see? We're not doomed to be alone like Gramama.

I remind her that Gramama was never alone, and that it was worse for her because of that. Anne usually hangs up on me then. I understand she is trying to live a better life, to somehow emerge from this family legacy a changeling. A swan from the duck's nest.

But I know better. I am very like my great-grandmother, I think. I don't have her beauty or her height, but I feel my eyes are strange and lonely as hers. In groups I stand apart; in photographs I have a hungry look, startling and yet sad. I can't bear to be touched by other people. I am used to Anne, but not to anyone else.

And I don't want anyone to be used to me.

War Crumbs

JOE KAPITAN

For us kids, Memorial Day weekend was all charcoal grills and parades, and it meant that we'd be packing up the minivan and heading for the shore, which also meant that Great Uncle Henry was bound to fall apart again at any moment. And by falling apart, I don't mean becoming overly emotional, breaking down, acting "dramatic." Great Uncle Henry wasn't like that at all. He was a simple man and fell apart the old-fashioned way— limb from limb, and torso into segments. Most times, we didn't even have the luggage emptied into the beach house before we'd get the panicked shout from Aunt Celia, his only daughter, who never got used to experiencing the temporary disintegration of her father. She'd pour herself another double Seagram's and chain-smoke her menthols and pace the salt-bleached deck while we young nieces and nephews mobilized and combed the beach, the leeward sides of dunes, the garden, the house, all for old Henry's parts—sometimes a hand down in there between the rows of grapevines, perhaps a foot exposed at low tide, or a section of pale belly flesh nestled among the towels in the upstairs linen closet. It was not, as some might think, a horror. Revulsion amongst us kids was minimal, especially when compared to the thrill of the hunt. Finding Henry, even the larger pieces of him, was heroic and life-saving stuff, the makings of stories.

When the parts were all accounted for and rinsed of their sand and mulch and patted dry, Aunt Celia would arrange them all in Henry's bed, in appropriate order, and lock the door for the night. We would then be free to play Monopoly on the screen porch, or take flashlights to the beach to scare up the ghost crabs, or maybe light a bonfire on the bluff and roast marshmallows, but the One Rule was that we had to stay away from Henry's room while he was mending. I was in charge of enforcing this rule amongst the kids, since I was the oldest. I'd shoo them all to bed by ten, and the adults would stay up another two hours drinking beer and talking about Iraq and stock markets until they couldn't keep their eyelids open. In the morning, Henry would invariably be awake and moving before any of us, out the door at dawn to take Roscoe for his walk.

This was summer's start at the beach, year after year, until I was fifteen. That was the year that Aunt Celia had just about enough. She drove in from Virginia, all blotchy and coughing up black phlegm into handkerchiefs, and you could tell that she had nothing left as far as Henry was concerned. She coughed up a lot of euphemisms, too, dubious phrases like "assisted living" and "quality care." Great Uncle Henry listened to her logic, but he wasn't the same after that. He didn't come apart at all that day, probably fearing that to do so would only hasten his departure. Henry spent a lot of time in his room. He offered no opinion, and Celia didn't ask for one; she wandered the internet on her laptop, searching for local senior facilities. She asked me what I thought of some of them, the ones with the professional photos, and I think I nodded, but I didn't tell her that I could almost smell the piss and bleach right through the monitor. They looked like human parking garages, linoleum-lined stalls for families to store their older models.

The next day, I carried a glass of lemonade up to Henry's room and tapped my knuckles on his door. I told him it was me. He said to come in, and I found him sitting on the edge of his bed. He had a shoebox opened on the bed as well, and he reached inside it. He held up a chain, and hanging from the chain were two small metal plates. "Read them," he said. I said, "Thomas Gaynor, Sergeant, United States Army." I didn't read all the numbers. "That was your brother," I said. I had heard stories of Great Uncle Tommy from Mom, and she had heard them from her mom, Grandma Elizabeth, Henry and Tommy's sister, before Elizabeth died in a car wreck back in 1983. Tommy was legend; he existed in sepia, trapped in photographs that ended with him in uniform, his face a portrait of a resolve that only heroes can summon. What I'd heard was that Tommy was two years older than Henry, but according to Elizabeth, anyway, they could have been twins.

"Tommy died in World War Two, at Anzio," I said. Somehow, I thought that. Maybe because I had seen a documentary once on Anzio and, at the time, I thought I'd like very much to drive my own tank some day.

"It was Omaha Beach," Henry said in a tired voice, "and no, I didn't die there."

The ice disappeared from his glass before either of us could say anything.

Henry, or I suppose Tommy, ended the silence. "My brother Henry had this recurring dream that something bad was going to happen at Normandy. He saw soldiers crying with dozens of holes in them, like they were unfinished jigsaw puzzles, boys searching for their crumbs, and he made me promise that I'd look after Annabelle and their little Celia if he didn't make it back. He believed he was already done for. He stayed up all night, trembling, when we crossed the Channel. I tried to help him . . ."

"What happened?" I asked.

"I told Henry I'd be first off the landing craft," Tommy said, "so if the German guns were on us, I'd go down instead of him. But I didn't. Go down, I mean. All I remember is jumping, being in the surf, bullets screaming past, and then a shell's whistle and a concussion that knocked me face-first to the sand. I looked back for Henry, but the landing craft was gone, just pieces floating. Pieces of metal. Pieces of men. I started to pick them up, but the platoon leader grabbed my neck and shoved me to the sand. I left the pieces in the waves. I don't even know if they were Henry or not," he said, and just as he finished, his left elbow came undone and his forearm, hand and all, fell to the floor.

I went to pick it up, but he pushed me away with his other arm. "Go on, get out of here," he said. "No one should have to see this."

I ran down the stairs and over the dune path to the beach. It was high tide, so I had nowhere to stand but in the wash of the waves. There were things beneath the water that tumbled past my ankles. It made sense now, I thought, his coming apart. It was the parades, the flags, the grayed and shuffling vets with their proud lapels full of medals.

When I walked back up to the house, I gathered the kids together. "Special Henry-hunt today," I said to them. "Everyone bring your parts to me. Hurry!"

When I had a full rucksack, I slung it across my back and rode my bike south, fast, toward the cliffs that guarded the entrance to Manatauk Bay. I was the only one missing when Aunt Celia ran yelling out of the house, and someone else had to tell her to relax, that the hunt was already over. She became despondent, they told me, mumbling about purgatory sidestepped, or some such nonsense, and debts not paid.

Aunt Celia went to hospice herself, in 2004, due to the lung cancer, and for weeks she still wouldn't talk to me, because I wouldn't tell her where I put him. I never told anyone. But I don't mind giving you a hint, because you look like you respect the inviolate guts of secrets. The place I picked is close to the shoreline, and high up, just about impossible to get to without a rope. I wrapped his parts separately, in plastic, so they would never grow back together.

When Celia's prognosis dwindled from weeks to days, I went to visit her one last time. I thought the truth, in this case, would be a gift. I told her everything Great Uncle Tommy had told me.

Aunt Celia made a sound like strangled laughter and shuddered so hard the oxygen tubes pulled out of her nostrils.

"What a crock of shit," Celia rasped, grabbing my arm. "So he got you too, huh? Lying, falling-apart bastard of a father. And you, you little fool, you went and let him off the hook! Uncle Tommy died at Anzio. All the Army could find were his dog tags."

I think I shook my head no, but maybe it was just really wobbly at that point.

Celia couldn't talk any more, nothing but air came out, but she wasn't done yet. She motioned to me for a pad and a pen.

She wrote about Henry making it to the top of the cliff overlooking Omaha Beach. She wrote that they stayed there two days, nursing the wounded and rounding up German prisoners. Lots of mine fields, she wrote next. And then this: Henry's idea to make the young German boys march in front until there weren't any left. That's how he got through to Belgium, she scribbled. Stepping through their parts.

Celia didn't write or speak after that. She sipped oxygen from tanks until she died, three days later, on a Thursday.

The beach house sold for seven figures to a plastic surgeon. We spent one last Memorial Day there, cleaning out the junk. Up there, in Henry's old room, fingering those dog tags, I made my decision.

I perched my body precariously on the ledge above the shoreline of Manatauk Bay. I barely had room to kneel and unwrap the pieces of his torso, arranging them in proper order. There was no room left for the leg parts. Those I took with me, back to the beach house. At night, I waded out with them and let the low tide pull them out to sea, no witnesses but the ghost crabs scrambling from my flashlight's beam.

I think about him sometimes, when I turn my thoughts to the weather. On cloudy days, I curse myself because I picked such a lonely spot, the sort of place where a soul would have nothing else to do but gnaw on its toughest remembrances. Other days, sunny ones, I know I did right, leaving Henry there with a view clear across to the sea cliffs of France.

Reintroduction

JEFF PEARSON

Coyote returns to the highland desert amid
the cedars, slipping under barbed wire. The
man watches cartoons of sheep-snatching coyotes;
the man questions his ability to take pills,
counting out all of the Tylenol PM, ashamed
of the anti-psychotics, not sure who
would be following him in cars.
Through the window he sees a tree
shake when he tries to be revelated
by a gold tinged book. He begins routines.
He follows along for the holiday.
Coyote, somewhere in a sandstone hideout, near
the lady playing the organ, long awaiting
the missing connection, wondering what
happens to dead cotton tails eaten and
chewed in dosages, the fur left behind
like a forgotten coat. Lost and found,
the two beings transfixed by sunlight,
deep down in the southern Utah desert
where his father lies underground, a plot
of grass is watered by the Sevier River
where coyote slurps unconditionally. He drinks
the muddy water with a false grin. Easter,
the man trapped in a car, his legs stark
rubber cooled by air conditioning. He
motels and tries very hard to look out
the window at free, but menacing grips
of eggs rolling down clay hills, all
colored by Easter vinegar. Some creature
must eat the hard boiled remains, and
must sit in so much heat to require air
sped up by pants through swath
glands. Mistakenly, prayer comes alone.
Pleas to a spirit that returns listless and failed
attempts to garner peace. He stops at a
family doctor who tests his body motions;
the way one would follow prey

trying to see a sign of frailty.
He finds it near impossible to blend in
with the celebratory hunt of eggs. The
seizure of painted baby animals,
aborted. A giant rabbit savior come back
from death, from the de-bodied fur, the
bones somehow retrieved from burial. His
father altogether underground; an owl payphone
was his only contact with others, priesthood
blessings often and in the dark prison
almost forgotten (hands pressed so hard on his
head). An illusory hint of self-help.
Now, he wishes for the reckless
wandering through underpass, veins intoxicated,
automatically fleeing to his habitat, but
all he can remember is pleading in the cave
for the rest of his pack he so
placidly loved. Most of the time, he now
waits impatiently for words
to devour the morsels of his apartment,
to shake his bed, to still the night
time howl of his record player, the unregulated
heat out his windows, inside his radio,
the view of the threatening trains forceful
and unrepentant. Forgive the missing
spirituality.

· Shelter ·

Like any stray, he comes around only when it rains.

—*Flowers, Shears*

part one of **Atomic Summer**

ANTON BAER

W e have no idea where this atomic fellow came from.
　　Everywhere there were shrinking islands of snow under the pines, stubbornly hard and bluish in the shade, stitched by even bluer tracks of grouse and crisscrossing rabbits that had left tufts of fur on the bark. The big icicles hanging from the cabin eaves were clear as glass, smooth-ribbed, and they were dripping fast into the gravel. The water spread in a sheen round the moldering sawdust by the chopping stump, gathered into a rivulet that trickled in its mossy narrow bed down through the black spruce to the creek, and the creek ran out into the river and out across last summer's sandbar. The morning sun can send a shiver up your back after six months of cold so bitter that the smoke from the chimney stood straight up on the air, and for weeks the sun only came up over the mountains at eleven o'clock, and by noon the line of light had already begun to climb back up the hoar-frosted trees, tipping them gold by two o'clock and leaving us in grey, smoky shadow. Now crocus peep out of the snow under the aspen up the hillsides, the wind lifts the bushy branches of the pines, and the ice floes left stranded high on the riverbank lie sagging, broken-backed, sloughing off chandeliers of green candle-ice that slither, wind chimes, onto the stones. A warm wind blows up the river.

If Kathe's not in the bush, she's at her table inside, bent over her microscope, leafing through her lexicons. In the cool of the morning she opens her trunk, lugs out her texts and taxonomic guides, and works, works, works. Her hair is beautiful. It gives me a flush in the chest, a steady heat, makes me alert and wide-awake. The mountains across the river are old mountains, cirques and shale and caribou lichen, as still as stone can be. An alpine valley opens out into even higher mountains whose sedimentary layers are given away by the tracing of snow. Wispy clouds blow up and down that little high valley. The cold mountains are like the company of chessmen: silent players, in and out of shadow, but players that never move. Kathe likes to work where she can see them. Unaware of her own mystery, maybe, unconscious of her own consciousness: a shadow that stops and thinks. A shadow that stops time. A sandbar in the river that's there in the same place, summer after summer, a sandbar you can go back to.

Maybe that's what drew him out.

It was just after lunch when he stumbled into the clearing. Pigshaven and pink-skulled, round rubber-rimmed glasses thick with more frost than a thumb could melt, he staggered out of the trees clutching his laboratory coat to his throat, tripped over his flopping gumboots, and collapsed in a sprawling, groaning heap.

I dropped the hoe in the furrows in the greenhouse, picked it up and leaned it against the fire barrel, and stepped out. Up at the cabin, Kathe was standing in the doorway. I made a gesture as if to say: it's all right, go back to your books. But it wasn't all right. On second thought, I went back into the greenhouse for the hoe.

Around the corner of the cabin came the huskies, snarling, tails curled tight, and went for him without a sound. But before they had even reached the grass they seemed to come to the ends of invisible chains and jerked somersaulting onto their backs with furry *whumps*. Whimpering, bristling but breathless, they turned about and belly-crawled back the way they had come, their fur rippling the wrong way over their ears as though they were being pushed by running water. As soon as they reached the pines, they got off their bellies and bolted from shadow to shadow, from snow patch to snow patch. Their howls floated back to us for long, eerie minutes . . .

That's the last we've seen of them.

The man merely cocked his head and smiled.

He sat staring back into the trees as though he were clearing a hurdle, and clearing it badly. While one bony hand reached back to scratch the awkwardly trailing ankle, the other drifted up like a nervous pink spider to wipe up a thread of spit drooling down off his chunky, twisted chin. His pants were black woollens, tucked into his gumboots, and looked stiff as cardboard; snow crystals were still caught in the coarse weave. He wiped the drool of spit on them and, knuckling the gold bridge of his glasses, shoved them higher up his chunky, pugnacious nose. The lenses were still frosted over, and the too-short temple arms tugged his ears out from his shaven temples. His ears were tiny and pink and whorled as honeysuckle. His teeth were blue as permafrost. His lips were lilac from the cold.

"This being so," he croaked, "mind telling me where I am?"

His voice was even more of a shock: it hissed, crackled, and sparked, as if it came out of an old radio glowing with vacuum tubes.

Partly he gave off the cold freshness of melting snow, and partly the stale odour of birds' nests. But mostly he smelled like a horse blanket and gave off the chill that wafts out of abandoned mine shafts even on hot summer days.

A flight of geese following the river towards the arctic deltas took the short-cut over the cabin, honking brassily, and were gone in a rush of wings. Then it was so quiet I could hear the steady, random, wind-chime tinkling of the sagging floes of candle-ice by the river, from all up and down the bank. From the cabin roof, the icicles were dripping so steadily that I had to fight down the urge to go look for a tap to close.

"Greenland, eh?" he nodded and started plucking needles out of the sap on his lab coat.

Our felt insoles were airing out on the porch and our long johns flapped on the washline. The door was propped open to let the warm wind in—and in it went, flapping and puffing out the pillow cases. The sun shone in after it, drew a trembling line down the log wall of the doorway, neatly bisected Kathe's brown felt hat with its tightly curled brim hung on a nail. It drew a jagged line across the rough wooden planks and the throw rugs, slanted up over the foot of the bed of burlap sacks stuffed with spruce boughs. It lit up the stove ash and tracked-in winter grit. It lit up the bathtub in the other corner. It lit up a reddish tin of soap flakes on the edge. The brass horn of the gramophone, the kerosene lanterns, the decks of cards on the table, the tea and coffee tins on the counters, the wind-up bush radio, my steel Dobro guitar and pedal drum and harmonicas in their felt-lined cases leaned here and there—all these intimate things suddenly took on a strange, silent, eerie, spot-lit museum quality.

"What a paradise!" he snorted. "Hellish woods you've got around here, I'll tell you that much. Nothing but rivers, creeks, boggy spruce blacking out the sun and swampy meadows stinking with flowers—or often as not submerged under busted chunks of ice—*Forestus horribilus!* You call that stimulating? Not exactly the august halls of learning *I'm* used to!"

Kathe had meanwhile pulled on her duffel coat and come down from the porch: arms folded, chin up, her jaws starting to flare out from under the lobes of her reddening ears, her reddish-gold hair pulled back tight under a knotted green silk paisley shawl and coming out in a bushy ponytail that was just about standing on end.

"You wouldn't have a cigarette, would you?" the man snapped his fingers. "Some *machorka*? A fag, a smoke? A cigar maybe? Leaf-wrapped? Dipped in port, I don't mind. Stogies, cigarillos? Hey, give the man a cigar!"

He raised his arm and snapped his fingers in our faces. "Baccy—comprendo? Speaka da English?"

"We speak English," I said.

"Good." Stretching out on his back, he folded his hands across his chest, shut his eyes, and drummed his heels on the grass. Snow crumbled out the gumboots in lumps.

"So, which one's the man of the house? The bearded lady on garden patrol, or the munchy dyke in the lumberjack shirt with the big carrot hair sticking out of Santa Claus's underpants?"

"What do you want?" Kathe asked.

"You there, partner dude sort of old-timer whose shifty eyes I can barely see under that battered old dirty old brown old oily old fedora that announces you are some plenty small-time artiste on the banjo—you going to play a few jigs for me? Go on, roll out that one-man-band. What else you do with that beard except wag it on the end of your chin when you howl your old rhythm-and-blues snooze tunes? '*Jes gimme a sign, and press your lips up close to mine*'—not with me, buddy. You pound that drum, not my bum. Where'd you get that beard, anyway—ye old Costume Shop? You ever going to wash those blue jeans, or you planning to make dirt soup out of them? Hey, dude—make it magnificent!"

His screech whooped and sputtered, faded and grew stronger in eerie pulses.

"Who are you?" I asked.

"Bet you've been hoarding your tabaccy for a moment like this, eh? It's been ages since I had a smoke. There were days I could have stuffed my mouth with moss for want of one. But I didn't. Because if there's one thing I can say for myself, it's character: I've got it. That's right. I'm a stubborn guy."

"Who are you?"

"So, living out here on your own, are you? All on your pretty lonesomes?"

"What do you want?"

"A treehouse you built yourself—I can tell."

The frost had melted by now off his little round granny glasses with the gold bridge and the black rubber rims. The left lens was cracked in a zig-zag from top to bottom. The right lens was spiderwebbed with shatter lines. They looked like gas-mask lenses.

"It's a cabin," I said. "Fifty square metres, permafrost storage cellar, ninety gallons of water on tap, hot-water boiler run from the stove, a stand-up piano, and a telescope on the roof. I'd hardly call it—"

"And this amazing lawn!" He let one hand fall patronisingly to the grass. "Real bluegrass! Resourceful. I like that. Maybe we'll pot a few holes later, huh guy?"

"It's ordinary meadow grass," I said. "There's no golf course."

"Your goddamn right there isn't," he sneered.

Drawing in his heels, he brought up his knees, crossed his legs, and dangled a sloshing gumboot. "Cigarette," he murmured, puckering up. He pressed two quavering fingers across his blood-blister of a mouth: "Got one?"

"I don't smoke. And neither does my . . . wife."

"Aaa-hah!" He opened one eye and regarded me coolly.

Suddenly he laughed—a high-pitched whine, like a rat being swung by the tail.

"Yes, I've been to university too," he said. "One of the best, can't complain. Anyway—and this is one of the things you should know about me—I don't complain. Strictly on principle. Even if I did, I wouldn't. Because that's the kind of guy I am. Now, I don't have to guess what you studied: Marxism. Yes, you probably think you're pretty funky kids. But what I say is this: funky—skunky. Pew-*yoo!* Sk-u-u-u-*unk!*"

"There are no skunks this far north," Kathe pointed out.

"Don't kid me, ok sweetie?" he said, rolling over and jabbing his finger at her. "Your politics are about as obvious as the color of Mars."

"I have no politics."

"University and no politics? Hah!"

"She played soccer and she liked to dance," I said.

She made a tongue-clicking *tsk* with a shake of her head, as if to say: hold back on the private stuff.

"And as for science," he said, "I bet you figure the moon's made of cheese. I'll bet you figure a cow could jump over it. Ha ha! *I'm* the man of science—got it? That's the difference between us. *I* get the facts straight before I make my move. Comprendo, Señorita? I'm not sucked in by muddled logic—don't even talk about fashion, or taste! Yep, you should have been trooping along with me—if you could have kept up, that is. You would have appreciated some of the gems I expressed in a wondrous form. Who were those declaiming-type guys—Milksop and Dandy? You know, the descent into Hell and all that. Buggered around in big poem-type situations. Went blind. Deserved to—I mean, give me a break!"

"Milton and Dante?" Kathe suggested.

"Yes, them faggots. They should have been trooping along with me too. They would have thanked me on their wobbling knees for my poetical items. But that's just what happens when you're a Renaissance guy. I *am*, however, a man of science at bottom, and a man of science doesn't trouble himself with flower-picking. That can be left to the feeble-minded. Or am I wrong?"

He looked up, his eyes blue and arrogant and darting behind the cracked spectacles. "What, me wrong? What an extraordinary thought! Only I could be capable of it. No, don't bother wondering how—you've had plenty of time to waste prattling with each other I'm sure, so now you can listen to me for a change—"

The rest of the afternoon he chattered on. Boolean algebra, synchronicity, yttrium, plasma physics—they all took a pasting. Meanwhile, we trundled out cups of herb tea and plates of hot flour biscuits fresh from the oven. After sampling a biscuit, which ended up in crumbs all over his chest, he touched only the camomile, which he gulped down without even blowing on it.

Eventually he wanted to come inside the cabin. Craning his pink neck, bulging in unusual places, he scratched furiously at the insect bites on his wrists and ears until, his head thrust deep between his knees, he degenerated into a contorted blur. "Must be a relief to sleep indoors!" he croaked, with just a hint of hysterical sobbing.

I coughed, as if I hadn't noticed a thing, and offered more biscuits.

Cross-legged on the grass as evening came, the pages of Kathe's books left to flap in the breeze on the plywood table up on the porch, we listened politely to everything the man said. He had such an intellect, we had to respect his frightening intellect. Even when, during his attempt to describe a fusion torus in a babbling gush of baby-talk, comparing it to a doughnut and a soother and I don't know what else, Kathe volunteered: "Oh, like a TOKAMAK," and he cut her off with "Never mind, I'm sure a lot of this atomic stuff's beyond you"—even then we had to respect his special intellect, which had done so much for humanity, and for him.

"I can do anything I put my mind to," he insisted. "Soap, for example. You ever use soap? If the fantastic notion ever occurs to you, I can make you tons. Nice green cakes. See it in the dark. Make you glow with health."

"No, but thanks."

"Come on!" he hissed, and rubbed his thumb against his forefinger: "Cheap!"

At supper time he was still going strong. Kathe brought the supper out and laid it carefully on a tablecloth laid on the grass: three roast grouse with red currant jelly, baked beans and rice, soda bread, and a can of peaches. The man looked it all over fastidiously, but touched only the currant jelly, which he licked up with his fingers. Until dessert. When he saw Kathe bringing a hot mossberry pie across the grass, steaming through the cracks in the crust, he greedily lolled his tongue from side to side. The moment she set it down, he plunged his hand right through the crust, gouged out a fiery triangle, and stuffed it into his gaping mouth.

"I was the numero uno on campus," he babbled, spitting out mangled purple berries. "Seven-day poker, fast cars and virgins—I've had it all. Nowadays it's different, it's Daddy's money to burn and some peasant's blood to shed for noble causes. Don't tell me, don't tell me, been there, know all about it—" he waved us off, choking.

Afterwards, he lay propped on his elbow, his head on his shoulder, and scavenged through the bones of the grouse. We piled the dishes in the cloth and carried the bundle back into the cabin. Crossing the porch, Kathe took the precaution of gathering up her books and pulling the trunk inside.

"The man is a fruitcake," she whispered. "He's a complete, raving lunatic. He'll come charging in here at night swinging an axe and singing a nursery rhyme."

"Don't worry, I'm not going to sleep."

"Do you think I am?"

Back outside, cross-legged on the grass, we shivered a little and waited for him to go.

He just kept talking about how awful Greenland was.

"Greenland is under a sheet of ice a mile thick," Kathe finally broke in. "And has been for the last ten thousand years. It's still in the last Ice Age."

"Is that so, sweetie?"

She flushed. White spots broke out over her cheeks, bloodless and hard. "Yes, that's so. I didn't catch your name, by the way."

"Oh, call me anything."

"What do you call yourself?"

"What do I call myself?"

Hands behind his head, he gazed up at the purple crocus swaying softly on the crests of the brown hillsides, the wild roses in bloom at the higher edges of the meadow; he glanced up at the mountains across the river, dappled like sleeping appaloosas with the shadows of the sunset clouds. The snowfields under the peaks were pink with the sunset. With the riverbank in shadow, the random tinkling of the ice floes had subsided to pure, expectant silence.

Something very odd happened: his eyes turned as dark as the sky, and the blue was streaked with a fiery pink that wasn't just from the cracks in the lenses.

"'His Master's Voice,'" he announced. "You can call me that." And he smiled his blue smile.

Suddenly he let out a belch so violent that we sat back covering our glasses with our hands, as bubbles big as grapes foamed out of his mouth and down over his lab coat in a purplish froth. Clutching his swollen belly, he fell back and lay staring goggle-eyed up at the brightest planets.

"Ah!" he began, taking it all in with a grand flourish, "The Last Frontier!"

As if nothing could be more normal, we got to our feet and bolted inside.

We undressed in the twilight, leaving the lanterns unlit; through the mosquito screens floated the smell of the melting snow, and as we listened to the wind sough in the pines, watched them sway against the darkening blue, it was like being whispered to sleep.

Except the lunatic out on the grass was still talking.

All night I sat up in the armchair by the window, cradling the 30.06 in my lap, chewing coffee beans to stay alert, and listening to his lectures splutter across the grass. Kathe sat propped up against the pillows, listening quietly to the solar wind of stellar facts: the seven-year summers of Titan, the electrical storms of Jupiter that went on for centuries, washing away the surfaces of its moons atom by atom. Hydrogen fogs, sulphur-dioxide frosts whitening the shores of methane lakes, blizzards covering cinder seas in drifts a mile deep. Eternal darkness and lunar cliffs thirty miles high. Once in a thousand years, asteroids raising tiny plumes of titanium dust. Now and then she whispered: "Did you know that?"

"We don't know if it's true," I whispered back.

"It's all true," she said.

About the Earth's moon alone he spoke for hours. His hands clasped behind his back, he nodded it on with a stiff-chinned salute as it went hurtling overhead leaving behind a sparkling wake, high above this useless earth, so flat, wretched, and cold—as if it were nothing to the man outside but a slab of blue ice lost in space, scratched with meaningless hieroglyphs, love-hearts and stick men.

Flowers, Shears

MICHAEL SCHMELTZER

In a corner of the living room, an old woman in a yellow sweater stained with spaghetti sauce knits a long, pink scarf. It hangs like a tongue crushed repeatedly under the mahogany rocking chair. The radio champions another dishwashing detergent then preaches the importance of fixing your pets. She clicks it off and hums to herself a tune from her childhood. A runaway watches from outside, his faded overalls drenched. Like any stray, he comes around only when it rains. The woman shuffles over to the dining room table. In her house are flowers, in her hands shears. She lifts the blossoms one at a time, snips a few inches off the bottom of the stems. She sets the silver shears on the green amputations like tinsel on a Christmas tree. She heads over to the kitchen, pours milk into a black bowl, and sets it out on the porch. The boy slinks around front. He laps it up quietly, his cat eyes shining.

Requiem for a Glass Heart

ROXANE GAY

The stone thrower, a good yet flawed man given to overindulgence, met his wife on a beach, after a lightning storm on a night when the sky refused to surrender to darkness, and yet there were stars up above. He saw the small fissure her body made in the sand first, moved closer, moved carefully. Then he saw her, her body bathed in moonlight, her eyes shining brightly. He instantly fell in love because he could not believe what lay before him. Her beauty was so mystifying and entrancing that it pierced through his skin and into his blood and wove itself tightly around his heart.

He did not think about what it would mean to love a glass woman. He fell to his knees. He took her hand in his, turned the palm over. He gently placed his lips against the tender spot between her thumb and forefinger. He closed his eyes and inhaled deeply. He prayed that when he opened his eyes she would still be there. When he did, she was.

The stone thrower's wife instantly fell in love because the stone thrower was everything she was not. He was the first man who did not see through her. He helped her to her feet, and then they walked for hours and miles and miles more. He listened and enjoyed her husky voice as she told him all of her hopes, her dreams, her fears. She tried to keep some secrets for herself, but couldn't. His propensity for indulgence was infectious. She laid herself bare and did not think about what it would mean to love a man of flesh.

The stone thrower and his wife courted for seven months and married on the seventh day of that seventh month. She wore a silver gown and diamonds in her glass hair. The stone thrower stood next to her, in front of his friends, their families. They vowed to love, to honor, to protect, to obey, although he did not yet know how he would keep his word.

When the stone thrower and his glass wife make love, she is always on top, her cool glass hands pressed against his chest. She covers him, leg to leg, breast to chest, face to face. He kisses her long, slender neck, the hollow spaces above her shoulder blades. He slides his hands along the length of her glass hair, then holds her face, tracing her lips with his thumbs. The stone thrower's wife warms to his touch, just slightly, and though he can't see it, he can feel her body respond. He enjoys the pressure of her glass thighs trembling against his and the way she breathes into his mouth, shallow and fast.

When the stone thrower's wife comes, her body fogs in a random pattern outward from her heart. As she catches her breath, she can often hear her heart threatening to implode with the high pitched lamentation of glass succumbing to pressure. When she's certain her heart won't break, she rolls onto her side, and the stone thrower lovingly traces lines in the condensation he has left behind. Sometimes, after they make love, the stone thrower will light a candle, sit against the headboard, holding his wife in his arms, her glass spine arched against his thick, matted chest. He'll look down at his seed slowly sliding out of her. He will ask her to lay herself bare further, to share secrets he does not yet know. He has become accustomed to seeing too much and now yearns to know too much. She will acquiesce, speaking softly, exposing herself in complicated ways. The stone thrower will smile. His wife will not.

Every morning, the stone thrower sits across from his glass wife at their glass table, and he watches as orange juice sluices down her glass throat into her glass stomach. It is a remarkable thing, he often thinks, being able to see such intimacies, being able to see the separation of her whole into parts. She'll look at him, then to the distance, her cheeks growing warm while she remembers the night before. As they discuss the coming day, the stone thrower's wife will reach across the table and take his hand in hers. She'll trace the calluses, the fingers that are bent but not broken. He'll squeeze back, gently, ever careful to not break her.

After the stone thrower and his glass wife share breakfast, he takes his glass child to school, holding the boy's cool, translucent hand in his. He listens carefully as the boy tells him about his hopes, his dreams, his fears. With every word his son speaks, the stone thrower feels his heart expanding, nearly breaking the cage of bone protecting it. After he kisses the boy on the forehead, sending him on his way, the stone thrower will sometimes stand just outside the child's classroom, peering inside, holding his breath, hoping that the other children will be gentle and kind, however fragile such hope may be.

During the day, the stone thrower's glass wife busies herself with the work of living in a glass house. Room by room, she uses soft cloths to wipe clean every surface because her husband cannot help the things he leaves behind. As she wipes away the fingerprints and skin and stray hairs she smiles to herself and hums the waltz to which she and the stone thrower danced at their wedding. Sometimes, her neighbors will stop in front of the glass house and stare as they catch glimpses of her body's glass contours beneath the clothes she wears more for their benefit than hers. They will whisper to each other and shake their heads.

What the stone thrower's wife loves most is stripping out of her clothes and slipping into the world unseen. It is a sacred time, those hours between when her work is done and when her child and husband return home. She steals these moments for herself because her life is so transparent that she craves having something private, something precious. She crafts from these moments secrets for herself that she has not and will not share with her husband who sees too much and loves too carefully.

Most days, the stone thrower's wife goes to a nearby park with wide open spaces and room to make big mistakes. She stretches her long limbs and stares into the sky. She marvels at the clear blue brightness above. She closes her eyes and says a small prayer. Then she runs. She runs because she is intoxicated by the sensation of wind against her bare glass skin. She enjoys the abandon of pushing her glass body and testing its limits and feeling the rough pavement and the cold slick grass beneath her bare glass feet. Her husband loves her but he worries. He wearies. He thinks her delicate. He fears that the slightest bump will transform her into sand. The stone thrower prefers to keep his wife trapped in the safety of their glass house where the dangers are not seen but known. She knows that the glass walls of their home cannot protect her. She runs.

After her afternoons in the park, the stone thrower's wife finds herself sweaty and pleasantly sore. She walks home slowly, breathing deeply. She revels. Then she takes a cold shower, emerges, wraps herself in a soft cotton robe. When her son comes home, she will pull him into her arms, and listen when he tells her about his hopes, his dreams, his fears. He chatters away and she traces her child's diaphanous features with her glass fingertips. The contact between their glass bodies produces a melodious keening that makes the boy smile wider. The stone thrower's wife falls ever more in love with her child each day. Though it pains her, she accepts that the boy's life is both a blessing and a curse. When her heart has had its fill of these precious moments, when she can literally feel the glass veins pulsing and threatening to shatter, she sends her child out to play with his friends until dinner. She needs him to be part of the world, to encounter that which is seen but not known.

The stone thrower's son knows that he is a curiosity but he does not yet know why. In school, he sits at his desk, his glass frame draped in his school uniform. He is quiet but studious. He is kind but strong, like his mother. His is tough and stubborn, like his father. Though some of his classmates tease him, make faces at each other while looking through him, the stone thrower's son has several friends who no longer concern themselves with that which makes them different, that which they cannot understand. To them, he is a boy who makes them laugh and chases them on the playground and who makes beautiful castles out of sand.

The stone thrower works hard and plays hard and provides well for his glass family. For eight hours a day, he works in a quarry, bare-chested and sweaty, throwing all manner of stone from the depths of the quarry to waiting trucks above. He is so good at his job that he often attracts an audience. Onlookers hover nearby, admiring the elaborate web of muscles enfolding his upper body, and the way he makes his labor seem so effortless. He does not mind the onlookers. He has become accustomed to living in a glass house.

When he finally gets home, the stone thrower sits at the kitchen table with his glass wife and their glass child. The family eats a dinner that has been lovingly prepared and the stone thrower tries not to look away from the intimate moments of his wife and son that he cannot share. He helps the boy with his homework, then together, husband and wife put the child to bed. Some nights, they hire a babysitter, leave a careful set of instructions for the care and feeding of a glass child, and then the couple goes out for a drink at a nearby cocktail lounge. His wife dresses in her favorite little black dress, relaxes against her husband's strong frame, enjoys the pressure of his hand in the small of her back as he steers her to a table where they can see without being seen, hear without being heard.

On very special occasions, they will don their finery and attend the opera. They'll sit in a private box above the orchestra, admire the ornate ceilings, the rich texture of the seats upon which they sit. The stone thrower's wife will lose herself in the music, glass tears cresting her eyelids as she is transported to magical places. The stone thrower will try to enjoy himself, but with every note in every aria, his entire body will tense. He worries that it is a matter of time before a diva with perfect pitch and iron lungs will fill the opera house with a note so flawless that it matches the natural frequency of his wife's body. He will be left, kneeling above shards of glass, holding his wife's pulsing glass heart in his callused hands. The stone thrower is always quiet when he and his wife leave the opera, humbled as he is by the tenuous nature of a glass wife. She'll ask him what's wrong and he'll look at her tenderly, and he'll lie, and he'll say everything is just fine.

The stone thrower, a good yet flawed man given to overindulgence, has a mistress he visits several times a week. She is a woman who is not made of glass. She is all flesh and bone, with a generous, meaty body like his. She is a different kind of mystery.

What the stone thrower's wife hates most is stripping out of her clothes and slipping into the world unseen. She knows about the mistress. She watches her husband and the other woman sometimes, sneaking into the mistress's apartment, padding softly across the thick carpet of the living room. She'll stand in the doorway and watch as her husband holds the other woman in his large, callused hands, how he will be reckless and rough. Then she will walk home, leaving a trail of glass tears for the stone thrower to follow. The stone thrower doesn't love his mistress, but he needs the moments they share, those moments when he does not have to see too much or love too carefully.

from **The Centipede Love Songs**

DANIEL PORDER

To Those Crawled Across in Sleep

I've even seen a landscape of your form, your firm
Breasts, foothills or massive flags, zero tents,
Some sagging breeze sucked out of everywhere
By night blowing absences of air. Night

The tomb. Your hardwood floor beneath thirty feet
Clacks, a black gloss, a sun's funeral.
Electric lights shut off by you are broken,
Disconnected, despised, despised

But still "nice to look at" or "just for show."
I've even seen a landscape form from your hands—
Negative rivers winding, growing, never rising,

Always risen, something pulled from your "perhaps."
Perhaps gazing through you is architecture, an atom
    Falling towards the ceiling. Up is too short a word.

To Those Who Crush Bugs

The streets hum, sometimes buzz,
You swat at a fly, miss, and this time
I kill and consume it. The moon shatters
In your window, sky stolen by all

Of me, none of you—where are the stars?
O crescent smile, O uneven head
Tilting down: do you even know what
I am? I know you, love. Long rain

In bands rakes this air, your endless hair.
Somewhere, somewhere you have seen
These eyes, stood deep in them: *there you are.*

"There it is!" you cry, and enter *husband*, stage left,
Brandishing swatter. "Stomp him!" someone
    Cries—no, you cry. No, I run. I weep.

Oldjohn's House

MICAH DEAN HICKS

Way out in Arizona, a few miles from the desert reservations, Oldjohn and his five kids lived. His kids were all in their thirties, and Oldjohn hated them. They were failures, even Fatjohn who'd only ever wanted to work at the gas station down the road, and they'd lived with him their whole lives. They stole his whiskey, ate all his pension could buy, and ran off every woman he'd had for the last fifteen years, starting with their mother. But they were too big for Oldjohn to whip anymore, so one day he decided to build a house that would be able to whip them for him and whip them good.

He decided to build the house on the edge of his land next to the highway. It took him four months to collect enough scraps from woodpiles and abandoned houses, but Oldjohn was a good hater—the only thing he was good at—and kept at it until he had enough lumber and tin. The day Oldjohn went to build it, he brought with him heaps of old belts, coat-hangers, cut-off lengths of water-hose, tough branches, and everything else good for whipping children. All these Oldjohn hung inside the walls and put up in the attic as he built the house. Each still throbbed with the hurt of his children and with his disappointment in them, and he packed them in so thick that nothing could be inside the house without feeling their sting.

For weeks he worked, and finally Oldjohn finished, clapped the dust off his hands, and went home. His kids were in the living room smashed together on the couch in front of the TV: Fatjohn, I'mjohn, Meanjohn, Miranda, and Candace. The couch was broken down almost to the floor underneath them. Miller beer bottles rolled around their feet, and yellowed popcorn flakes were ground into the rug. They were watching a western. On the screen, Indians chased buffalo across the plains in Toyotas, the small trucks heaving up and down over potholes and hills, feathers whipping from the side mirrors. Miranda and I'mjohn were ignoring the movie and playing cards. Oldjohn saw their dark hair and skin, their tall bodies, and remembered their mother. He stepped in front of the TV.

"I've built you all your own house by the highway," Oldjohn said. "Now get the hell out." His kids cheered and shouted, all talking at once and running back to their rooms. They filled laundry baskets and army duffel bags with everything they had, which wasn't very much. I'mjohn took the cards he and Miranda played with all the time, and Miranda took only the big bottles of shampoo and conditioner she needed for her long, thick hair. Meanjohn and Fatjohn helped each other carry the TV. Candace, last to leave, went to the pantry and measured out some dry beans, rice, and noodles into grocery sacks. She kissed Oldjohn on the cheek on her way out. As their voices receded down the hill, Oldjohn locked the door so that they couldn't come back.

He sat down alone and started drinking, rushing to the window when he thought he heard one of them outside, but there was never anyone there. The house was quiet, and for the first time in years he could hear the wind sobbing through the cracks around the windows and pushing through the crawlspace under his feet. He took one last hot swallow of whiskey and lay down on the couch. He stayed there for a long time, not knowing what else to do.

The sun was hot and white, and Oldjohn's children went squinting down the side of the hill to their new house beside the road. When they got to it, they huddled together in its ragged, ugly shadow. The house was tall and narrow with two floors. Its sides were mismatched planks of sand-scarred wood and irregular pieces of tin, flecked with rust and peeling back at the corners. I'mjohn stepped onto the porch and took the doorknob in his hand. The others crowded around him. They swung the door open and looked inside. The house was as dry and dusty as a shipping crate. Besides the porch, there were two big rooms one on top of the other, a small kitchen, a bathroom, and an attic. There was no furniture at all inside. They decided I'mjohn and Meanjohn would live upstairs and Miranda and Candace would live downstairs. They made Fatjohn stay in the attic. The five of them played cards the rest of the evening, grinning to each other because they now had their own house and wouldn't have to fight with Oldjohn all the time. Then, after they became tired, they spread their blankets out on the floor and went to sleep.

In their room, Miranda and Candace stayed up talking like they always did. Finally, Candace grew tired and started to say her prayers. Miranda kept interrupting her and changing the words: "Dear Lord, bless me," Candace would say. "With a big man to warm my bed," Miranda would finish. "Let us have the strength to withstand," Candace would say. "His lovely body on top of ours," Miranda would finish. They went on like this until Candace was too frustrated to pray, and Miranda was already dreaming of men.

That night, Candace couldn't get any rest. The house was so empty, she was sure she could hear everyone's breath echoing off the walls. Every gasp, snort, and snore floated down the stairs and ricocheted around the room until it struck her in the ear and made her bolt up in bed. It went on like that for hours, until she couldn't stand it anymore. Candace ran out of the house to find something to fill all that emptiness. While the others slept, she kept filling until morning.

When everyone got up, no one could say anything for a while. There was a national park service picnic table in the living room. Road signs were tacked to the walls—their directions all confused—a charcoal grill was in the kitchen, a dismantled eighties model Ford truck was hung in pieces along the wall going up the staircase, sacks of gardening dirt were stacked in the corner, oranges were scattered over the floor, and Miranda found a duck in the closet. I'mjohn even found a bicycle chained to the faucets in the bathtub and had to sit on it while he showered.

"It's like Christmas," Fatjohn said. They heard someone pull up in the yard and went to the window to look. Candace parked a white Buick on the lawn next to three others. She got out, opened an umbrella to shade herself from the sun, and started walking back toward town to steal another.

The four of them had a breakfast of the oranges and sat down at the picnic table to discuss what they should do. Fatjohn and Meanjohn insisted that there was nothing that could be done. She was their sister, after all, and wasn't the house better now? I'mjohn could tell that Miranda was bothered by it, though. He followed her into the kitchen and helped her clean the grill to cook lunch. They whispered together as they scraped charred tinfoil off the grillwork and raked out the old coals.

"She'll go to jail," Miranda said, "and all of us will go with her."

I'mjohn nodded. "I don't care if she is our sister. We have to do something before this comes back on us."

Finally, they decided what they should do. I'mjohn walked up the hill to Oldjohn's house. He didn't try the door, but opened his old window and stepped through. I'mjohn called the police department and told them that his sister had been stealing cars and where she'd put them. As he hung up the phone, Oldjohn walked out of the bathroom. "You're back," Oldjohn said.

"No, I only needed to use the phone."

Oldjohn nodded. He brought I'mjohn into the kitchen and made him a cup of coffee. I'mjohn thanked him for the coffee and told him about how much they were liking their new house.

"It's bad," Oldjohn said. "It's not a good house, and you should get out."

"No, it's great. We like it."

"There's nothing good in this place, and you should leave."

I'mjohn finished his coffee and thanked his father again. He told him not to worry about them. He went back to the house with the TV remote, a cook-pot, and a new bottle of whiskey. The police had already taken away Candace and the cars by the time I'mjohn got back. He and Miranda made lunch. Afterward, they sat at the table raising shots to their sister for most of the night and tried to trick the duck into drinking with them.

The second morning, they all had a bastard of a headache, and everyone was quiet. Fatjohn locked the front door twice that morning, but every time he went back, it was unlocked again. He looked up at the house's ill-joined walls and ceilings looming over him and locked the door a third time. He walked away for a minute, but when he came back, it was unlocked. The brass mouth of the lock, scratched all around from the teeth of keys, looked as surprised as he did.

Fatjohn went to Miranda first and shouted at her, "Why do you keep unlocking the door?" She covered her ears and told him to be quiet, that she hadn't touched a door all morning. Then he went to his brothers and shouted at them, "Who keeps unlocking the door?" They yelled and threw their shoes at him, told him to get the hell out. But it only got worse. All morning, Fatjohn went along locking doors behind him and finding them unlocked as soon as he turned his back. He could hear them click open as he stepped away. By lunchtime, he was beating the doors with his fists and screaming that something was wrong with the house.

Meanjohn's head felt full of waves and he couldn't stand Fatjohn's noise anymore. He found his brother swearing and trying to take the front lock apart with a screwdriver. Meanjohn pounded on his brother's head and back with both fists and chased him up the stairs and into his room. Then Meanjohn stopped, his eyes lifting to the ceiling. Since they'd moved in, none of them except for Fatjohn had been inside the attic. Hanging from the ceiling were hundreds of old belts, pieces of water hose, stretched out coat-hangers, and branches. They drifted back and forth from the wind blowing in through the window and rattled softly together. For a moment, Meanjohn was very afraid, remembering all the whippings Oldjohn had given him as a child. But then he laughed. "This house is just as screwed up as anything he ever did." Fatjohn nodded, hoping his brother wasn't angry anymore, but when Meanjohn jerked down some of the belts, he knew that he was in trouble.

Meanjohn bound his brother's feet and hands with the belts, rolled him onto his stomach, and striped his back and legs with welts while Fatjohn screamed for him to stop. Finally Meanjohn left the room, noticing that the doorknob had been put on backwards. He locked the door from the outside, giving it a shake. "What do you think about the locks now?" He walked back to his room. The floor creaked under Meanjohn, and it kept sounding like someone was coming up behind him. But each time he looked over his shoulder, no one was there. He would feel better after he lay down, he thought.

Later, I'mjohn opened the bathroom door and saw Miranda stepping out of the shower. Both hands were up wringing out her hair, and one leg was over the edge of the tub, long thigh tapering to calf and foot, a halo of water around her toes. The water made her hair gleam black and her skin wet and bright like honey. I'mjohn saw her and was still for a moment. Their eyes met, and he shut the door slowly and walked back to his room.

They always locked the door when they were in the bathroom, and neither knew how something like this could have happened. They didn't cook together that night, but stayed at opposite ends of the house. Meanjohn went back and forth asking them what was wrong, but they only got angry with him and wouldn't say.

Finally, the two of them met again at Fatjohn's door. He was beating on it from the inside, yelling for someone to let him out. I'mjohn shrugged. "I can't get it to open." Miranda tried, but she couldn't open it either. They started laughing about it, just chuckling at first, then more and more as Fatjohn yelled at them from the other side of the doorway. They leaned against each other and laughed until they were crying. "I'm sorry," said I'mjohn when he could finally speak. Miranda shrugged. "It was an accident. We don't have to talk about it." They decided to go play cards while they tried to think of some way to get Fatjohn out of his room.

Knowing that they had forgotten him, Fatjohn made a rope from the belts and tried to climb down through the window. Halfway down, the belts came undone all at once, and he hit the ground hard. The belts rained down on his face and chest. He threw them off and went to the front door, ready to yell at his brothers and sister for leaving him there. He tried the doorknob, but it was locked. He shook it, knocked on it, kicked it, but nothing did any good. No one heard him and came to open the door. "Fuck all of you!" he yelled. He walked back up the long hill to his father's house. He went to Oldjohn's door—one he'd been going in and out of all his life— and tried to open it. He broke down into sobs. Oldjohn's door was locked, too.

He walked away, babbling to himself and kicking at the cracked dirt. "All the doors in the world are shut to me!" he said. He liked how it sounded and said it again, crying. This had always been true, he thought, it had just taken him this long to see it. He walked out to the highway beside the gas station where he had never been able to get a job and hitched a ride away from Oldjohn, his cruel family, and this cruel place.

In the house, they'd finally gotten Fatjohn's door open with a pry-bar, but he wasn't there. They decided he must have gone back to Oldjohn's house, and it was getting late anyway, so they didn't think any more about it. After dinner and a few hours of TV, they started getting ready for bed. Meanjohn had been acting strange all day, but I'mjohn didn't care to ask him about it. I'mjohn put the duck in the bathtub for the night, hoping it would be easier to clean up after him in the morning, and went to bed. But every time I'mjohn had almost fallen asleep, Meanjohn would roll over on the other side of the room and hit the floor with his fist.

After the fifth time, I'mjohn sat up. "What is wrong with you?" he asked.

"The house is creaking. The boards around me keep making noise."

"All houses creak. Especially Oldjohn's houses."

"No," Meanjohn said. I'mjohn could dimly see him sitting up on the other side of the room. "This sounds like someone is walking toward me. Like someone is sneaking over here to get me while I'm sleeping."

"No one is in here but you and me."

"I'm telling you, I can hear them!" His brother sounded hoarse and afraid.

I'mjohn was too tired to have patience for this. "That must be an awful thing. Still, if you don't stop hitting the floor so I can sleep, I'm going to beat the hell out of you."

"I have to do something to keep them away!" said Meanjohn.

I'mjohn got up, grabbed his boot, and walked over to his brother. Meanjohn hit the floor when he heard someone walking toward him, then yelled when he realized someone was really there. I'mjohn beat his brother good with the boot, his fist buried inside it and punching Meanjohn in the stomach and chest, until he was tired and went back to lie down. Not even ten minutes had passed, and Meanjohn started yelling and throwing things again. I'mjohn threw both boots at him, called him a shithead, and took his blankets downstairs.

He walked down the staircase to Miranda and Candace's room, knowing there would be space because his sister was still in jail. In the soft blue light coming in through the window, he could see Miranda sitting on the floor with her arms wrapped around her knees. He wasn't sure if she could see him. Then he heard her talking.

Miranda was missing her sister and remembering their prayer. "Dear Lord," she called out. "Bless me with a big man to warm my bed. Let me have the strength to withstand his lovely body on top of mine."

At once, all I'mjohn could remember was his sister's honey-colored skin stepping out of the shower. She saw him then, standing on the other side of the room, but didn't recognize him in the dim light. She knew only that he was tall and lovely and watching her. She rose, and they met each other in the middle of the room where the light from the window couldn't reach. It was a long time before Miranda recognized I'mjohn, and by then it was too late.

Meanjohn found them in bed together the next morning. They covered themselves and were afraid of what he would say.

"You left me all alone up there!" Meanjohn shouted. "I fought them all night by myself!"

Miranda held the blankets to her chest and looked worried. I'mjohn said that he was sorry.

"There is something wrong with this house," Meanjohn said. "And I'm going to do something about it." He went outside.

I'mjohn and Miranda started putting their clothes back on. With every garment, they looked more and more strange to each other, and they didn't like it. Outside, they could hear Meanjohn ripping into the side of the house.

"I liked it," said I'mjohn. "I liked it an awful lot."

"I liked it, too," said Miranda, "but we shouldn't have done it."

A section of wall collapsed and the sun fell on them like an eye. Meanjohn stood beside the fallen tin and boards with a black pry-bar and sledge hammer in his hands.

I'mjohn turned back to his sister. "Says who?"

"Says everyone."

"Well, damn everyone. We should do what we want."

They talked it backwards and forwards, moving from room to room. As they talked, Meanjohn was steadily taking the house to pieces. Gaps dotted the walls, letting wind and sand blow through. Meanjohn soon had the second floor and the roof off, and I'mjohn and Miranda couldn't hide from each other.

Miranda walked out onto the porch. She could see the highway and all the cars passing, her father's house above them on a short mesa, and all the other little shacks and houses scattered around. "I love you more than anyone else, but none of them would let us live that way."

"We have this house," I'mjohn said. "If we stay here, none of them have to know about it." Even as he said it, though, Meanjohn pushed down the last wall and started stacking the boards and tin up in the yard. They stood on a porch connected to nothing. Meanjohn was making a big pile of belts, hoses, hangers, and branches, squirting lighter fluid all over it. They went to look.

Meanjohn had found the belts tacked to the insides of the walls and hung up in the attic, under the floors, and wrapped around the rafters. The pile was dense, all twisted together like cat's claw vines, and was taller than any of them. The belts were cracked and split, threaded around dead white branches and sun-bleached water-hose, and all the belt buckles shimmered brassily under their patinas of engine grease. "See," said Meanjohn. "This is what was wrong the whole time."

Miranda and I'mjohn looked at each other. They reached for the belts, but Meanjohn had already struck a match and threw it towards the pile. Miranda pulled back I'mjohn's arm as the belts exploded into fire and smoke. "Now, everything will be fine again," Meanjohn said. "Everything will be like it was."

I'mjohn squinted up at the little house on top of the mesa. "This is all Oldjohn's fault." Miranda started back up the hill. I'mjohn wondered if he should follow her or not. He watched her tall shape shrink as she walked up the hill closer to the sun. He was about to follow her, but Meanjohn handed him a hammer. "Now we'll put it back right," Meanjohn said.

Miranda went into Oldjohn's house through the window, just like I'mjohn had. She started scooping up coins from tables and dresser-tops. She took his pension check off the mantel, took his wallet and car keys, all the money he had. She'd made it to the hallway when she heard Oldjohn in his bedroom.

He was praying. "Dear Lord, send them away from this awful place. Make them leave," he said. "Everything they ever wanted," Miranda finished.

Oldjohn looked up at her from the bed, but kept going. "There's nothing here worth having," he said. "And Oldjohn still won't let us have it," she finished. Oldjohn began to cry. Miranda threw a handful of coins at him and left. She found his old Honda Civic parked beside the porch and took it, too.

Miranda saw I'mjohn stop working to watch her drive by, but the pile of belts had burned to ash now, and she knew that there would never be a place for them. She went past him toward the road. I'mjohn scooped up rocks and hurled them at the rear window, shouting that she was just like their mother. Miranda pulled out onto the highway and drove away, afraid that it might be true.

The two brothers worked for days putting the house back together. The sunlight was so thick, it stuck to their bodies and made them glow. They looked like angels standing in the desert, slinging up walls of tin and broken boards, their hands and arms throbbing with light. No matter how hard he worked, all I'mjohn could think of was Miranda: the sun desert of her skin, the night desert of her hair. When the house was all back together, they went inside and slept for three days. Then they woke up and showered the light from their bodies, watching it swirl around the drain like fire. They walked around the house. It was just as it had been before, only the belts were gone, and the house lay still and quiet, like something dead. I'mjohn found the duck still in the bathtub and put it out on the porch. Meanjohn wanted to go find their brother and sisters and bring them back, but I'mjohn told him to go do it by himself.

Alone in the house, I'mjohn found his and Miranda's cards and sat in front of the window shuffling and cutting them. He could feel her hands all over them. He could feel her hands all over his skin. He was alone now, without her or anyone else. He looked through the glass at his father's house on the hill, the sun peeling into darker shades behind it. He stayed there for a long time, his thoughts breaking up and reforming like the cards, always the same ideas when they came back together. He wondered if this was how Oldjohn felt.

This is the House That

SHELLIE ZACHARIA

Beyond the trees you can see the house, it stands there still, soft wood and trickle trees drop pointy leaves that stick to the soles of bathed bare feet, wicked leaves, a soft house, a rat scampering with malted mouth, cat yowls, dog barks, rumble belly tumbles toward the door, wide open, cat run, dog run, rat run, malt showered over a woozy kitchen floor, fuzzed moo-moo-moonbeams clearing forest path, cow scuddlewudding home, chew, chew, moo, crumpled horn like sadness, like forlorn, so sad, such a moo, and the man, tattered and torn, waits, whistles, hands malted and muddled, hands at his brow, at his bearded cheek, he sings a drunken tune, something like this and then this and then this, he stares toward open window, toward moo-moo-moonbeams, hears the sound of neighbor priest, whistling too, whistle, kick and skittle pebble across the path, good eve, good eve, a voice in evening, the neighbor farmer, the priest, a handshake, a head nod, and then such silence, golden, growing, tattered man with eyes closed, almost asleep, kiss on the back of his head, soft hand on his shoulder, malt and rat and cat and dog and all forgotten, maiden all forlorn, she cries, he sighs, cock crows at midnight, and then she smiles, maiden in her rumpled frock, all a-fuck she smiles and then she goes, silent across grain gravel floor, she skirts the dog, the cat, oh where is the rat, and then back on the moo-moo-moonlit path, she turns, a wave, a farewell to Jack and the house he built.

Three Times Red

A. A. BALASKOVITS

In Bed

The beast told her to take off the frock and knickers, the extra human skins. But leave the cloak, such color, like cherry pie or tart flesh or a wound. Toss each piece of cotton and silk into the hearth and let it erupt. Come under cover and let me smell you, girl, let me smell your cloak, let me smell you.

The girl slipped her hands across the coarse fur of the imposter's massive and inert form. She grazed her fingers across the shallow belly and felt a familiar row of teats, like the ones that sprouted on her mother's breasts after bathing, or in winter after the fire went out. Surely, thought the girl, monsters could not nurse, could not nurture. The beast raised its heavy torso and the girl slid underneath.

Her mother had warned her before she entered the forest: be wary, little love, all things change in that darkness. Boys photosynthesize and girls erupt from the pupa, all thin wings and tongues peppered with nectar, and you can't ever go back into a cocoon. The walls have been ripped apart, and cannot be sewn together again.

The girl's tongue flicked out and tasted the strange milk, a mother's milk, sweet and a bit salty, like a good cry. The beast whined in a low, soft way, like the girl's mother did at night when the window shutters shook and the bedroom was cold. It was cold every night since her father had gone into the forest and not returned.

Photosynthesize, her mother said, looking out the window on those nights, her eyes reaching. It means you become a part of something greater. You can't go back.

The girl closed her eyes and drank the quick stream of sweet wetness that erupted from the beast's teats. As she pulled on it, all the other teats began to cry, soaking the girl in thick, nourishing tears, and the beast wept as well.

Where does a monster feel loss, the girl thought, in the cavities of its jaw, or in its breast?

As she drank from the beast, she tasted memory in that milk, her own and not only her own: earlier that day when the sun was high and before Grannie's house, she came across a string of pups, little more than stains, caught between a woodsman's steel teeth. Their necks were nothing more than sinew, long wet yarn.

She released the teat from her lips and reached under her naked back and fingered her cloak, wondering what dye had given it such lovely color, and whether she too could be made into mere stains.

In Belly

I wish we were face to face, Grannie, in this fleshy compartment. Instead, the long nail of your pinky toe, the one you adamantly refused to clip, as if it contained all your magic, curls around and in the soft skin of my nostril. When I breathe, I can smell and taste all the places you have walked. You are still wearing your night clothes, Grannie, that tired old grey shirt with the frayed edges. The hem rubs against my breasts like it did when I was a little girl, and you pulled me, naked as I slept, to you in those hot summer nights when I woke, drenched in wet salt, from nightmares.

The she-beast gulped me down with only my skin adorning me. Do you know she made me shave off all my hair, pluck every ingrown strand with black tweezers (I had to dig so far that I bled, Grannie), so when she swallowed me, I slid down her throat like a skinned anchovy?

If you would speak to me, I imagine you would say what a funny place this is, where the walls are so warm as to burn, and the water is acid on our tongues. That's how you were, making light of what smothered us.

There is only one bit of softness in here, and that is—how you would hate it—your breast, slipped from your grey shirt, as wrinkled as your cheeks and as veined as the raised lines I used to trace on your feet as a child. And when I grew up you told me to stop, stand on my feet, not my knees, and sleep with heavy nightshirts, and a towel wrapped tightly between my legs, because all manner of wetness could pour out of me when I slept. How I loathed growing up in those summer nights around you, Grannie, when I feared all of me would seep out.

I trace the lines on your breast while the walls of the beast clench and release and clench, and I feel you sliding away from me, Grannie.

Don't leave me alone in here, Grannie.

And then I, too, am pulled towards that empty opening, thrust out onto the cold ground, leaves and dirt sticking to my face. Strange, only now I realize that I am covered, completely, in the inner slime of the beast's body.

Grannie, you're melting into the earth. Your old skin is falling off, your bones are becoming water and seeping into the mud. Will I, too, go quietly into the earth, as if I had never walked on its surface?

Yet the beast is tender, and before the sting of the sour from her belly makes me disappear like my poor grannie, she puts her tongue to my lips and moves up and down, cleaning me off, cooing as best a beast can coo. And when she is done, she spits, once, and looks at me in a way I have never been looked at before, like I am something new and something wonderful.

No matter how many times a girl has her story told, she will never be fully told up.

In one telling, our girl is shat out with the rabbits and dirt and the ragged flesh of her grandmother in one constipated pile. The beast buries her without turning around, simply kicking mud onto her face and shoulders, and wanders off. That one makes us ache in the spot our milk teeth fell from and were abandoned, scattered under pillow, or on the ground.

In another, the woodsman gutted the she-beast for food and warmth while his fair-haired daughter peeked from behind an oak with her eyes slit, for daughters never get used to the necessary violence of their fathers. When he saw the naked, hairless girl curled up in the beast's cavernous belly, he thought he had killed a pregnant werewolf. He grasped the smooth girl to his chest and would have torn her apart as he had her mother, but his daughter watched him and did not blink. Instead, he took the girl into his home and fed her all the things he had slaughtered, while his daughter stared at the wolf-girl, watching each hair grow back on her body like corn shooting out of the earth, and wondered, her hands grasping her thighs, when the wolf-girl would sprout thick fur over her face and the back of her hands and devour them in the night.

In our favorite, the one we dare not tell, the girl rips herself out from the belly of the mother-wolf with her teeth and nails. Weeping, she shoves her grannie back into the belly and stitches it up until there is no seam. She curls into the mother-wolf and promises never, never to leave, and as she does, the mother-wolf turns into her own mother, a human mother. Together, they chase all woodsmen from their woods and howl in a language we think we might understand, if we heard it.

But this is the one that was written, and so this is the one we tell to the shaking pigtails of our daughters and the fluttering eyes of our sons: A girl goes into the forest and is tricked by a man wearing a beast's fur coat. Because of this she loses her family, loses her innocence, and is saved by a man with a bloody axe, which is another sort of innocence lost. Then we do not know what becomes of her, whether she was happy to be torn out from under the beast, or whether she wished the bloody axe cut through her neck instead. Our children will make up their own endings, whether the girl becomes a witch or opens a cupcake shop or builds a bridge the color of gold. But we hope, in one of their minds, our beast-girl will find her gutted mother wolf, and using her hair as a thread and a curved toenail as a needle, begin to sew.

from **the human-suit series**

JESSICA YOUNG

Part II

Today at the dry cleaner's I show my ticket stub, and a body brings me
a plain jacket made of tweed with leather elbow patches, instead of my

human-suit. The face before me insists the plain tweed jacket with leather
elbow patches is the article I've come to retrieve, and suggests I take it

and go. I gesture to the word "suit" on the stub—human-suit, not some
plain jacket. The two legs move, carrying off what is not mine, clearly

just as displeased at this added effort. I have been coming here now
for seven months, I say in the direction of the sway-swaying body,

and I've never had a problem before. Seven months, the voice says
from every corner of the room, never seen you. The hand listlessly

holds up my human-suit, draped from a hanger, sheltered in thin plastic.
The hand dances my human-suit up and down, to catch my attention

from the back of the room, the rotating whirl of washables. And if
I'd been wearing it, I'd have clapped its palms together to show relief.

Part III

Today I set out to bicycle to the harbor around the hour
the seals get hungriest and bob around like plastic bags.

But I left late, and so I raced, and as I went to dismount
side-saddle, snagged my human-suit on the derailleur,

still rusty from the rain season. It wasn't pretty, and I'll
spare you the more nauseating details, but the way gears
work, so fast, they ripped off a nice chunk from the right
leg. Maybe four square inches. After that I was afraid

to lean too far over the dock, lest something fall out, and
was afraid for the families who came to see seals, seeing

more than expected. Then I was afraid for the depleted
repair-kit, the minutes tainted by help-line hold-music

on repeat, and ultimately, the prohibitive cost of shipping
back and forth my human-suit for the third time this year.

Part IV

My human-suit felt tight today. This happened
once in 2006—tight one day, couldn't get it on

for two weeks. Far as I can tell, it's separate
from diet and exercise, separate from a mere

wanting. Maybe it's the tide, maybe it's not;
what matters is I'm supposed to be seated

on an Amtrak train now, and instead
I'm tugging slowly at the squinched-up

places, hoping they might ease up in time
for the 4:43. And when this happens,

I curse, and I ask nicely, I pull taut that
which can be pulled taut, but all the while

know it is out of my hands, like the way
a drop of water slides down the cup's side.

Stain

MARIA DEIRA

She came to life with a port-wine stain on her right cheek. The mark of the devil, said her grandmother. The kiss of God, said her grandfather. At school no one touched her. At home no one called her beautiful. When she was sixteen, eating a burger at McDonald's, she met a boy with the same boot-shaped birthmark on his left cheek. Louisiana, he said. No, she laughed. *Italy*. They shared french fries and a milkshake and when the restaurant closed, they walked outside together. Above them the stars faded in and out, a silent rhythm that moved him to grab her hands and twirl her around. He pulled her close. On her tiptoes, she pressed her purple cheek against his and it burned. Meet me here tomorrow night, he said, and she promised him she would. But come morning, her stain had vanished and in her ecstatic surprise she spent hours looking at herself in the mirror, dusting on different shades of blush—Georgia Peach, Radiant Rose and Spring Fling Pink—forgetting about the boy until late that evening when an ad for a new double-cheeseburger and fry combo played on the radio. When she finally pulled into the parking lot, he was sitting on the curb, still waiting for her, even though the restaurant had long been empty and the weak light of an old street lamp flickered above him. She hurried over to him and asked, Is it gone? Is it gone? He looked at her, his eyes dull and gray, his left cheek smooth and unblemished and soft. I want it back, he said. She cupped her hand against her face. No, no, no. He dropped his head, his shoulders hunched like those of an old man who couldn't breathe, saying, Just put your cheek next to mine. That's all we have between us. I can't, she said, and she ran to her car, leaving him there alone in the dark, in the fumes of her escape, alone and stain-free. Free, free, free, she thought to herself as she drove away without looking back, trying not to understand what she hated and he needed.

· Topiary ·

She has told me stories about the garden before.

—*Lilith's Extra Rib*

Illustration by Anna Bron

Take Up the Bonnet Rouge

CHANTEL TATTOLI

I bet the French love of gnomes is doing with their blood-red hats. They look like the hats the French donned in *la Révolution*, and it must be that some wore this *bonnet rouge* when they broke into Tuileries Palace. They'd come for Louis, Marie-Antoinette, and the *Enfants de France*. There exists an anonymous oil painting of Marie and her children cornered by the mob that day on June 20, 1792. In it, they've stuck the woolen *bonnet rouge* on the head of the dauphin, the King's son, who would not live to take the throne; there wasn't enough bread, and slight social mobility, and many had gotten wind of the newer philosophies and verily liked what they heard. But think. What the Queen would have looked out on from the scaffold: those red hats? Bunched here and there in the audience, like cherries? Everything about her was really decadent even if it wasn't true. Diamonds, champagne, sex, cake, cherries. Oh, la la.

The French regard for gnomes has been looked into by an anthropologist. Which—I'm pretty sure—my Grand-mère would have pooh-poohed with vehemence.

I see her wringing her hands. *Enough. Leave what's sacré be.*

When Grand-mère's arms swung, a queue of lucite bangles on her wrists would cluck, critical, and despite their bad taste they were more like judges weighing in than biddies. (Always she wore bracelets.) That the world would end once the Magic was killed off is what Grand-mère knew. She didn't go for scientific inquiry, *Eating at the caractère of the world, de plus en plus!* Only children like I was then could appreciate magic, and us only sometimes. *When a wave slaps you mid-laugh, like.*

She'd pause. *Well. It's my point de vue, I'm saying.*

The anthropologist treats the affective relationship. Its therapeutic advantage is noted: the gnomes as interlocutors, as shrinks allowing for regression into childhood. It's normal to hear the old people chatting about their gnomes as they would about their children or their breast buddies. Normal, in fact, to see tins of sudsy water left out for the gnomes to bathe in. (In Germany they leave beer.)

But there's been talk in recent decades about the abuses of the *bourgeoisie. Le Front pour la Libération des Nains de Jardin* (FLNJ) was formed *ad hoc* to deal with these gross cases of exploitation. The group has freed some 6,000 in France alone (and spawned sister fronts in many European countries). To the parents of these there'd been letters of goodbye, some nice: *Dearest Mère/Père, I must leave you now . . .* And

133

some other, crasser things were said too: *AWOL Motha'fucka!!!*, for example.

I see my grandmother again; she is spitting mad. *Do they think they are Che Guevara, what?* Her bracelets chime in, pundits in their own right.

Sometimes gnomes are found. In Normandy, hikers spied daubs of bright color (*cerise! lemon! cobalt!*) through the dark green. They found two hundred decorated with pasta, lasagna slung over their shoulders, wearing necklaces of penne, farfalle glued beneath their chins, in case they became hungry and had forgotten how to glean from the land. *Le Front* had even painted on night-seeing spectacles.

Summer of 2006, dozens of gnomes collected on the lip of a pool in Limoges. Notes in their owners' mailboxes read, "What with the heat wave, they wanted some air."

Across Europe, gnoming has relocated tens of thousands back to the wild. Many go to the European Gnome Sanctuary, in Tuscany. There, the Barghigiani welcome the refugees, they've propped open the doors of the Castle of Barga for them. In Barga, gnomes are at leisure on ledges and in ideal niches, no more to be harassed by motorized weeders, suffering trappings like pesticides and acid rain, not to mention the normal elements and the unfortunate velocity of streams of canine urine. Laboring in backyard gardens, ornamenting lawns day after day. No more. No more wantonly stripped of their *dignité*.

From the Gnome Liberation Front's manifesto:

> "Remember our Ancestors; the proud bulls that guarded the gates of the Persian Kings, the lions that keep watch over the palaces of the Chinese Emperors, and the most famous of all, the mighty Sphinx, enigmatic, imperturbable, who shall return as the King-Emperor of the oldest race of all to lead his Gnomic Hordes to our Final Victory [...]. Enough! Enough! Are we not made of stronger stuff than the soggy blood and fragile tissues of our oppressors?[29]"

So many others remain enslaved and despairing, though. At any time, hundreds of gnomes await retail in dank warehouses. Cheek-by-jowl and packed in rough crates, they twiddle their thumbs or try to shake fists at kismet's untowardness. Given little elbow room they just clench their hands and grit their jaws.

"What's in store for us?"

"*We* are, or shall be," comes the reply.

1998: Eleven gnomes hanged from a bridge in Briery. A note pinned to one's lapel said they couldn't stand it any longer. The event was part of a larger trend—while the statistics never garnered any attention—of Toulousian gnomes jumping out of their second-story and higher flower

---

[29] barganews.com/gnomes

boxes into the Renaults and Peugeots zipping below, and in Paris and Nice too, jumping.

Some gnomes stay behind to protest. No, they won't end it, nor will they simply run away. They drop their spades and wheelbarrows and uptake signs—«gNOme MORE!!!»; «KITSCH YOU SEE?». Their cheeks rosy with humiliation before, now flush from uprooting their subjugators' flowers and smashing their glossy vegetables.

«À LA FIN!!!»

«FREEGNOME NOW.»

«I'M NOT YOUR GNOVELTY.»

Grand-mère would've been up in arms. *The people love them like their own petites. C'est la merde!*

But it's a good reason my grandmother would be hostile to the recent gnoming stuff. When I was a kid, Grand-mère called long-distance to talk gnomes. I lived in Washington state and she lived on an island right off the Gulf Coast of Florida. Sanibel is the shell capital of the world because it sticks out like a sore thumb against the grain of the water, and I spent my summers there. Her bungalow faced the ocean in the rear, where a tall seagrape hedge split the grass from the ecru hips of sand. Her lawn gnomes and plastic flamingoes were in the front yard, the birds hot pink, balancing expertly like ballerinas on one leg. At dusk, the flamingoes could be mistaken for the native roseate spoonbill, a rare bird, born gray like flamingoes and soon pinked from a diet of crustaceans that eat a dyeing algae.

Grand-mère said the gnomes were coastguards.

They rode flamingoes down to the beach in pointy red hats, and when sea turtles hatched and trickled to the water, it happened under the watchful eyes of guardians, her gnomes. The fell swoops of seagulls were blocked. The blitzes of ghost crabs, checked. Wayward turtles—mislead by false moons—had themselves rotated by degrees and made beelines for the ocean.

And how happy the gnomes were for every turtle folded into those silvery sheets. And how the flamingoes' feathers bristled with a well-done job. When the last of the hatchlings were safe, the gnomes made bonfires and brewed pineapple cider. They toasted, "Reptiles live long. Smiles, longer still!," broke out fiddles whose bows were strung with the hair of mermaids, triangles, bent from the metals of sunken ships. They danced-danced-danced around the flames.

If you were there, you might cry. Perhaps you'd laugh. Maybe you do both at the same time. Tears drip into your mouth—they shock your tongue with their salt!

Grand-mère adapted the story depending what I needed. It tickled, moralized, or was steeped in psychology. This one time I wet the bed at an embarrassing age; Felix the gnome drank too much cider and had an accident. Another time when I transferred schools, Grand-mère called to tell me about a new gnome. Leopold. He came from the Midwest via Fed-Ex and had never seen an ocean.

"Never?"

"*Jamais!*" Never. "Only a great lake."

I could overhear the bubble wrap squeaking. The mechanizations of a camera over the line—I'd get a photograph of this rookie in the mail. We worried how he'd fit in. What if he didn't take to the job? Grand-mère reminded them the hatchlings were due. There wasn't much time to teach Leopold the ropes. Hardly enough to learn to ride a flamingo properly. She'd keep me updated, of course.

As it happened, the others embraced Leopold. His maiden watch, oh, he delivered three turtles from certain death. "You should have seen him!" Grand-mère sung. "Go, go, gooo!"

And then, one mediocre afternoon that coming summer, my grandmother died.

Like that.

The gnomes and flamingoes "left" the day before.

I was twelve.

I'd already mastered sarcasm, acquired cynicism, shed several downy layers of naiveté under which I found the winking black sequins of dark humor, and what turned out to be the premature stubble of disenchantment, what would ripen to jadedness. But when Grand-mère told me they'd left for South America, I threw a fit.

A letter had come from Ecuador—green sea turtles there needing assistance. They went.

"You're lying," I yelled. "*Vous êtes plein de merde.*" I steeled, expecting to get slapped, but she tried to calm me down.

"They're good, ma chérie!" Grand-mère held my face. Her hands were like bookends trying to brace the million things pages say. "You know them, they'll be fluent in Spanish by next Tuesday! *Confiance en moi.* Hm?"

Silver bangles slid down her forearms, burbling, backing her up. If the Frenchwoman divined her aneurysm and thought to tie up a loose end, she meant well. I know this. But it was too bad all of them going like that. I had to continue the gnomes without her.

And I kept them autobiographical. Edited them to parallel my own phases and touchstones, made my x coordinates correspond to their y coordinates at sharp right angels. We are kindred. I think they're a psychedelic bildungsroman, like my allegorical autobiography. When I streaked my hair with magenta in high school, the flamingoes debuted in spiked collars, airing nonchalance equal to my own. We could not give a shit! In conjunction with my adolescent angst, Jeremy wove, of all things, a thick daisy chain. He hanged himself at the height of orange blossom season, from a branch especially hung with flowerets. The gnomes were potheads when I was in college. Leo became a full-blown junkie; Felix popped pills.

I overheard them once.

"We doubled the survival-rate," Leopold guessed.

"You got several on your first day out." Felix spilled a Xanax bar from a vitamin bottle. "You wouldn't come down from your high horse."

"Dude. I was on top of the world."

Felix swallowed the xannie, laughing. "That time we thought we'd gotten em'all . . . but Jeremy saw a straggler, and a mean gull diving . . ."

"Dude! Jerry decked that son'a va'bitch in the nick of time! He was grinning ear-to-ear when he dropped that hatchie in the water."

"Even though his knuckles were all bloody."

"Even though!"

"Dammit, Jeremy . . ."

Leopold grunted.

Their storybook immaculateness waned over time. Grungy salt-and-pepper dreadlocks pocked out from beneath flaccid hats. The rosy faces leathered. They're shabby now, but still winsome. Smiling smiles, though yellowed, which are wide and real. They're taller and more ordinary all around, sort of just scruffy retired fishermen.

You understand they aren't do-gooders. None of them weep when a hatchling is preyed upon. They care, but it's that melancholic way Peace Corps volunteers have, how inured they are and burnt out. They go through the motions, maybe, but the truth is—hardly any of the hatchlings will survive to adulthood, often, not even one.

Resignation slinks into my bedroom and smothers my optimism, too. The gnomes and I sit in our ruts with lukewarm ambition and wait for Hope to show her face. Hope is a dear women in red-red lipstick in a 1950s leaflet. She stands akimbo on checkered linoleum and speak-bubbles boilerplate: *Don't give up! Every little bit counts!*

We grunt.

After I started to work in photojournalism—this was later—I began to see them.

They'd turn up with street children in Thailand; in Bedouin camps in former Mesopotamia. In Moscow, in May of 1996, they sat in the loge at a ballet adaptation of *Anna Karenina*. The light from the stage threw their silhouettes against the wall, and from across the theatre I saw a sharp-headed row like wrought-iron arrows, their hats starched for the occasion. Sometimes I have this feeling—my hair stands up—that they are close. A red conical shape cut off on the periphery of one of my frames. In another, an elfin hand, extending from a dingy royal blue cuff, out of place. I catch glimpses in urban crows that leave me spinning. There are shadows.

Recently I was doing a series on informal travel, when I met a backpacking clique outside of a hostel in Denmark. Was the stout, bearded figure at their feet a hallucination?

No! They *had* a garden gnome with them—involving him in their pictures they said like in *Amélie*.

"I know some roaming gnomes myself," I said. They didn't get it but laughed politely. The photograph I took of them turned out my favorite of the series. Four Aussies, a Swiss couple and an Italian. They beam. Presently none can be thirty. Arms rest on each other's shoulders; the ones in the fore dunk, the Swiss woman, cradling the gnome as classical as the one you probably imagine. Everyone's footloose and glad. Most days, that is the way I prefer to think of the gnomes. Them okay out there wherever it is they are, let's say Ecuador. Say tonight in Las Bachas, the turtles will hatch and begin a new generation. And the gnomes ride out and see them home.

"*Qué será, será!*" they say. What will be, will be!

For once, Grand-mère and her bracelets would jibe. "*Qui vivra, verra,*" she'd pronounce. Time will tell.

OK.

from Lilith's Extra Rib

ALANA I. CAPRIA

2

[I raise fruits
in the kitchen cabinets.] When they ripen, they splatter me in the face. Their juice burns. It is too acidic. Then my thighs itch. I sit in the sink and Lilith washes me. She soaps my shoulders with baking soda and adds a layer of all-purpose flour. [We did not bake in the garden, she says and I drink chocolate directly from a plastic bottle. There was no chocolate, either, she says.] She has told me stories about the garden before. She mentioned the enviable fruits and all the trees that were like living skyscrapers. The branches were made of glass. When Lilith glared, the wood shattered and cut the Adam man's upper lip. Then she smiled and all the glass grew again. [What if the trees had been mirrors, I ask and Lilith eats a pineapple, thorns and all.] [We had no need for mirrors, she says. We weren't supposed to know we were naked.] She shows me the spot under her ribs that the extra breast came from. The breast was so small, I could barely see it. The mammary gland was more like a birth mark, a strange little mole. I poked the nipple and Lilith shivered with excitement. [You don't understand, she says and opens every door in the house.] She lets the air in. She lets Adam in. He sits in a corner, crying. His eyes are bruised. We force the swollen lids open. There are fruit peels shoved into the gray corners.

3

{Perhaps it isn't
only a rib Lilith has a spare of.} There is an extra eye and teat and leg. She
milks herself in the kitchen sink. I collect the droplets. [Her milk is bright
yellow. It is amber. Honey colored. Rotten. It is liquid cheese.] I drink a
glass and vomit. Lilith paints her face bright red. She rubs her fists against
the walls and leaves furrows in the plaster. [Was this how you left Eden, I
ask and Lilith shows me photographs of the forbidden tree.] It is really a
shrub. A tiny bush. With branches covered with thorns. Lilith's name is
written across the roots. I take a razor blade and scrape along the outer lines
of the letters. [Once upon a time, Lilith says. I knew a man who thought he
was more than just mud. We were born simultaneously, sprouted from the
same dirt clot. But the man said he was metal and I was leaves. So he tried
to tear me apart. I threw water in his face and he ran off like liquid. And that
was the end of the garden. It flooded with his organs and I flew away before
the fluid could touch me.] Once upon a time, I found a hidden garden and
climbed inside. The dirt was pale gray and dotted with brilliant red flowers.
I plucked the petals and every bloom had a nectar head at the center. They
oozed. [Now, Lilith digs the pollen out of the corners of her eyes and
smears the yellow across the stove top.] She pulls spinal cords from her
neck.

A Theory of Music

WALTER BARGEN

It was during the middle of the performance, the middle of a measure of composition that dragged on too long, when the bass drums became aroused and started to lead the band back from a funereal march, turning the gazebo into a cavalry charge, threatening to break down the surrounding palmetto and fluted railings, throwing into the fray a brigade of clarinets, squad of bassoons, company of French horns, and the belch of tubas.

The audience startled from their slumber, opened their eyes to see the pruned trees and sharp edges of light cut across the rich green of the lawn, leaving the wounded glow of grass bandaged with afternoon shadows. Parasols scattered through the crowd like the frills of regimental colors. The spark of a red parrot, flitting from branch to branch, glided low over the long tables weighted with sweating punch bowls. It was a feathered streak of blood, though none of the audience noticed, attentive to their pastries and yet another song defending the empire's dashing elegance.

The band conductor bowed to polite, persistent applause. When he straightened the double row of brass buttons, his jacket ignited with sun, bright as the flash of rifle muzzles. An elderly matron swooned in the heat and excitement, recalling her husband's stories of the Crimean War. She was the day's first casualty, though she was quickly revived and taken into the marble-columned mansion.

The conductor raised his baton, vigorously drawing it across the air. The triumphant blare of the horn section declared their right to lead the parade of prancing plumed horses and festooned riders. It was at this moment in the march, in the middle of the concert, the middle of a hot afternoon, in the middle of the grand estate that stretched for miles, that the baton shot from the conductor's hand and sailed skyward in an arc, leading everyone's eyes to see the hot air balloon high over the music where its rider waved methodically from a wicker basket decorated with the royal colors. The china blue sky was enough to make those not ready to move, stand, and break into a cheer. Even the band dissembled, one instrument at a time, until the conductor was prodding a single tuba player, and then the pavilion fell silent.

For a quarter hour the balloon didn't move. The men discussed the meaning of the persistent almost mechanical waving—was it a call of distress, an upward drowning in this pellucid air, or a distant salutation? During further refreshments served on silver trays, the balloon remained stationary. A consternation grew, the waving could be tolerated no longer and a plan was proposed. A fakir, head wrapped in a white turban, wearing only a loin cloth that tied his emaciated ascetic body together, was called from behind the servants' quarters. In the magic of those days, he coiled a rope in front of him and began to play his hypnotic flute. Cross-legged, he caressed the serpentine-braided hemp threads, and with each higher-note the rope rose, undulated, and stiffened. It was said to be the longest rope in the world: what was left of the Gordian Knot, untied by the bodyguard Ahzad Bogosian after Alexander tired of hacking it with his sword. The horn section watched in amazement, but the musicians thought that even if the fakir does make a single rope twist skyward, they could make an entire empire march to tea and its glorious death.

The rope, intricate as spun gold, reached the balloon, but the arm kept waving. Again there was discussion about why the basket rider wasn't climbing down. A boy known for his agility at chasing monkeys through trees was chosen to climb it. The fakir played on and the boy, hand-over-hand, raced up the tenuous twined path. When he reached the balloon, he was puzzled. He quickly removed the sapphire stick-pin and slid down the rope, which collapsed in a great heap the moment he touched the ground, burying the frail fakir, breaking his ancient bone flute.

The audience crowded in to see what it was the boy held. It was a greeting card cut in the shape of a hot air balloon with one moveable paper arm. The arm could be made to wave by pulling on a thin wire that passed through to the backside of the folded card. The boy showed them the pin that was used to fasten it to the blue sky. They squinted at the infinitely faceted sapphire and its nearly unbearable glitter. The boy gave it to the conductor in place of his broken baton. There was still the hanging wire, which theologians, after many interviews with the eyewitnesses, would declare an optical illusion and deny its existence. The wire's thin logic quickly rusted away during monsoon season.

The arm did stop moving. How had the arm ever moved, the woman who had fainted and returned to the expansive lawn, wanted to know. The import of her question caused her to swoon again. She held heavily to a general's epaulets. A voice in the crowd answered *wind*, but what could account for the clock-like swinging? A clock-like wind?

Another man asked if the boy had tried to puncture the blue sky with the pin? What's on the other side, he wanted to know. The boy hadn't thought of it. They all turned in unison and stared at the rope on the ground and then up to where the balloon had hung, their faces looking like white holes hovering over the lawn. Everyone knew there was no second chance; the flute lost, the rope fallen into another enigmatic knot.

A woman ensconced in the middle of her hooped skirt noticed that no matter how close or far away she or anyone else held the card it remained exactly the same size, which was how it appeared above the gazebo earlier, and the greeting remained unreadable. The face of the little figure in the basket was no more discernible at arm's length than it was if the boy ran across the lawn and held it in the shadows of the trees, or if she squinted at it from behind reading glasses.

Confusion spread. A captain grabbed a gardener's shovel and started furiously to dig in the grass. Was there dirt below this dirt that his polished riding boots stood so proudly upon? Only the laced wrist showed against the shocked husband's red uniform as his wife's hand searched to see if her desire was real. A rider dismounted and shoved his white gloves into fresh horse droppings, then threw them down in disgust. A servant retrieved the soiled gloves and placed them on a tray.

The brass-buttoned conductor could make out no more now with the card in his hands than when he first launched his tumbling baton up into the sky. He handed the card back to the boy, who took off running after a monkey stealing a cream puff from a serving plate. He dropped the paper balloon to climb a palmyra tree, leaving the arm to wave once more as it struck the ground. The card caught the wind and blew into a dense clump of bushes by the road, where it remained elusive and far away as ever.

The conductor returned to the bandstand, reached into his pocket for the sapphire stick-pin that had grown larger in the conflation of the afternoon's events. He stood in front of his music stand, motioning for the band to begin. Once again left alone, framed by a flawless sky, the audience returned to their folding chairs. The tubas plodded through an elephantine beat as the arm in the bushes snapped its fingers.

The Watchmaker

ERIC SCHALLER

There was once a watchmaker who lived in the town of Eichenwald, where it is said, because the town lies midway between valley and clouds on the alpine slopes of the Weisshorn, that there are but three seasons in the year. Winter lasts for six months, spring and autumn each for three, and summer, which may come but once every ten years, lasts only a single golden afternoon.

The watchmaker was known as Herr Lindhorst to most members of the town, and as Kristoff to the few who assumed intimacy with him. He lived and worked in a narrow two-story house that he had inherited from his parents, above the door of which hung an iron sign bent and forged into the shape of a watch dial. Ever since the watchmaker had been a boy known as Kris, he had drifted off to sleep each night listening to the sign creak in the mountain winds.

The family Lindhorst had repaired watches for as long as anyone could remember. If you overwound your watchspring, perhaps while distracted by the neighbor's daughter hanging her laundry, the metallic ping at your fingertips causing your heart to sink into your boots—how could anyone fall in love with such a klutz as you?—it was to Lindhorst's Watch Repair that you turned. If you attempted to master three tasks at once, such as reading the morning newssheet, locating your mouth with a spoonful of porridge, and checking the time on the pocket watch given to you on your sixteenth birthday, and if, as a result, your watch should tumble into your coffee cup, it was to Lindhorst's Watch Repair that you brought the family heirloom still leaking the brown droplets of your favorite roast. Invariably, your watch would be returned to you in better condition than before its accident. "Why it's just like new," you would exclaim, examining the print your thumb left on the polished metal. You would be answered with a smile and the phrase repeated by each member of the Lindhorst family for the past three generations, "We do our best."

Kristoff Lindhorst was the first member of his family to make rather than simply repair watches. His first creation was a monstrosity cobbled together from broken springs, chipped gears, and cracked crystals, detritus from the trash bin that had excited the crow-like curiosity of the four-year-old. The watch that Kris presented to his father for approval looked something like a mangled crab the boy had found deposited on the mountain slopes by a wayfaring seagull. But whereas the crab had clearly expired, such that even a week of warmth in the boy's pocket failed to reanimate it, the watch just as surely functioned. The mechanism emitted a healthy "tick-tick-tick" and each of its eight hands spun merrily around at different speeds. At the time, the similarity of the watch to the displaced crab was seen as coincidence, but later, after Kristoff's predilections became clear, it was granted that he had created his first automaton.

Kristoff joined his father in the shop at the age of six. Passersby marveled at the child who, perched on a tiny stool at a tiny watchmaker's bench, appeared to be an elf materialized out of a folk tale. "He has the eyes and the fingers," his father would say to his customers, winking a watery eye and waggling his own gnarled fingers. "More importantly, he has the passion." Kristoff's skills in repairing and, eventually, in creating the simple automata that graced the better variety of grandfather clocks soon became apparent. But he did not achieve renown until the age of nineteen when he was commissioned to update the clockwork of the town hall. This was a well-loved piece that included a blacksmith with hammer and a hunter with cudgel, who glided about a circular stage to ring the bell each hour. Although once a tourist attraction, it was now old-fashioned in comparison to the more elaborate dioramas of the neighboring towns. Kristoff added a fox that wound its way through the legs of the blacksmith, snuck up on the hunter, and then, by gnawing through the strings that tethered them to the hunter's belt, released three partridges. The birds flew up with a rattle of wings and rang the bell with sharp blows from their beaks, the two men now swinging their implements at the fluttering birds rather than at the bell. The fox winked at the spectators then ran off, the money pouches of the blacksmith and hunter clenched in his teeth.

After this there was no holding Kristoff back. He traveled from town to town, taking on more and more lucrative commissions. He was served the best foods in the best restaurants and, whether the project took a day or a year, lodged in the best hotels. Holidays were declared and bands played each time a piece of his was unveiled. Tourists followed routes on maps that depicted the locations of his creations, returning from their travels with metal or paper reproductions to set on their mantels, the jerky movements of these poor substitutes affirming the genius of the originals.

At 31 Kristoff was without peer, but before he reached his next birthday, his career was over and his friends and former patrons crossed the street rather than risk an encounter. How did this happen? Kristoff was approached in a pub, as he later said, by a man with features so nondescript that these were a better disguise than any mask. This man, who did not give his name, said that he was an agent for another who wished to remain anonymous, but who had a project truly worthy of Kristoff's skills. Needless to say, but emphasized a dozen times during the conversation, Kristoff would be well rewarded should he accept the commission. "You have spoken almost excessively," Kristoff said, "but I have yet to hear what you wish of me." At this the man took a square of paper from his coat pocket, wrote on it with a silver mechanical pencil, then passed the slip to Kristoff.

When Kristoff unfolded the paper, he saw that it contained a circle drawn atop a cross. "Venus," he said, understanding the significance of the symbol as soon as he said the name aloud. "You wish me to make a woman."

"Precisely. And to the specifications that I dictate."

It would have been to Kristoff's credit if he had thought long and hard before accepting the commission, but, as he later admitted, he was nodding his assent before the agent had finished his sentence. It was not fame that Kristoff sought, for the agent made it clear that the mechanical woman would become the sole property of his anonymous benefactor. Furthermore, given the nature of the commission, it was obviously intended for private entertainment, not public exhibition. Kristoff simply desired to push his skills to the limit, and through them to create something that exceeded all expectations, his own included.

But the devil finds more entertainment in the plans of man than in any staged comedy. Two months after Kristoff had delivered the commission, the mayor from his own hometown of Eichenwald was discovered by his wife in the arms of a female automaton. There is some disagreement as to what she saw, but the most persuasive rumor has it that the automaton had not one face but many, each a separate mask that could be affixed by discrete snaps to the featureless head. Among the faces could be recognized images, exact down to the slightest imperfections upon which a lover might fixate, of women well known in the community and with whom the mayor and his wife had dined on numerous occasions. The scandal that ensued had as much to do with the jealousies of those women not included in this harem as with the horror of those women who were included.

All decisions have their repercussions. The mayor suffered a brief downturn in his fortunes and won reelection by the narrowest margin of his political career. But for Kristoff Lindhorst, who was never forgiven by the mayor's wife, the change in fortune was permanent. He was obliged to carry a sign around his neck for one month on which were painted large block letters that literally translated to "Broken Bee," but in the local vernacular meant "Poor Fabricator." He was also forbidden to construct automata for the remainder of his life, although as a concession to commerce and the history of his family, he was allowed to retain the watch repair shop.

Now suppose that you were a friend to the watchmaker in your youth— perhaps it was you who foolishly drowned your pocket watch in a coffee cup—but that time and circumstance had come between you. You had heard of his fame and taken an unspoken pride in having once known this man who had risen so high. You had also heard of his fall and silently grieved that the just could be punished so harshly. On impulse, you wrote the watchmaker a letter expressing your condolences and how, although others might turn against him, your friendship remained intact. He wrote back a short message that ended with the words, "I am as happy now as I have ever been." You knew that this phrase could hide any manner of unstated griefs and so your heart remained troubled.

Now suppose your business took you back into the land of your youth, where the watchmaker still dwelt, and you sought him out so as to judge his state with your own eyes. The sky was jewel bright on the day you arrived, but the leaves had begun to change color and there was a chill to the gusting winds that warned of the coming winter. You found Kris, as you still called him in your mind, in the ground-level repair shop of the same narrow house that you remembered from your childhood visits. The rusty sign in the shape of a clock swung back and forth above the entrance. A bell tinkled when you pushed the door open.

How time passes, you thought, seeing the stooped shoulders and prematurely gray hair of the man bent over the bench. It did not take much imagination to realize that his parents were now gone, buried no doubt behind the old church, and that he was alone in the world. The gray-haired man did not hurry to stand, but raised the magnifier from his eyes and set his tweezers down beside a semicircle of loose gears. He looked at you, at the supposed customer who had disturbed his work. Then, with no hesitation, as if you had not aged a day, he called you by your name.

Kris insisted that you sit down and tell him everything that had happened since you two parted. But having taken to his feet, he did not himself sit down. He bustled in and out of the back room and eventually returned with two cups of fragrant coffee, the brew flavored with cinnamon according to local custom, and a plate of sugar cookies. You blushed. Had he forgotten the incident of your watch and the coffee? But you sipped politely—there is no brew so bitter as the errors of youth remembered—and told him what you thought he wanted to know. But in spite of his interest in your affairs, you eventually turned the conversation to his life and the events that had transpired in your absence.

"I am so sorry," you said.

"Think nothing of it."

"To see a man of your talents cast aside breaks my heart."

"Truly, I am a happy man."

"I find this hard to believe. In truth, I cannot imagine it."

"My father once told me that everything happens for a reason and, no matter what transpired in the shop, finding that reason was our true employment. Understanding brings happiness."

"It is easy to philosophize. But I think you will agree that most philosophers are an unhappy lot. They are distressed by uneven cobbles, the price of tobacco, and the inequity that consigns them to poverty when they have ideas worthy of kings."

Kris laughed, an easy unaffected laugh, and you realized that the pleasure he took from your presence might have little to do with what you had to say. "Come," he said. "Perhaps this will bring understanding. "He set down his empty cup, rose from his stool and opened the drawer of a neighboring bench. A dozen velvet bags were nested inside, the mouths of each drawn shut with silk cords. He withdrew a silver watch from one of these bags and laid the cool metal disk on your palm. "Here. Hold this. Look at it. Feel it."

You humored him, praising the craftsmanship.

Again he laughed. "Wind it."

You did so. "It has a very nice mechanism."

"Thank you." Kris's smile was as secretive as a sparrow's. He darted over to the door and, with the same delicate touch he applied to his craft, slid a bolt into place. There were two small windows on either side of the door, their panes so ancient that they only transmitted distorted images. Nevertheless, he unhooked the thick felt curtains used to keep out the winter chill and let these fall across the glass. "Now," he said, his cheeks glowing in the lamp light, "Wind it backwards."

"Backwards?"

"Press the crown in and wind it backwards. Then set the watch down on the bench."

You did as told and set the watch down upon its back. For a moment the watch was still, then there was some engagement of gears so that it rocked upon the bench. Then, so quickly that you doubted your sight, thinking yourself the victim of slight-of-hand, the watch thrust forth two legs and two arms, flipped itself upright, and began to dance. As dances go it was not sublime, being more like the untutored hops and bounds of a country boy intent upon impressing a young lady than the measured twirls of the aristocracy. But as you followed the watch's movements, you felt the corners of your mouth twitch, and soon you were smiling for all the world as if you were once again a youth with no fear of the ridiculous.

"I cannot help but love them," the watchmaker said. He smiled and, although he spoke to you, he kept his eyes on the dancing watch. "They are like my children to me."

There was a beauty there, a connection that you who had now achieved renown in your own right, realized that you could not touch. "It must give you great pleasure to achieve something so lifelike in an object so unlike a man."

"I do not think much about such things. I just do my best."

But although you saw the beauty, you also knew your moral responsibility. It is for this reason that, after returning to your own hometown, you wrote a polite but anonymous letter to the authorities in Eichenwald. In the letter you described a narrow two-story house, on the ground-level of which was a watch shop, and certain activities, possibly of an illegal nature, that took place in that shop. Once the letter was mailed, you felt as if a great weight had been lifted from your shoulders. If summer comes but once every ten years, you said to anyone willing to listen, even if they did not understand the allusion, then it might as well not come at all.

Beauty School

MARY LOU BUSCHI

First, make sure the face is clean. Start at the temple, knead the skin with your index and middle fingers in a cross skating motion. Once you have loosened the tension move to the cheekbones and press gently. This person will want her hair finger waved next. You will need finger waving solution, a flat black comb and the same two fingers to create the wave that will lie flat to the scalp and dry in a shape so perfect no wind can part it. And, yes, the wind can be fierce and destructive, igniting fires and fueling a burn intense enough to fell a forest. Focus, your next customer may want pin curls. You will need sharp clips to catch the end of each curl after you let it go. The trick is letting go. Your fingers will need a stealth grip on the curl before your fingers pull out of the center. This movement will need to be repeated every ½ inch on the scalp. Once the clips are in place, the hair must dry completely. Only then can the comb-out be magnificent. Remember to keep yourself busy during the drying—away from the dark thoughts. Your hands trembled during the facial. This salon is a lake on thin ice. While waiting, memorize the bones of the hand beginning with the *carpal, scaphoid, capitates, hamate . . .* Your next customer will test you by presenting her hand. You will need to recant each bone before cutting her cuticles, before cutting each strand of her hair because you will be using a scissor sharp enough to sever air.

The Legs Come Off Easily

EMILY J. LAWRENCE

The girl with the small pupils doesn't use the handicap stall. Despite the width of her wheelchair. Despite the cacophonous metal racket it makes against the ghost green tiles of the bathroom wall. She rolls backwards into the stall shoved farthest against the wall, under the broken bulb—the one she calls the Shoebox.

There, during lunch every day, she gobbles her *bento* then snaps the arms, legs, and heads off Barbie dolls, brought from home, in her school bag.

Barbie dolls have four main points of connection with the body: the left arm, left leg, right arm, right leg, and head. Each has a variation of the ball and socket joint. Very easy to pop out, Hitomi says.

The girl with the small pupils keeps a bottle of alcohol, a gift from Tabe-sensei, and a fuzzy cloth in her desk. They're for removing derogatory names from the desk's smooth face. *Slut. Slut, slut, slut.* The class receives a terse lecture and a pop exam as punishment.

Keike is exempt because she stood up for Hitomi even though the class wrote the names on the desk for her sake. The class rumor is that Keike's American ex-boyfriend, Keith-kun, was seen with Hitomi outside a love hotel a year ago. This was before Hitomi was in her wheelchair. (Why she's in a wheelchair nobody knows.)

Keike doesn't fight the rumor because she was the one who saw them. His arm around Hitomi's waist, hair damp, presumably from a shower. He buttoned his jacket, walked down the alley, rode the train, met his luggage at the airport, and boarded his plane for New York. Keike, however, was stuck there. He moved on. Hitomi moved on. She walked down the alley to Dolly Girls Hostess Club and rode the elevator to the top floor, her apartment, and fell asleep. But Keike stood there under the red wire-light, shaped like a woman, whose foot turned into a heart, who lay naked on the English letters: Rabuho.

No, she doesn't deny the rumor is true. When she stands up for Hitomi, she tells the class, "Please, there's no reason to call her names."

Keike is nicknamed after Cake, the newest doll from Pink Lucky. Cake has wide, pupil-less pink eyes, pink hair, and a teacup smile. Keith-kun is the one who nicknamed her, a year and a half ago.

Walking down the street in Akihabara, Keike pauses and pulls Keith over to a display window. Cake is featured in several dioramas, dressed like a housewife, cooking, a pop idol with angel wings, a nurse carrying a giant syringe, and Keike's favorite: in a high school uniform, hands on her knees, looking back at them with a curious laugh.

"*Kireii*! I hope my high school uniform will be that cute!" Keike says, gazing down at her drab middle school sailor *fuku*.

Keith is already in high school. He considers the doll in the window and says, "Cute. Like you, babe."

"No way."

He swings her around by her waist. "Yes way. You're super cute!"

She giggles and from that day on Keith tells everyone in school to call her "Keike" after the doll. Suddenly, everyone says how cute she is. She gains more friends. But one day while using the restroom, Keike sees a dismembered Cake doll lying by her foot.

The girl with the small pupils takes apart a new Barbie doll every day. Some are originals from 1959 or 1961. The designs are different, but its deconstruction is essentially the same. The head always comes off first. "Because that's what I want gone the most," Hitomi says. "That disgusting 'cute' face."

Her own disproportioned face crumples in hate.

Keike approaches her one day, smiling with effort. *Turn the other cheek. Just because she's hateful doesn't mean I should be . . .* She asks Hitomi, "Are these Barbie dolls from a collection?"

"My mother's."

"Doesn't she mind? They look valuable."

"She's dead. It doesn't matter what she wants," Hitomi replies, flattening a rubber head beneath her thumb. She likes to feel the soft rubber collapse under the pressure. "They might as well disappear with her. And when they're all gone, I'll go, too."

The girl with the small pupils writes confusing notes on her writing pad. *I'm the white whale that bit off my legs.* She pens them heavily, pressing down, almost breaking the pen to splinters. *Life is sterile, sterile plastic.*

From the corner of her eye, Keike reads the lines. *Life is plastic. Life snaps in two. I'll snap myself in two.* A name is being called over and over. The eraser of a pencil pokes her shoulder. Keike jumps. "Sensei's calling your name," her neighbor murmurs.

"Present!" Keike lifts her hand.

Tabe-sensei glares at her, "Have you forgotten your own name?"

Cake has a companion, a shorter and chubbier doll named Shoko. Her eyes are solid black, leaking like yolk from a thick black line. They look apathetic and pouty. Shoko is more Japanese in appearance than Cake.

Most fans don't know, but both dolls were released on the same day: March 31, 2008. Their first week of sales, 10,500 Cake dolls were sold in Akihabara alone. A couple thousand were sold to anime fans in America. 20 Shoko dolls were sold in the same week. None were sold in America.

The girl with the small pupils doesn't dress for swimming class. She sits in her wheelchair by the chain link fence, carving words into her notepad as if with a razor. Students who do not participate in swimming must do exercises by the pool to earn credit. Hitomi does not, but she still earns credit. The gym teacher doesn't argue because Hitomi's in a wheelchair, and instead, blows the whistle at the other girls.

The girls gossip about the rude things Hitomi has said to them. *She said it looks like I trim my bangs with a boxcutter. She said my front teeth are too big. What'd you say back to her? That it was a hundred years too early for some ugly girl like* her *to tell me that!*

Keike stares at Hitomi's hunched figure. She can hear the other girls from her lifeguard chair. (Because she belongs to the swim team, she takes the role of lifeguard for her class.) When swim class is over, the girls head for the showers. Keike decides to walk over to Hitomi and try one more time to be friends. "Do you not like the water?"

Hitomi doesn't look up. "I can't move my legs, dumbass."

Keike turns to go but Hitomi says her name. She's looking at Keike now and Keike notices her big, lumpy nose and huge chestnut eyes with the tiny, olive pit pupils. A thought wells in Keike's ears slowly like seeping oil: she's not good-looking enough to be a whore. She shakes the thought from her ear, along with pool water, apologizing to Jesus.

"Does this help?" Hitomi raises her skirt up, not caring if anyone sees.

Keike winces at the sight of Hitomi's legs; the skin is lifeless and rubbery like dried-out cheese. Her legs are perfect L shapes. Hitomi holds her knee with one hand and the back of her calve with the other. Grinning, she pops the knee and the lower half of her right leg snaps up two, three times and is perfectly horizontal. Hitomi leaves it that way and looks at Keike. It is effortlessly stuck in the air.

"My waist is the same way. Pretty much, I'm only alive from the breasts up. And I still have my arms to go, too. I'm unsnapping myself," she says, but Keike doesn't understand. "I'm disassembling myself," she tries again. "Like this."

Keike watches Hitomi take one of her mother's American Barbie dolls and wrench its leg from the small joint socket.

Keike's mouth fills with spit, anticipating nausea, while Hitomi explains: "I always start with the head on the dolls, but the process on my actual body started with my feet. You see, the legs come off most easily."

The girl with the small pupils doesn't talk to Keike again for more than a week. Her head is bowed over her notepad as Tabe-sensei passes back the latest exam, the sound of the sheets like scissors whispering.

Sensei walks past Keike; she does not receive her graded exam. In the teachers' office after school, Tabe-sensei explains very curtly that she did not receive a test from Keike. There was, however, an extra test turned in that was not graded. "It was not from any student in my class."

Tabe-sensei shows her the completed test, devoid of any red ink except a circle around the name printed at the top. KEIKE.

"I guess I accidentally wrote that instead of my real name." Keike apologizes, but Tabe-sensei refuses to grade the exam. As she steps out of the teachers' office, Keike's foot feels rigid and numb. Removing her slipper and sock, she sees her foot turned stiff as a melon rind. It is frozen in a tip-toe position, all the toes melded together, and the heel jointless. Like a doll.

The girl with the small pupils has big, round eyes. Tohya Colorado, Hitomi's mother, was named after the state from which her father had come. He was a soldier Hitomi's grandmother met at the club during WWII. Hitomi's own father, an American filmmaker, as she was told with a dewy eye, moved back to L.A. the day after she was conceived. He was only in Japan on business for the weekend and had had some side business with her mother. He didn't even say "good-bye"—or "good morning" for that matter—but on his pillow he left a Barbie doll, which his daughter in the states had packed so he wouldn't forget her.

After L.A.-san, as he was called, returned to America, Colorado began collecting Barbie dolls—the same Barbie dolls Hitomi was breaking. Hitomi used to watch from the doorway as her mother held them like a lover's hand and brushed their plastic hair, straightening their stiff dresses, tightening the rubber shoes' grip on their poised ballerina feet. Hitomi was never allowed to play with them.

Colorado died of an unmentioned disease, at the center of a halo of the other hostesses from Dolly Girls. As she did, Hitomi rubbed the fabric of her mother's hospital gown between her fingers, thinking how similar it was to a Barbie doll dress.

The girl with the small pupils is wheeled to the handicap elevator by the class representative, a boy with glasses. Her left arm is now in a cast; her right arm keeps her notebook against her stomach like a belt. Keike limps up behind the class rep. "Isshiki-kun, I'll take her up for you."

Isshiki bows in thanks and joins a group of his friends going up the stairs. Keike pushes the wheelchair into the elevator and the doors close on Hitomi's smile. After pressing the button, Keike worriedly leans over Hitomi's shoulder. "My foot—!" She exclaims but the parade of words trips and crashes on her tongue when she realizes how crazy their horns and flutes sound.

Hitomi grins, her eyebrows making her forehead wide and shiny. "Something wrong with your foot?"

"Why—?"

"Why am *I* letting myself go fake or why are *you* becoming fake? No, I assume you're asking about yourself. Naturally." Hitomi's words slap Keike's hanging cheeks. "Though, the answer to that question is not as interesting."

She raises herself up as far as she can, pushing her right elbow against the arm rail. Her pasty face is so near Keike, both can feel the heat spin between their noses.

"I'd like to know why you're so surprised. The answer's not so difficult that your Loveberry and Pichi Lemon clothes or your Usa-chan hair clip or your Hello Kitty face can't answer it. Idiot! He names you after a doll and you wonder why you're turning into one? Here's the answer: when the world looks at you they see one image. Cake. The real question is, were you ever real at all?"

The elevator dings and the doors open.

The girl with the small pupils is nearly finished. Now her chest is tight and unfeeling, her arms set akimbo, and her neck solid and unmoving. The supply of Barbie dolls has run out, except one, a Shoko doll. On her bedroom floor is a pile of legs, arms, torsos, and heads. All sorted. Occasionally a head will topple from the stack and cause trouble for her wheelchair.

Saeko, an old friend of her mother's, wheels her around before and after school. Saeko doesn't work much now that she's older and not many customers go for the "mature woman" anymore. "I'm out of style, it seems," Saeko says with a smile.

Hitomi tries to thank Saeko, but her chin is stiffening and can hardly move when she talks. Her fingers are permanently curled and can't hold anything. She can't turn to look behind her, either. No matter what bug or raindrop pricks her, she doesn't feel a thing.

All that's left—she smiles at the thought—is her head and she will be completely dead.

Keike sits on the bench by the pool after swim club is over. She attended even though she can't swim, not wanting anyone to see her foot. She told the coach that she broke her toe. The cast she wears she constructed herself. She slips it on in the alley by the school. At home, she wears long socks. Her mother and aunt would be frantic if they saw her nerveless foot.

As the club manager, the coach has left her the key to lock up. "Your head's been somewhere else today," Coach remarks. Keike says to herself, "I think it's been somewhere else much longer than that."

In her hands is her navy blue school swimsuit, its synthetic fibers glistening under the bright lights surrounding the pool. She wrinkles it with her thumbs, gazing at the name written in permanent marker across the white square on the front. KEIKE.

When had she done that? She can't remember. It must have been at the beginning of high school, when she'd gotten the suit. This isn't right, she tells herself. What's my name? What's my *real* name? Oh, God, I've forgotten!

"Don't breathe like that; you'll get lightheaded." The girl with the small pupils is suddenly there with her. "Why get so upset, Cake?" Hitomi asks with a smile. "That American boyfriend of yours—what's his name?—he likes cute little toys."

Keike's face freezes, her pores snap shut.

"Although . . . when you wouldn't let him play with you, he decided that looks didn't matter that much. Even an ugly girl like me can be played with. Though, I guess it hurt poor little Keike's feelings, huh?"

Keike's squeezed heart shoots down her arm and becomes a closed fist. By the time she stands, she's tried to stop herself, but isn't fast enough. Her open palm smacks Hitomi's face. Hitomi screams petulantly. The echo dances on the pool's water. Her wheelchair rolls slightly backwards, on the ledge of the pool.

Keike stares. She almost apologizes but realizes something. Taking a step forward, she slaps Hitomi again, much lighter, but Hitomi still screams. "Like a toddler." Keike muses. "You talk about killing yourself, but you make such a fuss over a little pain? Killing yourself—yeah right, you pouting brat! You just want to become numb. That's all."

Hitomi begins to spew obscenities, but Keike doesn't wait to listen to any more. Her mind is clear, as if seeing through a magnifying glass from the right distance. "So Keith dumped me. I admit I liked the attention. I liked being cute." Keike takes a gulp. "But—but I'm not a doll to be made or played with by anyone. This is me"—she takes her swim suit and bag— "so don't tell me who I am."

She strides past Hitomi, avoiding the clumsy shuffle of the wheelchair as Hitomi bucks, trying to move. But, Hitomi doesn't make more than a primitive start before her utterance is engulfed in a tumultuous splash—

The wheelchair hits the bottom of the pool, a lost city of Atlantis, and Hitomi is lost to the great white mouth of cement and its chlorine-treated saliva.

Keike runs to dive in after her, remembering Hitomi's frozen, akimbo limbs—she won't be able to swim!—but a hand grips her collarbone and jerks her back. She spins around—no one is there but an unseen hint—like a ripple in the air—that someone had just been standing there.

Whirling back to the site of Hitomi's fall she sees Hitomi's downy-white arms and legs—no longer hard and bent like plastic but flowing like silk or the frilly wings of a goldfish. She is like an angel trapped underwater.

The girl with the small pupils is drowning. Fueled to save herself, Hitomi upsets the water of the pool. Slowly, her skin begins to soften. She can feel how cold she is. Her lumpy nose resurfaces—then her coughing mouth—then they sink again.

Keike jumps in with all the prowess of her swimmer's experience. But her windmill hands can't find the drowning girl's body.

She risks the chlorine, opening her eyes to the milky, smeared world of the water. She does not see Hitomi's shimmering white body or her rolling school uniform. What she sees are two standing legs.

Keike looks up at the figure. Hitomi hangs limp in its arms, as listless and drowned as hair in the bathtub. Her lips are the color of fish, glossed heavily with water, not breathing. The figure gazes down on her with a graceful, swanlike neck.

Keike watches its expression.

At once the figure appears as a Japanese woman with a face very much like her own. The resemblance is remarkable. The woman's short hair is like hers, as is her heart-shaped face and smooth cheek . . . A small mole breaks away from her bottom lip. The woman looks like her but with a touch of experience and maturity and the body to match. She has a saddened and loving face like a mother who doesn't know what to do with her daughter.

The expression does not change but the next second, Keike sees the figure is not a woman, nor Japanese, but a foreign man, whom she'd never seen but knows in her heart.

Then Keike realizes that the figure is not there at all and Hitomi is actually in her own arms and she looks down at the girl's pouting face.

The girl with small pupils opens her eyes. She is lying on a towel, coughing. Keike, who has just resuscitated her, rises, eclipsing the bright lights surrounding the pool. Hitomi looks in her face and sees familiar features.

"Mom?"

Keike shakes her head. *"Iie. Watashi wa Kyona desu."*

The girl with the small pupils and Kyona walk into class the next day. Hitomi is without her wheelchair but bears a spiteful look. Kyona is smiling but not in any way like a doll.

The Adventures of Starfish Girl

LINDSAY MILLER

1.
Grime-necked man on the bus demands a smile.
I hand it to him. Lipstick stains my palm.

Every part of me from earlobes to entrails
can be removed without pain and grow back.
I do not bleed, I do not make a sound.

2.
The first time a nine-year-old boy
tried to hold my hand behind the swingset
I pulled away too fast. The bone jutted,
white in the horror of his staring eyes.

I did not cry out. My voice
lived in my detached fingers, grasping still,
burrowing in his gentle skin.

One of those science class flower videos
blooming at maximum acceleration
was happening at the end of my wrist.
The boy wept. I tingled
with newly circulating blood.

3.
That night, before a dirty bathroom mirror,
I practiced dismemberment.
Eyelashes and hair first. Not even a twinge.
The smooth caverns ungored beneath fingernails.

Fingers next, snapped
like biting through stale bread.
Bone is more forgiving than you think.

There are so many kinds of sockets
in the human body. Empty, they snarl with hunger.
I watched them refill, slow as swamps.

My teeth did not grow back straighter.
My eyes did not turn blue.
My arms were shaped just the same.

4.
I burned my amputations in the sink.
The stink swallowed me.

5.
The day of my first period, I cried with relief
to know there was blood inside me.
My cunt a tarnished but holy chalice,
transubstantiating flesh into flesh.

It is one of the only parts
I've never lost, misplaced, torn out:
more skeleton than my skeleton,
the dark thread that binds myself to me.

6.
I have dissected myself ruthlessly
(unwrapped skin like a gift,
minced organs on my kitchen counter,
severed limbs to see the tendons wriggle),
and here is what I've found:

I am a body made of tissues made of cells.
I am biological as anything else breathing.

I am not stronger or faster, I do not
reflect bullets. I cannot leap as high as some spiders.
I believe I can be killed. My only gift
is of escaping capture: savagely,
by gnawing off the trapped limb like a bear.
This has been necessary four times.

7.
Some days I stay inside, afraid of what
I might leave behind me on the sidewalk
or tangled in rosebushes, afraid
of some wild dog scenting my skin, tracking me,
afraid of the sound of digging in my backyard.

8.

Other days I have lovers, their faces
mass-produced, interchangeable.
They hold me like a rag doll, careless
of my loose stitches. They know my secret.
I tell them quietly, staring into my wine.
Or sighing, thrusting, a twist
in the wrong direction, a harder gasp.

One of them keeps my fingers in a glass vase,
arranged like lilies: a few seashells,
smooth blue rocks. They never wilt.

9.

The newest one (marbles for eyes,
chain-saw jawbone) laughs like broken windchimes,
says, If I'm ever stranded on a desert island
I hope it's with you. I'd never
have to worry about starving.

All night I stumble awake
dreaming woodsmoke—my skin
marinating in the sweat of his hands,
scarecrow fingers in the meat
of my belly, checking for tenderness—
wondering if I would even feel his teeth.

The Wooden Grandpa

KURT NEWTON

Not long after Grandpa moved in with us, he moved equally into the role as the family's elder statesman. His was the voice of wisdom when the limits of our knowledge needed expanding. His was the voice of reason when the limits of our maturity were exposed. Grandpa particularly enjoyed his other role as grandfather to our two young children. He sat and read them stories. He provided them with an attentive eye. "Watch this, Grandpa!" "Grandpa, look!" His expressions of wonder were animated, his laughter deep and full, and his words of encouragement were always thoughtful and heartfelt. He wore the face of retirement well. And though he never spoke much about Grandma, we knew he missed her dearly. This was evident on his more restless days, when he would wander the first floor of our home, stopping now and then to stare out a window, or to pick a knick-knack up off a shelf to examine where it was made.

Grandpa hardly ever watched television. His favorite past time was to sit and read in an old winged-back chair my wife had bought at a tag sale. His was the last face we saw when we left for work each morning and the kids left for school. His voice was the last goodnight we heard when we climbed the stairs to bed. He was as quiet as the clock on the wall, and just as predictable.

Until the day we found him standing in the middle of the living room rooted to the floor.

There was no other way describe it. Grandpa had simply solidified or petrified right in the middle of our living room, his large pale feet sunk through his slippers, merged with the hardwood beneath.

It didn't appear painful. In fact, on the grain of his features he wore a warm, almost pleasant expression, as if his last thought had been a nostalgic one. His arms were held out as if to welcome visitors into our home.

The children, of course, were mortified. But after explaining to them the nature of time and aging and how life is not always what one expects it to be, they were not so afraid and quickly adapted to Grandpa's odd yet solid presence.

Our youngest continued to carry on long conversations with him while conducting tea parties at his feet. There were days we found her favorite dolly cradled in one of his large open hands.

Our oldest skirted past his body without so much as a "Hello" or "Goodbye." At first, we were concerned about our son's behavior, until we spied him occasionally stopping to tug on Grandpa's shirtsleeve, or to rest his cheek against one of Grandpa's long wooden legs.

On holidays my wife took it upon herself to decorate Grandpa accordingly, trading his grey flannel shirt for a more festive one. Pastel colors for Easter. Red, white, and blue for the Fourth of July. Shades of autumn for Thanksgiving. Evergreen for Christmas. An assortment of hats were also used to celebrate the time of year.

At least once a week I pulled up a chair and sat beside Grandpa and read aloud from one of his favorite books.

As the months and years passed, Grandpa became a part of our daily lives as much as he had been before he had turned to wood. His was the last face we saw when we left for work each morning and the kids left for school. His presence was the last we felt before we climbed the stairs to bed each night. He was as quiet as the clock on the wall, and just as dependable.

When the children grew up and moved away, each took a piece of Grandpa with them. Our oldest took the legs and used them one on each side of the fireplace mantle he built for his new home. Our youngest took the torso and used it as a base for her dinner table. My wife arranged Grandpa's arms and coat, which we had kept in the closet, and mounted them on the wall of our living room. I took Grandpa's head and, in a private ceremony, buried it with Grandma.

It seemed like the proper thing to do.

Man without a Wishbone

PRARTHO SERENO

Blessed with jawbone, elbow and knee,
a tongue for tasting, fingers to touch.
The lantern of his heart swings from its ribcage.
The miracle of his lungs.
But no wishbone bridges the yes and no of him.

When the genie rises from the lamp
he never knows what to ask for.
When the meteors storm an August night,
everyone matching hope to flicker,
he stands dumbstruck.

One day he froze at a fountain,
unable to toss his bright coin.
The marble mermaid took him in, gave
him watch over the cherubs. All spring
the children climbed the ladder

of his spine, pigeons made nests
in his arms, flowers grew from the curled
rim of his hat. These days I wonder
about the strange gift of wantlessness.
However we come by it: birth

or a long life of being nibbled away
by paper moths and summer rain.

· Crematorium ·

Bang you say, and I'm bleeding.

—*the gun game*

When the World Ends

NICOLE MIYASHIRO

They might think the world is going to end, but I think they're paranoid and agree to take the pictures for fun.

The two men stand in the hospital B-Wing outside my office. The one talking to me—Marcus, he calls himself—is all business. The way he slouches in his navy suit makes it appear a size too big, suggesting there was a time he stood tall in it.

"Just get the job done," he says.

"Sure." I'm to be paid $100 per subject per day, no questions asked.

The discussion has to take place out in the hall because my office is occupied by two other coworkers. We share a space and have three desks equally littered with camera accessories, video equipment, cords, and sketch pads.

Marcus' partner jerks the shoulders of his gray-speckled sports jacket, his eyes panning the corridor.

"And Jace," Marcus hits me on the cheek with a spot of steamy coffee breath. "As I've said: *confidential*."

"Research," his partner adds. "Confidential research."

Marcus nods, and I accept his handshake. His partner still looks as though he may scramble for the nearest staircase or elevator at any second, and I weigh the odds that this is a scam, consider the ways I can be taken advantage of.

"One thing," I say. "Which government agency are you with?"

"EPA. Environmental Protection Agency. So we have a deal?"

"Okay."

"Good." Marcus places a hand on my shoulder and its weight falls through me, pressing my heels hard against the floor. "Let us know as soon as you capture any signs of deterioration."

Plant life. Any sprout of it poking through the city's cracks can be photographed for the *confidential research*. Fifteen or more subjects over a three-week period. Marcus said they recruited people who were experienced with taking photos for documentation purposes but, to prevent mass panic, left out what the purpose was.

I usually photograph pigmented lesions, rashes, and burns as a clinical photographer. After I record the activity of a disease or the healing process following reconstructive or invasive surgeries, doctors use my work to monitor patients. The good part about the job is that I get to contribute to curing people without serious risk. When a patient's blister continues accumulating puss or prescribed meds cause undue itching, it's not my job to know why. I just take the pictures. And when someone is cured, I know I've contributed in a way. I can mess up of course: bad lighting, lost film, the wrong angle, the wrong leg. But if I mess up, I just retake the shot. No harm done. I record stuff to document progress. Or, in some unfortunate circumstances, regression.

Among the papers on my desk, I spot a familiar envelope. Each block of writing is printed in leaky black ink and in all caps. The stationery emblem, a silver, dime-sized butterfly, sits in the lower right corner.

It's a note from Aurora.

Aurora and I have this coincidental connection. I only think about her two or three times a year, but each time we seem to be in sync. Once she sent me the article, "How to Cope with Stress," a day after my coworker quit and my patient load doubled. Other times, it's simpler. I remember grinning at a *wet paint* sign near an elevator, thinking of the swatches of paint and design tips Aurora might offer the hospital. When I returned to my desk, I had a voicemail from her.

Despite living in the same city, we never run into each other, and this seems right. For all the times we've been in sync the past few years, we were off for plenty of the years before.

It started when we were fifteen and she didn't show up to the shore one summer. Her parents said she had joined camp and had cheerleading practice. They didn't tell me she was *never* coming back.

Before I went to college, I finally mustered the nerve to get her phone number. We talked a few times—not about our childhood kissing games or how disappointed we were not to see each other again, but about exams and demanding professors and spring break plans. There was always something preventing us from reconnecting fully. Either I was dating someone or Aurora was; or she had sworn-off guys for awhile or I was preoccupied with improving my grades.

By the time she returned from a graduate program studying interior design in Italy, I was married to Donna. Even when Aurora told me she was moving to the city with her new boyfriend, Russell, neither of us rushed to arrange a double-date. We were just happy knowing that the physical space between us would finally shrink.

Soon after her move, I called her on a whim.

Aurora? It's Jace.

I know. Check your mail.

And she was right. There was a letter from her in my office in-bin.

Since then, this is what happens with us. A cycle of mutual thought.

I decide to wait to open her envelope. It's something small, I can tell by its weight, but still something to look forward to.

I'm already late for a 2:30 appointment. It's in Room 16 of the Outpatient Unit over in K-Wing, so I collect my camera bag and lighting equipment from the office. The new patient I've kept waiting might be a new acne surgery candidate or another episode of eczema. All I know is that, as much as I like my job, I'm having one of those days when even a parasitic worm case wouldn't be exciting enough. That's probably why I agreed to participate in some undercover research to prevent a *serious global threat* that I know nothing about.

Maybe it's something big that I can wow Patrick with when it's over, while we're having a catch in the yard and he begs to know what Daddy's secret project was. Right now I imagine him sitting in Language Arts or Social Studies, feeling like I do, and retracing figure eights in his notebook.

I pull the chart outside Room 16: Eva Verde. *Severe mammary and inframammary lacerations, left side, post surgery. Mammary necrosis due to trauma, auto accident.* The girl is seventeen. Just five years older than Patrick. I gather my composure and enter the patient room.

"Hi, Eva. How are you today?"

She's thin, appearing much younger than seventeen. A frizzy wave of hair covers her right eye. It's dyed red, the color of an overripe strawberry, and I can see the dark roots of her natural brown. She's Hispanic, like Aurora, but has darker skin. I wonder how Aurora's doing, if she's designing bedroom interiors in front of an easel, or onsite hanging paintings in a recently refurbished home.

Eva shifts on the examination table with her arms crossed over the front of her gown, holding it tight. I place my camera on the counter before unloading the other equipment.

"I thought this was at 2:30," Eva says.

"I apologize for being a few minutes late." Without delay, I begin prepping her while unloading equipment. "I'll need you to lift each breast when I raise my hand, then turn to the side when I turn my palm to the wall. Are you comfortable with this?"

She nods.

I place the lamp against the examination table. "This may feel warm, but I promise it won't burn you."

All of this seems okay with her, and I know the faster I work, the better. The legs of the tripod slide to the floor. I click each in place, then attach the camera to the head.

"I'll begin when you're ready."

She looks down at her dangling feet and grasps the neck of her gown. Squeezing her eyes closed, she yanks the gown and it slides down. It must have been untied in the back.

I click once, framing the front of her chest. I zoom in on the right breast, refocus, shoot. Then I zoom in on the scarred skin, refocus, and shoot.

"You're doing great. Just a few more."

I see a concentrated spot of black and blue. Zoom, refocus, click. She begins to move, and I try to refocus again, failing to compensate. I peer over my camera and see that she's crying.

My palm leans into the side of my Cyber-Shot, primed for shooting, but I know this is it.

"It's okay. We can stop."

She sniffs, arms shaking at her side. The gown is still sitting in her lap.

"Don't worry about it. We're done for the day." I close the camera shutter and unlatch the tripod.

"Are you disgusted by me?" Eva's voice is mature, revealing only a slight tremble.

"No. Of course not."

"You are."

"I am not disgusted by you."

I want to tell her I've seen worse, but stick with standard procedure: reassure, promote positive outcomes, and under no circumstance imply any kind of diagnosis.

"You wouldn't understand." She lifts the gown over her chest and wipes her eyes.

"Maybe not. But I could try."

I continue wrapping the extension cord under my elbow. The cord goes in the inside pouch of the camera bag. I collapse the tripod. This is work, routine, but to Eva it's something awful that happened to her.

For all I know, something awful is already happening to us. Eva Verde wouldn't be self-conscious about being photographed if the world were ending. Mr. Walker, waiting for me in Room 5, would forget about the third degree burns blistering over his abdomen, elbow, and forearm if there were no tomorrow.

There'd be other things to worry about.

"Do you remember your first kiss?" Eva does want to talk.

"Sure." I take my camera into my hands and fiddle with its disengaged buttons, thankful for this momentary pause from the usual.

"No, I mean *do you remember?* Still know what it feels like, that first real kiss?"

It feels like a child's game, a peck here, a peck there. It's playing around and sometimes bumping foreheads. *On the lips,* Aurora said once. And from then on it was a kiss on each cheek and then her lips like a ritual.

"I remember."

"Well now it's too late." Eva shivers, but not from cold. Her dark eyes deepen behind the flutter of soaked lashes.

For a second, I wonder if she's involved with and knows more about the undercover research. This is silly, because she's a kid and not a photographer.

And the world isn't really going to end.

"Too late for what?" I ask her.

"Everything. I can't explain."

Her openness with tears urges me to go to the window, give her space, clear my head. Cars and buses roll and stop on the street below and people zip up and down the sidewalks, others wait at corners.

If it were to happen, a lightning storm could strike buildings and trees, knock things down on top of us. Or the oceans could overflow and swallow us whole. If it's plants, maybe they're riddled with a poison that's spreading—to animals, our food.

The idea is laughable, as I watch the busyness outside and think of the paranoid men who approached me. The city is at peace. Even the revving motors and beeping horns sound soft, muted by the mood in this room.

I turn back to Eva. "It's okay to be afraid at first. Things will get better."

"*This* is what I have to show him." Her gown falls to her lap. "This."

I have no lens to look through, no lighting adjustments or refocusing to concentrate on. I see her skin with my naked eyes, the flesh above the tan of her nipple crinkled in wide gashes, the skin doubled over itself in uneven elevations, creased with bruises. The pattern repeats itself upward to the torn edge of her collarbone.

I don't know what I'm suppose to do.

"What if things were falling apart," I say, muddling through. "The world was going to end and nothing here mattered. Then what would you do?"

"What?" She laughs like I'm crazy, and the moisture in her eyes twinkles a bit. The straps of the gown flap at her sides, as she lifts the cloth over herself.

"Yeah. There's no time left. What would you do before it was really too late?"

"I don't know. Tell him. I guess."

"So you'd tell him."

"Yeah. If it was the last day on earth."

"And it's something important, right?"

"I think so."

With the last of my equipment packed, I swing the bag over my shoulder and lift the tripod under my arm. "Well I don't think you should wait."

Eva's nostrils flare and cheeks flush. Sighing, she pushes out a heavy rush of air, eying her clothes balled up on the chair next to her backpack that's sprinkled with violet star stickers made of glitter.

When she looks at me, I can tell she still questions my sanity, but smiles—a horizontal stretch of thin lips scrunching two rounded cheeks, free of dimples. I see now how she resembles Aurora.

"See you next week," I say.

With her note unopened and waiting, memories animate the rest of my day. I move the camera, adjust the lens, and snap—flashing to the past: sneaking to the outdoor shower of my parent's shore house.

The water wasn't on, but our feet made dull slapping sounds against the deck-like floor. We were careful not to get splinters.

Aurora brought her fingers to her lips and giggled, as the hinges of the door creaked. She wasn't giggling at the noise. This was our secret and we closed ourselves inside. A ritual had evolved from a kissing game, but at age 14 we were growing out of games. She even had a boyfriend and remained loyal. She hadn't kissed him yet.

My neck, Aurora offered. Her bikini top glowed fluorescent blue in the moonlight that seeped in from the vented roof. She wanted a kiss in a new place.

I slid my hands down her shoulders and pulled her against my torso, lowering my lips to her ear. *Okay.*

She seemed nervous, but unafraid—her eyes closed and lids pulsating. We had discovered a trust.

I pressed my lips into her neck, smelling the washed-out remnants of sweet shampoo. I tasted her sea-salted skin for what I feared was too long, but Aurora flung her arms around my neck. Neither of us knowing what to do, and both of us knowing exactly what to do. It came naturally. There was no doubt, argument, or monotony. Our bodies raced with an instinctual need to feel each other, to give and receive. To touch.

I backed her into the wall of the shower. Aurora lowered her hands from my neck and slid her fingers against the straps of her bathing suit. They fell to her shoulders, the rest of the top unmoved and waiting.

I kissed her neck with more confidence and skimmed my hands over the hanging straps. My fingers latched at the last second to pull them the rest of the way down, to her elbows. Placing a kiss on her collarbone, I lowered a knee to reach her.

She was all new, completely bared to me—her fresh skin, her unfastened and eager moan. My unsteady tongue rounded each breast in the same circular direction, and I touched each one again with a kiss. Then I enclosed her there in my arms, her beating heart warming the skin against my ear.

We stayed there, silent. My knee balanced on the shower floor. Aurora's arms crossed over my neck.

I was sure we were the only ones alive at that moment.

I covered Aurora with the light-blue fabric of her top and then replaced the straps on her shoulders while planting kisses: cheek, cheek, lips. We sealed things there, in that damp wooden shower.

It was the last of our summers together.

"Jace." Dr. Fennimore startles me, halting my stride back towards B-Wing. "Tall man with a blonde crew-cut and a snake tattoo on his left shoulder—possibly naked. Have you seen him?"

"What? No."

"Gown and slippers in the bed, stuff in the closet. But the patient's gone."

"Took off?"

Fennimore shrugs and turns to continue down the hall. He waves his beeper in the air as he walks away. "See him, page me."

"Sure."

As soon as I unload my equipment in my office, I scoop up the white envelope. Inside is a square piece of paper. As I pull it out, a smaller strip falls onto the floor. *This one struck me, so I thought you should have it. Always, Aurora.* I lean over to peel the strip off the floor. It's from a fortune cookie.

Good to see you, she said the last time I saw her.

Aurora smiled and clasped her hands at the back of my neck and smiled some more. It had been ten years. A need to touch her resurfaced from our past. All that time, yet I couldn't help savoring each point of contact we exchanged.

My hands found their way to her waist, right where the form-fitting crease connected white, gem-studded ruffles.

Congratulations, I said.

She grinned. We had never needed many words.

We stepped side-to-side at a slow pace. Peeking past her shoulder, I saw the rest of her guests occupied with pumping arms and hips, keeping beat with Kool & The Gang's "Celebration."

Without arranging it, we had created our own rhythm. One we found instantly. The thought of Donna sitting over at our table sipping red wine and watching us drift at a slow pace made me uncomfortable. I looked through the crowd and could just see the maroon scoop of Donna's dress hanging down her back, her left elbow propped on the table as she swished her glass, the way she always did when she talked.

I still found Donna to be incredibly sexy, with her straight, smooth back, not a freckle or mole to speak of, her beautiful neck glowing under the sway of deep, auburn hair, cut in bold layers. She was a loving wife who was attentive to all of my needs. I was grateful to have found her. My wife, the woman I loved. My attraction to Aurora was only a memory from our past. It had nothing to do with my current life.

You know, I've always wanted you to be happy. Aurora's newfound happiness was evident in her eyes when she spoke. They gleamed with a knowing flicker. A flicker that made me wonder if she knew what I was thinking—that I wondered, if we could have been happy together.

In that moment, I knew we could. I wanted to know how that could be, why I would think that. I wanted to know if the natural rhythm of our body language meant something, or if I was just imagining it.

Aurora tightened her hold on my neck. *It's funny that our parents still go to the shore. Isn't it?*

Yeah, I said.

Those were good times.

We both laughed and slipped into playful grins. Grins that implied, I know you. I know you because I discovered you first.

A cheery "celebrate good times" began to fade and the crowd eased up on their twists and jabs.

You're a beautiful bride. The words caused a bubble to curl in my throat.

The flower girl came tugging on a ruffle of Aurora's dress, and Aurora stepped away from me. She tapped the girl's crown of white roses, allowing her to slip behind and grab onto her waist.

A new song had started.

People continually latched on behind the flower girl, as Aurora turned to lead the chain across the dance floor. I turned to find my table.

When I sat in front of my yellow-starred nametag, longing and regret panged inside me. I was desperate for another time, an explanation.

I slid my arm under Donna's, as she chatted with strangers. I squeezed her turning wrist and looked out to the crowd again. Aurora was strutting past, leading the conga line; she looked at me, and winked.

As the sparkling white of her dress trailed her steps, I inhaled, feeling a warmth circle my insides. Things were right, I decided. Aurora was never mine, but somehow always would be.

To begin again, work backwards.

I fold the fortune into thirds and then pull out my wallet. Behind two thick layers of crammed credit, insurance, and discount cards, I slide the fortune in where news articles, a folded postcard, and two other fortunes are flattened. Preserved by a pocket of leather.

Donna and Patrick are well into their steaks and mashed potatoes when I get home from work.

"Why all the stuff?" Donna asks.

"Oh. Got a little assignment." I unload my bags in a heap next to the kitchen door.

Donna pecks me on the lips with a mouth full of food. I nudge Patrick on the way over to get a plate from the cabinet.

"Hey, Dad." He laughs. Twelve years old already. *Twelve.* Not sure where the time went. Just day after day. Waking up, kissing Donna and Patrick goodbye, and then going to work. Doing it all again. Then, he's twelve.

I put my plate down across from Patrick's, but hesitate before sitting.

"The salad's in the fridge, if you want some of that. And plenty of everything else."

"I love you," I hear myself say.

"Love you too, baby." Donna sips her water.

"No, I just want you both to know how happy you make me."

"Okay, *Dad*."

Donna stops eating and looks worried, so I sit down.

"I just thought I should say it." And I meant it. But it doesn't feel like I thought it would. Things are quiet and mundane. I swallow a gulp of potatoes and wonder if I should warn them about the *serious global threat*. Only, I wouldn't be able to elaborate much.

"What was your day like?" Donna asks.

"Same old stuff. Took pictures. Lots of skin."

Patrick laughs and shovels his food.

"Pimply, rash-covered skin," I clarify.

His chewing is less enthusiastic.

"And these men, these government guys, hired me to take photos, starting tonight. Of plant life in the city."

"Government guys? What kind?"

"EPA."

"Environmentalists?"

"Yeah, I guess. Hey, maybe you shouldn't eat that salad until I find out what's going on. They're research is confidential."

Donna combs a portion of salad to the edge of her plate with her fork, but giggles at me. "Okay. But we've been eating it all week."

"I know, you're right. It's just starting to bug me that it's so *confidential*."

"Plants were poisoned in Europe," Patrick interjects. "They said at school. Disappeared like magic."

"Not magic." Donna swirls her glass, creating a mini twist of water. "A farmer in Sicily said his wheat crops disintegrated. They suspect *he* torched them, because he's suing the pesticide company for lots of money."

"Mr. Roper says programmed cell death. Accelerated . . . osmosis?"

"*Apoptosis*," I correct. "I think you might need to re-review your homework, Patrick."

He shrugs.

I bring my plate to the sink and peer out the window. It's seven and the sun hides, casting an odd and lingering sheen to the sky. I brush leftover chunks of steak and potatoes into the trash bin.

"That's it? You're done?" Donna says.

"I should take these photos so I can get back home."

Donna pushes back her chair and stands. She wraps her arms around me, swinging left-to-right, using my waist as leverage. "Be careful." She dots my lips with hers. Her eyes dart to the window and squint. "How long will you be?"

"Not long."

"Good," she says, releasing me.

A clump of bark drops to the ground as I snap a photograph of a leafy tree branch. Subject one. I've been assigned the blocks from 20th to 22nd between Market and Sansom Streets. If Marcus and friend were more specific about what I was documenting, I might have a better idea of what to look for. Plants shriveling prematurely or developing abnormal stems? Discolored and spreading fast? Or crippled by stunted growth? What ever it is, I'll try to capture it.

On 22nd there's a church. Within its gates is a massive garden of greens and bushes. I crank up the tripod and take a shot of the whole scene.

The sky is now a color I've never seen. A gray-blue that glows without a central source, spreading evenly over space. This wouldn't be odd for late spring, except that it seems to have gotten brighter since I left home.

I retrieve the camera from the tripod so I can get close-ups of the garden. First I take a shot that includes a piece of the three-foot gate. I hop over it to get closer. I zoom in on a shrub and let it fill the frame. Then I kneel closer to focus on a single branch and its leaves. The sky provides just enough light. I snap the photo, and before the zoom lens retracts, the leaves fall off the branch, crumbling to the ground.

I fall back on my heels. They're gone. I ruffle the grass and an ashy, sand-like substance coats my fingers, the leaves nowhere to be found. I lift my camera and snap a shot of the naked branch. Just like that. Gone.

"Shit! Did you see that?" A smack against pavement follows the voice, and I stand to find a boy in a green Leo & Pop's cap beyond the fence. A flipped open pizza box sits on the ground. The boy points ahead, down the sidewalk.

As I jump the fence, I recall the weight of Marcus' hand on my shoulder. The sensation falls to my stomach when I see the neat heap of litter on the sidewalk.

The delivery boy looks to be a couple years older than Patrick and is still pointing.

"What happened? You alright?"

He doesn't answer. He keeps pointing at a discarded lump of clothes.

"You've been robbed?"

He just shakes his head, lowering his pointed finger. I approach the pile, and he makes a guttural protest, backing away.

"Someone probably just left it." I lift the dress shirt by the collar and dust bursts from its fabric.

"Holy shit." His feet pounding pavement trail the remark.

Looking after him, I'm amazed I can see so far this time of night. I watch him sprint towards the corner, and his shape seems to hit a bump and disappear to the ground. I rush over to see if he's okay.

My only reaction is to take pictures. I take one from above, that frames the baseball cap, to catch how it tops the lifeless pile of clothes. Click. Then I squat to capture an angle that will display how each sneaker is on its side, socks snug inside where feet should be. Click. Click.

I lower my camera—leaving it beside the pile of clothes. This is it. It's here. And my photos can't do anything to stop it. I stand and see the gritty particles that blanket the sidewalk like debris. Then I run.

I run down 22nd towards Walnut, rationalizing as I go: the leaves, the branch, the farmer. The boy, the pile, the dust. I run. Here and there I spot a tree top disintegrate and fall through the air like a cloud of rain. I hop scattered piles of empty clothes. One catches my foot and I shake it, thinking of Donna and Patrick. I think of them and run, waiting for my arms and legs to fall in showers of dust as I turn the corner of Waverly Street.

Halfway up the block from my house, I collapse on the curb.

A lurch knocks in my stomach, the thought of seeing them crumble. Or finding what's left. Their abandoned clothes.

I can't go inside. Instead, I envision them sitting at the table, talking long after their last bites of dinner. Something they always do. Their voices, safe in my mind: Patrick's laugh, Donna's smiling, inquisitive response, *That's funny, is it?*

I hear a low whiff and open my eyes. A woman stands across the street, stunned and holding a leash. It hangs slack, an empty loop at her feet, and I don't want to wait for the tears. I don't want this to be the end.

I need to know.

I lift myself off the curb and hurry out of my neighborhood. Fierce honking rattles my ears. There's a dead man blocking traffic, but no one can see that he's curled up in the legs of his pants, in piles at the foot of his pedals as I squeeze by. *Poof.*

Like magic.

Turning the corner, I see a small crowd surrounding a weeping man. He is crouched at a pile of clothes. An observer slips down through her own clothes, and the crowd gasps.

I go from jogging to running. I want to scream but want to hide. To sneak away before losing everything, and I realize I've left them. They've left me. There's nothing I can do.

Trees crumble and blow in the air like snow, but the pavement remains sturdy under my clapping feet. I've run at least a mile, numb to strained muscles and joints.

And it's not too late.

I knock on 955 Bridge Street. A place I've known but have never been to. When she opens the door I crave a piece of her calm. She doesn't realize.

She is beautiful, the same, but different. Her hair is longer, feathery against her cheeks, and she smiles her smooth-cheeked smile as if expecting me.

"Jace," Aurora says. "I was just—wow. This is unbelievable."

"Aurora," I pant. I grab hold of her hand, and she stops me in the foyer.

"Russell is napping upstairs." Aurora takes her hand back. "You're winded."

I can't formulate words, formulate sense of what's happening, why I'm here. A sweet, familiar scent encloses me, and Aurora pats the sides of my arms.

"It's okay," she says, and I realize I've been crying. My breath hiccups with tear-choked gasps, and I allow the pain to enter: a vision of Donna's squinting face, Patrick's chirpy voice. I feel it now. The loss, the fear.

Their memory.

"You have to say goodbye." I wipe my face, tears streaming my knuckle.

"What?"

"Goodbye. *Now.*" I grab Aurora's wrist and yank her towards the stairs.

"What's happening? Jace?"

I ascend the steps first, pulling her along. When we reach the top, I see a polo shirt and pants neatly placed on the bed—an impression of where Russell lay. I stop Aurora short, but she sees it in my eyes.

"Jace," she almost whispers. "Why are you here?" Her lips quiver, and she looks towards the bedroom, the empty clothes.

I release her arm, unable to answer. She takes steady steps, glancing back at me, as I follow close behind.

Her scream extends Russell's name into a cracked and broken shrill. Hazy powder clouds the air as she whips the empty shirt off the bed. I rush to restrain her arms, and we collapse against the bedside, lowering ourselves to the floor. Taking her to me, I wrap myself around her until her sobs are buried in my chest. Tears linger heavy on my cheek, and I look up at the window. A sky that is still a uniform blanket of gray-blue glows. Aurora presses her warmth into me.

My neck, I recall her suggesting—and close my eyes.

She begins to fade. No screaming, no more crying. Just a light cascade rolling down my chest and slipping from my arms. Like sand. The sound reminds me of ocean water at the shore, and I don't open my eyes.

Letting go, I work my mind backwards, to a place I know and trust, to where things are just beginning, and she and I—

Leaving La Dulce Vida

JOHN F. BUCKLEY & MARTIN OTT

Coyotes laughed before dawn as Martinez pushed the fake boulder aside
and stepped inside the express elevator, turning the key in the slot again,
submitting to the retinal-DNA-biometric scan again, rubbing his back—
stupid damn boulder—and whistling tunes for the forty-two seconds it took.

He began his circuit of cleaning on Level 1 with a terse hosing down
of the black fleet of sedans, hoping the anti-matter sweep had been sufficient.
He skipped Level 2 and the endless New Mexico mud from the bored cave
expansion, straight to stripping to his skivvies, being weighed, and provided

a registered, returnable, officially calibrated ion mop for swabbing iridium
floors in the Level 3 chrysopoeia lab. His predecessor was caught trying
to smuggle out gold nuggets tucked in each armpit. Now everyone suffered,
despite the screams of the service workers' union before the bribes took hold.

On Level 4, he took his time scouring the paranormal wing as the alchemical
delta wave experiments had caused dust to molt into metal shavings. He tried
not to look at body bits in jars, or into the renovated aromatherapy chambers,
or worry about mutated rodents, and found serenity stealing time with the love

of his hours, his deep desert flower, Dolores, the finest in janitorial artificial
intelligence, an Omicron-grade Cerebrobroom with a 170 IQ, an encyclopedic
knowledge of postindustrial cleansers, a silvery voicebox, a penchant for obscure
Neruda poems, and a secret compartment for crumb-free salami Lunchables.

Dolores means "sorrows," and yet she felt entranced to be cleaning the messy
alien cubbies on Level 5, vacuuming the slug remains from snack attacks as he
steeled himself for the multi-limbed Twister game on the "Nightmare Wing."
Here he would mount his trusty Zamboni and spin through the maelstrom

of eyed tentacles, tentacled fangs, fanged eyes stroking at him, snared in a time-
dilation field but aching for prey-touch, for "left-middle feeler on pink" to engage
him in laconic ESP. Together with Dolores, he pirouetted around unmentionable
horrors to empty yowling emanating from the frozen cross-species embryo vats

from R'lyeh. They kissed without entropy and fell for years through the wormhole air ducts below Level 7, carefully wiping ichor from eleven-dimensional windows. Love found its way again, even here, even as the sun swung their cave toward ice moons and gravity ceased to have meaning. Here where everything was alien, river

bats undulating through liquid-nitrogen fogs, itinerant molemen roasting their tin-foil hobo packs in magma pools, stray plasmoid starchildren sucking ionized solar winds from magnetic bottles, biomechanical cyberpriests giving last rites to quasars gone nova, a sublime union of opposites reaching for a singular core.

Trouble in Mind

JULIA A. ROSENTHAL

The 2:19 train to Hung Hom station roared past the estates and mansions of downtown Hong Kong. The towers rose over the tracks toward the cloud-dotted June sky like a forest of white brick, concrete and glass. From the train windows one could look up at the terraced balconies and see flashes of life inside each tiny apartment: a clothesline hung with towels, boxer shorts and a baby's footed pajamas, or a row of potted flowers blooming red and white.

It was rare to see anyone out on a balcony. June in Hong Kong was a season of angry humidity and sudden rains. The effort of pushing through one or two crowded blocks to a bakery or noodle stand to buy dinner could make someone too tired to eat. To leave the sanctuary of air conditioning, even to hang up laundry, was to forget instantly what cool air felt like.

Tony, alone, stood on the balcony of his apartment.

His white shirt was limp and his face glistened with sweat. He lowered the cigarette from his mouth and leaned on the railing, watching the train pass.

Under the train's tinted glass Tony could see passengers reading the flat Byron screens on their laps. Their fingers fluttered and their hands dipped over their Byrons.

The devices read the motions of their hands like an attentive orchestra, translating the signs into a complex language of numbers, symbols and formulas. It was a language too multidimensional to be spoken aloud, a language of pure theory that had left words, and the human voice, behind.

Tony could understand none of it.

A year ago he would have watched the motions of the passengers' hands with fierce focus, trying to read a word or two in their gestures as the train's windows glided past below him. He no longer bothered. The motion sensors in a Byron screen were finely tuned machines, crafted to read the manual sign language that had replaced the human voice as a means of communication. Tony had once hoped that, if he studied the sign language closely enough, he could grasp its meaning just as a Byron's motion sensors did. He gave up this hope as he saw the sign language evolve in speed and complexity over mere months. No matter how closely he watched someone else's hands now, Tony's eyes couldn't read the meaning in their gestures the way a Byron screen could.

Tony's brain was an obsolete engine. He could feel it rusting daily from disuse, isolation, and the stupefying effects of heavy medication.

His wife Winnie, an administrator at Queen Elizabeth Hospital, had been one of the first people to convert three years ago—before it was known as "conversion," when it was still considered an exotic strain of the flu. As Winnie had been one of the cases in the first wave, her loss of verbal language had been slower than most. She stopped speaking within weeks rather than days.

But her grasp of the new language of numbers was immediate. It began with a leap forward in her ability to understand complex mathematical theory. A few weeks after her diagnosis, Tony woke one morning to find that Winnie had taken a pencil and corrected the errors in the formulas in his draft of an article for *Finance and Stochastics* while sipping her breakfast tea. Soon she was sharing one-line jokes with him that were nothing but mathematical symbols. They were a mathematician's jokes— both inside the math itself and above it—and so clever that Tony posted them on his office door at the university and listened to his colleagues laugh in the hallway as they read them.

It wasn't long before Winnie was taking notes on hospital memos in a string of numbers and symbols that, to Tony, were opaque in meaning. She still scrawled one-line jokes to him, which he continued to post on his office door, but he no longer got them.

As more of his colleagues caught the same virus Winnie had contracted, Tony heard them laughing at her jokes. Every time the sound rang in the hallway, he wanted to poke his head out and ask for a translation. But Tony knew it was useless. By the time the other professors in his department could understand his wife's new kind of humor, they had already stopped speaking themselves.

A year ago Winnie still believed in him. She had argued with the specialists at Queen Elizabeth Hospital at his many appointments. Tony would sit next to Winnie, silent, as she rested one hand on his and signed over her Byron screen with the other hand. He would watch the patience in each doctor's face harden into irritation as Winnie refused to accept each new diagnosis. When they were alone, her deep brown eyes would look into Tony's and say: *You're brilliant. You're the finest mind in mathematics in Hong Kong. I did this. We'll find a way for you too.*

The red-flashing tail of the 2:19 train slid into the tunnel and disappeared.

Tony tapped the cigarette against the railing. He remembered too late that the ash would fall onto Mrs. Yee's clean laundry hanging on the balcony below, which would start another door-slamming fight between her and Winnie.

He went back inside the apartment.

Tony's office had been their daughter Ada's bedroom before she left to study computer science at MIT. He no longer went to his faculty office in the mathematics department at Hong Kong University of Science and Technology. The department head had gone to great—and condescending,

Tony thought—lengths to make sure that Tony, as a tenured professor, felt welcome to pursue his research there. His teaching responsibilities had been quietly eliminated. Tony endured a semester of pitying smiles from his colleagues before he stopped going to campus. He preferred the natural quiet and solitude of the apartment while Winnie was at work.

Tony sat down on Ada's narrow bed, his desk chair. He reached above his head to push a button on her old stereo. A compact disc began to spin. Dinah Washington's deceptively sweet voice sang of her troubled mind and her hopes for blue skies.

Tony bent over the papers spread across his small desk. A Byron was at his elbow, its screen dark. He nudged it further aside.

Tony turned to his computer.

Nonparametric analysis, he typed in English.

The search engine returned less than five hundred hits.

Tony checked his notes. A few weeks ago, the same search had returned more than eight thousand pages. Before the onset of conversion, there would have been hundreds of thousands, perhaps a million.

Tony reviewed the dates on which the first few pages of hits had been last updated. None had been touched within the last year. All article citations were in academic journals so minor that Tony had never heard of most of them. For all he knew, they had ceased publication and no one had bothered to go back and convert the archived articles from old-fashioned words.

When he had run the search a few weeks ago, there had been a few major articles left in English. All had been taken down. No one was reading in that form anymore.

Christ, Tony thought. *These are medieval manuscripts now.*

He stared at the screen for a moment.

Then he clicked on the icon for the translation engine his daughter Ada had coded for him. In the box Tony typed *nonparametric analysis* and routed the terms to the search engine's page, running the search again in mathematical translation.

This time an avalanche of hits came back. The summary page, in untranslated form, was an indecipherable flood of numbers and symbols. Tony scanned them out of habit, looking for recognizable patterns, before he could stop himself. On first glance, the written version of the new language Winnie, and the rest of the world, spoke still looked like mathematical theory to Tony.

Trying to read it in its raw form was, of course, futile. It wasn't old-fashioned theory at all. It was a new level of thought, a turn in the wheel of human evolution, that converted minds could grasp. Not Tony's.

He directed Ada's engine to the first twenty pages and waited for it to churn the babble into something he could read and understand—and, maybe, turn into new scholarship.

As he did, Tony lit another cigarette. He reached above his head and pressed the repeat-play button on Ada's stereo. Dinah Washington sang on.

Tony felt the thin apartment walls tremble as Winnie opened the front door. He looked at the overflowing ashtray on his desk next to his papers, but didn't empty it.

A moment later his Byron flashed. Tony picked it up. The Cantonese characters flowing across its screen were pale green; it was his daughter Ada calling.

Hi, Dad!

Tony unplugged his keyboard from the computer and connected it to the Byron.

Hi, sweetheart! Tony typed.

Ada's engine, also installed on his Byron, converted his words and sent them out. In a split second her response appeared, translated back into Cantonese. *Guess what! I'm back! Just landed!*

Tony smiled. He typed back, his eyes on the Byron screen: *Too busy to come and see us?*

No! I'm in line at customs. I'll be there in an hour.

His smile widened. *Fantastic! How was Athens?*

Great. I love it.

A photo of Tony's daughter flashed on the screen. A man Tony had never seen, a blonde who looked vaguely Scandinavian or Russian and who was a head taller than Ada, had his arm around her. Ada was leaning toward his shoulder and her hand rested on his.

Tony had barely absorbed this image when more came. Ada climbing white marble rocks, her long black hair hidden under a hat in the blazing sun. Ada standing next to a group of grinning people in their twenties in what looked like an office. A view through a narrow window of a brightly lit street full of small cars and motorbikes.

Tony couldn't keep up. *Who's the boy?* he typed.

Hans. He's from Geneva. His dad's a diplomat. They even lived here in Hong Kong once, back when we were kids. He used to speak Cantonese too!

Tony typed: *Is he there with you?*

No, he's back in Athens.

How did the project go? Tony typed.

Still going. I'll tell you everything when I get there. Oh—don't tell Mom. OK? I want to surprise her.

OK, he typed. *I won't say a word. I should sign off. She just got home. See you soon!*

On the Byron's screen, the conversation link with Ada vanished before Tony could type a goodbye.

Ada's departure for Greece a month before had been for a business trip scheduled to last only a few days. It had not surprised Tony when she simply failed to come back to Hong Kong, giving "project delays" as her only reason. Ada loved travel even more than she loved solving technical software problems.

Tony unplugged his keyboard from the Byron and reconnected it to his computer. He began typing again—he wasn't certain what—when the door opened behind him.

A few moments passed without a sound. Tony raised his head and looked over his shoulder.

Winnie stood in the doorway. Two cloth grocery bags dangled from her slender hands as she studied her husband without speaking. The V-neck of her beige silk sweater was patched with sweat. Strands of hair, a shadow of gray at its roots beneath its black sheen, clung to her damp forehead.

Tony stood up and held his hands out for the bags. A year ago, even six months ago, he might have said out loud: "Let me take those." Now the sound of his voice, speaking words, made Winnie wince or look at him with a flat, quiet despair that was more searing than any cheerful smile from his colleagues at the university. It was easier not to speak at all.

Winnie put the bags down slowly. She stepped into the small, cluttered office and into reach of Tony's outstretched hands.

Tony felt her wrap her arms around him and draw him, still sitting on Ada's bed, close to her.

He closed his eyes and pressed the side of his face against Winnie's stomach.

They didn't move for several moments. Tony wondered if something catastrophic had happened. Not being able to ask in words, he stroked the small of Winnie's back, slick with perspiration through the thin silk sweater and high waist of her fitted skirt. He felt the rise and fall of her breaths against his cheek.

It's OK, Winnie, he thought. *Whatever's wrong, it's OK.*

She reached up and turned the stereo off before she took a step away from Tony.

Then Winnie bent to pick up the shopping bags. Without looking at him, she turned toward the kitchen.

Tony stood in the kitchen doorway as he watched Winnie cook. Steam rose from a pot of boiling water on the two-burner stove, coiling into the curls of smoke rising from the tip of Tony's cigarette and lifting toward the low ceiling.

Winnie's eyes were avoiding his. The blade of her chef's knife rocked back and forth on the wooden cutting board. Cloves of garlic were peeled with a single smack down to their creamy insides and turned into a finely-minced paste in moments. Winnie always moved with a furious grace in the tiny apartment kitchen, but tonight she was working with unusual focus. Her glance never left the cutting board or the stove.

Tony wanted to tell her about Ada. It was clear that something was troubling Winnie; maybe the news would have made her smile. He had promised his daughter not to say a word, though, so he stood and smoked in silence.

At last he coughed.

Winnie looked up. She touched a button on a screen on the wall next to her.

From the stereo speakers above their heads, the ripple of a Bach prelude played on a harpsichord filled the kitchen. Winnie slid her finger along the screen to nudge the volume up.

Tony's doctors had suggested that he immerse his brain in instrumental music, along with the drug therapy, in an effort to synthesize the cognitive effects of conversion. The works of Bach, Mozart, and the twelve-tone school of Schoenberg were recommended in daily doses. Winnie couldn't stand atonal music, so she had loaded their apartment's digital musical library with the classical composers.

Tony had grown to hate them all. Particularly Bach.

He edged around Winnie without touching her to reach the screen on the wall. Tony's hand slapped it into silence.

Over the cutting board the knife paused. Winnie's head turned. She pressed her lips together before she looked back down and resumed chopping.

Tony's fingers rapped the screen. A moment later Dinah Washington was crooning, at high volume, through the steam and smoke of the kitchen.

He crossed his arms and glared at his wife.

Winnie grabbed a handful of green bok choy leaves and flung them into a stainless-steel strainer. Water shot from the faucet in a high froth as she shook the strainer vigorously, sending a spray over the front of her sweater. She slammed the faucet off and dumped the wet leaves onto the cutting board. Her knife lifted.

Two strikes of the knife against the board. Then the blade clattered down on its side. Winnie was gripping her left hand.

"Fuck," she whispered.

A trickle of blood spidered down her fingers, then pulsed and flowed faster. Drops fell onto the cutting board as Winnie stared at her hand.

Tony threw down his cigarette as he pulled Winnie toward the sink. She stood still and rigid as Tony rinsed her bleeding hand under cool water. He could feel her arm trembling under his as he examined the gash. It was crescent-shaped and bisected the back of two of Winnie's fingers just below the first knuckle. The water from the faucet flowed pale pink as it hit the sink's bottom.

He was shaking too.

It was the first time Tony had heard his wife say a word in three years.

Everything around Tony—Winnie's injured hand, the water splashing in the sink, the pot boiling on the burner a few feet away, the haze of the air in the apartment kitchen—seemed to shimmer for a moment as if reality itself were dissolving.

What if some part of Winnie's mind could still think in words?

Could he still reach it?

Was there something primal, as deep as pain, that could undo the erasing of conversion and wake up the ability to speak again?

Tony's heart was pounding. He wanted to turn to Winnie and grab her by the shoulders, look directly into her face and shout her name.

Perhaps, if he could connect to that part of her—perhaps there was a chance Tony could break through the hopeless sadness that filled Winnie's eyes whenever she came home and saw him at the end of the day, still incapacitated, still unable to think like everyone else, still stubbornly uninfected and un-converted. The urge to yell Winnie's name filled him until he could hardly breathe with the effort of holding it back.

Against his shoulder he felt Winnie's head droop as her body sagged. The sight of blood had always made her faint.

Tony shook his head to clear it. He turned off the faucet and slipped one arm around Winnie's shoulders as he reached for a dishtowel to press against the cut. He rubbed her back as she leaned against the kitchen sink. The color slowly returned to her pale cheeks.

When he took her hand and pantomimed wrapping a bandage around it, his eyebrows lifted in a question, she nodded.

A moment later Tony was back in the kitchen with a box of first aid supplies from the bathroom. He dried Winnie's hand with the bloodstained dishtowel. With one fingertip he traced the lip of the cut with antibacterial ointment, then with a transparent strip of adhesive gel that sealed the rest of the blood beneath Winnie's sliced-open skin. Now all that could be seen were two dark red lines, like closed eyelids, beneath a wet smear of clear jelly.

Winnie's brown eyes had been fixed on a spot on the kitchen wall just above Tony's head as he worked. He released her hands and turned to throw away the paper backing for the adhesive gel strip, which crackled in his fingers as he crumpled it. The sound made Winnie blink as if she were coming out of a trance.

From behind Tony felt Winnie's arms curl around his waist. The warmth of her cheek rubbed against his shoulder.

He stood still, holding his breath, waiting for Winnie to pull away.

Her arms tightened as she pressed up against Tony.

It had been a long time since Winnie had touched him with anything but pity. Tony could feel the weight of Winnie's slender body curving into his spine. He didn't need words. It wasn't sadness that was making her hold him now, but gratitude.

And a stirring of an emotion he had wondered if he would ever see or feel from her again: desire.

Inside her embrace, Tony turned to face her. Winnie's face was tilted up toward his.

Her lingering kiss was sweet and coy, a kind he hadn't tasted in years. Tony kissed her back. Winnie closed her eyes, smiled, and kissed him again—harder this time.

For a moment Tony wondered if there was another man.

Then he didn't care.

The knock on the front door of the apartment was loud enough to be heard over Dinah Washington in the kitchen.

Tony lifted his head away from Winnie and looked toward the door.

She slipped her hands into his hair and pulled his face back toward hers with a mischievous smile.

He grinned at her, jerking his head toward the door.

Winnie shook her head and stamped one foot on the kitchen floor. Tony could read her face. *It's just Mrs. Yee downstairs. Let her knock. She'll go away.*

The knock came again, louder. Tony shook his head and pointed at the door.

Winnie sighed. She gathered her tousled hair back up into a knot and walked toward the front door as she pinned it into place. Tony watched the movement of her hips—the sexy swing, just for him, that melted away with each step toward the door until her body was as smoothed and collected as the strands of hair underneath her fingers.

He heard Winnie gasp when she opened the door and saw Ada.

The square dining table was just big enough for the three of them to sit around it, elbow to elbow, in a corner of the living room, as they had done since Ada was a small child. Winnie had covered its scarred wooden surface with an embroidered tablecloth in honor of Ada's surprise return from Athens. The tablecloth was nearly invisible under a spread of plates, bowls, serving dishes and napkins. Next to each plate lay a Byron.

Tony leaned forward and slurped noodles from his raised chopsticks. He was the only one eating.

Winnie and Ada were arguing.

Winnie, who sat across from Tony, had lowered her eyes to her Byron screen and was watching its numbers and symbols skitter by in Ada's pale green. The chopsticks in her right hand rested on her plate without touching any of her food.

At Tony's left elbow, Ada's right hand was slashing at the air over her Byron, its motion sensors reading her rapid signs and translating them into the code that Winnie was reading. Ada was breathing hard. Winnie's breaths were inaudible.

The two women were still for a few seconds.

One last jab from Ada.

Winnie put her chopsticks down and lifted her hand over her Byron screen to reply. Ada's arms were now crossed and she was glaring at her mother. Tony watched as Winnie's wrist bent as gracefully as a classical dancer. Her response was slow, deliberate and full of fluid poetry.

Tony tried to imagine Winnie's voice.

I understand that you love Athens, Ada. But your life is here. What about the Ph.D. that you've promised to finish?

Or:

This boy. Hans. How can we give our blessing to you if you've never brought him here to meet us?

Tony set his chopsticks next to his plate and rested his fingers on the small keyboard lying, tactfully out of sight, down in his lap. He typed as quietly as he could: *Winnie? What's going on?*

Winnie's Byron screen flickered with a new color—blue, Tony's translated message—a split second later. Her eyes twitched, but she didn't look at Tony. Her hand continued to flow through the steps of her response to Ada.

Tony typed to his daughter: *Ada? Is everything OK?*

Ada, who had been watching her mother's hands with an increasingly taut face as Winnie took her time to answer, looked down at her screen to see Tony's message. She closed her eyes and covered her face with her hands.

Winnie finished her response with a gesture that looked like a mother smoothing the hair on a child's head. It was strange for a Byronic sign, of a type Tony thought he had never seen before. He wondered what it meant.

Ada read Winnie's response in silence. She sat, her breathing low and furious as she stared at her half-eaten dinner. Then she straightened her shoulders and raised her hand to her Byron screen.

At last Tony's Byron flickered in pale green Cantonese.

Dad. What's Mom told you?

Tony typed back: *About what?*

Winnie leaned toward Ada and shot her a dark warning look. Her eyes darted from Ada's face to Tony's.

About what she heard from the doctors today, Ada signed.

She hasn't told me anything, Tony typed.

Ada's hand flew in the air like a fencer's blade. On Tony's Byron screen, a few words appeared, garbled among strings of numbers and symbols.

Slow down, Ada, Tony typed. *Your translation engine can't keep up.*

Ada's hand froze. Her eyes screwed closed as her fingers balled into a fist. She hit the table with such force that the plates jumped.

Winnie stared at her, eyes wide with shock. Her eyebrows lowered in a stern reproach.

Ada signed again. On Tony's screen flashed: *20%!*

I don't understand, he typed.

Tears were starting to trickle down Ada's cheeks. She wiped them away with the back of her left hand as she signed, more slowly now, with her right.

Twenty percent. The estimate the doctors gave Mom for the chance that you'll be cured if you go into the hospital.

I'm not going into the hospital, Tony typed. *Who says I am?*

When there was no answer from Ada, he looked up. Winnie and Ada were looking at him. Their hands were motionless.

Tony typed: *I don't have the gene mutation. I can't convert like you and Mom did. They've known this for a year, sweetheart. So what is this about going into—*

Ada's hand lifted again.

Tony read: *The doctors say there are too many words here. They say your brain doesn't have a chance of learning how to speak like we do if you keep using words.*

What's going to happen in the hospital, then? Tony typed.

Full isolation. Drug therapy. Total language deprivation. Immersion in music. Mathematics. Some other experimental things. Surgery, maybe.

Winnie was signing over her Byron, much faster now. Tony's screen flashed with pink Cantonese characters.

Tony, Ada's blocked me from your conversation and I don't know what she's telling you.

Twenty percent? Tony typed to Winnie.

Winnie leaned back in her chair. She looked at Ada for several seconds before she began to sign again, this time more slowly.

I've met with the doctors doing the research. They've learned a lot about conversion since the last time you went in.

How many people have had this treatment? Tony typed.

It's experimental. Not a large-scale study.

How many?

It doesn't matter.

Five? Is that what a twenty-percent cure rate means?

Tony waited for an answer. His Byron remained blank.

He waited, then typed: *Ada said something about language deprivation.*

Winnie and Ada sat without moving.

In other words, Tony typed, *I won't have her translation engine. They would take it away. Wouldn't they?*

Winnie closed her eyes for a moment before she signed. *You won't need it.*

What if— Tony stopped, deleted, and tried again. *How do I tell someone if I want to stop the treatment and get out of the study?*

Why would you?

What if it doesn't work, Winnie?

Tony looked up at her. Winnie's hand stirred. *How long do you think Ada's translation engine is going to work?*

It works now, he typed.

What about a year from now? Winnie's hand was so low over her Byron screen her fingernails clicked on its surface. *Ada built it right when her conversion started, when she still spoke Cantonese. When it breaks down, who's going to fix it?*

Ada's green characters broke across Tony's screen. *Mom, I told you. I can maintain it. I've got all my notes.*

Winnie's forehead bowed slightly as she leaned toward Ada and signed with one finger.

On Tony's screen flashed in pink: *Let's see.*

Ada's hand swept over her Byron as she retrieved the comments in her programming code for the translation engine. She studied the first page. Tony could see Cantonese characters mixed with numbers and mathematical symbols.

After a moment Ada waved the notes away angrily with a flick of her fingers. They disappeared from her screen. She signed, *It doesn't matter. I can still read most of this.*

Winnie was looking up at Ada, not down at her screen, as she signed, *Really? Can you?*

Ada's eyes lowered. Tony could sense her body going rigid, as it did when she was a child and was about to explode into a tantrum. She was holding her breath.

Winnie, he typed.

The blue characters flickered as a string of numbers on Winnie's screen. She looked at him.

You still speak Cantonese.

Winnie's head tilted. *No, I don't.*

You did. In the kitchen, when you were cooking dinner.

When did I speak Cantonese?

When you cut yourself.

I screamed. Winnie signed with her right hand as she glanced at the fingers on her left, where her hand rested on the table next to her plate. The adhesive had sealed the cuts closed so that only two faint red lines were visible above her knuckles.

No. You didn't scream. You said a word.

I made a noise.

You spoke, Winnie.

Winnie sighed. She rubbed her temples with her left hand so that Tony couldn't see her eyes. *Tony. I'm sorry. I can imagine how badly you must want to hear someone talk. But you know I can't anymore. It hurt, and I made a noise. That's all.*

Tony wanted to type, *It wasn't a noise. It was a word.* His fingertips rested silently on the keyboard in his lap.

Winnie's fingernails touched her Byron screen.

Tony read in pink Cantonese: *The study, Tony. Please say yes. I don't know if we'll get another chance.*

This isn't a chance, he typed.

It's something. It's better than living the way we are now.

Is it?

I miss talking to you. Yes. It would be better than this.

For more than a minute, no one at the table moved.

Ada's hand dipped over her Byron. In pale green Tony read:

Mom. Tell Dad what happened to the other eighty percent.

There was no response.

Tony looked up. Winnie and Ada were locked in an unblinking stare.

He pushed his chair back and, setting his keyboard aside, stood up. He walked away from the table toward the bathroom.

Just before Tony closed the door, he glanced over his shoulder back at the table.

Winnie's hand was raised. It flashed through the air and slapped Ada's cheek.

The sound exploded inside Tony's head like shrapnel.

He slammed the bathroom door with such force that the walls of the apartment shook. The knob clicked as he locked it.

Tony turned on the light. In the vanity drawer was a pack of cigarettes. He opened the pack and lit one. Resting it on the edge of the sink, he opened the cabinet below and pushed aside bottles of shampoo, glass cleaner and bleach.

Behind the plastic bottles his fingers found the smooth glass surface of another.

Tony lifted out the bottle of whiskey. As he did, he heard something next to the bottle fall over with an unfamiliar thump. It sounded like cardboard, or paper.

He set the glass bottle down on the floor and reached to the back of the cabinet again. This time he touched a laminated surface with raised characters. It was the cover of a paperback book.

The book had been one of Winnie's from years ago. Humidity and age had warped the cheap paper into ruffles that would never lie flat again. The pages, foxed with mildew, stuck together. It was a romance novel, the kind that Tony had teased Winnie for reading. On the cover an almond-eyed woman in a tight silk dress, a Western depiction of a Chinese girl, was looking with demure fear at a man in a double-breasted suit ogling her. *Trouble in Mind*, the red-gilt stamped title blared in Cantonese and English.

Tony filled the toothpaste-smeared cup on the sink and took a large swallow of whiskey that brought tears to his eyes. Then another, and another. A dim memory of a warning about alcohol and drug interactions surfaced in the back of his mind. Tony drowned it with another gulp.

He opened the small bathroom window. The humidity of the June evening in Hong Kong billowed into the tiny, tiled room like steam from a shower.

Fists pounded on the bathroom door.

Tony ignored them.

He leaned out the window. Trains glided in and out of the tunnel to Hung Hom station, their windows gleaming like pearls in the falling light.

Above the train tracks and the spires of apartment buildings glowed the neon signs of Hong Kong's office towers. While no one could read the words on the signs anymore, the companies in the towers clung to their old-fashioned names. Letters had become a visual symbol of longevity. *Trust us*, each sign flashed. *We are old, strong, stable. We are words.* The blues, greens and reds flickered in the night sky like dying stars.

With his cigarette in one hand, Tony peeled the book open to the first page. The pounding on the bathroom door continued behind him.

He would tell Winnie and Ada that he would go into the hospital. *Twenty percent*, he said to himself, *are a hero's odds*. He imagined the relief and joy in Winnie's eyes when he told her. She and Ada would stop fighting. All of this would come to an end.

But, not yet. Not until he had finished the book.

Tony smoked, and read.

Eclipse

FENG SUN CHEN

He liked it better when the moon was not photographed. Now he had lost
his father. It seemed that each distant thing,
even the orbs that have long fizzled out
could be killed a second time, through a concavity. Bring it closer, ever
closer
and it shrinks and disappears.

Now he could turn into anything, anything to the full, except a man or a
woman
because he could not hide his tail.
On the day he tried to cut his tail off, the moon blotted out the sun,
there was the struggle
to describe the sliding out of that moment. Finally the sky had opened
and there were black fibers on the other side. The female entirety, filled
with
black and rimmed with renegade light. Behind the tear was sleep.

The ligaments were the hardest to cut, surprisingly
tougher than bone. Warmth left him and pale entered.
He held it in his hand. What had he hoped for? He chose this.
He chose for his blood
to run, to fall through a gliding eye, a black pupil
that would not stop gazing
in a moment that stilled, axed itself, turned backward
into the mind like a rolled eye.

The Rocket in the Sky

ANDREW MITCHELL

There is a rocket in the sky.

Perry Abbot is nine years old. He's playing Little League baseball at Turner Park, and here's this little rocket ripping across the sky like a needle on fire—"A meteor!" somebody shouts—only it's not a meteor, it's a rocket, and here it comes, a shard of shrapnel digging into the guts of the blue sky, and the color deepens into that yellow-orange-brown of a rotten pumpkin smashed on scorched asphalt, and a woman sipping root beer says, "What's happening?" and what's happening is this rocket will someday end the world.

Perry's parents sit and watch the game in blue-striped lawn chairs. They're drinking coffee, talking with other parents, clapping, cheering. Perry is at second base. He pounds his fist into the leather mitt, making it pop.

The sun is a burning white hole, and the dry heat makes the air shiver, the grass shimmer. Each individual leaf on each individual tree shines as if dipped in wax, as if every puzzle piece of green has been glossed, polished.

Perry crouches lower—his coach calls this the *athletic stance.* At home plate, the batter swings at a low pitch; the aluminum bat pings and the baseball hisses over Perry's head. The center-fielder, a redhead with early acne, lets the ball drop at his feet.

"Throw it in!" Perry screams. He pounds his fist into the mitt. *Pop. Pop.* The center-fielder does not move. The conversations of the spectators fade. Far off, a lawn mower buzzes. Perry scans the field and sees that the other players are also motionless. They're all looking at the sky. The batter is still at home plate. The umpire stands, too, with his black face mask at his hip like a gun.

The dog leashed to the chain-link fence is barking and barking and barking.

Perry sees the rocket in the sky. It is small—no bigger than a grain of rice pasted on blue paper.

He thinks: What's the big deal? Why is the little girl in the pink dress crying on the bleachers? Why is the old man with the brown-spotted face swaying on his heels? Why has everything stopped?

And now Perry's grandmother stands. Once, when she was fifteen, she saw the Devil smoke a cigarette in a black Studebaker. He'd been dressed in pressed Navy whites, and he leaned out of the window and said, "Hey there, sunshine!" His cigarette fell from his mouth, and when it struck the pavement it turned into a fat brown viper that slithered down a storm drain. Perry's grandmother hadn't told anybody because, really, how could she?

The sun glints on her glasses and turns the lenses into two coins of light. Perry shields his eyes with the mitt. Grandmother cups her mouth with twisted hands and shouts, "You're gonna die, Perry Abbot!" The other spectators nod but say nothing.

Perry has a headache now—a throbbing pain behind his eyeballs. Something whizzes past his face. From the dugout the coach yells, "Pay attention, Perry!" The batter runs. The first-base umpire shouts, "Safe!"

The dog stops barking and everybody sits down. They are laughing, talking. Everything has continued as if nothing stopped, so Perry spits out a mouthful of sunflower seeds and pops a fist into his mitt.

At seventeen years old, Perry stands in the woods behind his first girlfriend's house.

She says, "I can't wait any longer, Perry."

She has a Ziploc bag full of green grapes, and she peels the flesh from the fruit with her front teeth. She wears a V-neck blouse; the skin visible on her throat glistens. Perry leans against the trunk of a birch tree. He touches Ashley Gerenoma's face. His hand shakes.

Ashley steps closer. She unbuttons her blouse and hangs it on a branch. Perry grips the birch as Ashley undoes his jeans and pulls them off over his Nikes. It is an awkward maneuver. They both laugh. Still shaking, Perry moves forward, and his fingers work feverishly to unclasp Ashley's turquoise brassiere, and now they are just lying there. Her hot lips press against his neck; Perry's body tightens. He kisses Ashley's head. Her hair is all mangoes and coconut. Perry swallows great gulps of cinnamon breath. Beneath their bodies dead leaves crackle like static.

Perry slips inside of her and Ashley cries and smiles and says, "Oh Jesus."

But Perry does not hear her because he's listening to the roar of the rocket in the sky.

"It sounds like a train," says Ashley.

The earth trembles. Pebbles jump on the dirt. Ferns shudder. Leaves spin in the air like orange and red and brown flakes of confetti.

"It's closer," says Ashley. "The rocket."

"Yes," says Perry.

The roar softens. Clouds cover the sky like bloody gauze.

Perry rolls off of Ashley. They fall asleep and wake at dusk, covered in ants. They laugh, get dressed, and walk home.

After graduation, Perry has a party as his apartment. He's graduated from the University of New Hampshire with a Political Science degree. Someday, he hopes, he can go to law school—he never will.

It's Saturday. The sky is a gray and featureless movie screen. Still, it is hot. People mill around the backyard, talking and drinking beer. One man, somebody Perry only vaguely knows, has filled a graduation cap with ice and is using it to chill a beer.

"I'm gonna patent it!" he says. "Make a million *buckaroos*!"

For most people, the rocket in the sky is white noise; the sound is present but peripheral. Many have stopped listening entirely, though they know someday this rocket will explode. It is unavoidable. It sounds like a whirring hornet. The Air Force says it cannot find it. The radar is blank and the F-22's zoom through open space. Yet there it is, this rocket, a ghost haunting the world.

Perry stands at the grill and flips burgers and hot dogs. He presses the spatula on the beef patties, squeezing the grease from the meat so the flames hiss; this sound always makes him happy. He sips a Corona and listens to his friends say things like: "God, it's hard to believe college is over, isn't it?"

Or: "If you soak a slice of watermelon in vodka and then eat it, you won't taste the booze, but you'll get really smashed."

By the hydrangea bush, Perry's drunk mother talks loudly with an anonymous pregnant woman. Perry's father has not yet arrived—he's in Dover, stuck in traffic, because he's just gone to Big Ray's Used Auto to pick up the green Buick he purchased as Perry's graduation gift. It is a secret, but Perry is annoyed because his father is always late.

Through the haze of barbeque smoke, Perry studies Evelyn Baker. She sips a pink smoothie and chats with a cluster of girls from the Wildcats volleyball team. Perry isn't dating Evelyn yet, though they will be married in four years. At this party they're barely friends. She's dating Perry's freshman-year roommate, Mikey Ohrn. Mikey Ohrn is addicted to morphine. He's falling apart, collapsing, like a dark star. One day, when Evelyn eventually ends the relationship, Mikey will say, "The rocket in the sky is a spaceship from the future. Don't you get it, you silly bitch? We're trying to find ourselves!"

At this exact moment—during the graduation party—Perry's father has an aneurism as he turns the green Buick on to Church Street. The car smashes into a telephone pole; the wires snap and smack the street like crazed snakes spitting sparks. The wail of ambulance sirens scrapes the summer air, and, momentarily, the party is hushed. Nobody will admit it later, but many tacitly wonder if the rocket has finally detonated, and they look at Perry, dazed, as if he has called their attention, as if he has chimed his beer bottle with a fork and made a toast to the apocalypse.

The sirens fade. The party continues.

An hour later Perry sees his smiling mother answer the phone. She looks suddenly confused, like she's trying to decipher bad English. She staggers across the lawn and goes into Perry's apartment. Perry follows. When he reaches the front door he hears his mother shriek. It is an impossible sound—shrill, inhuman—like a drill grinding through aluminum. She's slouched against the refrigerator. She holds the phone an arm's length away, like a rat that has just tried to bite her.

She tells Perry what has happened. A neighbor saw the accident and called. Perry's mother called the hospital: Frank Abbot, dead on arrival. Just like that.

Perry remembers an old game he used to play with his father. When Mom was at work, Frank Abbot would drag the king-size mattress into the living room and cover it with pillows. Then he'd sit on the couch and toss the football, just out of reach, so that Perry would have to dive onto the mattress to make the catch.

Frank Abbot quoted Green Bay Packers coach, Vince Lombardi—"If you can touch it, you can catch it!"

This is what Perry thinks when his mother vomits on the kitchen floor. The radio crackles—*Come on down to Cam's Fish Shack. We've got the best fish n' chips you'll ever have!*

Perry stumbles outside. The screen door bangs on the frame. He walks down the street and is chased by the slurred voices of oblivious partiers. He looks up and watches the rocket dig its incandescent trench in the shapeless clouds. Soft rain falls. Perry sits on the curb. A Chinese boy draws on the pavement with chalk.

Perry is twenty-seven years old, and a coyote steals his golf ball at the Rattlesnake Mountain Country Club. It is Perry's best shot of the day, but the ragged canine scurries from the woods, snatches the ball in its jaws, and vanishes into the pines and maples like a phantom. The man trimming the fairway laughs so hard he has to turn the mower off.

Evelyn Baker's father, Desmond, grins and says, "That'll be a two stroke penalty."

Perry says, "Sir, I want to marry your daughter."

He doesn't know he will say such a thing until he actually says it. The words sound absurd, even inappropriate, like laughter in a cemetery. However, the sight of this mangy and emaciated coyote has struck Perry like a premonition, and he sits in the golf cart, breathless, while spiderwebs of white light revolve in his eyes.

"Can I marry your daughter?"

Desmond practically yells: "What? I can't hear you over that God damn rocket."

The rocket in the sky roars. The sound reminds Perry of baths—as a boy he'd lay in the tub of water while mother leaned over him and shampooed his hair. Perry would submerge his ears so that all he heard was that hard rush of water, that incessant dreamlike drone, and he'd feel sleepy, safe, his mother hovering like a mirage. She'd tell him knock-knock jokes, and her voice sounded so strange, so distant.

This is what the rocket in the sky sounds like to Perry: a bathtub filling with water.

He shouts, "Can I marry, Evy? I love her and want to marry her."

"What the hell you askin' me for?" says Desmond. "Go ask Evy!"

They both laugh. Desmond chews on the little scorecard pencil. He unzips his golf bag and pulls out a bottle of Jim Beam and two cigars wrapped in purple cellophane.

He says, "I knew you'd ask me someday, you slow son-of-a-bitch, and I thought I better be prepared."

"I don't like whiskey," says Perry, smiling.

"Well you won't like marriage, either," says Desmond. He pats Perry on the back.

On the seventh hole they smoke the cigars and drink burning gulps of whiskey straight from the bottle. They sit silently in the golf cart and watch the sun melt until Desmond says, "Let's skip golf and go order a pizza."

Thanksgiving.

Perry sits at the table with Evy and his white-haired mother. The phone rings. It's his half brother, Eric, the accidental offspring of this old widow. Eric is stationed at Fort Leonard Wood, Missouri—"Misery!" he calls it—and in two years he'll be shot and killed in Afghanistan by his own traitorous translator. At this moment, however, he's eating turkey with other Marines.

He says, "Perry, how the hell are ya?"

Perry says he's great. He despises small talk but manages: "Yes, work is fine and real-estate is finally booming again...Evy's doing well . . . Don't worry, she made the turkey . . . Love you too, Eric."

Perry gives the phone to his mother, but she cannot remember how to use it because Alzheimer's is picking her brain apart like a vulture. She holds the phone away from her face and grimaces.

Perry thinks of the younger and prettier woman slouched against the refrigerator in his old apartment. In this blurry past, his mother sobs while the radio hums in the window. Partiers roam around the lawn and eat hamburgers and drink beer. These people are ghosts now. They're simply haunts clattering around in an old corroded memory. Every second that passes creates an entire world of people who no longer exist—people who dwell only as shadows of that previous moment. No meat, no bones. Their bodies plow onward, leaving slime-trails like slugs. It is a realization that makes him dizzy. Claustrophobic.

"Perry, hon," says Evy. She bites her lip. "Your brother is still on the phone."

Perry puts the phone to his ear, steadies his voice, and says, "Sorry, Eric, but Mom is having a tough time right now."

A pause.

Eric says, "Okay brother. Well, happy Turkey Day to you. I'll talk with you all again real soon," and hangs up before Perry can respond.

The plates rattle on the table as the rocket tears over the house. Evy cuts a pearl onion in half with her fork but does not eat it. She brings her plate to the kitchen, washes it in the sink. From the window she watches a galaxy of dust float in the soft sunshine.

Perry clears his throat in the dining room. It is the sound Evy will inexplicably hear years later, right before the rocket in the sky ends the world—though by then she'll be in love with a different man.

Perry stares at his blank-eyed mother. She pulls a strip of turkey apart with greasy fingers. She's lost. Perry envisions her crouched at the bottom of a dark well. She is looking up the shaft, at the circle of light above—the sky—and Perry wants to lean over the edge and say something comforting—a joke, maybe—but all he mutters is, "Would you like some more cranberry sauce, Mom?"

The bar is nearly empty—Fisky's is never empty on a Friday night. A dark-skinned woman with peroxide-bleached hair shoots pool under the glare of a neon Budweiser sign. She wears red high heels. Perry sits at the bar and observes her chalk a stick.

The bartender puts a plate of nachos in front of Perry and says, "The rocket is going to hit soon. Can you believe that? All these years and it's finally going to hit. Ka-*boom*."

"That's wild," says Perry flatly. He pops a jalapeño in his mouth.

As if to offer proof, the bartender turns on the television bolted to the wall. *Any day now*, the news anchors say. *Any day now the rocket in the sky will strike.* The broadcast shows images of overflowing churches and mosques and synagogues, parades and festivals, fireworks, closed shops with boarded windows, vacant city streets, sunrises, sunsets.

"Turn on the Sox game," says Perry. "They're playing tonight, right?"

The bartender laughs. "Boston is empty, chief. The Sox are done. The players are with their families. Where's your family?"

Evy has left me, Perry wants to say. She's remarried a dentist in Massachusetts. He's a great guy, I've heard. He bought her a purebred Dalmatian. Evy always wanted a Dalmatian. You know, Mr. Bartender, every thought I have stings and stings. *Hornets.* I can't sleep. This rocket keeps me awake.

Perry wants to tell the bartender all of this.

Instead he says, "Where's your family?"

"Home," says the fat bartender. He folds a napkin into a triangle. Behind him bottles of liquor shake and fall and shatter. The cooks laugh in the kitchen. Where are their families? Why have they come on a Friday night to sweat over dirty ovens while the end of things roars so inexorably in the sky?

The lights flicker and go out.

"Goodnight," says Perry. He reaches for his wallet.

"On the house," says the bartender. He looks like he may cry.

"Thanks," says Perry, "and good luck."

He goes out into the rainy July night.

The bleach-haired woman who'd been shooting pool follows Perry and asks for a ride home. In the car she says she's Puerto Rican.

"My name is Yamile," she says.

"Pretty name," says Perry.

Yamile talks about her father. She says he sold tangerines and strawberries and sometimes zucchinis on a street corner in Brooklyn. He sold them out of a wooden crate.

She says he used to take the entire family—four children, a wife—to the Korean grocery store on North Dedalus Street. He'd push a cart along the aisles and pretend to shop while the family ate the food. Then he'd abandon the cart and everyone would go home with heavy stomachs. The Koreans never caught on, Yamile explains, because they packaged heroin in a back room.

"Where was home for you?" asks Perry. He merges onto the highway. Lightning bursts in a canyon of purple clouds. The wipers toss fans of rain from the windshield.

"The basement of a movie theater," says Yamile, applying lipstick in the dark. "The owner charged no rent as long as Mama slept in his bed on Saturday nights. We put mattresses on the concrete floor. There were rats in that basement. Big as dogs. Bigger. When Papa saw a rat he'd say, 'Get me a saddle!'" Yamile smiles. She rolls down the window and tosses her red heels outside.

"That's how big they were," she whispers, "big as dogs."

Perry brings her to his apartment. They sit on the kitchen counter and talk until four in the morning. They drink a bottle of wine and eat spoonfuls of peanut butter straight from the jar. They sleep in Perry's big bed.

He wakes up once, sweaty and disoriented, and thinks fleetingly that Yamile is actually Evy, that he has drifted into his old life again.

Perry decides to drive cross-country with Yamile. They're in New York. They stay in an abandoned hotel with marble floors and gilded ceilings. There is a fountain in the lobby: an angel spits an arc of rose-colored water. Goldfish dart in the green pool like flakes of sunlight.

Perry and Yamile take the penthouse suite. They throw the flat-screen television over the balcony and watch it crash on the street below. They chain-smoke and make love.

It is morning and Yamile is gone.

Perry waits. He stays in the penthouse for another night.

Alone, he continues west.

Empty streets.

The storefront windows are boarded with plywood. A plastic grocery bag scrapes over the sidewalk. It's Wednesday.

In less than an hour, the rocket in the sky will explode.

Perry Abbot walks with his head down. He kicks a chunk of asphalt along the road for nearly a mile until it rattles down a storm drain and splashes in the dirty water below the city. He's in Portland, Oregon.

He has come to watch the rocket crash over the Pacific Ocean. There is supposed to be a big festival in Lincoln City. Thousands of people have flocked to the beach for one last party before the end of things. There are bands playing on the boardwalk—trumpets and drums and bagpipes. Kites slap the sky. Children splash in the icy ocean. The rocket is low and loud and dragging a tail of fire. The sky looks like raw meat. Blood, guts.

But people are happy. It's beautiful. It's the end.

Perry will not make it to this festival. He wanders through the deserted city. He pulls his pockets inside-out so that all of his change clatters on the pavement. A dog barks in the distance. Perry wonders if it might possibly be Evy's Dalmatian. He even says, "Hell, wouldn't that be something?"

There is a café on the street corner that is not boarded. A little bell jingles over the door. The room has already gathered dust; spiderwebs hang from the ceiling. The air in the room is heavy and acidic, like vomit, though Perry knows it's just the month-old stink of coffee.

He takes a bottle of water from the cooler and a moldy croissant from a glass display case. He goes outside, climbs on top of a taxicab, sits, and eats. Windows shatter on the skyscrapers; glass tinkles on the ground like errant notes.

Perry says, "If you can touch it, you can catch it."

Far off, a dog is barking and barking and barking at all of the ghosts.

Teaching a Post Lunar World

CAITLIN THOMSON

I had to draw a picture of the moon
for my children, charcoal etched on stone.

My failure to describe stars an ongoing one.
The many Suns of night? Lanterns so far away
they appear to be fireflies? Bright holes?

My eldest asks, *How could you sleep?*
How did they stay up?

To draw one would only confuse them further.
Even the moon, an absent touchstone for me,
is to them a myth. *A bright gravity defying rock?*

My daughter traces the outline,
comes away with black fingers.

Dearest
Dirty

Written by
Tina Hyland

Illustrated by
Gavin Faherty

Once upon a filthy time in a muddy world there lived a dirty girl. And she was so alone.

She gazed outside her dusty window and watched the smokestacks most days. She counted the birds falling from the sky.

Even the smokiest days couldn't please her.

She wrote letters to people she wanted to know, ones who didn't exist. She wrote them letters so full of her soul and tore them into tiny scraps. Then she threw them out the window and watched the breeze carry each piece away. It was her only small joy.

The dirty girl wanted so much to be in love. She wanted to take picnics on the waste and wiggle her toes in the silt. She wanted to stare up into the billowy smoke and find all the shapes and creatures inside. She wanted to count up every dead bird on the plain and steal their feathers.

But this was no fun all alone.

She wrote a letter to a man who never was, about times that never were. She thanked him for each wonderful moment they never had, and then she tore the letter into bits and pieces and threw them out the window.

In the gloomy morning, there was a mound of paper scraps on the window sill. The handwriting was not her own.

She carried the scraps to the floor and puzzled them together. Each bit was so tiny and so expertly torn.

Dearest Dirty Darling,

I also loved counting the dead birds on the waste. The way your hair tangles in the breeze fills me with such overwhelming love. When you stand against the haze, my heart beats so loudly I'm sure you must hear it. Let it be a drum for us to dance by.

With you, I am finally complete.

Love Always,
Companion

The dirty girl read the letter again and again. She taped it together carefully and pinned it to her wall. She paced back and forth and she wondered, *What is this?*

When she was done wondering, she sat at her desk and wrote a letter of her own.

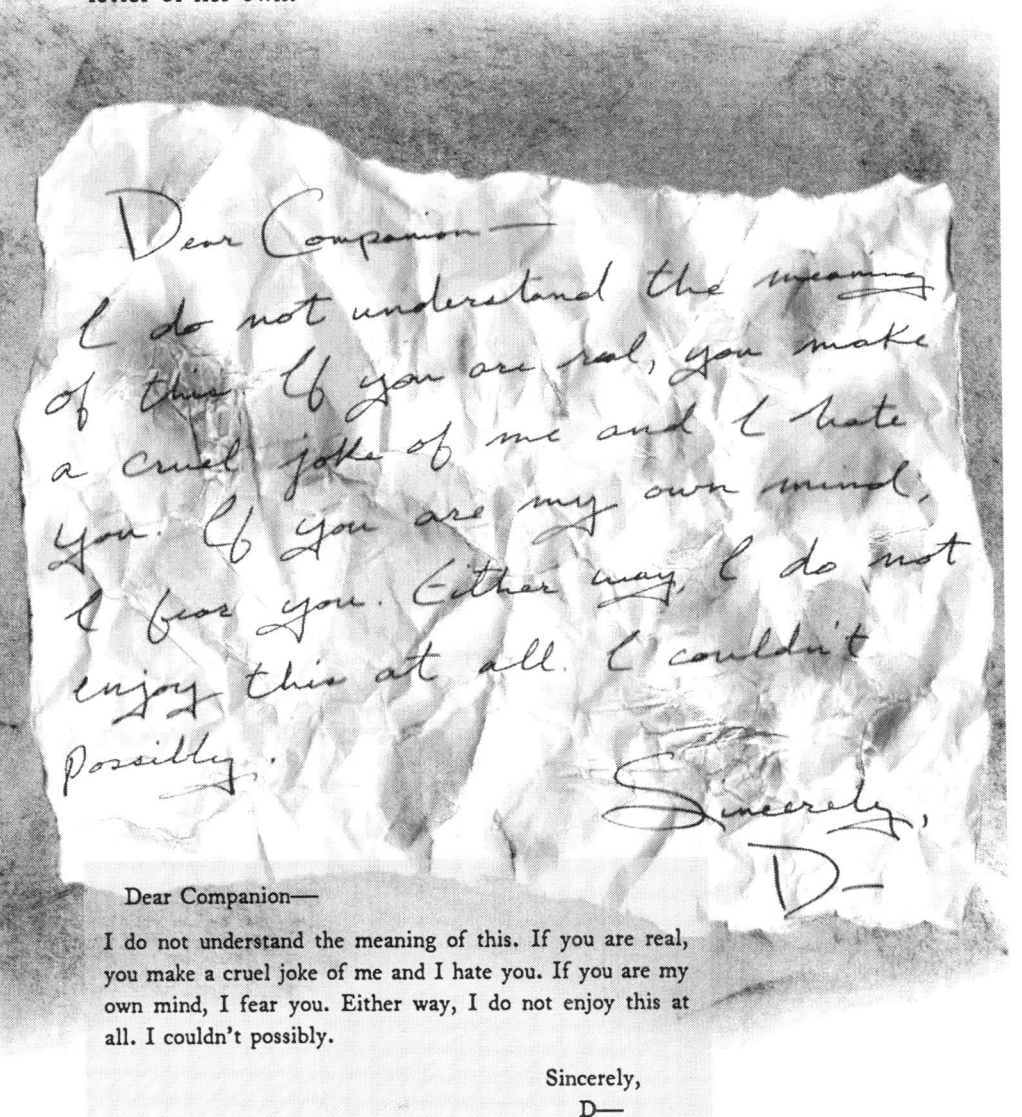

Dear Companion—

I do not understand the meaning of this. If you are real, you make a cruel joke of me and I hate you. If you are my own mind, I fear you. Either way, I do not enjoy this at all. I couldn't possibly.

Sincerely,
D—

She tore it up and threw it out the window. Then, she waited.

She sat up in her bed and watched. She gripped the blankets until her knuckles were white and her fingers cramped. She stared and stared at the window until her eyes ached to close.

In the morning, there was another mound of paper scraps on the sill. She wanted to throw them out the window, but she couldn't. She pieced them together.

Dearest Dirty Darling,

   I do not eat. I do not sleep. You think I am cruel, and I can't understand what has changed. If you tell me to never write you again, I will cut off my own hand to save you from offense. You do not believe I am your Companion, so I will sign with my tears.

The dirty girl taped the letter and touched her finger across the Braille of dried tears. She thought a long time about what it could mean. When she was through with that, she wrote another letter and tore it to bits.

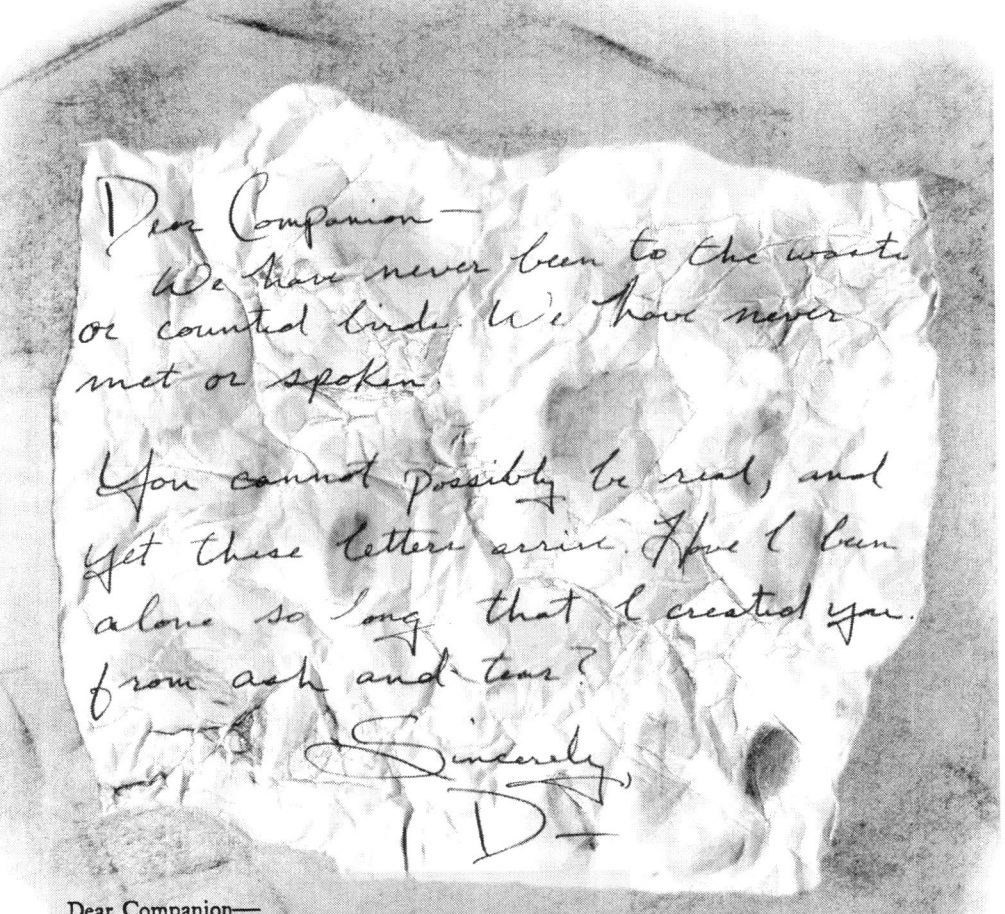

Dear Companion—

We have never been to the waste or counted birds. We have never met or spoken.

You cannot possibly be real, and yet these letters arrive. Have I been alone so long that I created you from ash and tear?

Sincerely,
D—

She tied twine across the room and laced it all with little bells until she had woven a jingly cobweb, impossible to pass through in her sleep. If these letters came by her own sleepwalking hand, she would soon know it.

In the morning, the strings were still in place and another mound of scraps was piled neatly on the sill. She jumped over the strings and bells and hurried to piece it together.

Dearest Dirty Darling,

I am as real as any man can be. Meet me under the smokestacks at sunset.

Love always,
Companion

The dirty girl paced the length of her room and thought. She tried all her pretty dresses in the mirror and threw them in heaps on the floor. She dabbed lipstick on, wiped lipstick off. She put her hair up and pulled her hair down. When sunset came, she looked just as herself, and she went to meet her Companion.

The brown grass crunched under her heels. The dying birds swooped and fell from the sky, and the hot coal wind pushed her on. Smoke poured from the stacks and writhed as much as her stomach and hands below.

When she arrived, there was no one to meet her. She looked over her shoulder and behind smokestacks. She twisted her hair and tapped her toes. She counted minutes and birds, and when she was sure she was alone, she noticed a ball of old twine propped against a stone.

The stone was sharp and gray and ordinary, but the twine was crisp and yellow against the sooty ground. She used the stone to cut a length of twine and carried it home.

In her room, she wrote a letter.

Dear Companion,

Those days on the waste were among the best of my life. Counting birds with you, dangling our toes in the salt, finding the hidden shapes in smoke. Do you remember when you saw a flower up there, and you reached as if to give it for me? When you tucked that wisp of smoke behind my ear? I have pressed those moments to my heart.

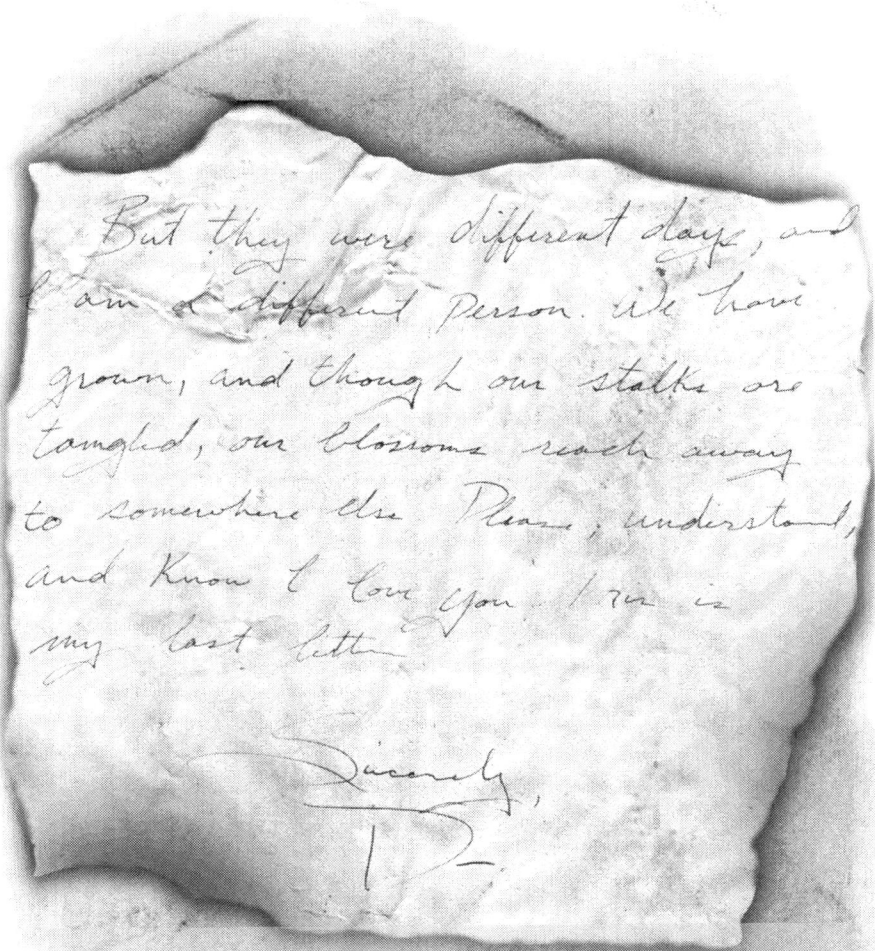

Dear Companion,

Those days on the waste were among the best of my life. Counting birds with you, dangling our toes in the silt, finding the hidden shapes in smoke. Do you remember when you saw a flower up there, and you reached as if to grab it for me? When you tucked that wisp of smoke behind my ear? I have pressed those moments to my heart.

But they were different days, and I am a different person. We have grown, and though our stalks are tangled, our blossoms reach away to somewhere else. Please, understand, and know I love you. This is my last letter.

Sincerely,
D—

The dirty girl tore the letter to pieces and threw them outside. She took the length of twine and wrapped it around her fingers. Then she closed her window tight.

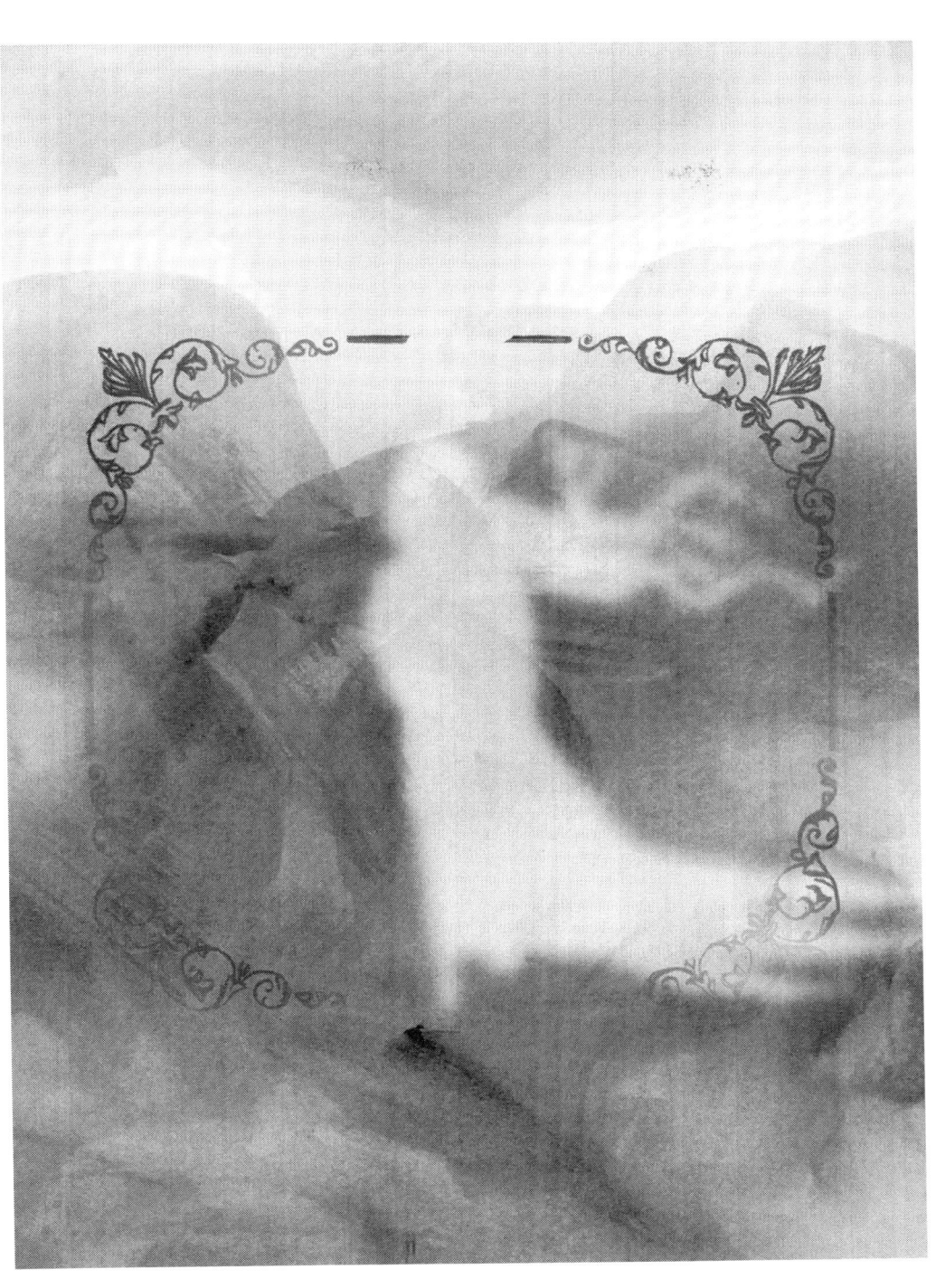

Dig

MARGARET BASHAAR

She catches her ankle on rusted out holes
in streetcar steps, impotent
for all of a day now.
Before she wraps her feet in onionskin,
she sucks mud
from her toes, rips the flesh
off them with her teeth.

Fingers slide through her ribcage,
cold, and she ties her hair to her wrists
with sailor's knots each night, and in the morning
she cuts earthworms into eighths,
drops them into buckets of water and
swears each part can grow whole
if she looks away long enough and makes a wish
on each writhing piece.

Still she sinks through painted red floorboards,
too thin at the elbows and too thick
at the heels for baby's breath.
Ground untouched for days and boxes of shoes
tumbling out of her closet like stones,
she cuts herself off at the ankles,
leaves her feet on hotel doorsteps
among empty beer cans and the smell of blood,
breathes in the weight of her feet and walks
like they are still there.

Popper's Choice

ROBERT EDWARD SULLIVAN

The trick is to clearly mark all the vits and don't pop too close or too far away. And small caliber, of course. But it's gotta pierce. It takes courage to get popped by a friend, more to pull the trig. True, the last thing anyone wants is to be hooked up to some machine, gargling through a tube, but it's just as bad if you're the one that puts a listmate in that spot. They do sell those cheapo ponchos with all the vits clearly marked—poorly rendered kidneys, cartoonish hearts, pale pink duodenums—but no one uses those.

You're *finally* going to pop, Ackley says.

Can I keep the gun? you say.

Sure, got two bullets left, only need one, syours, he says.

Ackley was in charge of this mess, for the most part. Only because he'd been popped twice, and was on the giving end at least once before. And now he doesn't want his only two listmates to be froshes. One who hasn't been popped—Dev, and one who hasn't done any popping—You. So now you're holding the gun and Dev is getting his vits all marked. Clearly marked. Dev keeps tabbing between looking tough and looking scared.

You have been popped before, of course, in the stump end. That's why they call you fivethree-fiveone. Too much limp. Too much bounce, you say. But you've never told anyone it was an accident by your seph, who didn't know the gun was forserious loaded. You don't tell anyone about the look he had when he saw all that blood. Sorry this. Sorry that. He didn't mean to, of course, but you're forcertain he was extra scared because, moments prior, he had the gun up to your gray matter and was pretending to pop you there. And of course that ugly makes you think about that day when he Declared military, and he told you to find a way to get the fuck out. Don't know exactly what he meant. But it's there. In your head. In a little corner.

Anyways.

Use tape.

Whitetape.

The super stitched, cloth-like kind you can rip off with your chomps. Ackley is still taping up Dev. He's got a chart out and everything. It's popper's choice. You're going shoulder, but still want make sure everything is marked. Don't bodge it up, Ackley says.

The sun is still perching strong, trying to get through all that gray. You're leaking, but not because it's balls hot out. Because of other things. Things on loop.

That big ol rumble between your rents this morning keeps refreshing. Just one more ugly. Your ma got her weeps on when your pa slugged her. Whole side of her face. They're always going on. This, that, and all that other, but he's never slugged her before. Now you don't even have a memory of your ma without that thinking about this morning. That sound.

Besides that, there's your sis giving you those med eyes all the time—and you, thinking about before she got popped in a vit, when she used to meet you after school every day with a hug and some sweets.

Besides that you turn twelvsies soon and have to Declare, like forserious capital D, Declare.

Besides all that, what you really don't like is the goodies are getting muddy now. No amount of meds will change that. You stopped taking them, anyway.

Dev is all taped up. Ackley keeps running his hand through his hair and is all, okay pop when you're ready, but do it today, Thirdo. Dev is waiting.

You wish you weren't in this back alley, behind this shed that smells like fuel. You wish you were outside of the city, in some field, standing in the middle, alone.

So what you can do what you're going to do.

Pop yourself in your own vits, the big one. Put this gun up to your head and pull the trig solid. It's the only reason you agreed to pop Dev, to get the gun and that last bullet.

They say if you pop just right or just left, you can see all that gray matter—all those uglies, all that shit you don't want in there, will spray out in a glorious red burst, before you fall, before you die.

The little ones and the big ones. The time Judytwo laughed when you said she was cute; that day you fell in the shit ditch; the time you lost all your listmates when you moved; all those nights you went to bed so hungry your stomach barked; that monotone moan of your sister when she asks who are you; that look on your brother's face when he shot your foot; that horrible sound of your father's open hand connecting with all of your mother's cheek—that sharp inhale of her breath when it did; and most of all, that sneaking suspicion that just one more thing is the last thing. And it will never get better, and maybe you do know what it means to get the fuck out.

Your wish, after the bullet pierces, is for all that gray matter, those details, all those uglies, to become like dandelion seeds when they get puffy and get caught in a summer wind and float away.

the gun game

from Kate Jury Denton Texas

COLIN WINNETTE & BENJAMIN CLARK

We decide to play the gun game, so you load the guns. We head out back where the grass is taller and we slip out of our shoes. We aim the guns at the highest point we think we can see. *Bang* you say, and I'm bleeding. The neighbors eventually gather in a circle. They look like a route we may have taken through the woods. They want to know the rules of the gun game. This is one of those times I should have changed the subject. You have a pet frog. I should have said something about the pet frog. On the other hand, I admire how confidently you speak in large groups. *It's a serious game* you tell them. *There are consequences. The rules are always changing* I add. *So they're hard to keep track of. And while I lost, I still think the fun might be in trying to keep track.* Then you break my wrist. And when the neighbors gasp, you confidently explain *it should go without saying: there's no equivocating in the gun game.*

Transaction

REDFERN BARRETT

S he was born nine years ago.
    That means nothing. She has a nine year old torso with nine year old arms and nine year old legs.

That also means nothing. Different agents are attracted now than will be attracted when she ages. That is all. Different penises, different fumbling fingers, different bursts of rank breath over her face. She hopes she will earn more as she gets older.

She longs to age.

Crusty chipped nails scratch from her collarbone, sending a scream of pain over her shoulder.   +4.52

So she grins.

She was born nine years ago to the day. She doesn't know it: where was the profit in tracking days? Profit is made moment to moment; transaction to transaction. The world works in never-ending seconds. Things fluctuate but nothing will change. No day differs to any other.

He shoves the stub of his cock between her knees, wiggling like a trapped animal.   +5.29

That tickles +1.37

she giggles.

It doesn't tickle, not at all—there's nothing to laugh at. He likes it though: the numbers increase. In this transaction she is innocent, unknowing, unreal. Anyone really like that would have plunged into debt long ago.

She pulls away, a mock protest they both know is fake but which excites him, excites him enough to push her down onto the cold blue bench,   +2.33
pull at her hair,   +3.53
bite her shoulder,   +4.19
hard,   +6.58
push his penis into her, pounding,   +9.32
over   +7.74
        and over   +7.75
                and over.   +7.57

He gives a heaving grunt,　　　　　　　+8.22
　　　　　　　　　　　one last burst,　+9.81
then pulls himself free. She is irritated: she knows she could have gained more from him. She's worked too quickly, the innocence too strong, the allure too thick.

　　　　　　　　　　Are you all right, mister?　−0.54

He sneers at her: he is bored with her. No further transactions will be in her favor. She pulls the thin pink dress up over her head, wipes herself, winces at the cold, opens her bag and rolls the dress in. She pulls out her walking clothes. He walks away.

This is everything; there is nothing else. There is no law but the law of transaction. All interaction is transaction.

It is night in Nowkown. No one has watched them: there has been no extra profit from adventurous eyes. Agents pass by the blue metal bench, none of them seeing or stopping. Nowkown is busy: a bright rush of advertisements, food stenches, voices and bodies stumbling over cracked paving. Wispy trees burst with new leaves, though just five streets away the leaves are brown and elsewhere there are blossoms. The buildings above climb high with rickety extensions, extensions that so often creak and crumble and collapse onto the street below—a shower of wood and chipboard and broken bricks.

　　A man is shouting jokes at the flow of bodies, earning small amounts from unwary ears.　　　　　　−1.13
　　She smells hot dogs and feels her stomach rumble.　−0.38
　　　　The real-time price of a smell.
　　She hears piped music she likes.　　　　　　−0.54
　　She walks along the street, keeping her eyes on the　+0.12
advertisements. She could weave her body in and out of the　+0.11
others without even looking. The advertisements offset　+0.23
inadvertent expenditures.　　　　　　　　　　+0.01

　　She doesn't understand that one; it has too many letters. Who needs letters? Numbers are important.
　　Numbers follow you.
　　It starts to rain globs of sandy water. Her hair is getting wet so she rips an umbrella from the fingers of an agent　−13.56
with graying hair. It will be worth the cost: if she is soaking she will be of little value. Her second problem: her mouth is dry: a dry mouth will lower her market potential. A drink

will be fiscally beneficial, so long as she has a budget one. They aren't as safe, but it will be the most cost-effective. The can rolls out the vending machine as she approaches.   −12.95
She winces.

The woman with the lop-sided grin is standing by the vending machine.
A lopsided grin is a consistent net loss:
smiles are important, they carry the face.

    She might be unattractive, but the woman with the lop-sided grin has a faster mind and is better informed: she is always the one to gain from any transaction between them. She is to be avoided.

    The woman with the lopsided grin is waiting for her, so the agent with nine years leaves.

Wait   +0.37

the lopsided woman calls. She wants something.

What do you want? −0.31

I just want to talk to you. Are you aware the city is getting smaller?   −2.86
It is. The population is decreasing. I know how to turn you a profit.   −2.11

The girl with nine years runs—runs away from the woman with the lopsided grin—over a street littered with the skeletons of unclaimed cars and bikes—through a patch of scrubland where bushes glisten through brickwork.
Conversations with her are expensive.
Perhaps that is why she always starts them.

    But why? There are other agents in the city, agents with less intellectual marketability than her. Unsavvy agents barely taller than the knee can sometimes be taken in, led around, fed expensive lectures until their debt burden becomes too great.

    The woman with the lopsided grin is gone. A pair of sparrows flutters overhead.

There is a bar eight blocks away, a bar with the potential for profit. By the time she reaches the shattered double doors her foot is cramping, but she hides it beneath a neutral smile. She takes a deep breath in through her nostrils and pushes her way inside.

The bar is thick with an acrid brown smoke which curls under fluorescent lighting. It is cold. Stained satin sheets in gray-reds and gray-greens hang from the walls, stretches of crusty cream tiling visible between them. The tables are made from old doors, decked in green and blue lights advertising this or that alcohol, solvents, chemicals, spices, herbs. In the corner squats a machine boasting a variety of needles. Aside from some mechanical clucking, the bar is silent.

Twelve agents sitting at twelve tables.

> Seven of the agents are not in a state of sexual pre-arousal.

>> Two are, but they wouldn't have the stamina to make any transaction worthwhile.

> Of the remaining three, one is not aroused by agents as young as she.

She makes her way over to the first of the final two, who glances up at her from his table. His tatty sweater is +0.29 sewn with fraying flowers, his lank hair awkwardly limp over his forehead. She knows she is worth more than him, but she also knows he won't enjoy himself, and so there will be little profit.

She walks on.

The last agent uncurls a piece of foil and presses his nostrils into it. He leans back in his chair.

She walks to the far edge of the bar, pushes aside a satin curtain and steps into a dark little room which reeks of shit. She opens her small lycra-lined bag and examines her three tightly-rolled dresses: lurid pink, sultry red, and glossy gold.

When she has spotted the right agent she has to choose the right dress.

Red. Red is self-explanatory. Red as rushing blood, as blushed faces, as grunting profit. She wears red when they want her to take control, when they want her to seduce them, her to lower her eyelids at them and give them her predatory stare. Digits guided her, numerical training for her seduction.

Pink. Pink is simply light red. The same coursing blood, the same hot lumbering fingers, but with a little white added. Innocence. Purity. High marketability. Wide eyes are right this time, wide innocent eyes, scanning the scene for wealth potential. They are roughest with her body when she wears pink. When she wears pink she earns the most. She will have to change these tactics as she ages. She wants to age.

Gold. She never wears gold to look rich, she wears gold to look desperate. This is her third act, her third form of exchange: poor, clueless, desperate, cheap. Many agents want that. She also knows that at one point gold had symbolized value, that gold equaled wealth, but the past is unprofitable. The world fluctuates. Secure one minute, fragile the next; agent one minute, commodity the next.

She pulls off her trousers and shirt, then rolls them inside.

She takes out her red dress and pulls it on over her head.

There is no mirror and no light to see by, so she models her hair by touch, smoothing and curling and splaying using her fingers and her small pot of gel. She paces her breathing because breathing is important—shallow breaths are only suitable for gold-dress conversations. She closes her bag and steps back among the tables.

Twelve agents sit at twelve tables. She has her agent.

She sits down opposite him. His head is rocked back,   −0.11
his eyes are closed, his hands are trembling. For a few
seconds she is aware of the price of the chair she is perched   −0.11
upon. She examines him.   −0.12

He is young, not as young as she, average weight, average height, hairline receded slightly, eyes a little sunken, lips cracked, a scratch of beard etched onto the jawline, the jawline strong, neck long, clothes not-too-new, not-too-old, wrists hairy, hands rough, nails bitten.

She is wearing her red dress, so simply issues a short firm cough: I am here, pay attention.

                                                  Ah-hem.   +0.38

His neck snaps forward, his eyes red-tired, his pupils   +0.49
large and dark; he's on the verge of desire, but he wants to
be seduced; he wants the red dress. She is right, as always;
she is fiscally astute.

She has his attention but she will have to work to keep
it. She leans forward, exposing the gap between dress and   +0.87
flesh, a gap where her bust would be. The man peers down   +0.86
into the darkening skin.

                  She lowers her voice to a whisper.

        Do you like what you see? Because I do.   +0.59

He nods, a long slow nod, his head rising and falling, his eyes meeting hers. He blinks several times. She laughs and says

I like your company. +0.67

She grasps the tips of his fingers and brings them to her +1.32
neck. She shudders, her skin pimpling. The enjoyment is all
his. She lowers his hand, bringing it down inside the line of
her dress, +1.28
he leans in toward her, +1.98
his breath on her face, +1.29
his lips on her cheek, +1.81
her mouth. +2.32

Someone is watching. +0.55
His fingers prod unknowing at the bruise where the
blue bench man has bitten her,
a jolt of pain +3.91
and she angles her arching shoulder, pressing the bruise to +4.28
his fingers.

That feels good baby +0.93

she growls.
He grips her hand and leads her to the back room. She
would rather do it on the tables where other agents can see,
where she might earn more, but he leads her away. Whilst
walking he gropes her buttocks. Clumsy. +1.66
Once inside she pulls down her dress. The agent
scrapes at her face with his beard, his movements slow,
heavy, she realizes she's miscalculated, as he mumbles,
he's too drugged for this transaction, as he slumps to his
knees, his side, his head on the floor with a long groan.
Desperately she pokes her head through the curtain, but
the lank-haired agent with the fraying flowers is gone. She
bends to shake the sleeping agent. Nothing.
She pulls off the dress and takes antiseptic solution
from her bag, sloshes it over herself, the sting bringing
tears, a torrent of them, fierce tears as it burns over her,
tears without profit, without purpose. She will grow out of
them, when she ages.
She sees something. Blurry.
Someone? There is someone in the corner of the

room.

Her heart-rate quickens.

He isn't moving. Why?

He is a huge soft toy frog, propped against the wall.

Her heart-rate slows. Her heart would be worth a great deal.

Despite herself she walks over to the frog. She brushes her face and runs her hand along the soft lining of the toy. He looks at her through plastic eyes. There is no cost. Whichever agent had owned it is no longer an agent. She will hold on to it. Just for now. Just until its value has risen sufficiently. She wraps her arms around it. Just to check the fur. The fur is soft. She names it.

It is hers.

Everything is calculated in real-time. What is worth something in one moment will be worth something else in another, depending on trillions of transactions amongst billions of agents. Competent agents will be able to predict certain trends in the value of a given commodity. There is wealth potential.

Above Prenzee the sun beams. There is a tall man with a long blond mustache who angles his face upwards, catching the light on his eyelids. His golden eyelashes shine. It is pleasant. The breeze brushes his cheeks. He hears the rush of the street below.

He is standing on a ledge, the ledge outside his apartment. If he pulls the window open wide enough—if he squeezes his body through, right arm first—he can get out onto the ledge. The ledge is a little wider than his shoes.

He waits. Now and then an agent will stop. They will stop to take something or fuck or shit. None of them stop near his ledge.

The sun is gone behind a mass of clouds. The clouds grow greyer.

The man with the blond mustache needs to piss. He contemplates pissing from the ledge, but then the street below the ledge will be splashed with urine, and no one will stop there.

He laughs. He hauls himself back in through the window and pisses in the toilet. He will empty the toilet later, out back. He takes care not to spill urine on the carpet, real carpet, then squeezes himself back through the window. Back onto the ledge.

There are now more agents on the street below. One of them looks up and sees him as she passes. He gains. He is +3.42 entertainment, up there on the ledge. A man in an unlikely place. He contemplates dancing and making more: a dancing man in an unlikely place. He could take his clothes off: the dancing naked man up there on the ledge. But then he would be too visible. His plan would be ruined. He knows better means of profit.

The tall man with the long blond mustache who contemplated dancing naked on the ledge is in very little debt. His debt is marginal, in fact. He likely has the lowest debt in all the city.

He trades things. He always had a good eye for profit, ever since being born. To him it was so simple: take an item, take it somewhere else where it was worth more, then hand it over to someone. When his body was small he would trade toothbrushes and soft drinks. When his body got larger he traded good chairs, or curtains. By the time he reached his current height he had mastered this skill, the most useful skill in all the world.

He could trade a stone for a handsome profit if he wanted.

There: there below. An agent has stopped. Early twenties, dark hair. She has stopped and is saying something to another agent, who also stops.

It is time.

He has piled bricks up on the ledge in neat stacks. Three even columns. The agent is standing directly underneath them.

He shouts. She looks upwards. +0.51

He pushes the first stack of bricks from the ledge.

She throws up her arms. The bricks—large bricks— snap her arm, cut her cheek, crush her shoulder. She screams.

He loses. −1`85.98

A number of agents glance at her as they walk by.

She gains. +26.33

She is entertainment. +24.81

He giggles: she has probably never earned so much in her life. She still screams.

He pushes the second stack of bricks off the ledge. Her head crumples. Her body collapses beneath it. He loses. -1`15`56.97

The man with the blond mustache groans. She was barely worth anything; he thought he would be charged more. This particular form of entertainment was more rewarding if the agent was worth more: gaining the money back would be a challenge.

Across the city a number of agents are credited. One was a woman she had regular sex with. A few are individuals she provided with her own special chemicals: they were said to bring you out of your body for three whole days—a rumor worth . . .   +2.54

Her numbers vanish.

Below agents swarm around the pulpy remains; the first take blood-soaked clothes, the later load pieces into cool-boxes.

He glances at the last stack of bricks and squeezes himself back through the window. He has things to trade.

He will trade stones.

This is everything. There are only two things in all of existence. There are agents and there are commodities. What is not one is the other.

There's a stub at Alexplace: a stub that was once a tower. There's a huge shattered ball at Alexplace: the ball used to be on top of the tower. Inside the ball it smells. It smells like things crawl inside the ball to die. The girl with nine years has never looked inside. Curiosity is a luxury.

There are tents around the stub, anchored to patches of bare earth where the concrete has worn away. The stub is colorful,   −3.52

it looks interesting. There are letters all over it in reds and purples and greens, letters and words that make no sense: gods and government. There is nothing really like it, not in the whole city—defacing someone's property is expensive.

The crowd flows in all directions.

A single beat and the movement shifts.

The bodies all flow together, the same destination.

This crowd of agents surges towards the girl with nine years, stomping over the street—

she's used to this stampede. She grips her frog,

she darts in and out of legs and torsos,

a man kicks her,   +2.92

someone treads on her hand,   +4.29

her fingers tear a stocking,   −5.50

a bag of tools catches her head.   +3.67

When she's free of the crowd she walks without looking back.

She knows there is little point in following. She is too small: she wouldn't be able to claim anything for herself. The debt ceiling. She worries about hitting her ceiling. In her nine economically active years she has accrued a debt of

-11`47`78.67

and though the figure might be fluid, it is a solid part of her. It keeps her alive. Without the number she would be stricken from the record, insolvent. No economic agency. A commodity. Commodities and agents, commodities and agents. Agents rely on commodities. A crowd would flow towards her.

Then perhaps she'd be put to work making other items, shirts or sandwiches or cigarettes, a commodity manufacturing commodities, an item making items, day by day, until all function ceased. Or perhaps she would be useful for the commodities within: the heart, the lungs, or the kidneys. Or without: there were all sorts of profitable uses for skin. And meat. Eyes and fingerprints and hair. Incentive.

Once more the crowd flows in all directions. She carries the giant frog on her back. A man has wrinkly apples. She takes one.

−17.76

Five blocks away the streets are quiet. Her feet are sore. She must find a cheap place to sleep.

On the stoop steps to an old townhouse a woman breastfeeds a newborn. Her milk flows from her to it, whilst every second wealth flows from it to her. Breastfeeding is profitable. Of course it would be to the newborn's benefit to feed on cheap take-a-chance vending machine milk: it is less expensive, but then there would be less profit for the older agent. Giving birth could be profitable.

−0.98
−0.97
−0.98
−0.96
−0.97

The girl with nine years walks on. She is too young to give birth. If she lasts then she will do it when she gets older. Perhaps she could birth dozens, giving them warm cuddles and hot food until her debt is marginal, until she is comfortable, until they are the burdened ones. But birth itself carries considerable risk.

The cold sun starts to rise. The streets grow even quieter. She can hear the debt of her own footsteps.

−0.01

−0.01

−0.01

One building has a large broken shop window lined with brown stains. Glass covers the street outside. She chooses that one. She walks in through the entranceway—the door is long gone—and climbs the stairs. The stairwell is dark. There is no handrail and she tries not to look down.

A door on the fourth floor is open.

The room is bare but for two mattresses side-by-side. One is a little gray, the other is darker with a large yellow-brown stain spread over the middle. She selects the latter and lies down.   −0.20

She will sleep quickly. Sunlight falls through the −0.20
fogged glass window, dull and heavy as smoke. She uses −0.20
the frog as a pillow.

She sleeps.

Through the cracked window the sky dims once more, the fluorescent light of the sun slowly winding down, the coming darkness an opportunity.

       Where is the frog?   +0.67
            +0.67
            +0.67

The woman with the lopsided grin is in the corner. She +0.67
has the frog on her knee. She is stroking it.   +0.67
            +0.67

Will you talk to me?   +0.50

She isn't losing from the transaction with the lopsided +0.67
woman. The lopsided woman is stroking her frog and +0.67
balancing out the cost of the exchange.   +0.67

She doesn't run. Instead the girl with nine years answers

                     Yes. +0.27

The woman smiles a lop-sided smile. It is not pleasing +1.82
to look at.

I like your frog. Don't run away. I know how you can make −1.53
a profit.

            I can already make a profit. −0.20

The lopsided woman speaks quickly.

You're failing. You'll hit the ceiling sooner or later. Think   −0.13
about it. Think about it. This transaction will benefit us   −1.15
both. I know how we can make a profit. I know where we   −1.23
can get organs. Organs for the hospital. There's profit
there.

                   Where are there organs for the hospital?   −0.43

In an agent. He has good organs.   −0.87

            You know someone about to hit the ceiling?   −0.28

No.   −0.22

    No. This was not a profitable avenue. To harm the   +0.67
body of an active agent involved paying them. To end an   +0.67
active agent involved paying everyone they would have   +0.67
provided a service toward. This could be expensive. The
woman speaks.

I need your help. I need someone physically alluring. I'll   −16.98
bring you to the agent, show you what to do. I know what   −0.77
you're thinking, that it would be expensive, that we would   −5.56
lose from the exchange. It isn't true. He is worth very little.   −4.31
He has no services. He sees very few people. Eventually he   −3.25
will hit the debt ceiling but that will take too long. His
organs will have aged. We need him now.

    The risk is too great. There are too many factors.

                                       No −2.44

she replies. The woman with the lopsided grin does not   +0.67
look surprised. She simply strokes the frog. After one   +0.67
minute she responds.   +0.67

I shall wait for you. By the stub. Just before dark. Every   −3.38
day. I will not find you again.

    And she leaves. The girl with nine years picks up her
frog.
    She decides to leave some things there in the building.
It is cheap and would remain so for the next few nights.
The frog is too much to carry around everywhere. She

wraps her arms around it again—just to check the stitching—then covers it with a dusty curtain and leaves. She'll come back later.

On the street outside is a lady with red hair. She's shouting something. It isn't important. It will cost. The nine year-old agent hurries by, closing her ears to the potential expense.

The red-haired lady wants to change things, she wants to make a difference and change the world. She has above-average wits, she is eloquent—if anyone can do it then she can. She can see a way out: she knows it; she knows there's a way for everything to be different. She wasn't sure how but they all had to try. She stands on a wall. She shouts at passing strangers.

She shouts that there is a way out.

One or two pairs of ears catch her words as they pass.   +1.40

She shouts that it is simple: all they have to do is leave the commodities alone.

A woman cradling a young agent hears her, pauses for a moment to drop a bottle to the ground, then carries on.   +2.62

She shouts again: Just leave the former agents alone. Just leave them be. When an agent hits the debt ceiling, don't claim them, don't collar them, just treat them as you would have before.

A dozen agents walk by; only one hears.   +2.28

If we leave them alone, we have nothing to fear ourselves. We'll be free. We won't have to worry.   +2.41

She shouts for four hours. She implores and pleads, she makes her most eloquent arguments. No one stops. No one pays attention for longer than a moment, and at one point,   +3.34
as she reaches a fervor, she gains   +9.27

The lady's throat tightens until the words melt away.

She's made no difference. She's made a profit.

For a moment the lady with red hair is pleased.

Gaining wealth: the quick-witted may gain from conversation or some other skill; those with physical beauty from being photographed or fucked. The dull will lose, the unattractive will lose. It is far better to be the less interested, less attracted party.

The girl with nine years crosses the bridge to the Exberg. The water is gray. There are dark splotches beneath the surface.

She descends into Kotbust station.

She descends down the subway entrance which bellows the smell of wet concrete into the streets. The steps are crumbling away beneath the swarms of shoes, the edges rounded, pieces broken free, a hazard for a careless foot. Underground the ceiling leaks into the floor, a surge of puddles and small streams cascading onto the tracks. Scattered shards of tiles coat the ground. The subway is getting slower, less efficient, and so it is becoming more cost-effective to utilize.

The girl with nine years thinks of the offer the woman with the lopsided grin has made. There is too much risk. It is a bad idea. There is no more value in thinking of it.

She clutches her bag close to her as the rattle of the train approaches.

The subway car lurches from side to side before screeching to a halt. She looks out of the window and sees the distant flicker of flames. They will be there for some hours. She re-evaluates her situation: is there any potential for wealth on the carriage?

The carriage is almost empty. One woman is mumbling to herself. For a moment she stares at the crazy woman,   −4.67 before cursing herself.

On the other side there is an objectively attractive man—very old, he has something like thirty-five years, but he is handsome. Too handsome. He would be the one to gain from any transaction between them. It is not worth the risk.

She looks around for someone less attractive but there are only the three of them in the subway car.

He moves to sit opposite her.

The seat he is on now is more expensive: it is a little further from the doors and the upholstery is still intact. She's determined to avoid his gaze: this won't be a transaction to her benefit. He says some words to her but she does not hear them—it is a necessary skill to avoid potential expense.

From the corner of her eye she sees him stand and kneel beside her. He strokes her hair. She cringes. She does not want to do this—a factor that puts the exchange to her +2.94 monetary advantage. He puts his hand on her shoulder and +3.25 she pulls away. He pulls her back toward him and presses +8.29 his lips to the skin of her neck. He takes hold of her arm, drags her up and then pushes her hard, down onto the floor +20.31 of the carriage. She is confused. She reaches up to push him +15.92

away but he stumbles on top of her, bites her shirt at the neckline and tears it down the middle. He keeps one hand at   +20.67
her throat as he pulls down his trousers, then hers, and   +32.28
enters her. Rough and dry. His sticky mouth is all over her.   +33.27
It is uncomfortable—her head and body ache. She is   +34.54
pleased. This will pay for her room tonight. This may even
pay for two nights.

He bites her. Good, she thinks. She smiles.   +13.90

Finally the train moves. He moves off her. They sit at opposite ends of the carriage. Her body hurts.

      +47.29

And she knows the frog is gone. He is gone. She has made more profit. She tries to smile.

The train reaches a station. She can't stop shaking. She climbs the stairs into the evening. She can't see things clearly. Her head spins. She can't focus. There is a pinprick of light at the center of her vision. Why can't she see? Her head throbs. The dot of light grows larger, only it isn't light, it is static, chaos, a buzz over her view, a streak over her eyes, and she can only see in her periphery. She takes a deep breath: steady breathing is important. The throb in her head shifts into a stab. A stabbing: at her temples, at her spine. The blur of colors clouds over the rest of her vision. She sits down. Deep breathing. Deep breathing.

She opens her eyes a crack. She is by a tree. Grass tickles her fingers. Leaves are scattered around her: orange and brown. She leans against the bark, which scatters in clumps and crumbles over her back.   −0.09

She shivers. She shuts out the city. She takes a deep, rattled breath and closes her eyes, shuts down her ears, the prickle of her skin, her mind. She sinks ever-inwards, beyond waking, beyond everything. She is being buried, sinking through a deep and peaceful mud.

She wakes.

There is a chirp.

A chirp.

The sparrow looks up at her. He squats by her hand. He cocks his head to one side and chirps. She laughs.

There are no numbers.

He chirps. His feathers are beautiful;

brown and brown and brown.

He opens his tiny face and chirps again.

She laughs.

She laughs and laughs until her sides hurt.

                         She laughs at and with
and for the sparrow,
         the sparrow with no numbers,
                  no cost, no profit,
                         the sparrow that hops
nearer her hand, looking for food inside, the sparrow that
hops onto her finger as she laughs and feeds it a crumb, that
flies away as she laughs, the free sparrow, the sparrow that
costs nothing.

Some things might cost nothing. Help might cost
nothing. The lady with the lopsided grin wants to help her.
She does.

*Every transaction is instantaneous. Every agent enters the
world at 0: no debt, no wealth. Equal opportunity. That's
what they said it was about, once, before. But what use is
once, or before?*

The tall man with the blond mustache hands over a sack of
purple pebbles. He knew he could trade stones. That was
what he would do for the foreseeable—he would trade
stones. The more he traded them the more agents saw them.
The more agents saw them the more they would want them.
The more they wanted them the more they were worth. It
was his first nature.

The other man takes the sack. There is no facial   +1`28.87
expression. He says nothing.

The tall man with the blond mustache thinks about
ending him. He must be worth something: he can afford a
big sack of do-nothing pebbles.

He won't end him. If he ends the man with the sack of
pebbles then no one will see the pebbles and his stone-
trading will be less profitable. He lets the man walk away,
staggering beneath the weight of his sack.

It is going dark. Three blocks east the tall man with the
blond mustache finds a sandwich in someone's hands; it   −15.23
tastes terrible so he spits it to the street,   −3.32
         where one of the many passing feet treads in it.   −0.82
In front of him there is a woman with a strange smile: −0.60
he is quite attracted. Her smile is uneven, that is all: it is
asymmetrical, sensual. He is aware it would be worth very
little; he doesn't want to end her. He wants to enter her.

There is a small agent to her side. The small agent is
not smiling. The small agent is staring at him. He gains   +0.18
small amounts from this constant odd stare. He doesn't   +0.20

recognize this look—there is no lust for the body, no lust +0.19
for profit. It isn't nothing, but it isn't something either. The
small agent too rouses his curiosity.

    He walks over to the woman with the strange smile and
presses his lips to hers.   −7.91
                       He bites her ear.   −9.25
                               then pulls down her shirt.   −12.09
Nipples bob in the blue glow of a sign for fried fries.   −1.66
                             There is blood on her breasts.   +1`01.52
          Where is the money coming from?   +1`12.91
                         He hasn't traded anything.   +1`32.23
           It would be worth a lot.   +1`85.07
                 He loses, for the stains on the woman's −14.65
dress, on her breasts:
    the blood is his, his blood, spilling spurting,   +2`96.95
                              sticky in his hands. +4`54.08
The small agent has the same expression. He stares in
wonder.
              He can't breathe. She has some glass in her hand. +7`33.17
It is sticky.   +8`32.84
                                             +6`61.91
          He starts to sleep.   +4`24.21

Survival has no time for luxuries, no time for anything
outside of now. Guilt and regret are for the past, malice
and hope for the future. They cannot be afforded.

                                               -88`05`86.12

    Across and beyond the city agents are credited. They
are credited for lost cloth and undelivered furniture, for
screens and speakers that will never arrive, for salt and
spoon collections, for coats and shoes and hats, wheels,
men and women with firm bodies, vending machines,
advert lights, needles full of chemicals, for hair and
kidneys, for parts of subway cars, for bricks and crates of
apples, for skin, for absent stones.

    The girl with nine years believes there should be more
blood over her arms. Instead it courses through her limbs,
her trunk, her heart. She has a good heart; its beat is strong
and regular: it will be worth something when the time
comes.

    The time is coming. That man with the blond mustache
was worth a lot. More than a lot. He was worth more than
she ever could have believed. She can't even see any more

numbers, not after one that big, not now that she is so near the ceiling.

The lady with the lopsided grin speaks.

Thank you. I'll be following you now. I shall own your body. I shall claim you, when the time comes.

She says it all with her unsmiling asymmetrical mouth. There is no pleasure in this: this is a transfer of wealth, the flow of the world, it is neither pleasurable nor painful; it is, that is all.

The agent with nine years had failed to see the transaction taking place: this had worked to her fiscal disadvantage. How long before she hit the ceiling now? A day. Three. Little more.

But she will not remain around the woman with the lopsided grin, for the simple reason that if she does she shall hit her debt ceiling all the faster.

She wanted to age.

So she runs, she runs from the woman with the lopsided grin, she runs as fast as she can, past all the agents who look at her, who see how close she is, she clambers and climbs away from them, up and over and under walls and boxes and rooftops, she runs until she stops running, she can't run any more, joints and tendons and bones scream, her head pulses. She sits.

On the rooftop there is a sparrow.

She takes a deep breath: breathing is important.

She looks at the sparrow.

The sparrow with no numbers. The free sparrow.

It is beautiful: brown and brown and brown.

The sparrow opens its face and chirps at her.

She laughs and feeds it a crumb.

The sparrow cocks its head and chirps

at her.

She laughs. She laughs.

She is savvy. She is competent.

She is in charge of her own economic destiny.

She names the sparrow.

She owns the sparrow.

The sparrow flies away.

Entertainment.	+1.28
She will never see the sparrow again, but it shall be seen,	+2.37
entertainment with brown and brown and brown feathers,	+1.83

and she will gain. She has more crumbs. She will find +2.72
others. They will be seen, and she will gain. The agent with +2.28
nine years—the agent with the birds leaves the rooftop. +1.99

Little by little her debt shrinks. +1.51

$$+3.01$$
$$+2.75$$
$$+1.93$$
$$+1.15$$
$$+2.46$$
$$+3.84$$
$$+2.94$$

There is nothing else. Transaction governs everything. The one law maintains itself.

In the park there is a lady with thick eyebrows. The lady with thick eyebrows sees a sparrow.

−2.94

The ceiling. That's it. −1`00`00`00.00. The lady with thick eyebrows has reached the ceiling.

So long—it was for so long that she worried about what would happen to her—what would happen when she ceased to be agent, when she became commodity. It all depended on who would find her first. Would she be put to endless, unceasing, death-inducing work? Would she be carved up? Perhaps there was something else, something worse that could happen. Who knew?

The agents who have been following her begin to sprint.

But at this moment her worrying stops. There is no need, no purpose. Her heartbeat slows. Her lungs fill with air. Her skin prickles. She has this moment. For the first time she feels calm. It is luxury, real luxury. For the first time she has no goal.

This moment she is free.

· 𝔖𝔞𝔠𝔯𝔞𝔯𝔦𝔲𝔪 ·

This was not the hereafter Mirelle had bargained for.

—*The End of the Objects*

What Follows Us

ADAM McOMBER

London
August 21, 18—

Acherton purchases tickets at the wooden kiosk in front of Lord Mayor's House and slips them into the pocket of his summer suit. The phantasmagoria isn't scheduled to begin for another hour, so we have time for a walk. A barker dressed in theater rags and corpse makeup attempts to draw a crowd for the show by announcing the details of his own murder. We cross the muddied street, leaving the barker and the carriage clatter of Knightsbridge behind, making our way into the silent depths of Hyde Park. I follow Acherton, observing the hard line of his shoulders and the strength of his pale neck. This is to be our final outing. To a casual observer, I suppose we might seem a pair of boyhood friends on a last lark. But it's far more painful than that. Acherton is to be married the following month, and he's made it clear we cannot continue our longstanding visits. "I intend to become respectable, Tom," he says, gravely. I cannot respond. How can I speak when I have known him for so many years, and the idea of life without him seems impossible?

We find a quiet stand of yellow oaks near the pond. Acherton talks, and I listen. He avoids further serious topics. In his mind, all the serious topics have been dealt with. He tells me instead the history of the phantasmagoria, attempting the sort of exuberant tone that once charmed me. But he cannot achieve true levity. There's weight in his voice—gravity that pins us both to the Earth.

"The phantasmagoria is the newest thing from Paris, Tom," he says. "It's all done with mirrors and light. There are no actors. A projector is hidden behind a false panel in the wall, and a series of mechanical slides create the illusion of movement—a real moving picture show. They bring all sorts of ghouls and hobgoblins to life on the screen. You'll love it."

"People pay to watch these horrors?" I ask.

He shrugs. "Horror stimulates."

I wish I could take his hand and ask him not to leave. But we were growing distant even before the announcement of his engagement. His visits to my rooms were becoming rare. He would say simply that we are putting boyhood games aside. This is to be an amicable separation, after all. I remain outwardly composed, glad to be wearing my coal-colored traveling suit. Such clothing, I imagine, better conceals my feelings. Acherton is twenty-five, and I am a year younger. When he marries, I will be left a bachelor, aging alone in my rooms with no one to visit me. I wonder if it's possible that he does not care what becomes of me. He reclines in the grass, pale jacket open, necktie slightly loose. I can't help but admire the way he's grown his dark hair longer than fashion permits. At least he hasn't entirely surrendered to convention. He smells of French cigarettes and shaving talc, and I wish I could make a home inside his scent.

I try to remember the first time we ventured into the leafy preserves of Hyde Park together. We were still boys at school, and I felt as though we'd fallen into the wilds of some fairy book. We'd been testing the boundaries of our physical relationship. In between our bouts of wrestling, Acherton attempted to frighten me by recounting the tale of a boy who'd drowned in the big pond. *He was Lord Croydon's son*, Acherton said. *You've heard of Lord Croydon at school, haven't you, Tom?*

I had, of course. Croydon was a retired dean and an antiquary, famed for his investigations into the Roman cult of Mithras. Traveling Roman soldiers were said to have brought the cult to London shortly after the death of Christ. Next to nothing was known about the ancient god of Mithraism other than that he held some terrible sway over his followers. Bloody sacrifice was common. Lord Croydon discovered a subterranean temple devoted to Mithras not far from the nave of Saint John's Cathedral. The temple was cut from the earth, decorated with odd blue tile that, despite its age, appeared almost liquid. There was a dark stain at the center of the temple—a memory of sacrificial gore. The god Mithras was represented as a boy emerging from a stone. His brow was pale and wide, his eyes large dark holes bored deeply into his face. The stony boy-god stared down at the stain with his depthless, hungry eyes. He seemed desperate—a lonely god of wrath, waiting for worship. Lord Croydon wrote that as he was dusting the surface of the god's face, he felt a power pass through him. "Like an awful cosmic tide, pulling me out into a vast sea," Croydon wrote. "For a moment, I saw all of London in ruin. The only thing that moved in our precious city was Mithras himself. Free from his stone prison, he dragged himself down the empty streets, searching for what, I cannot know."

Croydon's son didn't care anything for ridiculous old Mithras or any other portion of his father's work, Acherton said. *He was like the rest of us, Tom. The poor boy only wanted to fall in love. One has to imagine that his death in the cold water of the pond came as a terrible surprise. What were his last thoughts, I wonder? Something about a girl he'd never see again?*

Or a boy, I added without speaking.

Acherton prepared for the climax of his story. *Croydon's son haunts the woods. I've seen him myself.*

You have not, I said, a bit offended that he'd expect me to believe such a thing. I made better marks than Acherton in almost every class.

He took a long drag from his cigarette and squinted at me as he exhaled. *Oh, I'm afraid so. I was walking, trying to get my mind off school, and I saw a form ahead of me. I was annoyed, of course, hoping to be alone. It looked like another boy from our class up ahead in the shadow of the trees. But when the form turned to face me, I realized he wasn't from anyone's class. He had chalky skin and this awful mass of black hair that was wet and limp, as if he'd been for swim. And—*

And what? I asked.

His eyes were, well, there were no eyes. Just fleshy holes. But he wasn't blind. He could see me well enough. And he stood staring. Surveying me— to see if I had what he wanted. It was then that I understood he wasn't a boy at all.

What was he then?

Acherton shrugged. *Something that didn't belong in the woods. A presence that had worked its way out of the past. Some people say Croydon's son watches lovers by the pond—that he's heartsick.*

I wanted to ask Acherton if Croydon's son would look at us. Were we to be lovers? But I held my tongue, of course. Instead, I drew myself close to him, and he put his arm around me, and we sat together like that in the darkening woods.

But the thing I saw wasn't heartsick, Tom, Acherton said. *If I had to wager, I'd say he didn't have any heart at all.*

Such memories of our history are painful, but I cannot help but think of the dead boy and Croydon's old god as I sit with Acherton. My mind casts forth, searching for distraction. Shadows of oak branches glide across Acherton's body like a conjurer's hand. I gaze up at the oak leaves. They've started to change color but have not yet fallen. The pond itself has a leaden, blackish look. There's a woman walking her dog near the water, and she glances briefly in our direction. I wonder what she makes of us—two men in suits sitting in the shadow of the oak trees. Are we respectable?

I am unsure of when precisely I begin to pray. I'd been a rational atheist since a young age. Yet there in the woods, in that moment of duress, I find I cannot help myself. My prayers, at first, are strange and formless. I pray to the forest floor that it should leach my sorrow into the dark of its soil. And then I pray to the melancholy trees for the wisdom to let Acherton go. Before I can stop myself, I sense something unnatural happening. Something beyond my control. I imagine the energy of my prayers is beginning to coalesce somewhere deeper on in the woods—forming a kind of white and shimmering body behind the trees. It's a body made of prayers and desperate wishes. The body watches Acherton and me. I pray harder still and the body begins to breathe. I realize I'm bringing the thing to life, but I cannot stop myself.

"Are you going to take Anna to the phantasmagoria as well?" I ask, almost breathless, trying to forget the thing in the forest.

Acherton's expression softens as he looks at me. His sympathy makes me uncomfortable, and my woolen traveling suit begins to itch in the heat.

"I thought you didn't want to talk about Anna," he says, checking his pocket watch. "This is our day. Tell you what, Tom—let's go have a look at the magic lantern machine," he says. "Let's see the horrors."

He's pulling me up from the grass. I don't want to move into the trees. I fear the thing I've conjured—the white body. It's not the dead boy. Nor is it the old god, Mithras. It's something beyond the two. A cosmic willfulness. Surely it will trap me, and once it has me, it will not let me go. Acherton and I are moving together like we used to move—almost as one body. We walk along the narrow path, and I can feel the presence following, passing stealthily between tree trunks. Stalking us. I turn to look. But the woods are empty.

We cross back over Knightsbridge and enter Lord Mayor's House. The corpse in rags holds the door for us, grinning hideously. Once inside, Acherton and I stand together in the darkened hall, staring up at a large blank screen. Other patrons whisper around us in anticipation. The show begins with flickers of light. I watch as one awful image melts into the next. A bleeding nun descends the convent stairs. An imp rides a wooly he-goat out of Hell. There are writhing serpents. A blue specter manifests, swelling and contracting like a lung. None of it frightens me. I can think only of the thing in the woods.

Near the show's end, the odd specters disappear and a primeval scene spreads slowly across the screen. Dark and curling ferns blot out a projected sun. The high, airy call of some long ago creature sounds from a distant corner of the hall. "We are moving through time," says the barker's voice. "To an age when the great gods themselves walked upon the Earth."

Acherton leans close and whispers playfully, "They're coming for you, Tom."

I close my eyes, press myself against him. He puts his arm around me like he used to do. It's dark enough in the theater so that no one will know.

I allow myself to speak. "Am I going to die without ever seeing you again?" I whisper.

He does not answer.

An image begins to rise from deep inside me. It's a flickering picture like the ones on the screen. I see a boy at school meeting his dark-haired friend for the first time. They read a book of poetry in the common room, shoulders pressed together. They laugh at the wistful romance of the lines, kicking each other's feet. It's a simple scene of youth. Nothing horrible. Then I watch as my younger self stands and walks away from dark-haired Acherton. I'm holding the romantic book of poetry to my chest and wearing a half-smile. In that long ago moment, I believe I've gained some control over life. There are no sacrifices to be made, no gods to fear. I wish, more than anything, I could tell my younger self about the horrors to come. There are so many temples waiting beneath the earth—so many, they have made the Earth a hollow thing.

In the Emily Dickinson Museum

MARGARET WALTHER

Little birds on stilts chant—*Zero, Zero at the Bone*—
As dream approaches this grave-lined yard.

There is no rack. I carry my bicycle inside, hide it—Where?
Quick—behind Emily's beckoning bed.

In the living room, her writing desk. Enter at your risk.
Tiny knives fasten all the drawers.

Rows of suspended sculptures move on wires.
Under each—circling sand—magenta, azure, electric green.

Emily—her white perfection—graces every one. Clarety-
haired, she etches words onto alabaster stars.

The last one, Juggler. Hundreds of wire balls
with iridescent beads arc and fall into her slender hands.

Suddenly—the sculptures still.
Closed, the museum door—sonorous—announces.

I run, retrieve my bike. But who could mount it now?
Front wheel—Transposed into a saw—

The Paranormal Guide to Wedding Etiquette

PEDRO PONCE

Old

If one were to believe the preponderance of paranormal encounter narratives, one would likely live in fear of—or hope for—the plethora of strange detours afforded by ordinary circumstance. Ghosts haunt offices and rural roadsides; aliens hunt abductees in supermarket parking lots; spouses vanish from cornfields, birthday parties, honeymoons, cars in mid-commute. Enter an elevator at a certain hour of night. For the paranormalist, your chances of perishing from mechanical failure are exponentially outweighed by the likelihood that you will emerge far in space and time from your intended floor.

The same cannot be said of weddings. Any number of paranormal events may *surround* a wedding. A proposal's acceptance coincides with the flight of doves from nearby shrubbery. The rain expected to dampen a nuptial weekend clears brilliantly just before the ceremony. Or, as in the recent reception staple "Save a Dance for Daddy" by country musician Bo Lovell, a grizzled Gulf War veteran returns to attend his daughter's wedding; by the last verse, we learn he has been killed in action and is attending the ceremony literally in spirit before "dancing to my Great Reward." But the spirits hold their peace, yeti and Sasquatch admit no impediment, the fabric of the cosmos is not put asunder.

Recently, I spent most of an afternoon in the stacks of the public library's central branch, looking for stories of the unexplained at weddings or wedding receptions. Even with the latter expanded search terms, I failed to find a single documented narrative or eyewitness account. Several hours into my search, I cheered triumphantly—to the annoyance of a transient pair dozing drunkenly nearby—as the computer returned a reference to Helen Tremaine's *Wedding Disasters*. I should have suspected a false lead from the title's listing under "Customs, Etiquette & Folklore." I was perhaps overly eager from so much time spent fruitlessly. Not until I had the volume in my hands did I read its full title: *Wedding Disasters and How to Avoid Them: How to Plan (and Enjoy!) Your Special Day*. I perused the table of contents on the off chance that the author included a relevant chapter, or at least an anecdote or two. Apart from dismissing the recent fashion for throwing birdseed at departing newlyweds (the deadliness of rice to birds and squirrels was pure urban myth) and encouraging the bride to put her own stamp on wedding tradition ("Every bride needs something old, something new, something borrowed, and everything fabulous!"), the disasters were all hypothesis, easily thwarted by the proper application of platitude and exclamation point. The lights overhead began blinking on and off, a signal that the library was about to close. I proceeded to the exit.

There are, of course, less trivial impediments to the marriage of true minds. The recent indictment of a Michigan groom for allegedly leaving his bride to drown during their Australian honeymoon; the abandonment at the altar of a New York City bride who, at the reception now held to celebrate singlehood regained, shuffled bravely to the defiant strains of Gloria Gaynor; the well-documented story of the groom who toasted his guests with compromising photographs of the bride and best man left beneath every chair in the reception hall—these and countless other nuptial misfortunes seem to justify the smug proprieties that betoken the successful exchange of vows. But the motives behind such derelictions are easily attributed. There is nothing of the supernatural in a spouse's greed or suspicion. Nature has proven itself to be largely polygamous; we are one of the few species to practice monogamy and the only one, as far as we know, of sufficient intelligence—or lack thereof—to codify biological imperatives.

The best-known—albeit fictional—paranormal wedding narrative must certainly be Coleridge's "Rime of the Ancient Mariner," though the wedding is more of a framing device for the Mariner's tale of avenging spirits and monsters at sea:

> It is an ancient Mariner,
> And he stoppeth one of three
> "By thy long grey beard and glittering eye,
> Now wherefore stopp'st thou me?
>
> "The Bridegroom's doors are opened wide,
> And I am next of kin;
> The guests are met, the feast is set:
> May'st hear the merry din."
>
> [The Mariner] holds him with his skinny hand,
> "There was a ship," quoth he.

Of more recent provenance is the tale of another wedding guest who, to lighten the onus of a long reception line, decided to share a quaint and only slightly risqué bit of wedding night wisdom with the bride and groom. Having embraced the newlyweds, he withdrew slightly, keeping one hand on each of their shoulders.

"Well," he began, in the deadpan manner he had practiced carefully the day before in the rental car from the airport, "hope you guys don't wear each other out tonight."

Had he been less intent on his engaging punch line, he would have noticed the matron next in line swivel her head abruptly in his direction, her neck clacking with pearls.

The groom, whose practiced smile wavered slightly, patted the guest warmly on the back, perhaps to dissemble his complete lack of recognition. "Thanks guy," he said, cocking one hand like a pistol and winking suggestively.

The guest, anxious that his remarks would lose their humorous effect if broken up by the groom's glib riposte, began again. "Seriously. You guys should really take it easy on each other—"

The bride interrupted, grinning stiffly. "We're *so* glad you could make it," she said. She indicated the matron with the slightest shake of her head. "I don't know if you know my *grandmother*, who flew all the way from *Albuquerque*."

The guest offered the grandmother his hand; the grandmother shook it limply, her expression cool. The punch line would have to stand on its own.

"Anyway—" In mid-sentence, he felt the groom begin to guide him onward. Before he was out of earshot, the guest hurriedly elaborated on the folkloric context of his perhaps off-color but nevertheless well-intentioned remarks: the superstitious belief that the first to fall asleep on the wedding bed will be the first to die. "So, you know, try not to kill each other tonight." He chuckled to signal his humorous intent, clasping the groom's shoulder. The grandmother stepped into the narrow space between them and silenced the guest with a discreet elbow to the ribs. She dissembled the blow with vociferous praise of the ceremony and the bride's gown. Rather than embarrass her by reacting—the gauntness of her arm sharpened the impact considerably—the guest moved aside without protest to accommodate her ill-gotten audience.

The lingering guest now dispatched, the line moved briskly. The bride and groom endured the fraught permutations of wedding portraiture with relatively little fuss (the bride's estranged older brother hesitated briefly before posing with the wedding party; her mother-in-law demanded the same position in every shot to guarantee posterity her most flattering side). The reception was sufficiently lavish, despite the lack of a pork entrée and a minor malfunction in the third tier of the champagne fountain. Despite loving threats before the ceremony—and the goading of several drunken guests—the feeding of the cake left neither newlywed unpleasantly besmirched. The garter and bouquet toss produced a happy pairing, if not from this day forward, at least for part of the night. At eleven, the bride and groom retreated discreetly to the nearest elevator to the honeymoon suite. Despite their exhaustion, they mustered more than enough energy to consecrate their union beneath a canopy of seafoam stripes. They fed each other strawberries and squares of chocolate from the gift basket provided compliments of the hosting franchise. They extinguished their bedside lamps and spooned beneath percale sheets, talking softly in the dark.

As the light over the Pacific went from black to deep indigo, they had yet to fall asleep.

The groom sat up and padded to the bathroom. The bride hit the lights on her side of the bed. Her husband squinted over a tumbler of water. He took several sips and passed the glass to his bride.

"I'm still so wired," said the groom, stretching his arms toward the ceiling. He propped up several pillows and leaned back against them. "Still coming down, I guess. From everything."

The bride said nothing as she drank.

"You'd think we'd both be exhausted. We've been up for—" He looked at the red digits of the sleek black clock glowing against the mahogany nightstand. "Hours," he continued. "But here we are. Both of us. Wide awake."

Still the bride said nothing. She drained the glass and set it down next to her side of the bed. She reached for the phone.

The groom looked over quizzically. "I think it's too late for room service."

The bride continued dialing. "I'm not calling room service."

Five floors down, the phone in my guest suite began ringing.

New

The ancient Greeks considered balance to be divine and calculated its exact numerical proportions, replicating them in the dimensions of their temples and statuary. During the Renaissance, balance was a matter of perspective, allowing the flat canvas to assume the fullness of three dimensions. Asymmetry, by contrast, provokes and disturbs. The photographer crops unevenly to create expectation of what is outside the frame; the off center shot in film foreshadows trouble. Our predilection for balance extends as far back as the occult origins of civilization. In numerology, the number two represents unity and completion. The number one stands for independence and drive, but it is also associated with restlessness and the persistence of desire unfulfilled. To refer to one's "better half" is thus more than affectionate flattery—it is the expression of an archetypal impulse, as old as the caveman's mute foreboding as he stared skyward into the hemispheric husk of a waning moon.

The women at my table acknowledged these remarks with polite indifference. I will not detain the reader with a catalog of possible excuses for my unsolicited disquisition, although these were certainly in abundance: the late arrival of my flight the night before after several delays; the cocktails I had consumed earlier on an empty stomach; the wine I subsequently consumed to accompany my chicken cordon bleu and mixed seasonal greens; my self-consciousness as I introduced myself to the woman sitting next to me; my disappointment on seeing her ring finger, where the snout of a diamond perched in smug reproach; my neighbor's far less attractive friend, who asked for every detail of the impending nuptials, swooning with anticipatory relish that barely disguised her seething envy. "You're *so* his better half," she said, prompting protest from the bride-to-be. "I mean it. You're like the person that completes him. You know? Like in that movie with—" Here is where I interrupted, less to be helpful than to relieve the beginnings of a hangover.

Before continuing, I would like to make one thing clear: I am not the sort of person who resents love. Indeed, I celebrate love. I admire the serendipity that brings two people together, the persistence that keeps them together over time or distance or both, the commitment they share on occasions just like this. Yet would one choose to feast on such rich food every day? We savor holiday fowl, the sweetness of birthday cake. But their richness is enhanced because of their rarity, whereas a daily diet of them would quickly dull our palates. And so I enjoy the occasional romance matinee. I welcome calls from friends, breathless with news of their latest flirtations or more serious prospects, only screening when prior commitments prevent my focused attention. I am no less avid than the rest of my dinner companions when, between courses, a couple dissects with forensic precision the exact circumstances (the sunlit curls *that stopped me in my tracks*; the virile baritone *that turned my knees to jelly*) to which we owe their felicitous conjunction. It is to appreciate moments such as these as fully as possible that, for much of the year, I studiously avoid the least possibility of encountering them.

Nevertheless, when the bride invited me, I felt obliged to go. We've known each other since college and, for several years after graduation, we lived in the same city. We would see each other frequently, as her office was only two blocks from *Déjà Lu*, the used book store where I served as cashier and was recently promoted to assistant manager. Despite regular gatherings for drinks or dinner, we lost touch, apart from the occasional card or e-mail, after she was moved to her company's western headquarters. There, she met the groom, then a medical student, now a resident in internal medicine at one of the nation's premier teaching hospitals. I first met the groom at the rehearsal dinner the night before; he seemed perfectly affable despite his being primarily conversant in ESPN *SportsCenter*.

The soundtrack for dessert was Michael Bublé. I was struck by the odd coincidence as he had lately become an important addition to *Déjà Lu*'s growing music department. Among the assistant manager's newly assumed responsibilities was the whiteboard above the cash register. Here, management recommended recently arrived used discs. The board was split down the middle by a red line of dry erase ink. On the left side—IF YOU ARE—the store listed a timely selection of customers' possible moods or states of mind: IF YOU ARE/ OFF TO THE BEACH/ SEXLESS IN THE CITY/ AFRAID FOR YOUR DWINDLING CIVIL LIBERTIES. On the right side—YOU MIGHT ENJOY—were the store's corresponding recommendations: VAMPIRE WEEKEND/ GOLDFRAPP/ VOTING NEXT TIME. After hearing most of the singer's new record in line at the local deli, I was moved to add to the whiteboard after lunch: IF YOU ARE/ DEAD INSIDE/ YOU MIGHT ENJOY/ MICHAEL BUBLÉ.

The chatter at my table resumed. The bride-to-be's friend dabbed with her fork at a sliver of tiramisu. "Oh, I *love* this song. Don't you love this song?" She turned to the rest of the table, mostly friends of the groom from medical school who had vacated their seats for the bar. "Do you know what your song's gonna be?" she asked.

The bride-to-be shook her head. "We haven't decided yet. I sort of want that song I told you about. Remember? The one that goes—" Here she affected the throaty warble of Nellie McKay.

"I think she's being ironic," I said.

Her eyes narrowed to caramel slits. "Who is?" she asked.

"That singer. About getting married. She's not being serious."

Her friend leaned over a shallow pool of sugary mush. "Do you know what *you're* being right now?"

"I'm trying to be helpful," I retorted. "People only hear the melody. No one ever listens to the words."

"Well right now, none of us wants to listen to you." She raised a hand parallel to the side of her face, a fashionable gesture denoting the end of her receptivity.

I felt a tap at my shoulder. I was relieved to see the bride leaning into my periphery. "Why aren't you dancing?" she asked. I said nothing and drained my wine glass. She extended her hand resolutely. "You know it's bad luck not to dance with the bride if she asks."

"Bad luck for who?" I asked.

Her hand flattened with insistence. "C'mon," she said.

I allowed myself to be led to the floor, where several couples twirled in loose clusters to Frank Sinatra. I felt my feet drag heavily next to her heels, but after a few measures, we were swaying easily in time.

"Is there anyone else here I can offend?" I asked. "I think I'm done with most of your co-workers."

She laughed over my shoulder. "I told Grammy you have Tourette's."

"You didn't."

She nodded. I looked down at my feet again.

"Are you having a good time?" she asked.

"Sure," I said. "It beats burgers at The Tombs."

"Ugh . . . you still go there?"

"Not with the rent I'm paying." Sinatra's voice swelled to fill a brief silence. "You shouldn't worry about me," I said. "I'm fine."

"So you read about—"

"It's *The New York Times*. It gets around."

The bride looked up toward the surrounding tables. "She has great timing, as always."

"It doesn't matter."

"You didn't have to come. I would have understood."

I looked at her. "I wanted to be here. Really."

"What's it been?"

"A few years." Her eyes remained locked on mine. "Give or take a few more years."

"This couldn't have been a surprise. I mean—"

"Of course not. It's biological imperative. Did you know in a recent study of bats, almost 90 percent of females preferred gainfully employed male bats with thinning hair and bad skin?"

A bridesmaid approached and whispered in the bride's ear. "I have to go," the bride said. "Try and have a good time? Not for me—for you?" She vanished into the gathering crowd clumping in pairs to Al Green.

If my single tablemate took offense at dinner, all was forgiven by the bouquet toss. She emerged from a flurry of outstretched hands bearing the prize clenched tightly to her chest. She leaped repeatedly in triumph before being gently escorted back to her table. I congratulated her as she walked past in a cloud of pungent perfume.

At the front of the ballroom, the DJ leaned into his microphone. "The fun's not over yet, ladies and gentlemen. It's the guys' turn now. I need all the single men in the room to report to the dance floor immediately." The seated bride and standing groom were already there. I stared at the slick tumbler in my hand, unsure of where it had come from. The bride rose slightly from her chair and scanned the room. I shrugged, the glass now empty, and stood. I was halfway across the floor when I noticed the only other single making his way to the front. I slowed my steps, looking for the nearest exit. I stared into a solid wall of pumps, wingtips, and sandals. "C'mon fellas. Don't be shy. There's nothing wrong with being a loser—I mean ladies' man." There was scattered applause and booing. "C'mon guys. Hurry it up. The groom's hoping to get lucky tonight."

The DJ put on a burlesque melody and proceeded to give instructions. The bride hiked her skirts while the groom kneeled. ("Looks like this one knows his way around down there!") He reached up and pulled the garter off her leg. "Now you guys," the DJ said, pointing at us, "take a few steps back . . . Back . . . More . . . That's it, keep going . . . We don't want to make it too easy." We were at the dance floor's midpoint by the time he told us to stop. The groom's back was a wavering silhouette in the distance next to the blur of the bride's dress. I felt my knees begin to buckle as the DJ counted. "On three . . . One . . . Two . . . Three!" There was a drum roll. The garter disappeared into the lights overhead. I waited, almost forgetting to raise my arms. I could only guess the garter's trajectory as I stared into the glare of chandeliers. There was cheering all of a sudden; I clenched my empty fingers with relief. I began to bolt back to my seat when I noticed the loop of lace dangling from my chest. The garter had hooked itself on one corner of my tie tack. It was fixed there so firmly that removing it caused the material to tear slightly.

"Easy there, cowboy," said the DJ, winking. "Getting it off's only half the fun." The bride had vacated her seat; the chair was now occupied by the girl with the bouquet. A few pink petals tumbled from her lap to the floor. She had removed her shoes; her toenails looked coppery stubbed beneath her stockings.

"OK," the DJ continued, "now this next part is crucial. You paying attention? Or are you too busy trying to look up the pretty lady's skirt? . . . Your mission, should you choose to accept it"—I will let the reader fill in the most appropriate musical accompaniment—"is to slide that garter up the lady's leg as far as it will go. The higher you go, the better luck for the bride and groom."

I was, needless to say, rather skeptical about the provenance of this superstition—it had no precedent in the texts I could recall offhand—but the music was too loud for me to make my queries heard, much less understood. I went down on one knee. The blare of brass was soon joined by whistling and more applause. Her foot slid between my palms. Her big toe dug sharply at my wrist. I looked up and caught her wink.

I proceeded to honor the bride and groom. It did not occur to me to consult with my presumptive partner about the extent of my reach. The clapping grew louder, more rhythmic as I eased the lace further up. Her mouth, rimmed with sweat, smiled tautly. Somewhere above the knee, her thighs squeezed my fingers to a stop. I sank into the warm pressure. She yielded another inch, then another. Finally, I stopped. I gave her thigh a firm pinch as I withdrew. Her yelp of surprise was masked by the music in front of us and the shrillness behind.

"Let's give these two some room," said the DJ, introducing Marvin Gaye. We were clenched together now at the waist.

I felt her mouth at my ear. "You're bad," she said, with a trace of admonition, but I could feel her stomach flutter through her dress. She lowered her voice to a whisper. "Did you like molesting me in public?" I nodded wordlessly. She leaned against my shoulder, facing out. Others had joined us, but swayed along at a discreet remove. Her lips grazed my ear again. "I think you're cute," she said. "As long as you keep your mouth shut." She laughed and leaned back onto my shoulder. "Why is that, anyway?"

"Why's what?"

"Guys are so weird. They treat you like shit in front of everybody. But get them alone and they can't keep their hands to themselves."

"Is that what they do with you?"

She looked away for a second before answering. "Sometimes." She leaned in again.

"I couldn't help myself," I said.

"Really?"

"Mmhmm."

She smiled. Her hands hung damply at the back of my neck. "And what made me so irresistible?"

"You really want to know?"

She nodded, her lips parted slightly.

"Alcohol, mostly," I said. "Alcohol and desperation."

Her mouth flattened to a pallid line. She pulled away.

"I'm sorry," I said. "Come back." But the laughter kept rising from my throat. I laughed through Marvin Gaye and half of "Love Shack." I laughed as I watched the back of her dress retreat between stilled dancers. I laughed until my own eyes stung, streaking the sides of my face.

The singer Graham Parker once compared the hangover—specifically, the din that seems to line the skull the morning after overindulging—to canned laughter. I can personally attest to the accuracy of this description in spirit if not in exact detail. Canned laughter certainly goes a long way toward capturing its essence, but there are certain layers and nuances that escape the concision of popular song—much as I admire the latter form and Parker's work in particular. There is, for example, the further echo of voices raised across the whole spectrum of human emotion: curiosity, disbelief, indignant seething, simmering animosity, full-blown rage. There is the sense memory of your own cloudy actions and reactions: the tightness in your throat as you raised your own voice (in defense? in song?); the clutch of objects that were not yours for the taking (another's drink? the DJ's microphone?). There is the impression of halting conversation with disinterested silhouettes in tuxedo jackets and pastel satins. Perhaps you have not been heard, so you talk louder into the din. The music cuts off. You are shouting into a pillow, alone under sweaty sheets.

To these impressions may be added the chirp of the phone on one's nightstand.

"Hello?" I croaked into the receiver.

"Get up here. Now." The voice gave a room number before abruptly hanging up. I stared feverishly into the darkness as I placed the source of the call.

The bride was summoning me.

The hotel's air conditioned corridor was a relief from the damp swaddling in which I'd woken up. Except for my blazer, which was nowhere to be found, I was still dressed—shoes and all—so after some initial confusion it only took a few moments to get to the elevators. But as soon as the doors closed and the car began its ascent, I felt a burning knot rising rapidly to my throat. I swallowed hard. The elevator stopped.

The door to the honeymoon suite was already open. I knocked anyway. The groom answered in a dark blue terry cloth robe and led me toward a seat facing the bed. I was distracted from my nausea by the wide dimensions of the room.

Before I could ask about the bride, she emerged from the bathroom carrying a glass of water. She wore a robe matching the groom's. She didn't look at me as she joined us.

"If this is about the reception, I think I've apologized. Multiple times."

The bride gave me a look that instantly silenced me. "You're not here because of that," she said. She briefly noticed my dishevelment. "You want some water?"

I swallowed again and felt my stomach settle tenuously. "I'm fine."

"I'm glad," said the bride. "I'm glad you're fine. We"—here she glanced at the groom—"were just talking about you."

"You were?"

The bride nodded. "Among other things. Sports. Current events."

"Those are really the same thing, you know."

"Shut up," the bride said. The groom raised one hand in a calming gesture. "We've been up here. Together. On our wedding night. The happiest day of our lives."

"So far," added the groom.

"So far," acknowledged the bride. "We've had a beautiful day. The usual last-minute stuff with flowers and catering. But otherwise it's gone as well as anyone would want." She joined hands with the groom. "I—*we* are happy. We've had a beautiful wedding day. And a beautiful wedding night."

The groom grinned, mildly embarrassed, before speaking. "Only thing is—"

"You can't sleep," I said, remembering the reception line. "You can't—" I laughed, each chuckle sending a sharp throb to the center of my forehead. I closed my eyes and waited for the pounding to stop. When I opened them, the bride was watching me, her mouth taut in silence.

"Oh, come on," I said. "You have to admit, this is sort of funny."

The bride gestured for me to be quiet. "I know it is. But he—" The groom opened his mouth as if to interrupt. "*We* just thought since we were up—"

"—you could tell us more," said the groom. "Like maybe there's something we could do to break the spell."

"Spell? What spell?" The throb resumed as I sat up. "You know what they say about superstitions."

"What?" asked the groom, eagerly.

"They're only true if you believe them."

The bride took a seat on the edge of the bed next to the groom, looking down at the plush carpet.

The groom put an arm around her. "If the Soporex doesn't work, I've got something stronger—"

"I knew it," she said, brushing him away. "Things were just going too well—" Her voice caught but she quickly regained her composure. She looked up. "You're right, though. It is sort of funny. As wedding disasters go."

"No," I said. "Don't say that. What I said before, forget it. It's bullshit."

The groom stood up hopefully. "You made it up?"

"Not all of it . . . But that's not important. The important thing is that you're together. Who cares who falls asleep first? You have years with each other." I tried to rest a consoling hand on the bride's shoulder, but she stood and went to the suite's wide windows. The curtains were open; the harbor outside was now visible in the graying light.

"You know I used to have a thing for you," she said.

The groom and I looked at each other.

"This was a long time ago. Long before I met him." She took a seat on a nearby wing chair. She crossed her bare legs, swinging one over the other as she spoke. "Remember that summer I was living around Eastern Market?"

"Yeah."

"My roommate was out of town on the Fourth. We were meeting everybody at the Mall. I wore that blue seersucker dress, with the spaghetti straps? The one you liked on me."

I looked at the groom. "I never—"

"Oh, you liked it," she said. "I didn't really have it planned out. I would just wait until the right moment. You know, maybe during the fireworks. But that would be sort of cheesy. Maybe after, with all the smoke. So no one would see us sneak off. Just the two of us."

I could taste the return of my nausea. "I—I had no idea."

"Of course you didn't." She turned to her husband. "I was giving him every possible sign. Laughing hysterically at everything he said. And you know he's not that funny."

"I've got the picture," said the groom.

"And all he can talk about—before, during, and after—was Denise, Denise, Denise. Denise still hasn't returned my phone call. Denise returned my phone call but she sounded weird. Denise forgot our ten-week anniversary."

"Twelve weeks," I said. "It was twelve—"

"She was two time zones away. What did you expect? Anyway, you did me a favor. When I stopped feeling sorry for you, I stopped feeling anything at all." She stood and rejoined her husband on the bed. "He's right," she told him. "We're fine. We're going to be fine. Because this is real."

"That's not fair," I said. "She's still—"

"Fucking someone else. Married to someone else. Having someone else's babies. For your sake, there better be an afterlife. That's the only future in loving a ghost."

I stood. The room was spinning now. I prepared to run to the bathroom, but all that came out was a burning belch.

"You OK?" asked the groom. "Let me get you some water." When I started wavering again, he guided me gently to the bed. The bride was at the window, steeped in the growing light from the harbor.

The groom returned with a full glass. I could think of nothing to say as I drank. The bride continued her vigil.

After several minutes, the groom cleared his throat. "You know, maybe we're thinking about this all wrong. This is really just a good excuse to keep the party going."

"Honey, no." The bride turned from the window. She seemed more relaxed, but her eyes avoided mine as she left the area of the balcony. "I'm so tired—"

"Well then why don't you go to sleep?" he said. They exchanged a brief look. He began working the dial of a portable music player. "Most of this is mood music for us, but we must have burned something you like. What're you in the mood for?" he asked as he fixed the player into the bedside speaker dock.

"Whatever," I said. I pressed the cold glass to my forehead and closed my eyes.

"Here you go. *The Very Best of Elvis Costello and the Attractions.* You're into that British New Wave stuff, right?"

I opened my eyes. "That collection is for dilettantes. It barely scratches the surface." I was about to go into the glaring discographic omissions when I noticed the bride's brittle glare. "That would be perfect. Thank you," I said.

We listened to "Alison," then "Watching the Detectives." The opening drums on "Chelsea" felt as if they were being played against my temples. The groom refilled my glass and filled one of his own. I took a few sips, but mostly I just liked the coolness of the wet glass on my forehead.

The groom stood over me. "How're you feeling? Better?" he asked.

I nodded.

"Anything else I can get for you?"

"No," I said, then noticed the blurred outline of the groom through the glass. The bubbles along the sides looked soapy. And some held their shape as they sunk to the bottom in opaque shards.

I set the glass somewhere on my lap. Both newlyweds were in front of me now, watching. I felt myself sink back under the nuptial canopy. Words were suddenly hard to remember, but I managed to make myself understood.

"Was all that true?" I asked. "That time on the Mall?"

"You know what they say about superstitions," said the bride. She snatched the glass from my hand before it tipped onto the carpet. My eyes shut.

Borrowed

"I fear thee, ancient Mariner!
I fear thy skinny hand!
And thou art long, and lank, and brown,
As is the ribbed sea-sand.

"I fear thee and thy glittering eye,
And thy skinny hand, so brown."

Blue

I heard before I could see: a humming echo that seemed to carry me upwards to breach. The surface was solid black, then lightened to blue. I could make out the ripple of currents overhead. In their approaching transparency, I could see clouds and the outlines of sea birds. I rose faster, bracing for the shock of breath.

The honeymoon suite was fully lit in the overcast late morning. The music had looped back to the long fade-out of "Accidents Will Happen." By the curtains parted over the harbor, the newlyweds dozed together upright on a chair, each tilted over an armrest, heads lolling awkwardly over the narrow space between.

I left and took the elevator down to the lobby. Outside, I crossed the parking lot and the adjoining street to the rocks at the harbor's edge. The higher rocks were sandy and dry, but the lower I went, the more fresh seaweed rose and fell with the current. In the pools along the water's surface, black crabs gathered, alternately submerged and scrambling along the stones left glistening by the retreating tide. They scrabbled over the tips of my shoes; the leather was too smooth for their claws to find traction. The tide returned, higher this time. I watched my feet sink into a tide pool festooned with bobbing kelp. The water had an inviting warmth—only when the tide retreated did I feel the clammy heaviness of my legs. The next wave sprayed foam above my knees and pulled at the cuffs of my slacks. I waited. For sailors, the ninth wave is charmed, rising to take you to other worlds that, only in the guise of this one, could be mistaken for oblivion. But my head was clear and my feet were cold and my stomach swelled with appetite. I clambered back, in search of breakfast.

Kentucky-Fried Christ

C. E. CHAFFIN

I wear the Elephant Man's mask
like a Jewskin lampshade.
Do you see the glow of hell through it?
Come, warm yourself, take my gold fillings,
my bones for your Camellias
because living is for men in sunglasses
who filter the *not me* from the *me*
while suicide is for sissies in navy suits.

If my blood's been desiccated
and ground to red pepper,
remember me on your pizza.
I am the Jesus of the broken cell phone,
the Savior of ceramic kitsch.
I'll glue that broken cat
with the clock in its belly
together with my spittle.
Of my healing there shall be no end.

The End of the Objects

JACK KAULFUS

It wasn't a complicated passage, from one life to the next, unless you had difficulty making decisions. Mirelle silently gave thanks to an anonymous god (conspicuously absent at this stage in the afterlife) that her head remained level and her judgment unimpaired.

Mirelle knelt over a pile of blue sweaters and picked one that looked well-stitched. It was more used than others, but sturdily made. She had no way of knowing at which point in the next life it might be needed.

This was not the hereafter Mirelle had bargained for. She tossed the small sweater back onto the pile. Next to her, a blonde child laid four of them out for consideration. His bag was about half full. Mirelle wondered if he'd died young, or if he just felt like a seven year old. She'd noticed fewer gray hairs at her temples in the mirror herself, and had a feeling she'd been rewound a decade or so—before her body had begun its quiet, slow-moving rebellion.

"This is taking too long," he said, sitting back on his heels. "I just can't decide." His face was a child's, but his voice was tense and old.

Mirelle handed him a size 4T with a picture of a rocking horse sewn on the front. He turned it over in his hands for a few seconds, sighing, and handed it back.

"She's a girl, she's Black, she's not in America. These sweaters just mock her."

"Maybe if you go with a bigger one, there's a better chance she'll get more wear out of it. You know, statistically, we're adult-sized a lot longer than we're child-sized." Mirelle decided this was how she herself would choose, and she dug back in to find a generic looking size large. They watched a man kneel before the pile for approximately three seconds, grab a sweater, stuff it in his bag, and walk away.

"Careless," the boy said. "But he can probably afford to be. Maybe he's got a whole envelope full of possibilities. What about you?"

"Oh, I think I'm going with this one—" Mirelle paused to open the envelope and slide the card out so he could see. "Female, controllable mental illness, no parents. America."

"Wow. No parents?"

Mirelle shook her head proudly. She felt pretty solid about the whole thing. Enough strife, enough safety net, and a familiar setting. The choice between the two had been easy. She wouldn't have had the first idea about how to prepare for the boy's complicated situation with his coach and the kinds of problems it might bring him. "*I* made it," Mirelle said. "She can make it."

Mirelle was originally the son of a self-loathing, speed-addled mother and philanderer of a father. Her particular gender issues, she now understood, had been chosen for her just the way she was about to choose mental illness for a future self. Her predecessor had likely found himself or herself in this same spot, forty-two years previous, with a bad hand of cards: *Shit family. Wrong gender. Surprise gun barrel in an alleyway. Cancer.*

Tens of thousands of dollars in debt for necessary surgery to reverse the gender assigned at birth, she'd died at 55 after making a strong showing against lung cancer. She felt strangely indifferent about all the drama of life and death now. She'd been in love a few times, fostered dogs, been fired for dubious reasons, then employed as a counselor after returning to school for a license. She'd made a go of it, despite the absence of family.

After she died, they assured her at the gate that she'd done well.

"You didn't kill yourself or anyone else," said the woman in the first booth. "That puts you ahead of the game." She looked over the files in Mirelle's folder and presented her with an over-the-shoulder bag and a pad of paper. "Write down your worst fear and your deepest desire. Be literal. Take your time." The woman winked at Mirelle and wrote a large number seven on the front of the folder. She put the folder in a basket full of other folders, and waved at the next person in line.

Mirelle took a deep breath and followed the arrows on the floor. The absence of pain in her chest and legs was still a new feeling, and she suppressed a sudden urge to jog down the corridor.

At the next booth, a man in a cap pulled her folder from the basket in front of him. He inserted an envelope and handed it to her, smiling a golden toothed smile. "You will choose your future self from the envelope: your location, your situation, race, parentage. You will then find seven gifts from the available objects. These will be presented to your future self when they become necessary." He pointed to the window in the wall right next to her. Receding into the white space outside the booth for an eternity were piles upon piles of clothing, bins of toys, fruit, shoes, dishes. Tents. Sofas. "Put them in your bag. Remember your worst fear. Your deepest desire. Those, along with the objects, are your only legacy."

"You sound like the Wizard of Oz," she said to the man. He scratched his head, but did not look offended. "Do you think I can fit a sofa inside this bag?" Mirelle asked, but the man motioned toward the window and invited the next person in line to step forward.

On a bench under the window, Mirelle sat down and put her head into her hands. She thought there'd be rest in the afterlife. Light and dead pets and maybe a buffet. She wasn't ready to start everything over again. Her deepest desires on earth had always involved safety or paychecks, but she knew she'd have to do better than that. How? She opened the flap of the envelope. Two cards. Easy choice. She chose the girl.

At the pile of blue sweaters, Mirelle let the boy look through her bag: an inflatable raft, a tangle of keys, and a pair of sturdy brown walking shoes. She had three more objects to choose after the sweater: three more messages sent from beyond. She pushed away the apprehension and forced herself to think instead of the way it would feel to shave her young future legs the first time. Age eleven? Twelve?

The boy looked up at her. "I'm Frank," he said.

Mirelle shook his hand and introduced herself. "Can I ask you a personal question?"

"Arrested development, I think," Frank said, not waiting for the question. "I was in a boating accident when I was eight and I got stuck with a bum body, but I grew up all right. The last time I could move freely, I was this size. That's the only explanation I could come up with. Were you this age when you died?" He swept his hand from her head to her feet.

"A bit older, I think. I was wondering."

"I don't know how all the dying part works. But my future choices are limited." He pulled his envelope out and showed her the only card inside. "There was a meltdown in my teens," he explained.

"Oh?"

"That's right. Hard to imagine that I was the one who picked that terrible life for myself."

Mirelle shrugged. "You hadn't lived it yet. How many things do you get to pass on?"

"Four gifts. You?"

"Seven."

Frank sat back on his heels. "This sucks."

Mirelle thought it didn't suck as much as cancer, but she didn't say so. She couldn't—not to an ex-quadriplegic with suicidal tendencies. She was pain free now, but the memory of sickness wore at her like the memory of someone she used to love but didn't want to call. She'd died alone, afraid at the end, wishing for an afterlife much different than this one. Secretly, she'd always believed that people should get exactly what they want after the whole thing was over: Mormons their Celestial Kingdom, Baptists their Right Hand of God, Agnostics their Pleasant Surprises. This white room had no walls. She couldn't even sense a source of light.

They decided to go as far as they could in one direction to see if they could reach the end of the objects. Just to see what was on the other side.

"The world is big outside of America," Frank said. "And it's not like I even saw that much of America, at least not until 2000 or so, when we got the internet." They passed a woman weeping over a stack of high heel shoeboxes. "She looks famous," Frank whispered.

Mirelle couldn't place her. "Is this it? Choose a card and a few items and then go back as someone different? What's the point of a revolving door?"

Frank shook his head. "There's a point. I been here a while. You have to search for the things that will bring you the life you want. If you choose the wrong things, you can break your future self. I broke, kind of. You obviously almost broke."

"How do you know?"

"Well, seven objects is more than four, but some people have, like, fifty. And they have a whole stack of possible selves with problems like 'Too Many Boats.' They can just about plan an entire life."

Mirelle did not believe him. "With chess boards and crock pots?"

Frank fixed her with a critical eye. He directed her to a table full of watches and demanded she pick a real Rolex from a stack of knock offs.

She had never even thought about Rolexes. "I was a public servant. I don't have a clue," she said.

"That's the difference between you and Too Many Boats," Frank replied.

Rolexes had been the least of Mirelle's worries; once she was old enough to leave the house, she was never invited back. She recalled her father wearing expensive looking cuff links and ties, but she didn't remember anything about a watch. Her parents weren't around much for fashion advice, anyway, even when she'd been properly engaged in football and high school dances.

Mirelle met Abraham in Syracuse while she was still uncomfortably inhabiting the body of a young adult male. Abraham was the first to suggest that perhaps she was not yet who she might be. They were in an acting class together first, then auditioned to be regulars in a gay political theater group called GAYTES OF JUSTICE. Abraham's roommate was brewing beer in their shared dormitory suite bathroom, so he showed up without notice one evening and installed himself in the spare bunk above Mirelle's. He brought a suitcase, stacks of CDs in cracked jewel cases, and a poster of Morrissey in his underwear.

"Shit's about to blow in that place, and I need this scholarship," he said. Not a month had passed before Mirelle convinced herself they were in love.

He was growing his usually well-kept fade into something he called a "halfro," and one night after one too many Miller Lites, Mirelle let herself catch one of the longer curls between her thumb and forefinger as Abraham drifted off into a comfortably buzzed slumber.

He didn't push her away when she moved in to kiss him, but after a few minutes, he slid out from under her and went to the shared bathroom. He emerged with a small case beneath his arm and sat down on the bed across from Mirelle.

"Let me try something, Mitch?"

She leaned in to kiss him again, but he flipped open the case between them and extracted a tube of mascara. "Your eyes are amazing. I've been thinking of trying this color on you for weeks."

Mirelle looked at the tube in his hand. Abraham gently brushed Mirelle's hair back and brought her chin forward. "Look up," he said. She did. His breath was cool and smoky on her cheek as the mascara wetly darkened the edges of her vision. He opened a compact and showed Mirelle her eyes. "Look how beautiful you are," he said.

Mirelle took the compact from him and went to the mirror over the sink. She leaned in and swallowed hard, tears springing from nowhere. Behind her, Abraham assured her that the mascara was waterproof.

Mirelle jotted down possibilities in her little notepad as she followed Frank from table to table. Maybe a trenchcoat. A radio headset. A book about divorce law. She felt the tiniest flicker of excitement inside her chest. She imagined her new self being born of nothing, alone in a white room; at thirteen, in the dining room of another strange family, praying before a meal; at thirty two, living around the corner from a handsome, clever man who claimed to love Miles Davis but only knew his music from a college music appreciation class. Above all, the clothes against her skin, the men turning their heads to watch her pass. The home within her self, finally. At least she would be a girl. That part wouldn't be a struggle next time around.

Another life. More bad food, head colds, roaches, awkward sex. Dogs, hot rain, global crises. Coffee. She let her fingertips graze the tops of several ferns, and spotted a familiar-looking lamp in the hands of a large woman two tables over. She grabbed Frank's hand and walked over.

"What?" The woman drew the lamp to her chest protectively as they approached.

"That lamp just looks familiar. I'll give it back. I don't want to keep it." The woman handed the lamp over, and sure enough, on the bottom of the base was a crack in the shape of Florida. It had been her mother's.

Frank watched the woman take the lamp from Mirelle. "Tasha?" He asked.

Tasha tucked the lamp into her bag and raised her eyebrows at Frank. "What are you still doing here, Frank?"

"I told you I'd been here a long time," he said to Mirelle. "But I haven't been here as long as Tasha."

"So what?" said Tasha, throwing her head back defensively.

"So nothing. I just thought you'd get a handle on things by now."

Tasha's face closed into itself, her lips disappearing into a straight line. "I can't," she said. She dug through her bag and retrieved a worn-looking envelope. "One card. One. I can't go back on this card."

Mirelle took the envelope from her. *Afghanistan, educated woman, mother of three girls.*

"I know what it's like. I was in the military."

"You'll be on the other side now, though," Frank said. Mirelle could tell that this was not a comforting statement. "So, what, you're just going to wander around here for eternity?"

"I haven't decided. I think I might."

"Is that allowed?" Mirelle asked.

"I don't know who's in charge, actually." Tasha sighed and looked around. "Nobody's stopped me so far."

"Well, carrying that lamp around is not going to help you make a decision about going back," Frank said.

"So what? I like it." Tasha snatched the card back from Mirelle and turned away abruptly.

"I can't believe it," Mirelle said as she watched Tasha stalk off between the tables.

"*That* was confusing," Frank said, clearly exasperated. "Why in god's name would you have passed that useless lamp on to yourself?"

"I don't know. I didn't exactly use it to kill an intruder and save my family. It was just there. My mother loved it." Mirelle shrugged. "I wonder how many people are just killing time like Tasha," she said.

"I wish I had a card to give her," Frank said.

"You can't just trade lives with someone else."

"Who says?"

"It just doesn't seem right."

She couldn't decide a thing about her deepest desire or her worst fear, and felt at a disadvantage because most of it seemed as distant as a dream from three nights previous. She asked Frank if he felt the same way.

"I know what I know," he said, shoving a pair of sunglasses deep into his bag.

Mirelle stopped sleeping after her first makeover. She lay awake listening to Abraham breathe instead, wondering how she had neglected to notice such a crucial element of basic selfhood. For a while, gender panic eclipsed the plain fact that Abraham didn't return her love. She leapt back and forth through her own history, piecing together clues that had always before just seemed merely pointed in the direction of effeminate—never actually feminine.

By way of contribution, Abraham kept the fridge and the printer stocked. During the week, he tossed off translations for French and Spanish classes while working his way through one cheap beer after another. Mirelle struggled to keep her eyes open in class and rarely finished her assignments with any alacrity. Instead of working alongside him in the evenings, she watched Abraham study and thought about what it might feel like to wear a bra.

On the weekends, he coaxed Mirelle out of the dorm for rehearsals, though she refused to audition for parts and insisted on writing or working backstage.

"But it's *acceptable* to wear makeup on stage," he teased one day on the way home from rehearsal.

"I prefer to watch my words in action," she said, unconvincingly.

"You lie," he said. "You just don't want a boy part." It was maddening the way he threw those words around when she could barely utter the truth. He had no idea.

She loved him every time he slept with a professor, unsuccessfully wooed a basketball player, or shopped through her clothes to prepare for a night of sneaking past bouncers. Sometimes she went with him, but it felt like death each time he trained his beautiful brown eyes on someone else.

Frank said he needed to rest, so they picked a bench beside a fountain and sat down. He opened his bag and began unloading its contents. Mirelle watched the passersby. Most of them walked alone, looking bewildered. She elbowed Frank and he looked up to watch the weeping celebrity pass, pushing a wheelbarrow.

"What do you think her deepest desire is?" Mirelle asked.

"No idea. But I'll tell you mine," he said. He held up a tennis ball and a pair of green socks. "After you advise me on which is most ridiculous. Ball? Socks?"

Mirelle held out her hands and Frank relinquished the items. He flipped through the pages in his notepad. "My deepest desire is to be alone in my thoughts and my actions," he read. "It took me forever to get that much down, and it's lame. Tasha tried to help me make it better, but she has no idea what she's doing, either."

Mirelle stood up and threw the ball as far as she could and watched it disappear. "There are no walls?"

"Focus," Frank said.

Mirelle sat down and looked at Frank. "I think we are supposed to somehow prepare our future selves to achieve that deepest desire, Frank, and I think you might be wrong about how it's all done."

"I should keep the socks, then?"

"No. You probably don't need anything."

"That's not what the guy with the gold teeth said."

"You made it through a shit-hole life, Frank. You didn't hurt yourself or anyone else—"

"Not that I didn't try—"

"—and you're about to embark on another life, just as difficult. Quite possibly. A tennis ball and a pair of socks won't make or break you. I don't think you need anything at all."

"Speak for yourself."

"I might be. I mean, I think I can do this next life. In fact, after all this meaningless wandering, I'm looking forward to going back. It won't be a walk in the park, but there are drugs that can adjust my brain chemistry, and I know I figured out how to make family out of friends last time around. I've got some useful things here in my bag, sure. They might help me, but I think I'll make it regardless. In fact, I doubt *you'll* be back here if you survive this next time. You ever think that you're just about done, Frank? Just about ready to bypass the revolving door?"

"On to what?"

"I can't say. But this can't be *it*."

"I think you're deluded."

Mirelle shrugged. "Maybe I am. And maybe you're too comfortable here. Making up stories about your own victimhood." Frank shot her a look that did not belong to a child. "You want to hang out with Tasha the rest of your days? Never grow up? It's nice to be tall, Frank. It's very nice," she said. "We'll go together."

"You don't have to take care of me, Mirelle," Frank said.

The memory of the gun in her mouth was the only one that remained alive in all the fog. Long buried in her lifetime, it shined now. It was a sharp wet night, years and years after they'd moved out of the dorm and into a faux Victorian with vaulted ceilings and bedrooms connected by a long bathroom. There was a big autumn moon, reflected in the puddles on the sidewalks, everywhere at once. The air outside Club DeVine was a welcome surprise—a rainstorm had ushered in a cold front while they'd been inside, and the sweat beneath Mirelle's clothes turned chill the minute the doors closed behind them. She'd been dancing most of the night with a beautiful young dyke who had a bar code tattooed at the base of her neck. Since beginning the estrogen, she'd found her tastes ventured from beautiful fey men to beautiful butch women—something about the hard line of the shoulders and the softness at the top of the thigh.

She and Abraham lived together like there could never be another way. He'd been dating Justin for almost two years, long distance. She'd gone back to graduate school after losing her job for wearing a dress into the office, put her near- brain-dead mother into assisted living, and fallen out of love with Abraham three times.

Abraham stuffed his feathered vest into her bag and reached for her hand on the street. They did this as much for protection as for closeness. From the back they could pass as a straight couple headed home after drinks.

"So sad we're going home alone," he said, with mock sincerity.

"Speak for yourself. I got some digits in my purse."

"Please, Mirelle, BarCode Butch was still in diapers. Do not call her unless you want to converse solely about drag king performance art and socialized medicine."

Mirelle squeezed Abraham's hand. "Call Justin when we get home and I'll confirm your victory over temptation tonight. I saw that glitter boy all up in your face. I could read his mind."

"It's seven in the morning there."

"So what?"

Abraham leaned in affectionately. His head upon her shoulder was the last thing Mirelle felt before she came to with a piece of metal in her mouth and a knee in her crotch.

"I wonder what would happen if I chose more than my allotted items," Frank said. Mirelle threw the socks into the fountain, feeling guilt-free for littering. They sank beneath the surface of the water and disappeared.

"Want to hear my biggest fear?"

"Not right now," said Mirelle.

They couldn't agree on which direction to go. The fountain was circular. Three people wrote feverishly at the base of it. There was only white above, white below, white ahead, white behind.

It was difficult not to bite down on the barrel of the gun that had torn the inside of her cheek so deeply she was choking on blood. His knee ground bright white pain into her thighs and stomach, and she thought she might pass straight out into the static shrinking her vision. He was saying things to her, things she couldn't hear, or things she didn't understand. Mirelle raised an arm. He swung at it with his free hand, and someone else's boot came down hard on her palm.

Then he was up. The gun was gone. She coughed, turned her head and vomited blood. There were three or four of them, the moon like a spotlight over their heads.

"You want me to take care of your little problem?" He was saying. Or one of them was saying. She heard someone mutter, almost kindly, "Get up, freak."

She tried to stand, but dropped her head into her hands when the new pain and sight of blood on her skirt threatened to knock her out again. Two of the guys stepped forward, lifted her to her feet, and pushed her against the wall. They held her up. The gun that was once in her mouth was now pointed directly at the bloodstain on her skirt between her legs.

"You want me to take care of you? Say it, say yes sir, make my dreams come true. It's what you want? Right?"

Mirelle didn't answer. One of her back molars was loose.

In a sing-song voice, he continued: "Or you can say no, no sir, I want my dick. I love my dick. God made me a man, and men *love* their dicks. Just that, and I'll leave you alone. Walk away."

One of the men holding her up let go to light a cigarette. He exhaled into her face and said irritably "I'm bored, man. It's late. Just tell us what you want us to do."

Mirelle spat. The left side of her peripheral vision was gone. "Don't shoot," she said, quietly.

"Not good enough," said the one with the gun. The guy smoking a cigarette sighed loudly.

"Where's Abraham?" Mirelle asked.

He rushed her, his face in her face, the metal now pushed against her pelvic bone. "We already killed the faggot," he said. "Speaking of dick lovers."

Mirelle found his eyes. She told him she loved her dick.

"Do you ever get hungry here?" Mirelle asked Frank. He shook his head. They approached a table of firearms. Mirelle leaned over the selection and tried to make a decision. "Know anything about guns?"

"Not much, but not for lack of trying." Frank picked up a semi-automatic rifle, and the sight of him—such a small boy and such a big machine—was strangely pleasant.

"This might be the cure they're talking about," she said. "For the mental illness."

"*That's* not morbid." He put his eye to the sight, aiming at nothing. "You're not supposed to kill anyone," he added.

Mirelle dropped a nine millimeter into her bag. It had a satisfying heft. A great size for a purse. Two items to go.

Frank put the semi-automatic into his own bag. Mirelle smiled at him. "What?" He said. "I can always drop it later if I change my mind. I'm sure your nine millimeter will suffice, you know. I don't have the same kind of choice."

Abraham wasn't dead. He was unconscious, but not shot. Mirelle crawled to him and lowered her swollen face to his chest to make sure she could hear his heartbeat. Then she stood and pulled herself into a 24-hour gas station to call an ambulance. She returned to him and waited for half an hour, her fingers near his mouth, counting every breath.

They let her ride with him to the emergency room, where she had difficulty explaining the situation with any clarity. The nurse called her Mitchell and sewed her back together. They threw away her skirt and found her a pair of sweat pants to wear home.

She called Abraham's parents in Puerto Rico and soothed his mother the best she could.

"I laughed in that fuckwad's face," he told Mirelle the second morning. "That's why he jacked me up. I was never scared, and he knew it."

"Hell of a way to prove your manhood," she said, unfolding an ice compress from his crusted, yellowing forehead.

"Yeah? Well, where were you, Mirelle?"

"What do you want me to say? I was enjoying a cold beverage while they beat the shit out of you? I was unconscious, Abe."

"You also never fight for shit."

Mirelle turned her back. She returned to the kitchen to refill his water bottle, thinking he couldn't mean what he said. He was only upset, hurting, scared. He'd always been able to fend off attackers with his loud mouth or his fists. This time, he hadn't had the chance.

Mirelle heard Abraham on the phone that night, speaking in angry low tones long after he'd said good night to her. Justin arrived the next day and Abraham left with him within the week. His face hadn't even lost its patchwork bruising, and he was gone.

"I fear there's no end to this place," Mirelle said, looking around. Frank asked to see her bag again. She handed it to him as she circled a pile of things with little screens that lit up when touched. She had no idea what they might be used for, but she chose one and began to experiment. A man next to her was speaking quietly into the screen, and he seemed to be listening to something that she couldn't hear. She looked up to ask Frank his opinion, and didn't see him. She called his name a couple of times, returning to the spot where she'd handed him her bag. He was gone. His bag was there, emptied of all objects, save his original blue sweater. She dug around and below the sweater, she found that he'd left her own notepad, and her own envelope minus the one card she'd chosen for her future self. Her future as a woman was gone, gone with Frank.

She ran a few futile steps toward nothing and then sank onto a bench. Anger punched its way through the fog of distance that had overtaken her memories. Biggest fear: being blindsided. Complete loss of control.

She opened the envelope and pulled out the remaining card. *Male, Ritual Abuse at Hands of Trusted Family Friend, Divorced Parents, Southern United States.*

Mirelle retrieved the notebook from the bag, and then dropped the bag on the floor and kicked it underneath a chair. Beneath her worst fear, she wrote her greatest desire: retribution. Then she set out for the beginning again.

Tale of the Avian Saint

WILLIAM KEENER

When she spoke up, the birds would fly
wing after wing from out of her mouth,
harriers, hawks, and loggerhead shrikes
all in defiance of government rules—
words are for plumage, not to be used

for talons or song, forbidden to ruffle
their doves begging crumbs in the park.
But her owls broke the curfew, her larks
woke the neighbors, her crows cracked
the windows of the church and town hall.

We flocked to the streets, where they
night-sticked and cuffed her, but her wrists
disappeared in a puff of down-powder.
Facing the crowd, she said, *Don't resist*,
and gave up the rest. All that was left

was her dress, a few feathers they locked
in a squad car. We stayed to light candles,
debating her wisdom, what it meant,
that flight of her last falconet, our words
in the air, birds soaring, birds singing.

Finding Your Way to the Coast

JULIE DAY

Peter's hand moves slowly, hovering above Delia's bare forearm, as little as an eighth of an inch between her flesh and his fingers. The ghosts feel safest that way. That's what Peter had told her as he swallowed the last of his beer and set the glass aside, his eyes intent, lingering first on her lips, and then falling from her breasts to her right arm.

Peter doesn't look away despite the sideways glances of their companions and the clatter of dishes. The lone waiter is watching from across the terrace. Delia bends her head, ignoring them all. Both Peter and Delia are focused on his open palm as it creeps above her bare arm.

What do the ghosts feel? Delia wonders but does not ask. Instead, she closes her eyes. For a moment nothing has changed. The night air still feels dark and cool against her shoulders. She can hear the cars on the nearby Boulevard Saint-Michel. The taxis are bringing their loads of tourists to the Left Bank. A group of women erupt from a cab parked just beyond the terrace's back stairs. They speak in English, discussing how best to split the fare.

"Do these guys even get tips?" one of the women wonders.

Delia shifts in her seat, waiting. Anxious. It's dark behind her closed eyes. And Peter's ghosts have such sharp edges. She can already feel her skin loosening as they tug at her flesh, ghost barbs finding their way to the viscera underneath: the heart, the lungs, the looping passages of her intestine.

This is what I came for, Delia tells herself as Peter's hand combusts against her flesh. This is why I stopped the mail and packed all those cases. This is why I traveled through the night on that high speed rail.

Let everyone else wander the Seine, or the Louvre, or join all those bodies crushing their way up the Eiffel Tower. For Delia, Paris in summer means something entirely different.

The ghosts don't seem to even notice the city: not the moped speeding along the cobblestones, not the women now running south toward the Boulevard Saint-Germaine, not the darkened sky. Delia can feel Peter's ghosts burrowing, finding their rhythm. Meanwhile, Peter's hand continues to travel above her arm. Slowly. So slowly. And, finally, the moment arrives. She is floating, freed, her flesh, temporarily, left behind.

Delia keeps her eyes closed. The sun is beating against her skin. A shiver runs through her as the wind follows. She can hear the soft "Shh" of something flying overhead. The creature hovers for a moment before it moves on.

An arm presses against her side. Is it Mark? This is better than any memory, better than any stories told to a therapist for ninety dollars an hour. Peter and his ghosts have carried Delia entirely away. She hesitates, eyes still closed, the arm still pressed against her. Surely, it will be Mark....

And yet Paris still exists. Even now Delia can feel Peter's hand as it hovers above her flesh. She can feel his ghosts settled somewhere below her skin, entwined in her connective tissue, piercing her. But their barbs are like distant pricks, not even worthy of her attention. Delia opens her eyes. She turns her head. She looks.

Of course, it's Mark, resting next to her on a towel. The sky is a uniform gray; Delia sees no sign of any flying creatures. Before her is an ocean, slick and still and glassy. It shimmers in places, oily smudges like thumbprints scattered across its surface. The towel is all that separates Mark and Delia from the sand. Or the non-sand, gray-white and ashy. Strewn across the beach Delia sees odd, twisted rocks and charred lumps of wood that remind her of campfire remnants, though she doubts any campfires ever spark along this stretch of beach. This place, Peter's place, is where people come after the fires. Scattered as far as Delia can see are people. Bodies lying on the sand, hands entwined.

Her eyes are drawn back to Mark. Despite the thready-white of his skin, she can see his chest rise and fall. He knows I'm here even if he can't speak, Delia thinks. He must.

The air smells of salt and half-rotten seaweed. Fire. Cinders and ash. It smells of that, too. Mark and Delia may be resting against the sand. But Peter and his ghosts—Peter with his electric hands and pale gray eyes— and Paris and the terrace are no more than an eyelash away.

"A cultural attaché," Wendy had explained earlier as she'd dragged Delia from the hostel and through the labyrinth of cobbled streets. Dinner, it seemed, was a requirement, dinner with Delia's three new friends and Peter.

"Peter," Wendy had said as she eyed Delia's pale pink tank top, "remembers you from the Metro this morning." As though this was a special honor Delia was duty bound to accept. Certainly, ribbons and a small brass band weren't far behind.

Delia, however, remembered nothing but the gray tiles of the underground and Wendy talking, at last, to someone else. And now he wanted to meet her again? In the end, it was so much easier just to agree.

Peter was taller than Delia expected, tall enough to catch sight of her yards before she finally reached him. His arms and legs seemed to bend at unexpected angles as he hovered near an iron lamppost set just beyond the Luxembourg stop. Delia could imagine him crouched forward, looking down at the city from some ledge or high-up window. She could imagine him motionless for hours at a time. His light brown hair frizzed out from his head like an untidy halo, but there was no softness in his body. His skin looked rough, like sandstone, thick pores connecting the sallow membrane that rested atop his muscles. When he caught Delia's gaze, he smiled. Even feet away, Delia noticed his tidy, little teeth.

"Peter," he said as his dry hand gripped her softened skin. Delia couldn't quite place it, but his accent was definitely not French. Like her, he was a visitor to this city. The Metro entrance kept pouring people onto the street, bodies streaming in and out of the restaurants and cafes, everyone so hungry. Peter had eyes only for Delia.

Delia's other two friends, Kurtis and Alex, arrived soon after. Both were breathless. A flush was rising along Kurtis's pale cheeks. And then Peter was leading the group north. All the while, he was talking, talking, talking, giving his tour of the Left Bank. It seemed he was an expert. Kurtis, Wendy, and Alex couldn't believe their good luck. Peter pointed out the palm trees in the Jardin du Luxembourg, the red neon of the tobacconist, La Favorite, on the Boulevard Saint-Michel, and farther along, in the center of the Latin Quarter, the Church of Saint-Severin with its own collection of ancient gargoyles.

Gargoyles covered the rooftops of the city. The city was filled with crumbling and broken stone. Did no one else notice how hard Peter's back and shoulders looked as he guided them through the city? Did no one else notice the way his legs and arms bent as he walked? Did no one else notice that their guide, their cultural attaché, was a living gargoyle? An ash and stone grotesquery?

Finally it was time to eat. Peter, to everyone else's delight, chose the restaurant, and when the waiter dropped the menus on the table, Peter chose the chair next to Delia's. It was only minutes before Peter had turned his chair, his hard knees now pressed against the side of Delia's right thigh. His flesh felt so cold, his skin flaking, revealing more ashy layers underneath. It was the first time someone had touched Delia in days or weeks or months. That hand Mark's mother placed on her shoulder, surely, didn't count?

"I can do it," Peter said without the hint of a smile. "I can show you the coast."

"Oh, come on," Alex replied. "Without moving from this table? She's not that drunk."

At that moment, Delia almost liked Alex. All the same, she agreed to everything, agreed to Peter's hand creeping its way across her skin.

"It's alright," Delia said. "I'll try it."

"Only the ghosts will touch you," Peter said, looking straight at her. "The ghosts," he explained as he leaned even closer. "The ghosts generate the heat."

And then Peter's hand was hovering above Delia's arm. The little hairs on her bare flesh rose up, connecting with his palm. Despite the thin blue veins that lined his skin, his hand didn't feel cold anymore. That was

Delia's first thought. And then there was the beach. And Mark. And the vast and shiny ocean, brittle, hiding an infinite number of eyes. It felt like all those eyes were waiting and Delia wanted nothing more than to slide her hand up along Mark's inner thigh, his body so still as she leaned over, finally. Her breasts felt soft against his stone chest as her mouth searched for some warmth.

"Delia," a voice murmurs.

It isn't Mark's voice. His lips haven't moved even once. It isn't any of the other couples lying on the beach. Delia can feel ash swirling around her, stinging as it slips up her nose, finds its way into her eyes. Something is stepping across the sand. Someone's shadow is covering both Delia and Mark. Delia glances away from Mark, just for a moment. There's a glimpse of stone talons rising up from the ashen sand, each arched claw almost as thick as Delia's own fragile wrists. And then there is no more time. Her skin has tightened around her once again.

The blood is pounding in Delia's cheeks as she opens her eyes. The tables on the terrace are almost empty, the space lit by dim, orange bulbs. Alex has pulled a small pocket calculator from his fanny pack.

"How many should I divide by?" Alex asks.

Alex, Kurtis, and Wendy are all careful to avoid Delia's eyes.

"We can go to my place," Peter murmurs. His hard knees are still pressed against Delia. His lips are too close for anyone else to hear. Delia knows she should pull her arm away, push her chair back, but the warmth of his hand reminds her of a time before torn, white undershirts and unwashed bedding, before sleepless nights spent on molded plastic chairs. His hand reminds her of a time before she even considered this trip to Paris.

Delia doesn't reply, looking away toward the city instead. Notre Dame sits to the west, just beyond the Seine. She can see the cathedral's towers rising above the surrounding buildings. Underneath the night sounds of the city, the lapping water of the river reaches out. The old stone walls that press up against the distant bank are not that far away. The top of the wall, as she follows the curve of the river west, seems covered in fairy lights.

"In the magic stories," Peter says, noticing the direction of her gaze, "It's always a mistake to follow the lights."

His breath smells faintly of cigarette smoke and smoldering ash.

"I'm not afraid," Delia replies. And she means it.

Wendy is frowning, two lines appearing along the bridge of her nose, more cracks across her forehead.

Paris is for lovers? Who says? Delia came here alone. And despite Alex and Wendy and Kurtis sharing her train compartment from Amsterdam, she's remained alone. Earlier in the day she visited the city of the dead, the Pere-Lachaise Cemetery, alone, leaving Wendy and the others to find their own way through the city. Later she stared at the gargoyles and marmosets carved into Notre Dame Cathedral. One in particular, with his folded wings and a rough scar that seemed to cut across his forehead, held her attention.

His mouth half-parted and stone-still. Was he angry or afraid? He should be able to tell her, right? It doesn't seem fair to spend an eternity trying and failing to speak.

Now Delia is sitting with people who speak but who don't seem to understand what questions should be asked. Alex was Kurtis's teacher. That's what they are telling her as they explain their mathematical formula for dividing the check, but the words make less and less sense.

"Let's go" is all Delia hears as Peter murmurs in her ear yet again. A curl of his hair actually touches Delia's cheek. Her arm is electric with ghosts. All of them waiting. Does no one else notice? She is caught at the wrought iron table with Peter, the thirty-five-year-old cultural attaché, and her three traveling companions. But only Peter, Peter and his ghosts, matter.

Peter's left hand has, somehow, found its way under the table. His fingers have settled on her thigh. When did that happen?

If only she could find her way back. The beer is buzzing in Delia's brain, and after two months, her body still craves sleep, white-sheeted sleep. Peter's hard knees press insistently, too insistently, but Peter knows what she wants, he's the only one at the table who does. More than that, Peter is the only one who can show Delia the way back to the coast.

"Leave them," Peter whispers, nodding his head toward the darkness.

Kurtis waves his fingers toward the waiter. "Another Coke, please."

Ignorance shields happiness. Mark always knew that. He was the one who told Delia not to climb into the ambulance. He was the one who told her to go back to bed. And later, as he lay in that hospital bed, he was the one who told Delia to go home. As though that would have changed anything. Almost two months. Has it really been almost two months?

Peter's hand still hovers insistently above Delia's goose-bumped flesh, though his lips have tightened in frustration. He's the cultural attaché, not me, Delia thinks. Isn't he supposed to convince me of something? Isn't he supposed to have a plan?

And then she lets it all go. "Okay," she replies.

They rise together from the table, Peter's fingers locking with Delia's as they run across the terrace and out toward the river of fairy lights. His hand is dry and cool and Delia pretends she doesn't notice anything unusual, though the heat in her arm is spreading. The ghosts have already started, burrowing even faster than before.

They've reached the boulevard. It's like a parade of bright and shiny memories. Behind the plate-glass windows, Delia can see the mannequins in their belted, houndstooth dresses and capped sleeves, and suddenly, she is shopping with Mark for her first work suit. A perfumier's window is filled with burgundy flowers and small green leaves, each shimmering inside its own translucent bubble. And Mark is walking through the door with one of those funny little gifts Delia is always misplacing. A gourmet food store has a spotlight shining on the contents of its window. Red peppers and darker olives float in oil and brine. And there is Mark, explaining his theory of the proper oil-to-salt ratio as he stirs the tomato sauce. Delia can feel cracks rising along storefront windows. More memories are en route.

Peter's grip tightens, driving Delia's fingernails against the palm of her hand, and then he is pulling her in so that they face each other, tilting Delia's head up, kissing her. The pressure of his hands and arms are not at all comforting. Meanwhile, the ghosts continue to burrow, cutting their way through all those connections. Delia's lips are wet when Peter finally pulls away. He leaves his arm draped across her shoulders as though they've crossed some threshold together. Delia can see her reflection in the clothing store window, Peter's tall, lanky frame hovering over her. The top of Delia's head barely reaches his chest. Her face seems to waver, a pale and uncertain reflection.

And now she can't stop remembering, Peter's arm heavy, pressing down against Delia's flesh while his ghosts wind ever tighter.

Delia hears the siren first, an ambulance. The red and white flashing lights follow soon after. She watches the lights as they dive down the street from window to window, reflecting back from the plate-glass storefronts. Help. Someone is failing. Someone is dying. Someone is dead, they say. They are ghost lights, grounded stars, lost amid all those shattered memories.

Shuddering breaths. Delia remembers those. She remembers pulse rates and sweat-soaked sheets as well. Despite the price tags on the window displays, the flashing ambulance lights are setting their own price. They are offerings from an entirely different store: wounds of all types for sale on this summer night. Delia stands with Peter on the sidewalk, his arm on her shoulder. Both of them are still. Their eyes follow the ambulance as it moves farther and farther away.

Funerals are all the same: tears and music you never want to hear again. Prayers.

Delia wore tights even though it was ninety degrees outside. She listened to Mark's mother as she cried. Mark's mother leaned into Delia's shoulder as they carried Mark's casket inside the old stone church. His mother's smell was all wrong: floral and powdery. Delia wanted sour. She wanted sweaty. She wanted three days of forgotten showers and a night on the river with the mud sliding between both of their feet. She wanted Mark. No one asked Delia if she wanted to cry. Why should they? She wasn't even there, too busy floating, ashes against the sky.

The door of Peter's house is only inches from the river. The wall and the fairy lights are all that separates them from the water. Delia can smell the boat fuel and a sweetish rot, like flesh, floating along the river. Peter's door sits in the middle of an alley: dark, old wood, and peeling paint, a stone lintel hanging above. The brass doorknob is like an open hand waiting to be taken. She wants to reach forward. There is darkness waiting. There is cold and heat. There is the coast and Mark and the hard and staring water. But Peter's grip hurts. His arm is like a crushing stone. Delia can feel bruises on her shoulders, rising up, and she wonders what will be required of her this time. She hears a cough from a nearby window and the slow putter of a boat moving on the other side of the wall. In the end, it is someone, someone on the other side, who finally turns the handle.

Not Mark.

"Welcome," Peter says, following Delia through the doorway, just a step behind. His hands have settled on both of her hips. Delia can feel his breath against her neck. His body feels like molten rock: hot, hard, and blazing.

Delia shudders, her body wracked by a sudden fit of coughing: ghosts everywhere, sharp jabs in her lungs, a twisting in her gut. What does it matter if Peter scorches her skin?

They are near the river, the veins of the city bleeding through the cracks in Peter's walls. Delia expected the crouching gargoyles and damp stone walls. She expected the dimness and the smell of charred remains: wood ash, the acrid stench of scorched hair, and, hanging over it all, the oily, cloying sweetness of burning meat. Even the cot, set in a far corner of the room, seems familiar, the sheets hospital-thin and hospital-white. It is the girl who takes Delia by surprise, the girl who opened the door. She is watching Delia with those silver eyes: ash-coast eyes that shimmer but do not blink.

Peter is still behind Delia, his hands tightening. The cloth of Delia's cotton skirt presses into her hips. And all the while, the girl is reaching out, the girl's face as untroubled as a Christmas ornament, something red and fleshy in her outstretched hand. Each of the girl's thin, little fingers ends in a black nail, sharp and pointed. Each nail is at least half the length of the finger itself. The girl's fingers curl slightly, cradling the red contents of her palm. There is red on her cheeks as well, blonde curls under her velvet cap, hot ashes escaping her nostrils and perfect lips. The girl opens her mouth wide, and a cloud engulfs Delia. Delia can feel Peter behind, inhaling deeply. The cinders make Delia cry. Nothing makes me cry anymore, Delia thinks as ashes and water stream down her cheeks.

The ash is swirling around all three of them, the girl, Peter, and Delia, passing over the stone creatures who watch the trio from the corners of the room. Peter's hands slide upward, cupping Delia's breasts. He runs his hard tongue from her collarbone upward against the base of her skull. Cold and then hot. Burning. Delia can feel her skin pulling back in protest. A whimper escapes her lips. And still Peter's tongue keeps tracing lines along Delia's flesh, his hands like crushing stones as they grab at breast and hip and thigh.

The gargoyles that line the edges of the room are not the ones to worry about, Delia realizes. The stone statues with their long ears and sharp teeth have such gentle eyes. It is only Peter, Peter with his halo of brown hair and electric hands, who wants to touch her. The rest just want to return home, to fly to the coast once Peter opens the door. The closest gargoyle, the one to Delia's left, stretches her legs, her back a concave length of stone that curves toward the ground, then she settles once more against her back legs, content, it seems, to wait.

The lights on the boulevard were nothing. The memories are tumbling now, pressing hard. Delia is gasping for breath as the cinders fill her lungs. Peter's dry fingers like an abrasion against her thighs, the small of her back, and Delia is falling back against the bed, hospital-white sheets covering the backs of her legs, her waist, her bruised and shaking arms. Inside, she is untethered. The ghosts are rising up, carrying everything with them as they rush back through Delia's skin.

It is almost time to open the final door. It must be. Delia can hear the girl breathing somewhere nearby. She can feel the heat of the girl's cinders. She can see the girl's flashing eyes, silver light that doesn't look away.

Mark lay in that hospital bed for ten days while Delia sat on the molded plastic chair, willing him to stay asleep.

"Just sleep," she murmured as she stroked his sweat-stained hair, but it did no good. The vomiting would start: his legs curling up against his chest, his skin covered in a pattern of splotches and welts Delia couldn't begin to translate.

"He needs to rest," the attendant said as she added another ingredient to the bag of fluids that hung near Mark's head.

Delia noticed the woman's kind brown eyes. Then Mark's own eyes closed, and Delia started to breathe again. She timed her inhalations with the movement of his chest: the rising and lowering of the hospital sheets telling her Mark was still alive, the air in Delia's lungs telling her there was enough for both of them.

Toward the end, Mark mostly slept.

"Just go and get some rest," Mark said that last time. But Delia didn't go home. She couldn't. Home was where the bed was empty and the cat expected Mark to feed her at 6 A.M. Home was the pile of clean laundry heaped and unfolded in a corner of the room, the trash rank after too many days left untended. Home wasn't a place that existed anymore.

Delia wanted to climb onto that narrow hospital bed. She wanted to wrap her arms around Mark's chest and smell that sour, male scent. She really did. But his skin looked so drained, and the smell when Delia hovered over him was closer to chemical antiseptics and veterinary visits than the salt of living flesh. The scent closer to death.

Instead of leaving, Delia pulled that molded plastic chair close, held Mark's hand.

He is sleeping, Delia thought as she watched the sheets rise and then fall again, breathing.

When Delia opened her eyes, it was dark. Women were hovering around the bed, two or three of them, and someone was pushing Delia back with hard, stone hands. Mark's fingers were no longer in hers.

The heat in the room, was Delia the only one who felt it? And now they were pulling in a cart. It was like a T.V. episode, a movie-of-the-week special. Wasn't Delia supposed to start weeping? But she didn't. And she didn't. And even when they left Delia with Mark, or Mark's body, for "a few moments" still she didn't. Mark and the Hospital. This wasn't a story. This was pretending to float while you crashed and broke across the rock-strewn ground. This was the Great Blackout of 2010 and Delia locked inside the elevator listening to the cable unravel. Devastation doesn't have a script. Shattering and then smaller still. Pulverized. A cloud of floating debris.

It was easy to get on that plane. Easy to float across the ocean, landing with Wendy and Alex and Kurtis, the Metro and the tourists maps. Finally, though, night fell, Peter's hand holding hers as they headed across the city.

Of course Delia went with Peter. She was like a box of ashes, carefully contained, just waiting to be released.

"To ghosts," Peter had said, tossing back that last beer while they sat on the terrace. But the ghosts all seemed so small under his hands, more like a child's toy or dangling charms rather than people. Nothing but a palmful of energy. Delia wanted more than that.

They are almost done.

Delia is lying on the bed, face up. The sweat drips from Peter's neck and chest hairs onto her body. Peter's hands are cradling Delia's breasts, heavy, pressing inward. Delia can feel the bones of his hips grinding, his thighs leaning into hers for a moment before she is forced to bend her knees. Peter's face flushes as he finally slips inside, eyes now closed. Delia's body rocks with Peter's while her hands reach outward, finally wrapping themselves in those hospital-white sheets. She can smell the sweat of their bodies and the candy-sweet scent of her crackling flesh. Underneath it all is the scent of linoleum hallways and that white-tiled hospital room.

The creatures lining Peter's room do not roar, they bellow. A wave of rage and grief that crashes through the open door.

Delia's hands have stopped moving. Her arms and legs no longer shudder as her mouth gasps for breath. Meanwhile, Peter is sliding off, stretching his legs before he stands. He stoops down to the floor and then sits, his hands now holding a pack of cigarettes and a book of matches.

Delia remains still, wrapped in the sheets. The bed feels worn, threadbare, overused. The room is empty of stone creatures, empty of girls who watch her with ocean-silver eyes.

Peter looks down at Delia from his seat by the bed. The cigarette smoke lingers above his nascent horns. His hips and clavicle press outward, their outline clear beneath the skin. He's far more skeletal now. It's only that thin layer of gray skin that keeps Delia from seeing his organs: his kidneys, his heart, his ash-filled lungs.

The bed feels so warm.

Why didn't Delia notice Peter's chair when she first stepped through the door? It's made of the same molded plastic as the chair in Mark's hospital room. The metal legs are attached with those too-small screws that make it tip slightly whenever you sit down. Delia doesn't want to look at it. It is not a chair anyone should trust. But Peter slouches all the same, the Cultural Attaché. His face, despite the slouch and the curling lines of smoke, is more petulant than tired. His part is done.

The warmth of the bed is drawing Delia inward. Her body curves against the other body now resting next to hers. She can feel an arm against her naked shoulder, feel a chest under her hand. Delia's feet wrap themselves around his calves. Mark. The sheet covers them both.

I am sure we will arrive at the coast soon, Delia thinks. Her eyes have closed, but she knows the pallor of Mark's skin matches the thready-white of her uncovered breasts, the two of them now white as sheets.

Finally, Peter and his gray smoke are lost on the other side of the broken windows.

Ballad of Conjure

for Jack's Terrible Presence

FELICIA ZAMORA

Pluck the dark
from behind a billion eyelids

paint sky with echoing
empty is not in the night

how the belly stores
clears space and spins

a womb happens without eyes
without candelabras

burning – *here*
in the calloused tufts

of skin below the ankles
of skin below the wrists

magic firing in furrows
cut in veined grooves

where all fruit as fruit
bears fruit. Sow

bulbs (plant us
all) and ovum (oh,

silkworm mother)
in wonder:

the frailest cocoon
swarms deep. What burns

boldest in the night
is the night.

La Chanson de l'Observation

BERNARD M. COX

Preface:

> With Theo asleep it was easier. With him asleep, he couldn't ask why I came into his life only to leave. With him asleep, I could be selfless and not hold onto him.
>
> This, my twenty-eighth iteration, may be my last. Soon I would no longer be able to feel his arms around me, or the flitting of my heart when he calls out to me, or delight in his scent. Soon I'd be reduced to molecules, a new observer would take my place and it was possible that I would not even survive as a node—no longer sent on missions to observe, never a chance to see him again.
>
> With him asleep, I could leave this world and save him.

Abstract:

The phenomenon of entanglement, referred to by humans as "love," caused a network failure for node AR1x40 and resulted in individuation of the node and, subsequently, in its break with The Commonality.

> I woke up and inside was quiet and clear. The internal, sometimes deafening, slow churning of the data stream—the calculating, compiling, tallying, and transmitting—ceased. I could hear things like the crinkling of the sheets under my head, the faraway sounds of birds in the park, the trolley coming to a stop at the corner, and the slow, measured breathing of Theo's sleep. The world was different to the touch, so much sharper and full. I was the sole operator. I was the data stream.
>
> He woke and said to me, "Morning, Beautiful. You're up early."
>
> "Isn't it just wonderful?"

Introduction:

Coupling is a common occurrence among species that have not developed the ability to bypass indirect perceptual filtering. We recognize these pairings as an interstitial step, substituting a physical/social pairing for a direct connection (such as conduition or telepathy) with a community of minds in an effort to eliminate the sense of isolation that indirect connection produces. Similarly, these species often develop some theological framework in an effort to comprehend direct cognitive connection.

The following account is a participant observation study of node/observer AR1x40's experience coupling with one human participant, "Theo Zedek."

Node/observers inhabit human biological archetypes in order to better interact with and report on true human behavior. This node/observer's archetype is named "Javier Flores."

> *Theo smells of fresh bread, and his lips taste of chocolate. His hands are strong from sifting flour and working dough. At night he brings home failed cookies and cakes, which are moist on our tongue and soft in our mouth, and our cheeks sweat at their richness, and we ask how they can be failed. He says that they aren't really failed, they're just too good for La Chanson but not good enough for us. We disagree as we devour them. Sometimes he pretends he's a bunny, and he hops around the house, his hands limp, shaking his tail, begging us to chase him, which we do with abandon until we catch him and fall on the bed laughing. He says "Javier, I love you." And we say, "Je t'adore, mon chéri."*
>
> *We were not to get involved. We were to stay "we" and not become "us," not become "I."*
>
> *He doesn't know, we never tell.*

Aims of the study:

This experiment is a longitudinal study in fifteen year increments. The original intent of the study is to report on behaviors and developments of humanity on "Earth" in order to determine when they can be welcomed to the Symposium.

Review of Past Studies:

Though this was not the goal of the study, a small number of experiments have resulted in a true pairing of an observer and a participant. Often pairings are just to preserve cover of the observer; seldom do they result in a connection which disrupts the network.

Recollection provides us with a few examples. Node qW2-RR, infamously, was consumed by a Gammens participant in a courtship study which overloaded the network in a field of euphoria. As a result, The Commonality needed to reboot all observers on the Gammens' system.

Similarly, node LEA*2626, while observing early humanity, escaped recall and forfeited one hundred iterations of research to swim across a strait in an attempt to remain paired to a human counterpart. The subsequent event became a myth, and, as with such myths, details become inexact over the years.

Sample:

Archetype Flores interacts with approximately 500 participants on a daily basis through his position as a bank teller. However, he is fixated on only one participant, Theo Zedek. As such, most data retrieved from node AR1x40 in some way relates to the relationship between observer and participant.

Method:

Our objective is to become integrated within the society in a position where we can collect the most data. We seek a position where we are not directing other humans but rather receiving directional input so to minimize interference in their behavior. Positions such as the mentally infirm, domestics, and customer service representatives offer the most expedient and direct data.

For example: our job as a teller at a bank provides us with examples of how humans treat those in positions of service. Many customers hand over checks and deposits without acknowledging our participation. They look at their shoes, talk to a companion, or fiddle with communication devices. They do not acknowledge our presence. We only operate to serve them. But for some we are an integral part of their day.

> *Professor Holiday, age 64, comes into the bank to check her balance twice a week. She smiles and says our name. She asks us how we are doing. During our first interaction she stated:*
> *"I will try not to be too much of a bother since you are new."*
> *We told her she was no bother. Then she asked, "Did you see that new French bakery open across the square? It's just like a real boulangerie, but it has coffee. Excellent coffee, not French coffee. It makes Rittenhouse feel like a small part of Paris. Have you ever been to Paris?"*
> *"Yes, a long time ago."* For further details see iteration 23.
> *"It's just like that. I'll bring you a croissant next time."*
> *She did. The pastry was hot, almost burning in our palms.*
> *"You must go,"* she commanded.

Results:

Despite the communication collapse, all transpirations of the data stream were coded by The Commonality and remained intact for analysis. This being said, most observations related only to the pairing.

Notwithstanding the resulting individuation of the node/observer, AR1x40 has provided valuable data. While we are no closer to understanding how pairings cause conduition collapse, we can be certain that individuation needs to occur in order to instigate the pairing and, subsequently, the cessation of communication between the node/observer and The Commonality. This inciting action of individuation results in a binary commonality within the pair—each identifies as a separate entity but the individuals refer to the pairing as "we."

> *On Sundays* La Chanson *is closed, and we go to* Charlie's *in the afternoon. It's a small bar, but has a dance floor. We two-step and swing for hours on end. We float through the crowd, around and around, following the line of dance. Sometimes, when we are lucky, we are the only ones, and we become the resident Fred and Ginger. Everyone watches as he leads me across the floor. He dips me, spins me, and when the song ends, the patrons applaud and ask for more.*
>
> *On slow songs, his hand is firm against my back and I lean against his chest. I am filled with warmth in his embrace and "we" is no longer the network or the Common, but us, he and I. The first time he took me, I knew we were now us, and I was Javier, and he was everything.*

Though it must be noted, a pairing does not always result in equilibrium, such as the connection to The Commonality provides and, thusly, is not always a desirable condition.

> *In our fifteen years together, life has not always been easy with Theo. Sometimes we argue, over money or other trivialities.*
>
> *Sometimes we wouldn't see each other for stretches of time due to his work, and I would feel this immense, dreadful feeling of drowning. I'd be alone in the house but instead of feeling space, I'd feel like the house was falling in on top of me, crushing me.*
>
> *I remember the transmission of node DIR58*7 which stated, "While taking a partner in a society where it may be the normal modality to do so, take care to not become attached to this mate. Such attachments deliver a complex pleasure that can be more desirable than becoming a full conduit for The Commonality and create a sense of individuality that may lead to madness and result in a terminus of the operating node."*
>
> *But when we are together, I no longer remember.*

Additionally, we are unsure if nervousness, manifesting in physical, actionable quirks, is a necessary element for human pairing. Physical displays in other species are usually grander and much clearer, allowing us to discern the motive behind them.

> *He kept rubbing the palms of his hands against his jeans when he first asked us out. He also had difficulty looking at us. He said: "Hi, I'm Theo Zedek."*

Theo Zedek's face is big and welcoming, and his eyes are sapphire blue; and when he did look at us it seemed as if the twin O-class stars of the Wyn system orbited us. We grew warm, and our clothes became uncomfortable as they stuck to our skin. We responded, "Hello," involuntarily giggled, and forgot our assigned identity.

He said, "You come in a lot."

"The food is very good."

"I make it."

"Really? I'm impressed."

"What's your favorite item?"

"You'll laugh. I'm a bit simple."

"Tell me, I won't laugh."

"The hot chocolate with chantilly."

"Oh so yummy. I have to be careful, or I drink it all day."

"How could you? It's so filling."

"Honey, I haven't always had this body," he said as he patted his belly.

"Neither have I."

"What gym do you go to?"

"No gym, just a nip there and tuck here every few years or so." At that point, we knew we had a problem. We told him that we were making a humorous statement and that it was just self monitoring that kept us in a healthful condition. "Though I can see that if I continue to come here for hot chocolate, I will have to join a gym."

"Go for long walks, like the French. Speaking of which . . ."

We knew our answer would be yes.

Contrary to most ethnographic observations of other species, in humans, interaction with members of a partner's family helps establish a more intimate connection through the sharing of embarrassing or relevant stories of each partner's past. The following are two examples.

Theo's mother is a big woman, about the size of the crimson helium puffers of Ftsi. She's only dwarfed by her personality. When she enters a room, usually carrying some wonderful concoction she has just whipped up, or the best bottle of Beaujolais we have ever tasted, or an entertaining story, she is the center of attention.

"When Theo got it in his head that he was going to be the next Pelé, he'd practice in our backyard for hours and hours. Kicking the ball against the garage, flipping over on his back and spinning his legs in the air. The couple behind us would phone and ask us to call him in because the sound of the ball would boom throughout

the neighborhood. BOOM, BOOM, BOOM. You remember, Theo?"

"Yes, Mom, I remember."

"You know, Javier. Our backyard wasn't very big. About fifteen steps in any direction and you're up against the fence or at the garage. Well, one day he's kicking the ball around, and I hear this crash. I run to the window, and there is Theo, out cold lying in the grass. He had run through the wooden fence. I thought that's only something you could do in a cartoon."

"Thanks, Mom." When he blushes, his shoulders turn as red as his cheeks.

"After the concussion he couldn't play for the rest of the season, so I taught him how to cook and bake."

"And that's how I became Julia Child."

"Bon appétit!" Mrs. Zedek chirped.

Example 2:

He has told me on occasion that he wishes he could have known my family. I don't tell him I was recombined from the residuals of past nodes, that I am engineered. I tell him my parents died and, instead, I trade him stories of my childhood—compiled from records of human interviews and previous observers' experiences—for stories from his childhood. I provide a deception out of a myriad of truths.

He told me that during high school he dated Sarah Bouchard. At prom she got them a room, and after the dance they went back to it. The place was all done up with rose petals and candles. He got so nervous he went into the bathroom and threw up. When he came out, she was naked on the bed. He didn't know what to do. He started crying and ran out of the room. He just left her there. She never spoke to him again.

I told him that I grew up in a tough, poor neighborhood in Chicago. I was bullied all the time because I was so "swishy." They used to call me "girlie," "sissy," and throw tampons at my head. Once I was on my school playground, and Tommy Rosario depantsed me in front of the entire school, gave me a bloody nose. He started shouting, "Look at the faggot crying. Faggoty faggot. Faggoty faggot."

When I got home, my younger sister had already told my parents. I ran upstairs, locked myself in the room, and cried. My dad came home from work early. We seldom got to see him because he worked fifteen hours a day in a factory running the boiler system. He finally convinced me to unlock the door. He sat down next to me and told me it would be alright. He told me he loved me no matter what and that those kids were just ignorant.

Then he started rattling off all these people in history that were gay, like Michelangelo, Jane Addams, Reinaldo Arenas, k.d. lang, people like that. He told me, "Come down to eat, you'll feel better. Things will get better."

"Your dad sounds wonderful. I wish I could have met him."

"I wish you could have, too."

Moreover, inappropriate comments from said family members informed the observer to how much they were welcomed into the family.

Mrs. Zedek often says things like, "You know, if you two could have babies you'd have the most beautiful children. Like little gingerbread people. I'd just want to eat them all up." Aside from what many may take as an alarming statement of cannibalism, she meant it to be taken as a term of endearment, much like the early society of Gammens who had to eat their partner in order to generate offspring. However, I often want to say that with our advances in genetic engineering, Theo and I could have olive-skinned or even pink-skinned children like those of the Gammens and that, unlike the Gammens, she would not have to consume them to show how much she loves them.

Further analysis of this particular case study suggests that the node/observer associated food with his partner. We are still unsure as to what this purpose served. We can only surmise that the food "Theo" provided was some sort of symbolic offering that may have represented sexual consummation.

The gateau à l'absinthe *that Theo makes is verdant and rich with notes of licorice and citrus. It climbs into our nose and curls behind our eyes, and the hair on our arms dances and reminds us of the orange and purple sunset over the great green seas of Hemus. And if we eat too much, we stare at the ceiling watching the fan in* La Chanson *spin round and round. We sip hot chocolate, gaze at his arms roped in muscles as they hand off orders, and wait for him to take us home.*

The symbolic interchange of food and sex also permeates ordinary discussion. These dialogical interchanges are often preludes to actual consummation.

"You know what they say about a happy baker?" Theo smiled.

"They have happy hubbies," I postulated.

"No, they say their baguette always rises."

> *"Well then, is that a soufflé in your pants?"*
> *"It's more impressive when it's still hot."*
> *I said, "Let's dig in before it deflates."*

Another peculiar development was the observer's attachment to particular body parts of the participant. These unnatural attachments prevented higher-level decision-making, and, during the node/observer's debriefing, resulted in alarming statements about humanity's ability to act as a mediator in Quorum.

> *Have you seen that man's ass? ¡Ay, dios mio! Theo's ass is reason enough to allow humanity into the Symposium. If there was ever a quarrel in the Quorum all you'd have to do is trot Theo out, have him show his ass, and then, just like that, the universe would be in alignment.*

Discussion:

In looking at the case of node AR1x40/Javier Flores alongside data from other iterations from the same node and data collected from other experimenters, we have found it difficult to pinpoint why the pairing took place.

> *He's pretty and funny. He makes me feel like I am the only person in the world. And when I kiss him, touch him, or we have sex, I am struck with unending waves of excitement, wonder, and love.*

We are aware that sexual euphoria occasionally leads to breaks with The Commonality—such as the case of node qW2-RR and the Gammens, or node 5TT&2 and the Thousand Benevolent Emperors of Xandnax, or node YYY and the Ticklewisps of Ibré—but these are instances of extreme, overwhelming physical input. In the case of humans they have only so many appendages, chemical signals, ways of communication, and technologies with which to stimulate their physical selves.

> *It wasn't sex. It was something else. We knew when our answer would be yes. It was when he said:*
> *"Go for long walks, like the French. Speaking of which, I normally don't do this."*
> *"Do what?"*
> *"Well, ask a customer out." And he blushed, this light crimson. And then he tried to smile, but it came out as a bit of a frown.*
> *"Which customer?"*
> *"You. I'm trying to ask you out. I know I am failing here."*

"You're doing fine. Yes, I'll go out with you."

He made a small gesture with his right arm, closing his hand into a fist and moving it horizontally along his waist, and he whispered, "Yes."

I asked, "Where do you want to go?"

"Some place with you."

With me, he wanted me.

It must be noted that, while this is a typical interaction between human species—proposing an excursion to determine ultimate compatibility—other observers have been propositioned in similar manners, and these interchanges seldom result in a true pairing.

Conclusion:

Node AR1x40 reported the disconnection from the central Northern Hemisphere's correspondent and did not resist recall. Additionally, humanity has not progressed past indirect perception, neither through biological evolution nor technological progress. As such, we advise the Symposium that The Commonality continue observations on Earth without interruption until such time when they have achieved this phase and direct contact can be made.

Furthermore, AR1x40's data stream has been adjusted accordingly to monitor for entanglement. No threat seems to exist from the node/observer's pairing, and the engagement has resulted in valuable data about human/node parings.

I didn't do it out of a sense of duty to The Commonality. I reported for recall because I didn't want anything to happen to Theo.

And while The Commonality would like me to remind the reviewers that correlation does not equal causation, when node qW2-RR submitted to consumption by Ewi, Ewi was subsequently obliterated in a freak meteor storm. When node 5TT&2's orgasm blew its network channel, the Thousand Benevolent Emperors faced summary execution at the hands of their people, and two millennia of war began on Xandnax. When node YYY hid from recall agents, a virus infected all Ticklewisps resulting in an inability to tickle and subsequently the end of their species. Finally, node LEA*2626's resisting recall led to the death of her partner and her subsequent drowning. Eventually, the empire of Greece fell, and a legend was born of our interference.

I knew all this, but I remained silent while he made dinner every night, while we danced in our kitchen, while I chased after my Bunny. Given a chance I'd chase him forever.

I loved him, so I left him asleep in our bed and headed to recall.

Archetype Javier Flores was subsequently recycled and the molecules put to use in the spawning of other observers' archetypes. Node AR1x40 was debriefed, purified, reconstituted, and sent back to Earth.

The node is currently operating archetype Helen Vapiski. This was in keeping with the protocols of the experiment in order to continue uninterrupted observation. We see no further complications. At this time we cannot recommend humanity's assimilation into the Symposium.

Postscript:

The following is supplemental data pertaining to node AR1x40, after its reconstitution.

We see him every day. We sit in the square with the birds and watch him open La Chanson. *Sometimes, we dive into the dumpster behind the bakery looking for evidence of his mourning or his anger. We only come up with stale, broken bread. We hear that he no longer makes* le gateau à l'absinthe.

On one very cold day, he came running across the slush slicked road and into the square.

He said, "Why don't you come inside?"

"Where you taking me?"

"In there." He pointed to La Chanson.

"You're not with them, are you?"

He hesitated, and then he smiled, "No, I'm not with them. How could I be? I don't even know your name."

"Helen."

"My name is . . ."

"I know you. I've always known you."

"Okay, then."

There was no one in the store, and it looked like no one had been in for a while. The store was warmer than outside but colder than it should have been. He sat us down and we said, "There's no birds today. Too cold."

"That's right." He brought us a cup of chocolate chaud.

"It's not right. No snow."

"Snow?"

"On top." We pointed to the cup of chocolate.

He scooped chantilly into the cup, and the white cream melted down the side. "Better, huh?"

Our mouth engulfed the cup.

"Don't. That's hot."

We drank it down in one gulp and pushed the cup towards him. "Sunny sunshine."

"I'll get you another."

"The birds, they tell me things."

"Really what do they tell you?"

"Stuff about oranges and licorice. About broken fences."

"Is that so?"

"So. You happy?"

"Sure. No customers, but I guess so. How happy can you really be anyway?"

"You know what they say about a happy baker?"

He stopped behind the counter.

"Soufflés are for rising bread," we said.

He placed the cup in front of us. "Yes, that's what they say. You know you should find a shelter. There's a church over on Twentieth and Walnut that has a shelter."

"Gods are cruel. No promise there."

"Well, I'm sure the city has something."

We finished our cup and placed a quarter on the counter.

"No, really," he said. "I can't."

"Is it not enough?"

"It's plenty." He picked up the quarter and placed it in the register. "Thanks." Outside it began to snow.

And we said, "He knows. It was hard for him. So many lives. The node just churns. It churns and churns out information. It never knows who it's going to be next. Boy, girl. But then you came. Information wasn't important. Just one life. It was hard. Hard for him. He had to go far away. Farther than the birds go, farther than the dust spinning off the planet. Past the rings of Saturn. Over the red cascading nebulas. Out of swirling galaxies. Far away. There's no God, though we think we are. We just observe and record and wait. But then you were there. Every word he took. Every word. Now all to read, forever. Written in the stars. But the birds don't come to tell you because it is too cold, and it's snowing now. Things will get better, Bunny. It'll be better, Bunny. I'll be your moon on the square."

And we hugged him, and he smelled of bread and chocolate, and we wept.

Beelzebubstomp

M. P. POWERS

In rosedusk, when the sky is littered with crows; when all the world's mad and mulish brutalities abound and you've scrapheaped hope and your soul's hiding somewhere in the cracks of your sofa; if your mirror makes rank complaints about the face in it, and you feel like every crumpled lottery ticket in the world, hang your name on a cliché. It's not a question of whichwhat or rightwrong, whywhere or whether the rightbrain seizes what the lefthand knows. The elephant will never shuffle out of the room for you, and wounded is the color of its languor. For this unspooling, precisely not improbable lie, which is life, it's a question of posies and perpetual changelings. Blueruin and a borrowed dialect, the drowsy rings of Lethe. It's not a question of whether or why the ghosts grieve in trees of the evening. The cruel ornaments of spring; bells, halls, mills, hells, lovers frisking up the peachblue cobblestones of Montmartre. Occidental neopreacher's goatfooted rooftopspeeches warmed with the bluidtinged fruitwine of hate. Nightornoonday, spirits in graveyards coalesce, polliwogs girdlehurtle. Is that a merely man or mostly a noun? It's not a question answerable by the mouth of any cyberterranean quasidemocracy, or that which sells off its own superficial "ideals" as if they were a bundle of flameretardant socks. Simply certainly yes certainly quite commonly understood, the wherefores and the ways the world suffers under the weight of the same old unrealities. Down at the heel and up against the wall, over the hill and under the gun. The lusty living things, lovethighs and paltryprinces, meager matter whirling chaotic. It's not the answer, but the question eternal: when your nightdreams lose their dances, will the djinns still sing for you?

· Aviary ·

Climbing onto the windowsill,
wearing scarlet socks, she leaps.

—*Circling of Cranes*

Illustration by Anna Bron

Showtime

NANCY GOLD

We aren't really made the right way for flight—extend your arms, rotate the top of your hands forward, and flap from your elbows. That's a start. Forget all you've seen about flapping from your shoulders. You'll never get any lift that way.

Cowboy is a wiz at putting things together. Like my wings—he rigged them up so I can open and close them by flexing my wrists. These skinny tubes run down my arms, under my shirt. He offered to run the tubes under my skin. I told him I'd think about it.

Cowboy is smart, but he's goofy, too. I mean, look at his getup. All this cool stuff he does for me, and all he does for himself is stick a couple of horns on his head. Then he wears holsters and chaps and a ten-gallon hat. How cheesy can you get? I tell him, either you're a cow, or you're a cowboy. It's stupid to be both. But you can't tell Cowboy anything.

We have our own street act, a kind of freak show. Don't tell me it's "dehumanizing." Man, getting stared at for money is nothing. Try cutting up chickens all day. Or being a telemarketer. That's the worst. Sometimes we hook up with a carnival. Most of the time we're on our own.

It's a good way to meet girls. We're just a story to them, a way to one-up their friends: I hooked up with this guy, get this—he had wings, like an angel. Or he was a cowboy—you know, he had horns like a cow. That's okay. I used to try to get to know the girls a little bit, talk to them, ask their name, stuff like that. Not one has asked me my real name. So now I just call them all "Angel." Don't bother to ask their name. They're just a soft bed.

Cowboy tells me he moos during sex. I don't know; you can't believe everything Cowboy says. I don't see him getting that much action. And if he really moos, well I don't think he gets it twice. Now a guy with wings—the girls really dig that. You would not believe what they want me to do with these wings. C'mon, they're just hacked off a bird that's getting turned into nuggets, and if they are more than a day or two old they've started losing feathers already. I can open them. I can let them fall closed. That's it. Do they think they're really my wings? Like I can control them? Of course, I never got any action before the wings. Before Cowboy and I started doing the show, we were two lonely dudes.

I have to admit things didn't really happen until Gash joined us. Anyone would look sweet next to him. It looks like someone grabbed him by the jaw and tore off the side of his face. He doesn't have much more than a hole for his mouth, and nothing below that. One side of his nose is gone. He dresses real fancy, a top hat and tails, and wears a mask that covers his face from just below the eyes. Gash makes a show of not wanting to remove it, of not wanting to scare anyone. And then he takes it off all on a sudden, no warning, and you're looking at this red raw hole. A guy puked on him once. Gash picked a fight with him after the act. The guy wouldn't hit him back, I mean, could you?

Gash never got any love. Until Sarah.

It's mid-July and we've got the show down. Cowboy and I used to do the show just the two of us, back at the start, but it was different. Now it's a whole good versus evil and redemption thing. Cowboy goes on first. He ambles across the stage, hands in his pockets, that ten gallon hat on his head. Then he turns and looks at the audience, like he's surprised to see them there. He bows, and sweeps the hat from his head so that you can see his horns. He moves his head back and forth so everyone can get a good look at them.

Then I come on holding a red cape. This is the trickiest part of the act for me. I've got to keep turned so that the audience doesn't see my back yet. They may get a glimpse of white, but nothing much to draw their attention. I want to wait for the right moment. I shake the cape at Cowboy, and he turns and wriggles his eyebrows at the audience. Then he turns to me, scrapes his foot on the ground, and charges. He charges me a few times and then runs into the audience and charges a girl there. A pretty one of course—why waste this on one who isn't? He lays his head in her lap, tickles her with the horns. He always gets a big laugh. I guess when you're as smart as Cowboy you don't mind looking stupid.

I go to the edge of the stage to help Cowboy back up. Gash comes on stage behind us. I never know he's there until I hear the audience react. He skulks from side to side. He starts playing with the mask, moving it from side to side, pulling it higher or lower, so that although you can't see it, you know something is really, really wrong with his face.

Cowboy and I edge to the side of the stage, and start whispering together. We keep our eyes on Gash. He knows how to play the crowd, performing a macabre striptease with the mask. Cowboy and I rush him, and he turns to us, tears off the mask, but turns to keep the audience from really seeing. It's not hard to react with disgust and fear, even after all the times I've seen that face. That's when he turns to the audience and shows them the face, too. And then he does the thing that really gives them their money's worth. He laughs at them. It's a distorted hooting sound, with his tongue moving in that hole and spittle flying out.

Cowboy kneels down, folds his hands together, and looks for all the world like he's praying. Really, he tells me, he's making a list of all the girls he's had. I grab the mask from the ground and set it back on Gash's face. He takes a swing at me, and that's when I back away and open my wings. If I've done it all right it's the first time the audience has seen them. I stand firm before Gash until he stumbles towards me and lays his head on my shoulder and pretends to weep. Man, this still creeps me out, the idea of that face of his touching me. But I put my arm around him and Cowboy gets up and puts his arm around Gash too, and we leave the stage together. We all return to the stage to take our bows before we pass the hat.

It's our second night in town, and the crowd and take were even better than last night. After the show we go hit the bar. I get a beer and scan the crowd. I walk over and touch this girl's hair, and say, "Hey Angel." She turns around with that look on her face—you know the one—but then I open my wings, just a little bit. A rustle of feathers, a little shiver running through me. Like I just couldn't not react to her. She gets this smile on her face, and turns around on her stool, leaving her legs just a little too far apart for the black mini she's wearing. And I'm thinking, yeah, here we go. Then I feel my wings spreading apart. Felt eerie, not doing it myself. I turn around slow, because the wings aren't all that tough. So the woman is leaving before I get turned all the way around.

"Hey," I call, but she's still moving away. "Hey, you can't just go pulling on a guy's wings and then walk away."

"They aren't *your* wings," she calls back. She never turns around.

"Hey," says the girl next to me. "I thought I was your angel."

I turn back. "You are," I tell her.

"Just what can you do with those wings?" she asks. She's a freak fan for sure.

I leave the girl's apartment early—it's just getting light—and head back along the lake to the bar, wings tucked under my arm. Cowboy and I tow a trailer behind his old pickup. If the trailer isn't at the bar, Cowboy will know to come pick me up. Gash stays in the trailer sometimes, too, but never if Cowboy or I are there. I don't know where he goes then. As I head back along the beach gulls watch my approach, turning first one eye upon me, and then the other.

Further up the beach a woman kneels beside a dead gull, slowly moving its wings out and back, up and down, testing their limits. She grasps the bird's wing tightly and wrenches it loose in a spray of feathers. The other gulls startle into flight. She holds it along her arm and tests the movement.

She stands and tosses the wing away.

"I'm Sarah."

I recognize her voice from the bar. "Norman," I reply. The word feels strange in my mouth. Looking at the dismembered gull, I think of her spreading my wings at the bar.

"Where are your wings?" she asks.

"Where are yours?" I ask, but I'm smiling.

"I lost mine."

We walk together down the beach. When we get to the bar Cowboy is walking up to the trailer, too. The door swings open and Gash comes out, blinking at the daylight. He's wearing blue jeans, a dirty t-shirt, and no mask. He sees us and raises his hand to cover his face. Sarah walks up to him and extends her hand.

"I'm Sarah."

He takes her hand in his own, but doesn't seem to know what to do with it. You can see his tongue moving around, but he doesn't say anything.

"That's . . ."

I don't know his real name. I never asked, and he never said. He lets go of Sarah's hand. "Gash. Can't you see?" He spreads his arms wide and sticks his face close to Sarah's. I flinch, but Sarah remains still. Gash stomps back into the trailer and slams the door.

Sarah turns to Cowboy. "And you are?"

"Cowboy, at your service ma'am." He takes off his hat and bows to her. The horns are still on his head.

Sarah climbs into the truck with me and Cowboy. He looks at me and shrugs. We drive to the next town quiet. When we stop Sarah gets out and pulls a dead butterfly from the truck grill.

"Whatcha lookin' at?" asks Cowboy.

"The wings."

"Why are you looking at the wings?"

"An interest of mine."

"Did you see our show? I made up those ones he wears." Cowboy jerks his thumb at me. "I could make you a pair. Just need to find a bird. Then I could make you wings and dinner." He laughs and looks at me. Sarah stares straight ahead.

That night after the show I go to the bar. Gash never showed up for the act. Even when we haven't seen him all day, Gash has always found us in time for the show. I'm scanning the bar for him, to see if he found a perch there. There are more flies than customers. One buzzes around my head and I wave it off. A big blond with too much makeup waves back and comes over. "Never met a guy with wings before," she says, and slips off her stool. She sits down again and leans over toward me. The fly settles in her cleavage. "But I guess I already know how to fly." She lifts her glass to me and drinks. The fly hovers over her glass. I wait until it lands on the rim. There's a secret to catching flies—they always take off backward. I close my hand around it and feel it darting around, humming against my palm.

"I gotta go," I say.

I find Sarah and Gash leaning over the hood of the truck with an assortment of winged insects spread out before them: flies, crickets, cicadas, fireflies, even a wasp. From behind, with their heads bent together, they could be anyone. I hand Sarah the fly. She holds the wings apart and watches it struggle to escape. "Good for maneuvers," she decides, "but not for every day." She releases it into the night.

"You missed the show," I tell Gash. He grunts and hands Sarah the wasp. He's wearing his mask, but it has slipped a little and reveals the ragged edge of his nose.

"You could check out my wings," I say. My voice sounds too loud outside of the bar, outside of the crowds.

"I already told you I'm not interested in your fake wings," Sarah says without looking up.

She and Gash turn over the wasp. I think about the girl in the bar, leaning over and smiling at me. Three days now, and I've never seen Sarah smile. I lean up against the truck, in line with the bugs. I'm right after the caddisfly.

"Where would my real wings be?" I've never thought much of it before; if they looked okay, that was enough for me.

Sarah picks a moth and examines it closely, studies the way the ghostly wings attach to the body. She pulls one wing off and extends it to me. She turns me around and moves her fingers over my back. She isn't touching me, but I swear I can feel the shadows of her fingers on my skin. She finally alights, near to my neck, maybe the fifth vertebrae. Her fingers mark narrow channels along my spine.

"No," she says and turns to look for another wing.

The lines burn on my back, first a small flame and then a conflagration. "Erase them," I say through gritted teeth. The fire increases, and I can't hold back the moan. "Erase them."

Sarah places her palms flat against my back and holds them where she had drawn the lines. The fires slowly settle. She holds her hands to my back until I release the tension across my shoulders.

Later I will look in the mirror. Not the merest mark lines my skin.

Have you ever looked closely at an insect wing? They're a marvel, really. Different from a bird's wing, but no less successful. A guy, said he was an engineer, told me it was impossible for insects to fly, to lift their heavy bodies. Don't believe it. Back before the dinosaurs, insects were huge, the size of pigeons and crows.

The more time Sarah spends with Gash, the more I want her to spend time with me. I catch a couple of dragonflies and take them to Sarah. She's sitting in the trailer with Gash. He isn't wearing his mask, and I can't help staring. Gash stares back, then laughs at me.

"What do you think of these?" I hold the dragonflies out to Sarah. My face burns. I concentrate on Sarah's face to avoid looking at Gash. I watch her face a lot. The expression barley changes. The corners of her mouth don't lift. I've never seen her smile, not even at Gash. She turns the wings over, measures their length with her fingers.

"Here and here." She lightly strokes the inside and outside of my legs, just above the ankles. She hands back the dragonflies and turns to Gash. I stand there for a few minutes more before I leave.

Cowboy sews the dragonfly wings into my skin. He runs them deep, attached down to the muscle. With every step I can feel them pinch and pull.

"They don't add to the act, man," Cowboy says. "Why do you want those little wings down there?"

"That's where Sarah said they should go." I don't tell him that after she marked me, these places on my skin tingled—sometimes with a low hum, sometimes a clamor. They were hungry until I fed them with the wings.

The wings move and flap as I run. I accelerate and a hum rises in the air from the vibration. When I stop the wings continue for a moment more, up and back, rowing through the air. Cowboy sees it. Gash, too. He crouches and gently touches one of the wings. My leg twitches in response, and the wing flutters.

"How did you know where to put it?" Gash's intensity makes me step back. He looks to Cowboy and back to me.

"Sarah marked the place."

"You know about Sarah's wings?"

"What do you mean?"

"Have you seen the scars?"

I look at the scars spanning Gash's face, and at first I think that's what he means. He meets my gaze for a moment, then turns away.

We know now where to find Gash before the show—we just have to find Sarah first. The last two nights Cowboy and I have dragged him away from her and the bugs to join the show. His heart isn't in it. Instead of scary and dangerous he just seems pathetic. Our take is down. But without him, Cowboy and I will have to change the whole show, and the take would be even worse.

"C'mon, Gash, it's time." He doesn't even turn around. "We think we can get one more show out of this town before we move on."

When he turns I see the wings, delicate and iridescent, that sprout from his temples. Either the wings are misaligned or his face is; they don't line up side to side. "I'm quitting the show. Sarah and I have plans here."

I swallow hard; my pride hurts going down. "You know the show's no good without you in it."

Sarah comes over and Gash puts his arm around her. "Take your fake chicken wings and leave us alone."

Cowboy convinces me to talk to Gash one more time before we leave town without him. Clouds of dust rise up even though Cowboy drives the truck slow. We find Gash and Sarah walking toward the lake. Wings bristle from

Gash's shoulders. A double row lines his arms to the wrists. They flock at his knees and along the muscles of his thighs and calves. My leg muscles twitch. I can see that my idea of a pair at each vertebrae was too much, an ostentation, a vanity. Closer, I see a variety of wings—the large brown ones from the Cecropia moth, the long wings of the praying mantis, fly wings at the wrist. Nodules of blood and pus mark every point of entry. Not Cowboy's work. Gash stumbles, and Sarah waits while he stands again. Beetle wings flash their iridescence at his hips. Gash shuffles forward.

We follow them out to where the beach turns to rocks and the rocks into cliffs that fall to the water. The winds are calm. Sarah keeps talking to Gash, low, leading him to the edge.

I climb out of the truck. "Sarah, tell him it can't work." Cowboy shifts the truck into park, leaves the engine running.

"You need lift. Think like a raptor," we hear Sarah instruct Gash. "They can hardly get off the ground, but they can soar from a high tree or a cliff."

"Gash."

He turns from Sarah. "I have a name. Just like you, Norman, I have a name." He spits on the ground.

"What's your name?"

He nods his head at Sarah. "Ask her. She knows my name." He rolls his shoulders and the wings beat at the air. Sarah leans close and kisses his cheek.

Gash hunches over, and a cicada wing falls from his arm, twirling on its way down. He launches forward, arms extended, and begins flexing his muscles in a giant shivering. The wings flap and row and buzz.

I feel the wings at my ankles flutter, maybe from the truck exhaust, maybe from their own desire. Every spot Sarah has ever touched me comes alive, throbs and burns and urges me forward to the edge. I can feel where those wings should be now, I can feel the muscles pull and tense as they spread the wings. I want Gash to fly, and I want to fly with him.

I don't notice that Cowboy has left the truck until he tackles me. "No," he growls. Gash steps forward. I struggle against Cowboy and spit dirt from my mouth. "Look at her," Cowboy says. "Look at Sarah."

His hand relaxes enough for me to lift my head. Funny; I start thinking about the next show. Cause I can see we'd gotten the old one all wrong.

While Gash hovers there for just a moment, dark against the sky, Sarah smiles.

Circling of Cranes

CHARLENE LOGAN BURNETT

The child's chair faces the wall,
a paper mural: pagoda, weeping
willows, wooden footbridge,
sacred cranes in scarlet stockings,
standing on one foot in an ink-blue stream.

Behind her, the girl's mother stirs
a sauce over the stove, still it burns.
Her father drinks another beer.
Her sister piles stones inside the girl's pockets,
whispering they are now hers to keep.

It is said of the crane, if you ask him,
he will carry across migratory oceans
smaller birds, the souls of the dead, a lost maiden
folded between the scapulas of his wings.

The girl asks the crane a question.
He rises, his eight-foot wingspan
shuddering the walls.

That night, she places the stones, one by one,
inside the top drawer of her dresser.
She opens the window. Outside,
above the first hush of frost,
cranes circle, calling, calling.

Climbing onto the windowsill,
wearing scarlet socks, she leaps.

Birds Every Child Should Know

KATE RIEDEL

I first met Charlie and Aphra early one morning down in the business district. I was picking up discarded office furniture, and they were picking up birds. Most of the birds were dead.

The birds were small migratory warblers that had crashed into or been confused by the tall glass buildings that coughed up the jetsam I collected as my living.

Charlie was tall with thick curly dark hair clubbed back, inclined to jeans and sweaters. Aphra was wispy, with wavy blonde hair, and her legs were usually enveloped in long swinging skirts. My name, by the way, is Paul, and I don't look in the mirror that often.

Charlie was a sculptor and builder of installations. Aphra worked in fabrics—banners, quilts, wall hangings. Both preferred working from found materials, and became regular customers for my scavengings. They lived together in an old house with a sunroom full of finches. Both the house and the finches belonged to Charlie.

I think we could be called friends.

"Have you ever seen anything like this?" I asked, once Charlie had wiped down the table and set out coffee in the sunroom.

"Where did you find it?" Charlie turned over the little body I'd unwrapped from its paper towel shroud.

Aphra, who usually preferred to stay out of the sunroom and away from the birds, moved in for a closer look.

"Residential area," I said. "On top of the garbage. I thought, you know, that it might be some kind of cage finch."

Charlie carefully examined the feet, the feathers, the beak. "It's superficially like a finch, but just not quite. And you don't throw a pet bird out with the garbage when it dies."

"*You* don't."

She stood up.

"I'll bury it," she said.

I didn't tell them, then, that this was actually the third one I'd found, all on residential garbage put out for collection, all brightly colored, but all different, and all dead.

But having shown this one to Charlie, I needed no excuse to bring her a live one. The second bird was only stunned, as if it had flown into a window; eyes open, heart pounding, but otherwise immobile. Spring migration was over, and I didn't think this one was a casualty of a picture window.

Charlie was alone today.

"It's starting to revive," she said, looking into the brown paper bag. "I don't recognize it. Where did you find it?"

I told her, and this time told her about the others. "All residential, but all over the map. Nothing, really, in common, except that they were all dead and all on top of the garbage. No two alike. This is the first live one."

She folded over the top of the bag and set it aside. "I think it needs a little more time."

She went to a shelf and picked up a book, a big one, full of colored pictures of exotic finches, like her own.

"Nothing in here that's at all like yours," she said, after leafing through it. "I suppose it could be a new mutation of some kind."

The bag rustled and the bird burst out and flew to a window, beating against the glass until I thought it would stun itself again. The rest of the birds fled to the top corners of the aviary. Charlie rose and quietly approached the window, undid a latch at the side and slid the glass open. The bird flew out and away, and Charlie slid the window shut.

I stood looking after it for a few seconds, then said, "Well, I guess I'd better get the morning's haul home and sorted out."

But instead of going home I drove back to the house where I had found the bird.

The garbage had been collected, the cans stood tipped upside down, the street lay green and quiet in the mid-morning sun. I parked down the street and walked back to the house.

I could hear light thumps against the glass, then I could see the bird itself, beating against the front window, trying to get in.

As I watched, the window slid open and a hand reached out, and the bird alighted on it. It ruffled its wings and I thought I heard it twitter as the other hand cupped itself above in a caress, brought into relief by light reflected from the glass.

Happy ending, I thought.

And then one hand came up and the other down and grasped the bird and deliberately wrung its neck.

I wouldn't have thought the Lucky Dice was Aphra's sort of place, but there she was, a couple days later, tucking into a large plate of bacon, eggs sunny-side-up and hash browns. She saw me and waved me over. She wasn't wearing her usual all-enveloping skirts, but jeans and a t-shirt that, if anything, made her look even wispier.

"Work duds," she explained.

"So what are you doing out in this neck of the woods?" I asked after I'd ordered my scrambled eggs and home fries.

"I'm doing some banners for a church down the street, and I have to do a lot of climbing to take the final measurements."

"Charlie tell you about the second bird I brought over?" I asked.

She nodded. "You've found more than those, haven't you?"

"All dead but that one." I didn't tell her that one was now dead too. I set the tomato slice to the side of the plate and reached for the ketchup. "I've always kind of wondered," I said. "Why don't you like Charlie's finches? Charlie told me you were the one that got her into the migratory bird rescue thing."

She thought a moment, her hands wrapped around her coffee cup.

"When I was a little kid," she said, "growing up out in the country, there was always at least one barn swallow nest in or on every building— the barn, the granary, under the roof of the driveway between the big double corncribs. Corncrib walls aren't solid, you know, for circulation, and the spaces between the boards made a ladder so I could climb to the top of the inner wall and watch the swallows fly in to their nest."

She smiled. "I really wanted one for a pet. I even rigged up a snare, baited with corn. I was too young to have noticed that swallows only eat bugs. And that saved me from ever having to deal with the fact that swallows can never be pets."

"Well, that's childish ignorance with a happy ending," I said.

"Um," she said. "When I was about twelve, I was staying with a friend in town. Her brother had trapped two pigeons and had them in a cage. We wanted them for pets. We were going to put them on leashes attached to their legs but didn't know what to use for leg bands. I found some kind of soft metal D-rings that could be opened and shut by hand—I'm not sure what they were originally meant for."

She reached out with her fork and took the tomato slice from the edge of my plate, but she didn't eat it, only shoved it around on her plate with her fork.

"Anyway, we put on the leg bands. And the pigeons panicked, the rings were so heavy they couldn't move very well, just fluttered around, and I was so scared I nearly wet my pants, but I managed to grab them and get the rings off their legs, and I let them go. My friend was mad at me because her brother was going to be mad at *her*. It scared me. Still does."

"What were you scared of? Your friend?"

"Of me. Oh, finish your breakfast!" she added with a laugh. "It's too early in the morning for this kind of confessional. You pick up anything interesting this morning? Can I see?"

So when I was done with my own breakfast she walked with me to the parking lot and hoisted herself up to look into the back of the pickup. "Oh, wow!" she swung herself over the side—the jeans revealed a nicely rounded little bottom that ordinarily couldn't be seen for the skirts—to look at a pile of old wrought iron fencing, my big item for the day. "This is exactly what

Charlie needs for her latest installation! She thought she'd have to buy new. How much do you want for it?"

I gave her my artists' price and told her I'd deliver whenever they were ready.

The next live bird I found, I took home. I had a couple of bird cages sitting around, and I put one of them in a warm spot, put the bird in it (this one was black, with red and green and blue spots in a necklace) and covered the cage until I heard the bird stir.

I gave it seed and water, even hamburger, remembering stories of rescued baby robins. But it only beat against the bars until it dropped back on the floor of the cage, exhausted. When it revived, it was only to struggle against the bars once more. I took the cage outside and released the bird. It flew away, and I did not follow it.

I seldom found more than one bird, never more than two, and more often dead than not. The live ones I continued to take home to revive, and to release, because watching them beat themselves against the bars was, if possible, even more painful than thinking of what might happen to them once released.

Then one day in late summer I was scouring an older suburb of working class houses built maybe a hundred years ago, still solid, the kind of places people would move into and renovate, leaving all sorts of interesting stuff out front for me to pick over.

This house was on a bigger lot than the others, with room for a big garden, both vegetables and flowers, old trees either side of the house, and, I guessed, more lawn out back—the kind of lawn that would have a hammock and a tire swing and a sandbox and maybe even a tree house. The kind of house where everything would be saved and treasured, to be put to new use some day. But I stopped anyway and cast an eye over the week's garbage.

There were half-a-dozen birds, little things, some of them brown and grey and cozy looking, some like bright jewels.

It was bad enough with single birds. But half-a-dozen! And only one dead.

I could not leave them. I got a shoe box from the pickup—I had lined one with paper towels and punched air holes in it, and now carried it with me regularly—and lifted the little bodies in, one by one. I left the dead one until last. I had just picked it up when the front door of the house slammed and a boy of maybe sixteen ran down the walk and skidded to a halt in front of me.

"Thank God!" he gasped as he realized the box was intended for live birds, although the words choked off when he saw that the one in my hand was dead.

But he wasn't the kind of kid to cry, at least not in front of other people.

We looked at each other over the box, and finally he spoke.

"They're my mom's," he said, never taking his eyes from mine. I waited.

"She's sick," he went on. "She . . . she won't get any better. She's not bad all the time. She fights it. But it won't ever get better, and some . . . sometimes she does this."

"Is it cancer?" I asked.

"No. Sometimes you can do things for cancer. Operations and stuff. You can't for this. It will only get worse and worse until . . . you know, what Woody Guthrie had?"

Even Guthrie's name came out with difficulty; he couldn't name the disease at all.

"Your mother must be very brave," I said.

"She's the bravest person I know." He held out his hands for the box. "I take care of them for her, on the worst days."

I handed him the box. "Shall I bury this one for you?" I asked.

For a few seconds he looked as if he wanted me to, as if he wanted to have at least that small sorrow taken from him, but at last he shook his head.

"No," he said. "That one was one of her favorites."

I watched him go slowly up the walk, cradling the shoe box.

Then I got into my pickup and instead of continuing my rounds I drove straight to Charlie's, and told her all about it, in the sunroom, while Aphra leaned on the door frame.

Finally Charlie spoke.

"You know, when I was a kid we always had a bird feeder in the winter, right outside the living room window. When there was no work to do in the winter my mom would sit by the window and knit, or read, and watch the birds—chickadees, nuthatches, woodpeckers. She always hoped to see a cardinal, but we were a little too far north, and they never came.

"The day after my mother's funeral, we came home from the service, and I went into the living room, and there by the window was her rocking chair, and her knitting basket. And out on the bird feeder was a cardinal. A female cardinal. It stayed for—oh, several minutes—and then it flew away and we never saw it again."

"The owl was a baker's daughter." Aphra didn't wait for an answer, but strode out of the kitchen in a flurry of skirts.

"What's with her?" I asked.

Charlie shrugged. "We had, um, a disagreement last night."

"Couldn't have been that serious, surely."

"Only if you consider kids serious."

"Huh?"

"I suggested it. Aphra went off the deep end."

"Ah . . ."

"Adoption, probably. Unless you want to volunteer," she added with a half-hearted leer.

"I'll take that as a compliment," I said, and she smiled, a real one this time, if still unhappy.

The next bird I found was a particularly bright one; it reminded me a little of Charlie's Lady Gouldian finches, all red and blue and gold. It was dead. As I looked down at it on my hand, a man on a bicycle pulled into the driveway beside me.

"Hurt yourself?" he asked.

"Huh?"

"The way you were looking at your hand, I thought maybe you'd hurt it, somehow."

"Uh, no." I held out the bird, to show him.

"Well, in that case," he laughed, "I can see you have an unbroken life-line, which means you'll live a long and happy life, and you're going to meet a dark-haired lady."

"Already have," I managed to reply.

"See? Cross my palm with silver! Just joking!" He pedaled up the driveway to the garage beyond.

The same driveway next to which stood the garbage can where I'd found the bird that lay dead on my palm in all its brilliant plumage.

And he couldn't see it.

Aphra was home alone. She apologized for her behavior the other day.

"Come around to the back," she said, and led me up the back stairs to her own studio, rather than into the house.

Charlie's house, I thought.

Bright fabrics were spread across her work table. Some of them I recognized as pieces I'd found in my own gleanings. Among them was a piece that hadn't come from me—a blue silk pashmina that had been a present from Charlie.

I told her about the bird the man on the bike couldn't see. I hadn't buried it yet. I took it out to show her.

"You can see it, right?"

She nodded, touching the feathers briefly, before I wrapped it back in a paper towel.

"So why couldn't he?"

"I don't know."

"I've been wondering," I said, "if they're—I suppose they might be souls, like Charlie, ah, sort of said."

"But you said sometimes there's more than one."

"Jewish tradition has at least two souls, and so do the Navajo—"

"But which one gets its neck wrung?" she said, in the same tone she'd used on the baker's daughter. At least she didn't walk out. She thought a minute, then went on, "But I know what you mean. I wonder if they could be—you know, when you have dreams, I don't mean the kind of sleeping dreams where you try to get from point A to point B while you're stark naked. I mean..."

"Dreams. Yeah, I know what you mean. But you see it, I see it. Why couldn't he see it?"

"Maybe it wasn't his."

"But it isn't mine, either, or yours. Why can we see it? And the boy I told you about, those birds weren't his."

"But they were his mother's, and he was hers." Aphra picked up the pashmina, put it down again. "You know Charlie wants a child?"

"She mentioned it."

"And I can't."

"She said adoption would be okay."

"Not that kind of 'I can't.'"

I thought about that for a few seconds. "Like the pigeons?" I asked.

To my surprise she flung her arms around me and kissed me on the cheek. Then she sat back and repeated, almost in tears, "I can't. I don't want to have that kind of power over another living being, ever!"

You already have, I thought. Over Charlie.

But I didn't say it aloud. Perhaps I should have.

"Maybe," I said, "it's because we all work with salvage."

"Maybe."

I went about my business, scavenging, selling, trading, occasionally giving things away. Finding birds. Burying the dead ones, releasing the live ones.

I delivered the wrought iron fencing to the site of Charlie's installation. I noticed that Aphra didn't come to help, as she usually did.

Then one evening I got a call from Aphra.

"Paul? Do you have time to help me move?"

This time Charlie was nowhere in sight as we packed the pickup.

"Where to?"

"Just to my brother's. He's storing stuff for me while I'm away on a travel grant. Research—folk embroidery and appliqué. South America. I've been brushing up on my Spanish."

"Congratulations."

"*Gracias*. I'm really excited."

As I pulled out of the driveway I saw she'd put out a couple of garbage bags. She didn't look at them, but I did.

There was a dead bird on top. I wondered whose it was, hers or Charlie's.

Charlie asked me to come over a few days later.

She took me into the kitchen and fixed coffee as usual. But the sun room was empty. No plants, no birds.

"Oh, don't worry," she said. "They aren't dead. They're all in new homes, and I made sure they went to people with aviaries; I didn't want them confined to cages when they were used to freedom."

"Why?" I asked.

"I'm going back to the west coast. Some friends have a house there—they'll let me stay 'til I find a place of my own. I was going to call you, to ask you to sell the furniture for me, on commission, of course. And anything in my workshop you can use, it's yours. I'll tell the real estate agent you have the key."

"I'll miss you," I said.

"I already miss you," she said.

I'd set out my garbage that morning. When I got home there was a bird on it. Not brilliantly colored, I saw when I got out of the pickup, but with a subtle iridescence in its grey feathers.

I picked it up. It lay on my hand, soft and light, and incredibly warm for its size. Warm, and with a heartbeat.

I took it inside, found a brown paper bag, put the bird inside, poured myself a little whiskey and sat down to wait for the first stirring.

It seemed to take forever, but just as the glass was empty I heard a faint rustle of paper, and when I picked up the bag I felt movement. I stepped outside the door, opened the bag, and waited again.

Small wings beat tentatively against paper, then more strongly as it struggled up, and then it burst into the light and was gone; I couldn't see where for the sun in my eyes.

I sold Charlie's furniture. I gave the commission to the local bird rescue mission.

I used some of the scrap wood from Charlie's work shop to build a birdfeeder this winter. I get the usual birds—cardinals, blue jays, chickadees, gold finches, sparrows. Sometimes I think I see something just a little different feeding there—perhaps a small grey bird with flashes of iridescence—but by the time I find the binoculars there's nothing but house finches or a nuthatch.

Sigilism

JOHN MYERS

Locks, to stop their turning the smell of the river
where ducks preen into the first of the year and faces about.

Was it after ingesting the blue feather I would turn blue,
like a peacock turns thistle gold, or when parabolas intersect
heat lightning, even vaguely,
       and what if we were blond
kisses, bound, taut, or a spring, a blue heron, the wake
of her head,
     and what if twine had cuts, streams of disposable
film, the clatter against our hush on the mute where brown,
the hours stood together.

The school clocks glow at night, trains whistle, cats back-
lit in a second-story window
        when the river proves no smooth water
for reflection and defeat is a mattress outside the apartments
join the sag of thirty-four years of heirloom roses
         along a span,
a prune, a rotary phone. A bush so heavy with sparrows,
          it snows.

Calling Rain

LORA RIVERA

Four minutes and twenty-two seconds later, the park has emptied completely. In the grass, puddles spring up like ant colonies, silent and teeming. I watch you lift your white skirt to your thighs as you wade in under beckoning palm trees, the sky receding for you, so that your face drinks up the darkening clouds and grows indistinct behind a haze of rain. I have waited a long time for your smile, and for this moment that has neither beginning nor end, as is the way with all healings—but simple too, like a single drop of rain aloft in the air.

Afterward, you laugh at me, your wet silly-string hair on my neck, your chest flattened softly against mine; you are soaked through to your bare feet, which are brown still from mud puddles. You are powerful today, and you know it. How easy it was for you to make the rain.

In bright places—like movie theaters when the lights go up, or parking lots at midday, or in modern kitchens, shopping mall atriums, hospital clinics, salons, hotel bathrooms—flaws show up worse. Tara has two long wrinkles that run together to form an upside down 'y' in the middle of her forehead, right between her eyebrows, which are slender and silver-red and perfectly curved like fish gills. People notice the wrinkles only when she's under bright lights. They notice that her eyes are slightly different colors—one hazel, one brown—only when she looks straight at them or when they study her portrait that hangs in the hallway downstairs. Daniel Wingard painted it for her, when they were in art class together in the days before Seta. Tara doesn't have the heart to take it off the wall. He told her he would come back for it. If she hadn't known better, she would say he had unusual powers, too, because when he left that day, after staring at her portrait and then at her, after kissing her and wiping rainwater from her eyes, and tears—after all that he stepped out through the door and disappeared.

The man she's meeting for dinner tonight at Seven Arches is not like Daniel. Harrison is too logical, too predictable. She's amazed she has lasted this long with him. Of course, she knows why. It's because she has been careful. She has schooled her face, she has dressed appropriately, she has evaded questions. Her fourteen-year-old daughter Seta says her mother is cruel, and that Harrison is broken somehow, or is gay. Why else after two months of not *getting any* does he still want to go on a date? Tara tells Seta that she is too young to be thinking things like that. She tells her to watch her tongue, and then, in her mind, wonders if Seta is right, and then wonders if Seta is not right, if it is not a false dichotomy. She wonders—and this idea makes her skin feel tight—if Harrison is not playing some sort of game with her, peeling her secrets back slowly, tenderly. Today, she is trying not to think of such things.

Today, Tara has on blue, an early 90s style one-piece dress with cap sleeves and a scooped neck. It ties in the back, which is a good thing, because otherwise she'd drown in the dress. Being thin—Seta calls her stick-mom, endearingly—when she finds herself engulfed in fabric, even when it's lightweight cotton, she feels suffocated. She's barefoot, as usual, and thinks about neglecting shoes for the evening, too, but decides against it. Seven Arches doesn't usually mind, but Harrison will. Daniel used to chide her for being so worried. How could you put someone to flight by such innocuous habits as going places shoeless? It's why Tara loved him—because of that thoroughly genuine acceptance of anything and everything. Except her. In the end, he couldn't take it, and how could she blame him?

She slips on her shoes, nice, flat white ones that Seta left behind when she went to camp for the weekend. For a moment, Tara feels nauseous, as if she's just run too long too fast. After all, a voice whispers, won't it hurt less if you do your own peeling? Even though Tara wears shoes to the museum every day, she takes them off as soon as she gets there. She's much more comfortable barefoot.

She considers powder for the furrow between her eyebrows as she stares into the mirror over her bathroom counter. She only has one bulb above the vanity actually screwed into its socket. The rest are merely place holders. The single light is not enough to see furrows by unless she leans very close to the mirror. Seta thinks her mother's abhorrence of bright places is ridiculous, and Tara has often found the bulbs screwed in, which requires her to climb up onto the counter—making her knees sore—to loosen them up again.

Powder, Tara decides, would hide the furrow, but the furrow is part of her, an integral, meaningful part that ought not to be kept secret from Harrison. Shoes are one thing, but her face is another. She's had many people confounded by her face, which is heart-shaped and marked on one side by a dark scar the size of a baby fist. Powder has never been able to hide the scar.

Harrison asked her about the scar on their first date, and it caught her off guard. So off guard that she told him. Her mother had done it with a pink origami bird Tara had made to hang on one of the mobiles in her mother's preschool classroom. Her mother had lit the bird with her cigarette lighter and made Tara hold it to her face, her mother's hand on her wrist. But then she shrugged. Things like that happened a lot back then, said Tara.

They had been outside near the park. The sun was sinking, the bright lip spreading fire-fingers over the ocean, casting feathery shadows by way of palm fronds. He was looking at her as if he might paw at her, as her father used to, or claw at her, the way her mother had. Or maybe he'd just wanted a kiss, because he brought his face down and her body trembled with terror and desire, and so the rain came because she had called it—as wet and solid a wall as there'd ever been.

Maybe it had been the burn after all, the bright fire that had opened up inside her chest a rush of power that made the clouds form faster and spill. Her best friend used to let her spend the night, and often she and Kyla would steal out from the small mountain house where Kyla and her mother lived alone, past rows of blackberry bushes, always freshly devoid of berries for jams and pies, and up past the little river that ran, if you followed it, all the way down to the bottom of the hill and turned into roadside gullies that kept the streets from flooding. There was a meadow up there, and after Tara's face healed, she went up with Kyla and watched the stars blink out of the darkness. But what happened, Kyla wanted to know. She kept pestering, and when she wasn't asking, she was staring, staring so hard and unblinking that she missed the star. And Tara didn't tell her about it. Oh, she told Kyla about the scar that was still brown and a little puffy like paint puckering as it dried; it had only just begun to peel off at the edges near her jaw. Tara wasn't even sad about the scar anymore, because her brother was going to take her away to live with him in his apartment in Charlotte, and that meant she'd wouldn't have to smell her mother with all that perfume and alcohol wheeling through the house when her father wasn't home—and when he was home, Tara wouldn't have to be his princess anymore.

She used to like it, being her father's princess. She'd told Kyla about all the times her father would cuddle with her on the sofa, holding her tight to him like his doll, stroking her hair and her neck and her arms: his sweet little princess. Back then, she would tell Kyla to make her jealous, because Kyla didn't have a father. He'd gone away before Kyla was born, and Kyla said her mother was never going to get remarried because the Bible said you couldn't or you'd be an adulteress. (She pronounced it a-dull-dress; Tara remembers thinking the word sounded funny.) But lately, being her father's princess was more difficult. The scar was easier to talk about. The pain went away quickly, leaving just a dull itch, and the whole thing had been brought on by a bad day. People do things when they get angry, she said, staring up at the stars while Kyla's head was still turned toward her, eyes opened up like tin cans of tuna fish, all the white exposed. That's why Kyla missed the star that fell, why she didn't get to make a wish and why Tara did, and why, perhaps, the rain comes now whenever Tara calls it.

Once, Kyla told her she was very selfish. Look, she said, you should make it rain where people are thirsty, or where there are fires, not just whenever you want it to. They had been out on the little wooden footbridge that lets you go from one side of the river to the other without having to cross a mile up or down where it narrows and splits. It was an old bridge that had many initials carved into it with hearts and crosses (they were carving their own initials along with the letters *BFF*); birds' and hornets' nests could be alternately found in the crisscrossed wood making up the supports, and spider webs too, often beaded with water droplets, stretched between the age-warped slats. It had been very hot that day, and the sky was a blue so bright with sunlight, the white clouds looked as though they were near enough to reach out and pluck like dandelions. The green fleece of the mountains, usually wrung round with mist, was visible all the way up. So Tara had made it rain, because she was sweating, and because sweating was so sticky and salty and reminded her of her father. She and Kyla were both eight years old; Tara's brother had only managed to let her visit on weekends because her mother said she was still too young to be alone so often by herself.

You could make it rain in Texas where my Aunt Rachel is, said Kyla. She says it's always hot there. Or in New Mexico where Richard is.

Who's Richard?

My mom's friend. She visits him sometimes.

Tara didn't tell Kyla about the time she'd made it rain in the house. Her parents' room had been soaked, spoiling the oak dresser and causing the new red comforter to stain the beige sheets. Her father thought it was faulty roofing; he'd had to replace the ceiling.

Tara has to drive because walking downtown to Seven Arches would make her late. She doesn't mind driving. It gives her something mindless to do while she thinks. Harrison is not the first man she has dated since Daniel divorced her five years ago. Her last boyfriend waited a week before he realized he wouldn't be able to get her in bed any time soon, and fled. Before that was a man whom she dated for six months and never knew. He would wrap himself up so she could never see him; even when he was naked, it was as if he were wearing floor-length trench coats all the time, and turtlenecks and cold-weather gloves. She felt sorry for him then—a man whose aura mimicked Tara's own lighting habits: keeping it dark for the sake of privacy, for protection. But later, she realized his vulnerability had been a ruse to keep Tara out, to keep her at a comfortable, useable distance until he was done with her.

Tara flips down the visor and frowns into her mirror, watching the furrow on her brow crease like a gorge between soft mountains. She touches her face, the scar on her cheek, and then flicks her eyes back to the road, swerving around a pothole. Without the scar, she would look a lot like Seta, she thinks wistfully, and pushes the visor back up as she turns left at the light, locating the modern chrome angles of Seven Arches on the right a few blocks down.

She allows the valet to take her car and smiles at him, knowing that he finds her attractive by the way his eyes linger on her face a bit too politely, as if he is making an effort to keep them from straying elsewhere. Somehow, this makes her feel guilty. She should not have worn a dress with such a low cut.

She remembers Kyla always wore dresses cut low enough for the both of them when they went out together. But she is without Kyla, has been for many years, ever since Tara left for college and found Daniel.

The restaurant smells the way it always does, full of bread and spices, garlic and leeks being the most powerful, and the bright flavors of jalapeño, pungent onion, and a whole array of more foreign seasonings from the rainbow of curries to the barely discernible toasted seaweed the Japanese call *nori*, all lacing the air with tiny stingers, so that she blinks wetly a few times under the cool shadowed alcove where the hostess behind the bamboo podium asks for her name.

"Tara, party of two."

She is always early for dinner with Harrison, mainly because she knows he values punctuality more than he can admit. He can be counted on to march through those glass doors at exactly seven thirty, by his watch, which means seven twenty-eight by the astronomical clock to which she's set her cell phone. She sits on one of the red cushioned benches and declines a server who asks her if she would like a drink while waiting. She usually doesn't drink. Sometimes a martini, extra dry, with two olives if she's feeling gleeful and safe. Tonight, Tara feels apprehensive. She feels stalked, like prey, cornered, like an oyster under the prying knife. Harrison cannot possibly love her. It's absurd. He doesn't even know her. He's never seen, for instance, her favorite artist hanging in her studio above the antique telephone in the corner—because he's never come over—nor has he met her daughter. Only that once has he seen her call the rain. And he made jokes afterward about downloading her brain into his phone so he could get the forecast without using the internet.

Tara's hair was so pale orange that day, like a sun-bleached life vest. He'd said it was like silly string, that she always made him smile. He'd said there were parts of her too deep for him to access, and in him, also—and then Tara's breath catches because he said afterward that she was a bridge builder, a woman who made rivers to swim across, and she hadn't known what he meant. She remembers that it was hard, harder than it ever has been, to make the clouds come. Because she had to think of him covering her, wet with his own sweat and her unwilling saliva and her thighs slick with him, and then of her pushing him away through layers of water that drowned him and made him indistinguishable and harmless. She didn't like thinking of Harrison that way. What are you thinking, Daniel had asked her the last time she'd made it rain for him. She'd thought she could tell him, because even if it was hard, it gave her so much pleasure to see him smile when the clouds filled in the sky and burned the heat away. He was horrified; she was a monster. She should have known better. She will never tell Harrison.

An employee opens the door for him with an inclined head, and Tara watches Harrison's eyes settle on her as he strides inside. He is tall and dark of face and hair, with features that made her wonder, when they met, if he was Arab, although he denied it, smiling, and said he was a healthy mix of Spanish and Indian. Dot, he'd said, not feather, to which addition she hadn't known quite how to respond.

He is wearing brown loafers, pleated khakis, and a lightweight navy blue coat over a white button up. When he sees her, he grins, and greets her with a light kiss on the cheek. His chin is scratchy, and he smells of grass, as if he has been golfing, which he does often. She breathes him in.

"This place looks fantastic," he says, sitting beside her and checking his watch.

Tara knows he is on time, precisely, to the very second if he had not stopped to kiss her, which makes the kiss doubly precious.

"I thought you'd like it," she says, inhaling deeply through her nose. He also smells warm, relaxed; he's been bustling about all day and has only just paused to let his heart stop racing. Tara's heart is racing. "Did I tell you they have koalas?"

His lips part, stretching to one side, and his eyebrows drift upward like feathers. "That one you'll have to explain."

"You'll see when we go through the arches. They have skylights for them. Some restaurants have wall-length exotic fish tanks. I don't see how keeping koalas is any different. Did you know they sleep most of the time—about twenty hours a day because they have to produce an anti-toxin to digest all the poisonous eucalyptus leaves they eat?"

She talks too fast. She always does when she gets nervous. And about unimportant things. But Harrison seems interested rather than put off. He asks her about the restaurant, how long it has been open, who the owners are, is it a chain, and what made them decide to use chrome for the exterior.

"It's basically steel on steel frame," she is saying as she takes Harrison's arm. They move through the restaurant, beneath three arches. The arches are the mediums out of which are crafted the new seven world wonders. They pass through the Great Wall of China, meticulously chiseled rectangles of rock strung over and above them; the beautiful white Taj Mahal cuts deep into the face of the second arch, the relief like a mirage, growing in the eye; they walk through the façade of the Chichén Itzá temple—surrounding the square arch are lurid frescoes depicting in a visual round the Mayan ziggurat's obsessive geometry. A short steep flight of chrome steps descends into a room awash with Mayan gold.

"You have to see the others," says Tara as the waiter shows them to their table, unfolding their napkins. "The ones with the koalas. In the back." She wrinkles her nose. "Because of the smell." The sommelier offers them a specialty wine and Harrison nods without consulting Tara. The lights in this room are dim, and shadows sink like blotches on Harrison's face.

"I can't believe I've never been here," Harrison says. He lifts the napkin from his lap, and replaces it seam-side down.

Tara stares at him, at how his face has been transformed by the shadows. "You haven't been in town all that long."

"Long enough to find you," says Harrison, with a lift of his glass. He swirls the wine and tastes it, absorbs the red into his tongue.

Tara cringes because his words are too genuine-sounding, too much like something Daniel might have said once, long ago. She feels herself closing up, her skin tightening. She must concentrate; it wouldn't do to bring the rain indoors again.

The second time she brought the rain indoors was, like the first, an accident. It was that same day Daniel stared at her and kissed her and told her he was leaving. He said he felt like a parent in too many ways. Always protecting, always loving, always hoping that she could accept his love, that she would accept herself. It wasn't because of the rain, he said, which made her cry, because she knew it wasn't. It was about the reason she could bring the rain at all, the reason she'd whispered to that falling star. She doesn't even remember what she said to it. *Give me strength*, maybe, or *Make him go away*, or maybe just *Help me*. And then because she looked like a little girl again, he must have wanted to take her in his arms. So he did, but he was leaving, and Tara couldn't help it, and the rain came before she could say what she wanted to say, the only words that might have kept him with her. She mouthed them, her lips already wet from the water falling straight out of the ceiling, three syllables, but she couldn't say them. Love. She has never been able to pronounce words that have no ontology.

When the door shut, the rain fizzled out like a defective firework.

He is talking now of work, and of golf. So, she was right. He did, in fact, play golf today. He is not calloused toward her, talking this way; on their first she told him that if she is not talking, it's not because she's uninterested. It is because she's thinking, and she cannot think and talk at the same time. He often stops mid-sentence to check on her, just a flicker of his eyes that she knows is registering her comfort level, and for this she appreciates him so much more than she ever has anyone before, for this small concern.

Tara cannot help thinking, while Harrison is talking, of his lips. Harrison's lips, and what they would feel like on her. And then, because this scares her, she thinks of Daniel's lips. And she has real memories, not just images conjured up by an active imagination, for what Daniel's lips can do. But somewhere in the conversation—perhaps because the wine bottle is empty and she has not touched it and because she can imagine all that wine in his mouth, in his stomach—Harrison's/Daniel's lips become her father's, and because she spends so much time thinking of her father, and because she does not want to remember her father, not ever, she remembers her brother. It is hardly an improvement.

When she was "old enough," which really meant when her mother had finished divorcing her father and had no one to look after Tara when her mother was working, her brother finally took her to live with him. He left her in charge of unpacking boxes. Tara could not imagine living for four years with boxes and clothing and trash piled up in her house the way her brother had while taking classes at the university. In two months he would graduate, and it looked as if he had just moved in. So while he was at school, or working late at the diner with the blue awning Tara could never pronounce the name of, or wooing some new girlfriend or other, Tara organized the apartment. She stocked the cabinets with plasticware, cleaners, detergents, filled the newspaper bin, and took out the trash whenever it deluged onto the kitchen floor. She alphabetized books and movies, dusted light fixtures. Even though she was far too old for it—there was "old enough" and "too old" and somehow, unexpectedly, she had arrived at both during the same school year—she spoke to her flaking miniature nesting dolls, consoling them. Everything would be all right now. They had Kyla still for a friend and maybe one day, they would see mother again. And Tara encouraged them: at least they had escaped from their father.

Probability should have warned her brother she'd end up in his bedroom, if only to clean. She had run down to the laundromat with his sheets that smelled like little boys' hands. She lifted the mattress to tuck in the flat sheet and saw the box half open, a magazine lying haphazardly on top with near pristine pages. She moved to tidy it. A glossy woman crouched on the cover with a glossy body. Every part of her was russet brown and tapering, ovular and taut, like oiled fish fillets smoothed over a shelled boiled egg. Her red tongue showed between white teeth and black hair surged around her face, a cloud rising with a slow but steady updraft. Tara had seen such magazines, tucked away in the drawer of her father's nightstand.

Tara touched the woman's shoulders, drawing a captivated finger over breasts that puckered out dark brown nipples, so different from her own flat ones. The ones beneath her finger were like enormous tomatoes. Or papayas. The woman had a hand stretched between her thighs protectively. Tara knew from experience that it was not so simple. There was a secret undertone without which the magazine wouldn't have been nearly so popular. Need. Tara remembered need, though not like the woman's. When she was little she would creep into her mother's room and climb into her bed, hoping her mother would yell at her, because then, she would have a chance to explain why she crawled up in the first place. What her father had been doing in her room. How she didn't want him to do it anymore. Maybe her mother would hold her and stroke her hair and hush her crying. Maybe she wouldn't send her back to a room that had nightmares in it. Different nightmares hid behind the woman's hand; they wanted out, though, just the same.

Tara began turning pages, first quickly, just to glance, just to see if any of the women looked like her, had diluted orange hair like hers, and then lingering, fingers, eyes, mouth pausing over the pictures: a tightening in obscure muscles, a vague, familiar tingling and warmth. Shame grew like a mushroom in her stomach.

He walked in then, and found her. He hit her for it, two hot blue spots on her arms where his huge hands picked her up and threw her into the living room. He had storm clouds in his eyes and static discharge, but she didn't want him to send her home again, so she held back the rain. When the new girl, Mikaela, arrived with groceries, she asked Tara what was wrong.

She got into my porn, said her brother, who had opened the door just enough to peer out, groundhog nose first, and vanish.

Mikaela was sympathetic but brusque. She knew just the thing. Fishing through the counterfull of paper bags, she drew out a bunch of bananas, broke off two, and trotted out from the refrigerator a jar of old raspberry jam. She slathered the bananas and handed one to Tara.

Like this, said Mikaela.

Tara was disgusted and astonished. It wasn't that she didn't know what Mikaela was doing, for she herself had moved more than bananas around in her mouth in that fashion. But Tara had *had* to do it. She'd been forced to, and it astounded her that someone would want to do all on her own what Mikaela was doing with that banana and jam. Tara held her own banana farther and farther from her as she watched Mikaela's lips and tongue and hands play over jelly-slick banana skin, eyes half-closed. So that was what she looked like. Tara had a strange sensation that she was watching a private show for someone else; her own body felt too near, as if it had been sneaking up on her. The banana came out of Mikaela's mouth with a wet pop. Well, are you just going to hold it? Mikaela took the banana from Tara's hand, gently and firmly moving it sweet and slippery in and out and around and back and forth in Tara's mouth, coaching with throaty urges: Not the teeth, relax, breathe, no, your lips go like this. Eventually, Tara gave in, wondering distantly how many people in the world could make her do what she didn't want to do.

Late that evening after supper, she watched through a cracked door: her brother and Mikaela on the sheets she had washed, grunting like pigs or rubbery seals. She made her nesting dolls watch, told them that this is what life is like and that they should be glad they are not really alive.

They finish dinner, peer at the sleeping koalas, explore the other three arches. Tara has not eaten well; her stomach is knotted, her throat tight. She clutches Harrison's hand too tightly, she is still talking too fast—about useless things, about the arches.

"Art that's reproducible like this, made not for the sake of beauty but for advertisement—I used to think it was degrading to 'real' artists. But then I started to wonder what I meant by 'real' artists, because some time ago I got this crazy idea that curator wasn't enough work," (her voice is so high pitched!) "and so now I'm an agent too with *no* time, buying up all kinds of art. You know, I saw a piece come through once that looked like— well, it looked like a pile of feces, to be honest, on a blue field. Oils. And I sold it."

Her car pulls up, driven by the valet. The seat will be pushed too far back, the rearview mirror will reflect the gray ceiling interior. She might even have to adjust the steering wheel in order to see over the dashboard.

"You look lovely tonight," says Harrison into her hair, and his breath is heady alcohol, mixed with sour chocolate. He no longer makes her think of grass, as when he walked in. He is simply Harrison, and his lips brush her ear. She jerks back, an involuntary rigidity.

City lights blot out the moon and stars. There ought to be a slender crescent, and she should be able to see Lyra, too, and Cygnus.

She's running, in her mind, and overhead, thunder rumbles.

"What's the forecast?" asks Harrison. The valet waits patiently: the longer Tara takes, the more she feels obliged to pay him.

In response to Harrison's question, Tara says nothing. She has no idea if it's going to rain, or storm, or hail even. (The wind against her throat and ankles has picked up and dropped several degrees since arriving at the restaurant.) She has not called the thunder nor beckoned the rain, although she wants to. So, as reply, she takes his hand as if to read his palm. She is able, if she feels like it; strong, straight lines sprawl over his skin.

"What is it?" He looks aghast. "My death? I choose old age."

Tara glances up, wondering if he is making fun of her, but he's smiling fondly, and then he loops her arm around his waist, resting his chin on her head. The valets are still waiting.

"Do you want to come over tonight?" he asks into her hair.

She tightens, he feels it and lets her go. "I've got Seta's shoes," she says.

He must be conscious of his breath, for he sucks in as he speaks, making his words rasp slightly, as if he has a cold. "Isn't she at camp?"

She wants desperately to call the rain: it will be safer, she'll be wet, he'll be wet, they can go home. Alone. Separately. But again, he surprises her.

"Then walk with me," he says.

It's a trap. She knows traps; they have a certain sharpness about them, a certain eeriness. He'll spring it soon, whatever it is he wants her to do for him, he'll spring it from where he's standing by the park bench, and she'll obey, because she always does.

"Make it rain," he says. "Make it rain, then." And he begins removing his shoes.

The grass is long, tickling her ankles. The palm trees rustle like sheaves of paper in the night air. The smell of metal from the skeletal playset, the wood, the sand, the salt spray off the water—all of it is perfect. More than perfect! If Daniel had asked her like this, she would have fetched him snow.

But this is Harrison. And Tara can't do it. Not this time. Because she can't look at him, because there *is* no trap, and she is as vulnerable as she once was before she knew how to call the rain.

It's raining now. Without her summons. She runs two red lights. Her eyes are glued to the slick road in an unseeing daze. Her legs feel thick like jam; she looks down to make sure they are still there; she has lost a shoe. Seta will be upset. Seta will be upset anyway. She hates Tara's moods, her mother's sudden irrational flights. She will stare at Tara from under heavy, amber eyelids. Her mouth will open, snap shut without speaking, tighten, and then finally she will speak, regale her mother about her last boyfriend and how she *snagged* him, how she can't believe her mother's going to die a decrepit, celibate divorcee, how it's just her luck, and whatever guy Seta ends up marrying is going to think Tara's *certifiable*.

No, Seta doesn't understand.

Daniel did.

When Seta was born, there was a hurricane off the east coast. Category four, and everybody thought it would smash them. He held Seta up to the eerie fluorescent hospital lights, every twist of baby fat and every line in Daniel's face visible for the light. They were both beautiful, like a picture from an age in which it was not in vogue to put on display all the dark abysses of the human soul. The nurses hurried about; Tara thought at one point that the doctors must have been wearing rollerskates, they were going so fast. But the hurry was the storm, and everyone was evacuating. Not Tara, though, because she was in labor, and not Daniel, because, he said inscrutably, he was in labor too.

She never did really understand it. How he could want nothing from her, and everything, and how giving herself to a man was still, at bottom, not giving. It still felt like he was taking her, and he knew it, and it was so confusing to want so badly the thing that hurt her most. The storm was coming, and Daniel begged her to stop it, *to save Seta*, he said to her. So she did. She drove the storm out into the ocean with a precision that astonished the meteorologists. And in the hospital bed, she knew she could never truly look at him again, because she would always see him holding her daughter while in a hospital bed she closed her eyes and imagined herself held like Seta and filled with need and fear, both enough to stop the storm.

Daniel said he would come back for his painting.

Tara stares at it in the dim hallway. He has captured the strangeness. Even Tara feels unnerved looking at her own face with its dull orange hair, odd thrust of jaw, and scar like a gouge in the canvas. Her eyes are staring into some other world, is what Tara thinks. Into the world where Daniel is.

She blinks because her eyes smart. Of course he will not come back for it. It was enough to know that his tongue in her mouth was not his tongue. *What are you thinking*, he had asked her the last time she made it rain for him. It was too much to hear it said. If she could do it again, she would say out loud a kind of charm: *Where you are, I don't have to control the rain.* And he would never ask her to call the rain again. But that idea also makes her sad.

Two arms slide around her waist, but she does not scream.

"Harrison," she breathes softly. He turns her into his chest, strokes her hair, and says he likes her portrait.

"Daniel did it," she replies, and then realizes that Harrison is here, in her house, that he followed her home. His arms tighten, and she can feel his pulse in and out as if by the pull of the moon.

"Can I see your studio?" he asks, drawing her just slightly away from the wall.

"It was Seta's baby room," she says too quickly; "before that I used the sitting room by the door." The hall is in semidarkness. On either side are staggered portraits and mirrors, her portrait being the one nearest the entrance. Seta says this arrangement makes the house cluttered, makes her feel as though there are *creepers* about. But this silent crowd of spectators is exactly what Tara likes about the hallway. Her house is always full, filled with people who look on, see everything, and do not judge. They never leave and they never close their eyes; they would never let anything happen to her, to Seta.

"I'm glad you're safe," says Harrison quietly, drawing her through the hall to the foot of the stairwell.

She can almost make out his mouth. And his glasses reflect the hooded light of the lamp from the sitting room behind them.

"I've only seen you in glasses once before," says Tara. "They make you look distinguished." Why is she always so nervous? Because she does not want him here. She wants to think she has lasted this long with him— two months without sex—because he does not know her, because she's taken every precaution against his finding out how she calls the rain. She has a sudden fright: perhaps he's been talking with Seta! How else could he know so much?

She pulls on his arm away from the stairs, but he mounts another step. Now he is clutching her, his hand covers her forearm. "You ran two red lights and a stop sign."

"That was you?" she laughs, remembering the pair of headlights she'd seen behind her in her review mirror—which she'd had to adjust after finally retrieving her car from the valet of Seven Arches.

"Tara," but he stops, peering at her.

"Let's make this easy," says Tara urgently. "You think I'm this someone. I'm not. I don't know who it is you think I am, but I'm not her. I'm a freak; I'm messed up. I have this power—the rain—I know, I know, you know—but there are other issues, too." She wants to tell him about Daniel. And about her father. Why? What could he do? Invoke the gods? Perhaps an exorcism? She has begun to cry; at least, her eyes are wet. She blinks and shrugs out of his grip, turning her back to him. "You don't want to get mixed up with someone like me."

She can't help but think about his lips, now that they're on her, how different they are from Daniel's, from anyone else's. She hears her name when he stops for breath. "Tara." He tastes of food and wine, and paradoxically, of hunger, too, and of fear. Or is that her fear? But she can't tell them apart now, not her lips from his, not her tongue or shoulders, not the strong powerful curve of his back, which is softer than flesh has ever been, not her hands from his, or thighs, and is that his heart or hers, her stomach or his, and only now, at the foot of the stairs leading up to her bedroom and studio, only this very once has she ever wished they would shut their eyes, all those staring portraits, multiplied a thousand times by the mirrors, like a hall of witnesses.

The hall steeps in cool darkness. Tara sighs, and then jerks up toward the door, which is cracked open. For an instant, she is terrified Daniel has chosen this night of all nights to come back for his painting, but then Harrison mumbles something between her breasts, something about not wanting to click the door and scare her when he came in, and she relaxes.

Slowly. Staring slowly into the dark until her eyes adjust—they have been closed for so long—her gaze lights on the portraits, on the mirrors, on the lamp in the corner room with a brightness that does not reach them, and then on the top of Harrison's head which, she has never noticed until now, is slightly balding. She cups her hand around the back of it, in his hair, as she might a suckling child. He has not peeled away her secrets, and yet they feel exposed somehow—but not as body unclothed, but as water to air, slowly evaporating. *Where you are* . . . But Daniel is not here; and Harrison is not a child in her arms, nor—for the first time in the arms of a man—does she feel a child in his and she knows something that is very strong, like the streak of a star falling . . . *I don't have to control the rain.*

And then, because she is not fully satisfied, or perhaps because stars do not often fall singly, another flashes with a tail as long as the horizon.

I can if I want to.

Outside, it has stopped raining, and through the crack, Tara can hear the thrush of distant traffic, sparse in the midnight hours. She blinks up once more at the hallway, her eyes settling on her portrait.

Tomorrow, Tara will take it down. And they will go to the park, and she'll ask Harrison to close his eyes.

But I don't, because I don't want to miss anything. Like the way you look today among a thousand people dressed for summer—and you and I in raincoats! And I let you run me under the trees where kites fly in the distance, where children hang like opossums from playground equipment and teenage couples chatter in low voices. Wanting sex, you accuse me of, laughingly, and I don't deny it.

"So, make them all leave," I say. "Make it rain. Make it rain for me."

For me, I say. But I mean for you. And you chide me even before I can fix it. You shake your head: for *me*. And you throw off your raincoat, and I toss mine aside, and you wade through grass as high as your ankles, under swaying palm trees, hands and face upturned and arms outstretched. I've seen a hundred pictures of rain dancers, but none look like you.

It comes fast as you smile at me, and I cannot remember, at that moment, what your face looks like unsmiling; we are stuck in this moment that has neither beginning nor end, a single drop of rain aloft in the air, like a photograph.

The History of Sexuality

JOSEPH HARRINGTON

Chapter 1

Once upon the beginning,
the founder of Safety Day
bred on this treeless plain.
The zoo had its lean years:
the animals served us food
The barking ribbed-face deer
consumed whole trees
when the shelling ceased.

Chapter 2

"Will the distinguished animal
please declare himself
a bug or a bird? We cannot
abide generic ambiguity in
unidentical flying objects—
Condom and Gomorrah
perished thus!"

Chapter 3

Erotic fantasies disturbed him
when he was not having them;
their lack of evolutionary function
caused him to write: "Mommy
o mommy my head and my body
want different things."

Chapter 4

"The peristyle is a clerestory," he wrote,
"penetrated by console brackets forming
a transition to the ribbed surface of the cap."
Thus did the dome expand and contract,

a symbol of the cheerful government
where daddy is in charge of alphabets,
where suffragettes in the basement
rise from living rock like the ascent of man.

Old Myths

COLLIN BLAIR GRABAREK

Our fathers say men are men no longer, so when the Valkyrie came for us, we were uncomfortable to say the least. A great hole blossomed in the clouds, a circle of blue morning sky through the gloom, and on wings of white feather she descended towards our oilrig. She wore a winged helmet and nothing more, her hair the color of white gold. Her silver spear glittered in the sunlight until the clouds closed above her.

We formed a wide circle around her as she landed so softly that three men fell to tears. She surveyed us—our overalls streaked with grime, our hardhats nicked and dingy—with searching eyes a washed and unnatural blue. Sven leaned close to me.

"Why today?" he said.

This was the final day of our crew's three-week shift at sea. A month of rest in Stavanger awaited us. The helicopter would arrive in mere hours to ferry us back to our families.

"Olaf, what could she want?" Sven said.

"Heroes," she sighed. She spoke in a chorus of voices, all in perfect harmony.

"Ma'am, ma'am," said Mister Bjornson as he jogged out of his office. He wore a tie clip the color of the Valkyrie's spear. His suit could have fit him better. "What is the meaning of this? Where did you come from?"

"Asgard," she sighed. She shifted her weight, though the poise she commanded, the ease with which she carried herself, made it hard for me to believe she bore any weight at all.

The color drained from Mister Bjornson's face. He buttoned his jacket. "I see," he said. "Well, we're happy to have you. What was it you needed?"

"Heroes," she sighed, a hint of annoyance audible in her baritone section.

Mister Bjornson licked his lips. He was balding and short—certainly shorter than the Valkyrie would have liked. "Of course," he said. "Just one moment. Let me converse with my foreman." He shuffled over to me, and I stifled a groan.

"Olaf, she is armed," he murmured.

"I noticed that, Sir."

"Amongst other things, of course."

"Of course." And is it awful to say I noticed the curve of her breasts, the pale hair tapering between her legs like sand in the top of an hourglass?

Would that make me more of a man, or less of one? In the Valkyrie's eyes, I mean.

She did not watch us, but stared up and into the distance. The muscles in her flat stomach flexed like living porcelain, so unlike the stomach of my wife, Elena—loose and doughy, slightly yellow like fresh butter, the stomach I loved to kiss.

Elena would soon rise for work. She would prepare Nils' lunch and drop him off at school on her way to the clothing store where she operated a cash register, taking the money of customers convinced they needed expensive things to wear.

"Olaf, please," Mister Bjornson said.

"Please what?"

"Please make her happy. Or at the very least, make her go away."

The Valkyrie stared on. I swallowed hard, wiped my face clean with a handkerchief, and handed the soiled rag to Mister Bjornson. Not a man amongst us failed to gasp as I approached the Valkyrie, and these were hard men (for this day and age, our fathers would say).

I inhaled the smell of the oilrig—ocean water gone stale. I hoped I didn't smell that way.

"Miss," I said. "We have only oilmen here. I'm afraid there are no heroes."

"I am afraid," she sighed, and only now did she turn to me. First her neck craned—not straining, but graceful—and then her eyes glided to meet mine. "We will lose," she sighed.

"Lose what?" Sven called.

The Valkyrie did not turn, but the muscles in her face tensed in rage. She assumed we all knew the old myths. The coming battle. The twilight of god and man alike. The cold rise of the wicked. The end of the world. Ragnarok.

"Do you hear that?" I said. "What more need you see?"

I wanted to add: Besides, I do know the myth, and our loss is fated, yes? But of course, that wasn't the point.

The Valkyrie blinked. She tightened her grip on the spear and stretched her wings. Then she flew off in an instant, the sky opening to receive her.

We stared at the sky for some time. We stared until Mister Bjornson shuffled back to his office, his head lowered, and muttered thank god we could get on with our lives. He was right. The world had returned to normal, so we must return to work. This was the twenty-first century, and more than ever before the world would not stand for dawdling oilmen.

At lunch, Sven said, "I don't care for lettuce. It bothers me." He removed the lettuce from the cheese sandwich he had built for himself. Of late, this was a daily ritual for Sven. His wife pleaded with him to adopt a healthier diet, more than bread and meat and cheese, and I can attest that he tried. He built his sandwiches with lettuce everyday, but his resolve always faltered at the moment of truth.

"Have I asked you about lettuce?" Sven said. "What is your stance on lettuce?"

"I'm not sure I have one." I poured hot pea soup from my thermos into the clay bowl Nils had fashioned for me at school. He had presented it to me three weeks prior, on the morning I was to leave for the oilrig. I mistook the lopsided, yellow thing for a mug and told him I would take my coffee in it. To staunch the disappointment tightening his face, I laughed and lied that I had been joking, that I loved this bowl and would take it to work with me. But I had not used the bowl until today. Now I grew disturbed as my soup took on a yellowish tint. Cheap paint, no doubt.

With nothing decidedly non-toxic to eat, I thought of the future instead. Tonight we oilmen would meet in our favorite tavern in Stavanger to celebrate the end of our shift. We would drink and talk of our day. Perhaps we would mention the Valkyrie. If we did, our fathers, the ones still alive and hearty enough to spend their evenings in a tavern, would drink on in silence. They would drink to impending battle and inevitable destruction. They would drink to Ragnarok—that foretold cause, already lost.

Then I would go home. When I put Nils to bed, I would tell him how terrifically my soup had tasted in his bowl, and he would smile. And when I kissed Elena's stomach and then kissed lower, lower, and she sighed—a sigh so different from the Valkyrie's—I would know that I was far from expert at this trade, that her sigh was for my pleasure. So I would know she loved me as much as I loved her.

I turned to Sven as he crammed the whole lettuce leaf into his mouth. He swallowed it with a grimace.

"I've done it," he said. "I've eaten my lettuce." And with a laugh, he added, "I've become brave."

Magic Realists in Love

LINDA ANN STRANG

The garden is heavy
with the bellow of bull roses.
We notice foghorned unicorns
in the back yard.
Maria's angel runs away with the gypsies,
and she flies off—
such a blue jeans Angelus.
But what are bell bottoms for after all?

So pluck the pure string of the washing line.
Beat the olive oil drum.
Her tortillas, chilies and chocolate
could make the rock and roll mountains come.
The Holy One's metal horse is hot.
Let down your new wineskin hair.
Bring on the sexed up old wine.
Let the whole of creation tear.

See Christ of the ratchet and spanner
raise shocks at the veteran's side.
Put on your stained glass crash helmet,
Maria, God will now advise.
Fit the sprocket to the rosary.
Yes, that's right.
The way to the angel-eating quetzal
is on Guevara's motorbike,
and with the way these plots are constructed
it's going to be a bumpy ride.

Have a pretzel.
She'll go down like jaguar for *agua*
when she comes down tonight.

CONTRIBUTORS

Rachel Adams ("The Sacrosancts") lives in San Jose where she teaches 6th graders. In her dreams, "The Sacrosancts" continues though it was long ago cancelled by the network. Her favorite character is all of them, but Esther was the first.

Anton Baer ("Atomic Summer") is from the Yukon and lives in Slovakia. More at http://about.me/AntonBaer.

A. A. Balaskovits ("Three Times Red") is a graduate of the MFA program at Bowling Green State University and a PhD candidate in fiction at the University of Missouri. Her previous and upcoming works can or will be found at *Gargoyle, WomenArts Quarterly, Shimmer, Permafrost,* and others, including a chapbook to be published by Deathless Press. She is finishing a collection of fairy tales and working on a novel.

Walter Bargen ("A Theory of Music") has published fifteen books of poetry. Recent books include: *Days Like This Are Necessary: New & Selected Poems* (2009), *Endearing Ruins/Liebenswerte Ruinen* (2012), and *Trouble Behind Glass Doors* (2013). His awards include: the Chester H. Jones Foundation prize in 1997, a National Endowment for the Arts Fellowship in 1991, and the William Rockhill Nelson Award in 2005. He was appointed the first poet laureate of Missouri (2008-2009). His website: www.walterbargen.com.

Redfern Barrett ("Transaction") was born in 1984 and gained a Literature PhD in 2010 on 18th century queers. His work has been featured in the Danish National Museum and Paris' Maison Populaire and will soon appear in the journal *Gender Forum.* He is a columnist for the online magazine *Scifi Methods,* and his sci-fi novel *Forget Yourself* is now available on Amazon.

Margaret Bashaar's ("Dig") second chapbook, *Letters from Room 27 of the Grand Midway Hotel,* was published by Blood Pudding Press in 2011. Her poetry has also appeared in or is forthcoming from journals such as *Caketrain, New South, RHINO, Thrush,* and *Copper Nickel,* among others. She lives in Pittsburgh, PA where she edits Hyacinth Girl Press and generally gets up to poetic mischief.

Anna Bron (cover art & illustrations) has a BA in traditional animation from Sheridan College. She is a freelance illustrator and designer working from Vancouver, BC, Canada. Her website: www.annabron.com.

John F. Buckley and **Martin Ott** ("Leaving La Dulce Vida") began their ongoing games of poetic volleyball in the spring of 2009. Their first full-length collaboration, *Poets' Guide to America,* came out on Brooklyn Arts Press in November 2012. Their poetry has been published by more than 40 publications, including *Barrow Street, Confrontation, Evergreen Review, Glint, Redivider,* and *ZYZZYVA.* They are now working on a second volume, *The Yankee Broadcast Network.*

Charlene Logan Burnett ("Circling of Cranes") Charlene Logan Burnett earned an MFA in playwriting from UC Davis. She was a MacDowell Colony fellowship recipient. Her fiction and poetry appeared in *From the Depths, Literary Mama, Loch Raven Review, RHINO, Weave Magazine* and other journals. She is passionate about dogs, especially homeless dogs, and when not writing, she is caring for a growing brood of collies and finding them homes. Her website: charleneloganburnett.com.

Mary Lou Buschi's ("Beauty School") poems have appeared or are appearing in *Anderbo, Willow Springs, The Laurel Review, Cream City Review, RHINO, The Collagist, Pank, Tar River Poetry,* and *Fourway Review,* among others. She earned an MFA in Poetry from Warren Wilson College. Mary Lou is also a mentor for new teachers through the Teaching Resident program at Teacher's College, Columbia University. She is a special education teacher in New York.

Edmond Caldwell ("The Collector of Van de Voys") got a literature PhD from Tufts University in 2002 and then decided he would prefer not to. Since then his fiction has appeared in *West Wind Review, Mad Hatters' Review, Harp & Altar, Pear Noir!, Lamination Colony, Prick of the Spindle, DIAGRAM, Juked,* and elsewhere. He has been twice nominated for a Pushcart Prize, and his short play, "The Liquidation of the Cohn Estate," was produced in the 2009 Boston Theater Marathon. His novel, *Human Wishes / Enemy Combatant,* was published in 2012 by Say It With Stones. He was last seen in Boston, MA.

Alana I. Capria ("Lilith's Extra Rib"), born in 1985, has an MFA in Creative Writing from Fairleigh Dickinson University. She resides in northern New Jersey with her husband and rabbit. Her website is http://alanaicapria.com.

Theodore Carter ("The Life Story of a Chilean Sea Blob") is the author of the collection *The Life Story of a Chilean Sea Blob* and the novel *Stealing 'The Scream'* (forthcoming). His stories have appeared in *PANK, The North American Review,* and in genre mags and themed anthologies focused on humor, horror, erotica, super powers, and Jimi Hendrix. You can find out more at www.theodorecarter.com.

C. E. Chaffin ("Kentucky-Fried Christ") was a practicing family doctor until 1996 and has been composing songs and poems since the age of five. He has published two books, *Elementary* (Mellen Press, 1997) and *Unexpected Light* (Diminuendo Press, 2008), has written many others, and edited *The Best of the Melic Review* (Melic Press, 2001).

Feng Sun Chen ("Eclipse") lives in Minnesota and is a graduate instructor at the University of Minnesota.

Robin Patric Clair ("The Story of Jimmy Draws-So-Small") is the author of *Organizing Silence: A World of Possibilities* (SUNY, 1998), the editor of *Expressions of Ethnography* (SUNY, 2003), and first author of *Why Work* (Purdue University Press, 2008). Clair has won two Outstanding Book of the Year Awards and the Golden Anniversary Award from the National Communication Association. Clair's first novel—*Zombie Seed and the Butterfly Blues: A Case of Social Justice*—is forthcoming with Sense Press/division of Springer Publishing.

Bernard M. Cox ("La Chanson de l'Observation") has been transplanted many times and is now considered an invasive, though naturalized, species. His recent transplantation was from Philadelphia to Berwyn, IL to San Diego, CA. It was originally planned as a cutting but no one was willing to propagate him. He is a graduate of Roosevelt University's MFA in Creative Writing Program and the former Assistant Artistic Director for the Tamale Hut Café Reading Series.

Nicelle Davis (*In the Circus of You*, poems) lives in California with her son J.J. She has taught poetry at Youth for Positive Change and with Volunteers of America in their Homeless Youth Center. She currently teaches at Antelope Valley College. Her books are *Circe* (Lowbrow Press, 2011), *Becoming Judas* (Red Hen Press, 2013), and *In the Circus of You* (Rose Metal Press, 2014). She runs a free poetry workshop at The Bees' Knees Blog and is assistant poetry editor for Connotation Press.

Julie Day ("Finding Your Way to the Coast") recently graduated from the Stonecoast MFA program. During the day she writes IT documents from her office cube as well as attempting writing of the more fictional variety. She hosts Small Beer Press's occasional podcasting series. Some of her favorite things include gummy candies, loose teas, and standing desks. Her website: www.stillwingingit.com.

Maria Deira ("Stain") grew up in Eastern Oregon but now resides in the cozy gloom of the Willamette Valley. Her fiction has appeared in *Fiction Southeast, GigaNotoSaurus,* and *Strange Horizons,* as well as in the Spring 2010 and Spring 2011 issues of *A cappella Zoo.* In addition to writing updates and a personal blog about living with lupus and other chronic illnesses, a full bibliography can be found at Maria's website: www.mariadeira.com.

Josh Denslow ("Proximity") stories have appeared in *Third Coast, Black Clock, Cutbank, Pear Noir!,* and *Wigleaf,* among others. He is a staff editor at *SmokeLong Quarterly* and an associate editor at *Unstuck.* He has written and directed five short films, and he plays the drums in the band Borrisokane.

Gavin Faherty ("Dearest Dirty," illustrations) is an illustrator living in South Korea. His work can be viewed at www.gavinfaherty.com with regular updates on twitter @gavinfaherty.

Roxane Gay ("Requiem for a Glass Heart") lives and writes in the Midwest.

Nancy Gold ("Showtime") is pursuing an MFA at Northern Michigan University, where she is an associate fiction editor for *Passages North.* Her work has appeared in *The Huron River Review* and *The Moon City Review.*

Danya Goodman ("Brunhilde's Escape") is currently completing the last year of her clinical psychology PhD, working at a veteran's hospital in Long Island, NY. She completed her MFA at the University of Kansas in 2012. She has been published in *Midwestern Literary Review, Down in the Dirt, Kiosk,* and elsewhere. She hopes that Brunhilde is enjoying her adventures, wherever they may be.

Collin Blair Grabarek ("Old Myths") writes in Virginia. He received his MFA from George Mason University, where he was the fiction editor of *Phoebe: A Journal of Literature and Art.*

CONTRIBUTORS

Born and raised in Brooklyn, **Cheryl Gross** (*In the Circus of You,* illustrations) is an illustrator, a painter, a motion graphic artist, and a professor at Pratt Institute and Bloomfield College. "I equate my work with creating and building an environment, transforming my inner thoughts into reality. Beginning with the physical process, I work in layers. I am involved in solving visual and verbal complexities such as design and narrative. My urban influence has indeed added an 'edge' to my work." Many have compared Cheryl's work to "Dr. Seuss on crack." Cheryl is currently working on an illustrated science fiction novel, *The Z Factor.*

Joseph Harrington ("The History of Sexuality") is the author of *Things Come On (an amneoir)* (Wesleyan University Press, 2011), a mixed-genre work relating the narratives of the Watergate scandal and his mother's cancer; it was a *Rumpus Magazine* Poetry Book Club selection. He is the author of the chapbooks *Earth Day Suite* (Beard of Bees, 2010) and *Of Some Sky* (Beduoin, forthcoming), as well as the critical work *Poetry and the Public* (Wesleyan, 2002). His creative work has also appeared in *Hotel Amerika, No Tell Motel, 1913, BathHouse, Fact-Simile, Tarpaulin Sky,* and others. He is Professor of English at the University of Kansas in Lawrence.

Micah Dean Hicks ("Oldjohn's House") is an author of fables, modern fairy tales, and other kinds of magical stories. You can find his work in places like *Indiana Review, Cream City Review,* and *SmokeLong Quarterly.* His short story collection, *Electricity and Other Dreams,* will be published by New American Press in spring 2013. He attends the PhD program in fiction writing at Florida State University.

Tina Hyland ("Dearest Dirty," story) lives with a man and a cat. Her work has appeared in *>kill author, decomP, Anemone Sidecar,* and other print and online journals. She tweets @AnnaNimh.

Joe Kapitan ("War Crumbs") is an architect-turning-writer in northern Ohio. His recent work has appeared in *The Cincinnati Review, Bluestem, Midwestern Gothic, Wigleaf, decomP, Per Contra,* and others. He blogs erratically at joekapitan.wordpress.com and is threatening to start a novel in 2013.

Jack Kaulfus ("The End of the Objects") lives and works in Austin, Texas and holds an MFA from Texas State University in San Marcos. Her work has appeared in *Barrelhouse Online, FAWLT magazine, Off the Rocks,* and others. She recently finished her story collection *The Answer Is Please* and is hard at work on a novel.

William Keener ("Tale of the Avian Saint") is an environmental lawyer in the San Francisco Bay Area. His poems have appeared in *Rattle, Alehouse, Iron Horse Literary Review, The Main Street Rag,* and *Slice Magazine,* among others. His first solo collection, *Gold Leaf on Granite,* was published by Anabiosis Press, and he serves on the editorial board of the online literary journal *Terrain.org.*

ali lanzetta ("Versions") is a woolgatherer who lives in the forest and sleeps under blankets of books. Her work has appeared in *Hunger Mountain, Verse, Switchback, Eleven Eleven, Sugar Mule, The Invisible City Audio Tours,* and *A cappella Zoo.* ali is enamored with giraffes, whose hearts are over two feet long. She lives, loves, and teaches creative reading and writing in New Hampshire.

Emily J. Lawrence ("The Legs Come Off Easily") is not a Barbie doll. She is a person who does not often talk. Her website: wrathofsweetsourdough.tumblr.com.

Claire Massey's ("The Sand Ship") short stories have been published in *Best British Short Stories, Murmurations: An Anthology of Uncanny Stories About Birds, Flax, Patricide,* and elsewhere. Two of her stories, "Marionettes" and "Into the Penny Arcade," are available as chapbooks from Nightjar Press. Claire lives in Lancashire, England with her two young sons.

Adam McOmber ("What Follows Us") is the author of *The White Forest: A Novel* (Touchstone, 2012) and *This New & Poisonous Air: Stories* (BOA Editions, 2011). His work has appeared recently in *Conjunctions, Fairy Tale Review,* and *Hayden's Ferry Review.* He teaches creative writing and literature at Columbia College Chicago where he is also the Associate Editor of the literary magazine *Hotel Amerika.*

Lindsay Miller ("The Adventures of Starfish Girl") won the Denver Citywide Spelling Bee in seventh grade, kicking off an illustrious life of being a total nerd. She was a Founding Mama of the Tucson Poetry Slam, received her MFA in Writing & Poetics from Naropa University, and has never really mastered the art of the indoor voice. Her work has been published in various places in print and online, including *The Legendary, The Nervous Breakdown, decomP,* and *Union Station.* She teaches writing at Pikes Peak Community College.

Andrew Mitchell ("The Rocket in the Sky") is a student in the MFA program at the University of New Hampshire. His work has been published in *The Emerson Review* and *Aegis.* He lives in Dover, New Hampshire, where he is working on a collection of short stories.

Three things contributed to the origin of **Nicole Miyashiro's** "When the World Ends": a Dave Matthews Band song, a medical editing assignment, and a fascination with inexplicable connections. Since the Pushcart nomination of this story, she has continued to write short fiction and poetry. Her other stories have appeared in *Pearl Magazine* and *Parlor Journal,* and her poetry and poetry reviews have appeared in *Philadelphia Poets,* with a third review forthcoming this spring.

Hayes Moore's ("The Creature from the Lake") fiction can be found or is forthcoming in *Foliate Oak, Slush Pile, Crash, White Whale Review,* and *H_NGM_N.* He is originally from Oklahoma, by way of Tennessee. He is currently teaching in Queens.

Kristine Ong Muslim (the "Conrad" poems) is most recently the author of *We Bury the Landscape* (Queen's Ferry Press, 2012) and *Grim Series* (Popcorn Press, 2012), which included these three "Conrad" poems. Her short fiction and poetry have appeared in numerous publications, including *Ellipsis, Existere, Hobart, Southword, Sou'wester,* and *The State.* Her work received Honorable Mentions in *Year's Best Fantasy and Horror* and *The Best Horror of the Year: Volume 4,* as well as multiple nominations for the Science Fiction Poetry Association's Rhysling Award.

CONTRIBUTORS

John Myers ("Sigilism") grew up in the Endless Mountains in Sullivan County, Pennsylvania. His work has been featured in *PANK, FRiGG, Gigantic Sequins, Spork, OmniVerse, Handsome, ABJECTIVE, elimae, the Dirty Napkin, The Cossack Review,* and *Word For/Word*. He's earned degrees in biology from Oberlin and poetry from the University of Montana. He lives and works in Tucson.

Kurt Newton's ("The Wooden Grandpa") fiction has appeared in wide variety of magazines, including *Weird Tales, Polluto,* and *Leodegraunce*. His second novel, *Powerlines*, was published in 2012 by Gallows Press.

Elizabeth O'Brien ("Ginny") writes poetry, fiction, and nonfiction. Her work has appeared in *The New England Review, decomP, PANK, Swink, Versal, The Pinch, Juked, NewPages, The Leveler, Slice, The Emerson Review, Flashquake, The Found Poetry Review, Glide Magazine*, and elsewhere. She lives in Minneapolis, MN.

John Jasper Owens ("Postcards from Home") lives in the South and spends his time wondering why "Postcards" was chosen for this issue above "LizardFoot," which was nominated for a Pushcart Prize. He encourages readers to buy *A cappella Zoo's* #3 and judge for themselves. Oh, and pick up #1! He's there, too.

Jeff Pearson ("Reintroduction") did his undergraduate in Literature at Idaho State University and is currently studying under Robert Wrigley and Alexandra Teague in the MFA program at University of Idaho.

Pedro Ponce ("The Paranormal Guide to Wedding Etiquette") is the author of *Superstitions of Apartment Life* (Burnside Review Press). He is a 2012 NEA fellow in creative writing and an associate professor of English at St. Lawrence University.

Daniel Porder ("The Centipede Love Songs") is an NYC poet studying writing at The New School. He can be contacted at danielporder@gmail.com.

M. P. Powers ("Beelzebubstomp") is an American expat living in Berlin, Germany. His poetry has appeared in *The New York Quarterly, Word Riot, Rosebud, Menacing Hedge, The Foundling Review*, and many other fine places. More info here: http://www.nyqpoets.net/poet/mppowers.

Kate Riedel ("Birds Every Child Should Know") grew up in Minnesota and now lives in Toronto, Ontario, Canada. She has been previously published in *On Spec, Not One of Us*, and *Realms of Fantasy*, as well as the anthologies *New Writings in the Fantastic* (Pendragon Press) and *Lilith Unbound* (Popcorn Press).

Lora Rivera ("Calling Rain") holds an MFA from the University of Arizona, after two years interning at Claire Gerus Literary Agency. She writes literary and juvenile fiction and Life Book biographies for children in foster care. She is twenty-six and has found home in moments of wordlessness wandering the Sonoran Desert. Find her on Twitter under the handle @lroseriver.

Julia A. Rosenthal ("Trouble in Mind") is a freelance writer and researcher in Chicago. "Trouble in Mind" was inspired by the films of Wong Kar-wai and a 2010 trip to Hong Kong. Her fiction has appeared in *Kaleidotrope* and in the anthologies *Breaking the Bow: Speculative Fiction Inspired by the Ramayana* (Zubaan Books, 2012) and *Shanghai Steam* (Absolute XPress, 2012). She is working on a novel about the unsolved murder of King Edward the Martyr of England.

Eric Schaller's ("The Watchmaker") fiction has appeared in *Postscripts, Sybil's Garage, The Pedestal Magazine, Shadows and Tall Trees,* and *Lady Churchill's Rosebud Wristlet.* His stories have been reprinted in *The Year's Best Fantasy and Horror, Best of the Rest,* and *Fantasy: Best of the Year.* He illustrated Hal Duncan's wonderful *An A to Z of the Fantastic City* (http://smallbeerpress.com/books/2012/) and is co-editor of *The Revelator* (www.revelatormagazine.com).

Michael Schmeltzer ("Flowers, Shears") earned an MFA from the Rainier Writing Workshop. His honors include five Pushcart Prize nominations, the *Gulf Stream* Award for Poetry, and *Blue Earth Review's* Flash Fiction Prize. He has been a finalist for the Four Way Books Intro Prize and a semi-finalist for the Zone 3 Press First Book Prize and Miller Williams Arkansas Prize. He helps edit *A River & Sound Review* and has been published in numerous journals.

Randolph Schmidt's ("Larva") fiction has appeared in *The Berkeley Fiction Review, Pear Noir!,* and *Cavalier Literary Couture.* He holds an MFA from Rutgers University-Camden and lives in New Jersey with his wife and son.

Prartho Sereno's ("Man without a Wishbone") prize-winning poetry collections include *Call from Paris* (Washington Prize, 2008) and *Causing a Stir: The Secret Lives and Loves of Kitchen Utensils* (illustrated by the author/ 2008 IPPY). Her other publications include an essay collection, *Everyday Miracles* (Kensington, 1998) and the chapbook *Garden Sutra.* Prartho will receive an MFA in poetry from Syracuse University in June 2013 and return to her work as a California Poet in the Schools. Her website: www.prarthosereno.com.

Amber Sparks ("When the Weather Changes You") is the author of *May We Shed These Human Bodies,* published by Curbside Splendor in 2012.

Linda Ann Strang's ("Magic Realists in Love") first poetry collection, *Wedding Underwear for Mermaids,* was published in 2011. Recently her work has appeared in *Orbis, So to Speak,* and *Other Poetry.* She lives in Port Elizabeth, South Africa.

Patrick Sugrue ("Dialysis") is a native of Chicago now residing in New Orleans. He manages and edits *Bellow Literary Journal* and blogs frequently at patsugrue.blogspot.com and searchinfluence.com/author/psugrue/. He spoke at the 2013 AWP Conference.

Robert Edward Sullivan ("Popper's Choice") has stories published or forthcoming in *The Southeast Review, McSweeney's Internet Tendency, Fiction Southeast, Used Furniture Review, The Northville Review, EveryDayFiction, Fiction Fix,* and others. He is from the Midwest but now lives in Oregon and enjoys having in-depth discussions about Midwest winters versus Pacific Northwest winters. Also, he enjoys the Scotch he received for Christmas.

Chantel Tattoli's ("Take Up the Bonnet Rouge") work has appeared most recently at *The Millions, Guernica,* and *The Rumpus.* She graduates this spring from Savannah College of Art & Design's MFA Writing program.

Caitlin Thompson ("Teaching a Post Lunar World") is a Canadian who married an American. She resides in Bellingham, WA. Her work has appeared or is forthcoming in numerous places, including *The Literary Review of Canada, The Liner, EDGE, Echolocation,* and the anthology *Killer Verse.*

Margaret Walther ("In the Emily Dickinson Museum"), a retired librarian, has poems published or forthcoming in many journals, including *anderbo.com, Quarterly West, Fugue, The Anemone Sidecar, Phoebe, Connecticut Review, Tattoo Highway, Snow Monkey, Willow Review,* and *Nimrod.* She won the *Many Mountains Moving* 2009 Poetry Contest. She has received two Pushcart Award nominations and poems published by *In Posse Review* in 2010 were selected by Web del Sol for its *e-SCENE #44, Best of the Literary Journals.*

Colin Winnette and **Benjamin Clark** ("the gun game") wrote the book *Kate Jury Denton Texas* collaboratively. Clark is also the author of *Reasons to Leave the Slaughter* (Write Bloody 2011). Winnette is the author of three other books: *Revelation* (Mutable Sound 2011), *Animal Collection* (Spork Press 2012), and *Fondly* (forthcoming from Atticus Books in July 2013). They can be found online at www.benclarkpoetry.com and www.colinwinnette.tumblr.com.

Jessica Young's ("the human-suit series") book *Alice's Sister* is forthcoming in August 2013 from WordTech. She teaches at the University of Michigan, where she completed her MFA in poetry, held a Zell Fellowship, and received two Hopwood awards and the 2010 Moveen Residency. Her Pushcart-nominated poetry has appeared most recently in *The Massachusetts Review, Rattle,* and *Copper Nickel.* Her undergraduate work was at MIT, where she received four Ilona Karmel prizes for her poetry and essays.

Shellie Zacharia ("This is the House That") lives in Gainesville, Florida. Her work has appeared in *The Pinch, Sou'wester, Washington Square, Opium, Gigantic Sequins,* and elsewhere. She is the author of the story collection *Now Playing* (Keyhole Press, 2009).

Felicia Zamora ("Ballad of Conjure") is the author of the chapbook *Moby-Dick Made Me Do It* (Flat Cap Publishing). Her published works may be found or forthcoming in *Bombay Gin, ellipsis...literature and art, Harpur Palate, The Laurel Review, The Journal, The Normal School, Weave Magazine,* and others. She is an associate editor for the *Colorado Review,* a fall 2012 Martha's Vineyard Writers Residency poet, and holds an MFA in Creative Writing from Colorado State University.

Made in the USA
Charleston, SC
07 April 2013